BRINGING

The roar of the explosion rolled through the tunnel. For Reaper and Hausmann, it was like being inside a huge drum with a giant madman pounding on it. Their bodies' reaction to the stress of combat helped save both men. The headsets of the Liberator communications systems had saved their hearing. But they were still shaking from the aftereffects of the shockwaves as they got up from the floor. Enough of the lights had survived the explosion to illuminate the mine as the heavier dust and smoke settled.

"The next one could be a whole lot worse," Reaper said as he checked his M4A1 for damage. Hausmann looked at him questioningly, and Reaper nodded at the boxes and crates that were stacked up nearby.

Even if Hausmann hadn't been able to read Cyrillic on the Semtex cases, the crates marked CHARGE DEMOLITION BLOCK M5A1 2½-LB COMP C-4 were all too clear. A grenade going off near the boxes would literally bring down the house. After they were blown apart, Reaper and Hausmann would be ground into the dust . . .

THE HOME TEAM

HOSTILE BORDERS

Command Master Chief
DENNIS CHALKER, USN (Ret.)
with KEVIN DOCKERY

AVON BOOKS
An Imprint of HarperCollins*Publishers*

AVON BOOKS
An Imprint of HarperCollins*Publishers*
10 East 53rd Street
New York, New York 10022-5299

Copyright © 2005 by Bill Fawcett and Associates
ISBN: 0-06-051727-1
www.avonbooks.com

First Avon Books paperback printing: August 2005

Avon Trademark Reg. U.S. Pat. Off. and in Other Countries, Marca Registrada, Hecho en U.S.A.
HarperCollins® is a registered trademark of HarperCollins Publishers Inc.

Printed in the U.S.A.

10 9 8 7 6 5 4 3 2 1

THE
HOME TEAM

HOSTILE BORDERS

PROLOGUE

"Call me Ishmael."

"Ishmael? Who the hell is Ishmael? Have you gone dingy from the cold or something?"

"Didn't read the book assignments back in high school did you?" Ted Reaper said. "That's the opening line in *Moby-Dick*."

"Who the hell cares about a book about a great white whale?" Mark Jenkins said.

"Well," Reaper said, "it feels cold enough that icebergs and a couple of whales could float by and it wouldn't surprise me at all. Besides, *Moby-Dick* is a really big book."

"So?" Jenkins said.

"It would burn for a long time," Reaper said, as he hunched down.

Shivering with the cold, the two SEALs sat with their Teammates in a pair of open Boston Whalers far out of sight of land. The boats were part of the Special

Operations Command's preparations for Operation Just Cause, the U.S. invasion of Panama. The SEALs were set to practice a takedown of a simulated Panamanian ship. Intelligence had stated that such a ship might be used to move valuables or personnel secretly from Panama prior to the invasion. It was going to be the mission of the SEALs from Lima Platoon of SEAL Team Four to quietly take control of such a ship.

The SEALs were waiting offshore of the Florida panhandle, near Eglin Air Force Base, for their target ship to approach. Following the rule of "train as you fight—fight as you train," the SEALs were equipped to take down a ship in tropical waters. The only problem was, their present situation was far from tropical in terms of weather.

A cold front had moved down from the north and the offshore temperature on the water had dropped, dangerously so for the SEALs. They were all wearing the same uniforms, and carrying the same weapons and equipment, that they would be using on the Pacific Ocean side of Panama. The cold weather was knifing through the men, and each of them had suffered the cold before.

"S-s-s-son-of-a-b-b-bitch," Mike Nelson stuttered from his position crouching at the bottom of the boat, "just where in the hell is that target? I haven't been this cold since BUD/S."

Each of the men in the two boats had suffered through what was considered the hardest course of training in the U.S. military—BUD/S, Basic Underwater Demolition/SEAL training. Passing the course was the only way to get into the Teams. And gutting out the cold was one part of the training that caused a lot of the students to quit the course and return to the regular Navy.

"Shit," Jenkins said, "I wasn't this cold during BUD/S, and I was in a winter class!"

"Come on," Reaper said with a strained smile, "you think the steel pier wasn't colder than this?"

One of the trials of Hell Week, an unbelievable period of maximum output and suffering during the first phase of BUD/S training, had been known to generations of trainees as the steel pier. In the dark of the night, students were ordered to strip down and get into the water. Once they were good and soaked, they had to lie down on a pier that was made up of pierced steel planks. Not only would the cold metal just suck the body heat right out of a student, the instructors would spray the class with cold water from hoses and lawn sprinklers.

A lot of men quit training, dropped out of BUD/S, because of the ordeal of the steel pier. The students who got through it, and completed even harder evolutions later on, knew they could endure cold conditions, painful, gut-rippingly cold conditions. But during training, experienced SEAL instructors were constantly watching the students, keeping a tally of their time in the cold and just what the temperature was. Those instructors made sure that none of the students actually suffered from hypothermia, a cold condition that was life threatening. But there were no instructors floating miles out to sea in the open Boston

Whalers with the SEALs from Lima Platoon.

The SEALs didn't have instructors watching out for them, but they did have decades of SEAL experience watching them in the form of Chief Cousins, the platoon chief, in Boat One. In Boat Two with Reaper and his Teammates, was the platoon's leading petty officer, Intelligence specialist first class Garcia Santiago. The platoon's two officers had been intentionally left off the boats for the night's operation. They would be acting the part of observers on board the target ship, if it ever arrived.

Worried about his Teammate, Reaper moved over to where Santiago sat at the rear of the boat.

"Santiago," Reaper said, "I think Nelson's in trouble. The cold's getting to him bad."

"We're all cold here, Reaper," Santiago said. "But we have orders to hold our position until the target ship shows up."

"Yeah, I know," Reaper said, "but Nelson's stuttering his words pretty bad. That's not something he does."

"Nelson!" Santiago snapped. "Say bell, boat, and oar."

"W-w-what," Nelson said, startled at the odd order.

"You heard me," Santiago said, "say bell, boat, and oar."

"B-b-b-bell, b-b-b-book, a-a-and, and . . ." Nelson's voice faded in his confusion.

"Jenkins, Reaper," Santiago said, "tear up those pads in the bow of the boat. Get Nelson under them now, and you two crawl in with him."

"Chief," Santiago called out to the other boat, "we've got a man going into hypothermia here!"

"That's it," Chief Cousins growled. "Get him warmed up any way you can. I'm calling for a medevac and we're calling off this damned goat-fuck."

While Chief Cousins had his radio operator call back to command to get emergency transport out to their location, the coxswains of both boats were firing up the engines. Hypothermia was a very serious condition. The fact that Nelson hadn't been able to repeat the words Santiago told him to, and confused the ones that he did say, pointed out that the man was in real danger.

"The nearest medevac bird is twenty minutes away," Chief Cousins called over to Santiago.

"That's too long," Santiago said, "Nelson's in a bad way."

In spite of the emergency effort to warm the man, Nelson's shivering hadn't subsided. But the shakes were getting weaker and he was responding hardly at all to Santiago shouting at him.

"I'm heading in to shore," Santiago said. "The medevac can meet us partway if they get out here."

"Go," Chief Cousins said. "Don't talk, just go. We'll follow."

It was a close race to get back to shore and a warming shelter before Nelson went into shock. As it was, the man was suffering badly from hypothermia when the Boston Whaler grounded its bow on the beach. Santiago had used his squad's radio to call in rescue units and an ambulance was waiting for them when they arrived. Nelson was going to be all right and the rest of the platoon would recover quickly.

The target ship had never shown up. Back at Special Operations Command, Lima Platoon's mission had been changed—but none of the Army commanders had thought to tell the Navy element that the training operation had been scrubbed. The two SEAL officers from Lima Platoon hadn't known that their men had been waiting out on the water, poorly equipped to deal with the cold. It had been the Chief and the leading petty officer of the platoon, Cousins and Santiago, who had kept the training op from costing the first casualties of the invasion of Panama—well before it even began.

"Good call out there, Reaper," Santiago said the next day when the platoon was in their assigned quarters at Eglin. "If you hadn't noticed Nelson slipping, things could have been a lot worse for him."

"It was just the right thing to do," Reaper said. "Now that we know he's going to be okay, what's the mission for the platoon?"

"Don't worry," Santiago said, "we've still got a hot operation to go on. Just not one where we'll be sitting out in an open boat freezing our asses off. And you'll be partnered up with me. I need a good man I can depend on to keep his head on straight. Sometimes, we can only depend on each other."

Chapter One

The long nose of the H-295 Super Courier aircraft stuck out into the night, the propeller a spinning blur as it cut through the darkness. Dressed in gray tactical Nomex flight suits with black balaclavas worn underneath their Pro-Tec helmets, the heavily laden grim-faced men sitting inside the plane were still. Only the pilot at the controls was moving as he shifted his arms and head while flying the aircraft.

There was no talking among them, no joking or conversation. Voices would have been immediately blotted out by the roar of the engine coming in through the open side of the plane, the right side where the door was missing. The cold night air washed in through the opening as the plane continued on its flight.

Late December is not the time of year that San Diego has the great weather that it's well known for. At five o'clock on that Thursday morning, the sun wasn't due up for another couple of hours. The overcast clouds blocked the moon and the stars, further darkening an already black night.

———

A shrill whistle blast sounded out through the corridor, echoing off the hard walls as the lights along the ceiling came on. The area was silent after the blast of sound. Rows of individual six-by-nine-foot cells lined one wall. The facing wall was nothing more than a row of sealed windows, each one covered with heavy bars. It was the maximum-security segregation area of the Federal Building in downtown San Diego.

The silence was explained by the almost total lack of activity on the floor. In all of the cells, there was only one prisoner. As the head of one of the largest drug cartels in Mexico, Placido Pena was considered a very important prisoner, as well as a high-security risk. He was kept isolated from the rest of the inmates held in the building while they underwent trial in the federal courts across the street. Pena was exercised and fed only in segregated circumstances, especially now that his trial was drawing to an end.

"Do you have to blow that damned whistle every morning?" Officer Mitch Stevens said in the security control room just outside the isolation area.

Sergeant Keith Munson looked up at his shift partner.

"Look," Munson said, "if that damned drug lord wasn't on this floor, we wouldn't have to be here the day after Christmas and we could be having a nice long weekend just like everyone else. They even let his jury go home for the holidays and kept him locked up here in isolation."

"Everyone in the building knows what you think of this guy," Stevens said. "It's not like you keep your opinion a great big secret."

"Never forget that six brother officers were shot taking this guy," Munson said. "Both a DEA agent and a Highway Patrol officer were killed. He's facing multiple counts of drug trafficking, money laundering, and murder charges. If he hadn't been suckered across the border to help his brother, we never would have gotten him. It's not like the Mexican government ever would have moved against him. He has everyone across the border either in his pocket or so afraid of him they don't dare move.

"If I'm not going to be happy about being here, he sure as hell isn't going to be either. That sonofabitch has more money than God and thinks he can buy his way out of here with fast-talking lawyers. Well, he's going to learn that money won't buy him a damned thing here. He's supposed to get a minimum of two ninety-minute exercise periods a week. And he's to be kept segregated from the rest of the population. So I guess we'll just have to put him out early today."

Leaning forward at the desk where he sat, Munson keyed the microphone hanging on its long boom.

"Okay, Pena, rise and shine. You've got fifteen minutes before your exercise period. I suggest you dress warm, it's a bit chilly outside."

———

Placido Pena's name meant "tranquil," which was anything but his nature. He and his brother had risen to the top of a fiercely competitive business, drug trafficking across the border from Mexico. They had reached the pinnacle of their professional lives by being more ruthless than anyone else in their business, a field not known for its gentle work ethics. Even the vicious Colombian cartels had learned to respect the Pena family of northern Mexico—those who failed to learn that lesson died.

Dark, cold eyes gleamed out from a square face—eyes that had seen streams of blood flowing in the streets at their owner's order. That face had witnessed a lot of violence in Pena's thirty-seven years of life. Thick coal-black hair and a full beard surrounded a calm face that could show intelligence, charm, and evil.

In his orange prisoner's clothing, Pena stood facing his cell door as Munson walked up. Back in the control room, Stevens watched through the heavy Lexan window as Munson approached the cell. Neither officer was armed, they only had the can of pepper spray and radio on their belts, but they needed little more. There was no place for a prisoner to try to escape to on the floor. The Federal Building was twelve stories tall and they were on the ninth floor. Below them were secured floors that were normally filled with officers and other federal law-enforcement bureaucrats. Above them were the general prisoner-holding floors and the exercise yard on the top of the building.

Escape from the exercise yard wasn't considered a

major problem, the long drop to the ground prevented that. Fencing and guard stations surrounding the exercise yard prevented suicides from climbing up and jumping. And the rooftop enclosure was too tight a spot for a helicopter to land. That area was where the two officers were going to escort their prisoner for his ninety minutes of exercise and fresh air before breakfast. By the time his exercise period was over, the few other prisoners in the building would have finished eating and have been returned to their cells for the rest of their early morning routine.

"Okay, Pena," Munson said, "time to go walkies."

Standing at the open door, Pena said, "I will not be spoken to like a dog."

"You'll be spoken to in any way I feel like," Munson said with heat in his voice. "You may have been something on the outside, but you're just another inmate in here to me.

"Oh yeah, you used to have quite a life. Fast cars, faster women, parachuting, scuba diving, horse racing, smuggling drugs, killing cops, I've read quite a bit about you."

"I'm surprised you read at all," Pena said as he gazed at Munson. His dark brown eyes steadily looked at the man. The look resembled that of a cobra sizing up its next meal. It was the guard who first broke eye contact.

It wasn't quite anger that Munson felt at Pena's insult. It would have been hard for him to put a name on exactly what his feelings were just then. They weren't quite fear, but, for a moment, he definitely felt out of his depth with the man he was facing, in spite of the bars between them. He shook off the feeling and fell back into the morning's routine.

"Open Cell Six," Munson called out loudly. He knew that Stevens could hear him clearly over the PA system that covered the area.

Back in the control room, Stevens pressed the button that electronically opened the door Pena was standing behind.

"I've read enough," Munson said, "to know that you won't be doing much of anything for a while, other than rotting your life out behind bars. But that life might not be all that long. If the Feds don't give you the death penalty for that DEA agent you killed, you're still not off the hook. They're going to turn you over to California as soon as they finish with you next month. Then the state of California will have its shot at you for killing that officer during your capture. And California has the death penalty, too. Somewhere down the line, they're going to stick a needle in your arm. And the only way you can get out of it is to be as dead as your brother."

"Then I suppose I'll have to leave your gracious hospitality before that happens," Pena said coldly. "And my brother was killed because of a traitor we both believed was a friend. That is the person who will be punished for his crimes, not me."

"Move out for exercise, inmate," Munson said roughly, and he stepped back so that Pena could go down the hall ahead of him.

As they stepped up to the control room, both Munson and Pena stopped in front of the locked door lead-

ing to the elevator. Stevens pressed the button that unlocked the cell-side door. There was only room for a
few people at a time to fit inside the cage into which
the cell-side door opened. Only when the inside door
was closed and secured could the outside door be
opened. That kept any chance of a group of prisoners
rushing the door pretty much at zero.

As Stevens unlocked the outside door, he stood up
and left the control room.

"You going with us?" Munson asked.

"I want a smoke," Stevens said. "Besides, there's no
one else even on the floor. There's nothing for me to
watch besides a bunch of empty cells."

"It's colder than hell out there," Munson said. "You
sure you need a cigarette that bad? You should stay in
here in case something comes up."

"Just what could come up this early in the morning
the day after Christmas?" Stevens said. "None of the
other prisoners are going anywhere today, the courts
aren't open, and they're not on our floor anyway. Besides, with the observation cameras being out of order
in the exercise yard, we should be following the two-
man rule."

Munson looked as if he was going to argue further
about Stevens coming along for Pena's exercise period. Then he shut his mouth and appeared to think better of it.

"Suit yourself," Munson said finally. "You're probably right anyway."

———

The elevator that the three men rode up to the roof was very limited in its travel. Besides the roof exercise area, the elevator could stop at all of the prisoner-holding floors, the mess hall floor, and the processing area down near the first floor of the building. The stairwells were all secured at each floor and were well covered with security cameras. Munson and Stevens knew they were under the watchful eyes of their fellow officers down in the main control area. At least they were being watched until they got to the roof area.

"It's a bitch that the cameras are still out," Stevens said as the men rode the elevator.

"Well, it's not like the Feds or the city would spring for someone to come out over Christmas to fix them," Munson said. "This is the first dry day we've had in a while. Probably just some rain got into one of the junction boxes is all. It's happened before. The rooftop system is shit and no one is going to shell out any money to upgrade it."

"Not when they have guys like us to go stand out in the cold," Stevens said.

"Hey," Munson said, "you can always just stay inside where it's warm."

"What, and miss your sparkling company?"

Munson didn't bother answering Stevens's comment as the elevator stopped at the top of the building. The elevator doors opened and Stevens and Pena stepped out into the holding pen leading to the exercise yard. The small building that housed the elevator machinery and guard shack was on the west side of the enclosure. When the elevator doors closed, Munson used a key from his belt ring to turn a switch on the elevator control panel. That switch opened the doors on the back side of the elevator, doors that opened onto a small guard room.

The guard room had a heavy Lexan window looking out onto the exercise yard. Below the window was a desk with a small control panel on it as well as a telephone and microphone setup. Through the window, a guard could watch the yard and be able to call for help or lock down the area without leaving his seat. At the back of the guard room was a set of stairs leading up to the top of the small structure. Those were the stairs Munson used to climb up to the open guard position on the roof of the structure.

Pena and Stevens stepped out into what they called the cattle chute. The area was a short corridor of steel fencing that controlled the prisoner's access to the elevator door. An electronically locked gate at the far end of the chute opened out into the exercise area proper. Punching a code into the numerical pad next to the gate, Stevens unlocked it.

"Go on out and get some fresh air," Stevens said. "It may be your last chance until Monday."

Pena walked out into the exercise yard. The area was well lit from the floodlights pointing down into it from around the raised wall. A line of eight-foot-high fencing surrounded the entire roof. Inside the outer fence line was a walkway the guards could use to patrol all around the exercise yard. Bordering the inside of the walkway was another eight-foot-high row of chain-link fencing completely surrounding the exercise yard.

The ten-foot-high walls around the exercise yard kept any of the prisoners from being able to look down into the area surrounding the building—not that there would have been much for Pena to see at that time of year. At nearly 5:30 in the morning, the streets of downtown San Diego were completely deserted. Even the street people who normally camped around outside had moved indoors to seek shelter from the cold. For most of the rest of the country, the local fifty-four-degree weather would have been a balmy heat wave for late December. For the people who lived in Southern California, it was downright cold.

As he walked out into the exercise yard, Pena turned and started trotting. There was a small running track that led around the basketball courts that took up the center of the area. At the north end of the machinery structure was the air-conditioning housing. Up against the wall, right in front of the air conditioner, was a workout area for the prisoners, complete with weights and benches. To the south of the structure, on the outside of the holding pen leading to the elevator, were several tables and chairs, all of them secured to the roof of the building.

For Pena, his normal exercise routine would consist of a half hour of jogging followed by a forty-five-minute workout on the exercise machinery. In the world of the jail and prisons, being fit and hard kept you from becoming a target to the rest of the predators. Pena wasn't worried about becoming a victim of jail-house life. He never intended to join the regular prison population. He kept in shape for his own reasons. Besides, in his orange prisoner's jumpsuit, keeping moving was the only way he could keep warm in this weather.

Up on top of the machinery structure, Munson stood watching Pena jogging around the basketball courts. He was standing next to the small guard shelter, a short, six-sided booth with windows on all sides where a guard could stand under cover and watch the prisoners. On top of the shelter was a flagpole with the American flag flying from it. A pair of spotlights illuminated the flag so that it could fly twenty-four hours a day.

As he stood and watched Pena, Munson spoke quietly to himself.

"A half-million dollars," he said. "Enough money to start again anywhere. And it's not like the courts would convict him, not with all of his money. Fucking lawyers."

Reaching into his shirt pocket, Munson pulled out a small plastic bag wrapped in his handkerchief. Spreading the handkerchief out over his hand, Munson dumped the contents of the bag onto it. Tumbling out of the bag was a nine-volt battery and a small plastic cube about half the size of the battery. Though he didn't know it, the cube was an IR-15 model Phoenix infrared flashing beacon. What Munson knew was that he was supposed to snap the terminals on the bottom of the cube onto the top of the battery and drop it to the rooftop.

Holding the parts inside of his handkerchief to keep his fingerprints from the battery, he snapped the two pieces together. Invisibly, the light inside the Phoenix beacon began to flash. Though Munson couldn't see anything happening, under good conditions, the flashing infrared beacon could be seen for twenty nautical miles by anyone looking for it through a night-vision device.

Dropping the beacon to the rooftop, Munson reached into his pants pocket and pulled out a cell phone. Like the parts to the beacon, the cell phone had been given to Munson by one of Pena's lawyers inside an envelope that held a page of instructions and a thick wad of cash. The money had been a down payment to Munson for a promised half-million dollars. All he had to do to earn the rest of the money was follow the directions on the sheet. As an added incentive, the sheet also listed a secure Web site for an offshore bank along with an account number and a set of codes. On a computer at the San Diego Public Library, Munson was able to pull up a bank account, a secret account in the Grand Caymans. Not even the IRS could check this account without the long strings of numbers and letters that made up the access code.

Staring at him from the computer screen was his own name followed by a huge number, $450,000.00. More money than he could ever expect to make in his whole life. Enough money to drop a job where he was spit at and ridiculed by the prisoners he guarded. And when he retaliated to the abuse, the higher-ups in the federal system looked down on him. They even took the side of the prisoners most of the time. This much money was freedom, and he wasn't going to let it go.

Assembling and dropping the beacon was only part

of what Munson had to do. Before he burned the envelope and the instruction sheet to ashes, he had memorized the few lines on the sheet. Once Pena was away, Munson would be able to access the money in his account. How the man intended to get out of the building, Munson neither knew or cared. He was just supposed to act as if everything was normal, even to giving Pena a hard time. And, he was to make sure that Pena was exercised early in the morning.

There was nothing about the cell phone that looked at all unusual. Flipping up the cover on the phone, Munson watched as the small display lit up. Punching in the numbers 999-999-999, he pushed the little green-phone symbol. When the light on the screen went out a moment later, he dropped the phone back into his pocket.

Though his heart was still beating as if he had just finished a hard run, Munson's hands had stopped shaking. Now he would just see what was going to happen next.

Inside his pocket, the Global Positioning System locator beacon disguised inside the cell phone sent out a steady, coded signal up into the night sky.

Chapter Two

"We've got a signal!" the pilot of the Super Courier said into the boom microphone of his headpiece.

"Where away?" Garcia Santiago asked from his seat behind the pilot. The heavy load of equipment bags Santiago had resting on his lap, attached to his parachute harness, kept him from being able to lean forward easily. He could just see the visual display the pilot had mounted to the top of the control panel of the Super Courier.

"Just to our west," the pilot said as he pointed to the display. There was a Palm O.S. 5.0 personal digital assistant open in a holder attached to the control panel. The PDA was connected to an NMEA–018 GPS receiver. A map of San Diego was programmed into the Fly in-flight navigation system and was showing on the screen. A small flashing dot showed where the GPS locator hidden in Munson's cell phone had been activated.

The navigation and tracking system in the plane was simple, accurate, and made up of off-the-shelf components. Using the satellite system of the GPS network meant that the display was showing the position of the locator to within a meter of where it was lying on the rooftop. And the system was completely anonymous.

"We're less than five minutes away," the pilot said, "make ready."

Santiago turned to the other two men in the plane with him. They were both ex-members of the Mexican Grupo Aerotransportado de Fuerzas Especiales (Airborne Group of Special Forces) the GAFE. Both men had been in some of the Mexican GAFEs that had operated death squads against the guerrillas and the peasants who supported them in Southern Mexico during the 1990s. The massacre of civilians during the suppression of the guerrilla bands had led to a number of GAFE troops being forced to leave the Mexican military. Those men included Franco Reyes and Alano Falcon, the other men in the plane.

Neither of the ex-GAFE troopers were physically large men, but Garcia Santiago knew very well not to judge the measure of a man by his physical size. Before he was forced to leave the United States rather than face drug charges, Santiago had been a Navy SEAL. In the Teams, he had seen men complete physical acts you would not have thought possible by just looking at them.

During a more recent career working for the leaders of the Colombian drug cartels, and gradually moving north toward the border of the United States as his reputation grew, Santiago had developed a number of contacts in the criminal underworld as well as in the international mercenary community. He had been able to pick and choose his men for the mission. The two men with him were some of the best available and had been training with him for over a month.

Franco Reyes was an experienced parachute jumper with nearly eight hundred jumps to his credit. At five feet, seven inches tall and weighing 150 pounds, he was a slender man. But Reyes was big compared to the man sitting in his lap. Alano Falcon was only an inch or so over five feet tall and weighed only 115 pounds. But Falcon had a "won't-stop" attitude that kept him going in the worst of situations. Both men were in excellent physical condition, hardened by tough hours training with Santiago. Theirs was going to be a particularly unique part of the upcoming mission. As far as they all were concerned, they were about to conduct an airborne infiltration well behind enemy lines. Only this mission was going to pay much, much better than anything they had ever done before.

It was 0537 hours in the morning, Pacific time, as the Super Courier maintained its turn toward the locator signal. Below them were clouds that started from a base of nearly 3,000 feet and extended upward to rolling domes at 10,000 feet. The plane moved along above the clouds, maintaining an altitude of 13,500 feet.

At that time of the morning, none of the local airports were operating. Even the large naval air base on North Island, to the west of San Diego Bay, had no ongoing operations. The skies were clear, and there were no special radar signals painting the plane.

They were operating at a normal altitude for local civilian aircraft and had approached from the east to appear to be just another plane. Having slipped north across the border several hundred miles away in Arizona some time earlier, the Super Courier had drawn no attention from any U.S. Border Patrol assets during its flight toward San Diego. They were even following a registered flight plan that would take them from their takeoff point in Arizona out to sea to the Channel Islands and the airstrip on Santa Catalina Island. But the passengers on board the plane had no intention of going all the way to the islands.

The men were dressed to conduct a very specialized airborne infiltration. Each of them was wearing additional protective equipment besides his helmet, balaclava, and flight suit. Impact-resistant ESS Profile NVG goggles covered the upper part of each man's face. They all had on black Hatch Centurion nylon-and-foam knee and elbow pads, Kevlar-cloth Operator Tactical padded gloves, and Han Way Fly 2000 boots. The boots were specially made for paragliding with especially strong ankle support.

They all were carrying weapons, though none of the men appeared heavily armed. On the right hip of each man was a Omega VI Airborne model assault holster holding a Glock 19 9mm pistol. Reyes had an additional long pouch strapped to his left hip, opposite the leg holding the holster. Falcon was wearing a bulky padded chest pack over his harness, a pack that extended from his lower right hip almost to his left shoulder.

On his back, Santiago was wearing an all-black Vector 3 M-series skydiving harness/container. Inside the container on the back of the harness was a Performance Designs PD-193 main canopy. The canopy was a seven-cell construction made of low-porosity fabric and capable of being very precisely handled by an experienced jumper. In case there was a problem with the main canopy, there was a pack holding another PD-193 canopy in reserve below the main container. Like almost all of the rest of his equipment, both canopies were dyed black.

Normally, Santiago would have been using his personal Katana 120 canopy. That elliptical rig only had a surface area of 120 square feet as compared to the 193 square feet of the PD canopies. But he needed the larger canopy to properly support the heavy load he was carrying. Also, the larger canopy would let him descend at roughly the same rate as Reyes and Falcon.

The other two men were only wearing one parachute rig between them. Falcon was sitting in Reyes's lap because he was attached to the man by a tandem rig. Instead of jumping with his own parachute, Falcon would be hanging from Reyes, attached to his harness at the shoulders and hips. During the descent under the shared canopy, Falcon would have his hands free while Reyes controlled the chute.

For his rig, Reyes was wearing an RW Sigma tandem parachute system. Inside the main container of the system was an Icarus 400-square-foot canopy. There was a special drogue chute on the end of a long tether that would be deployed to help keep the tandem jumpers properly oriented in a stable position for the drop. While Reyes would be working the system and paying attention to the altimeter attached to his left wrist, Falcon would be sitting back in the Sigma tandem harness. The harness went around Falcon's shoulders, chest, waist, and thighs, holding him in a partially sitting position.

As the Super Courier approached the calculated release point indicated on the PDA screen, each jumper went over his gear in a last-minute check. Nothing had slipped or become unattached. Attached to the jumpers' right ankles and wrist altimeter were activated chemical lightsticks. Stripping off the shielding tape exposed the blue-green glowing sticks. On the right hand riser of each main canopy was another glowing lightstick, this one unseen inside the parachute container. The lightsticks would be too faint to see from the ground, but they would help guide the jumpers to each other through the clouds below them.

Each man pulled down a set of AN/PVS-7B night vision goggles that were attached to quick-release fasteners on their Pro-Tec helmets. The ESS Profile NVG goggles they were each wearing had been designed to be compatible with all night-vision systems. Flipping the switch on the upper right side of the goggles turned them on. Suddenly, each man saw the inside of the aircraft cockpit become starkly bright in shades of green while looking through the AN/PVS-7Bs.

As his last act of preparation, Santiago unwrapped a short length of ribbon he had tied around his left wrist, just above his altimeter, and wadded it up in his gloved hand. Acting as the jumpmaster, Santiago signaled to Reyes and Falcon to move to the open doorway.

The two men were clumsy but had practiced this set of motions over and over again, first on the ground and then while sitting in the Super Courier they would be using on the jump. There was no danger of them accidentally falling through the door and out into the night sky.

The indicator for the aircraft kept closing with the pip showing the calculated release point for the drop. Looking down out of the plane, all that could be seen was a dark rolling sea of clouds. There were no gleams of the city that was supposed to be stretched out underneath them.

Pulling his headset off, Santiago disconnected himself from the aircraft's intercom system and moved into the doorway. He crouched in the open door of the plane on bent legs, his hands on either side of the doorway. Looking forward, Santiago could see the pilot's hand clearly. As the release point approached, the pilot started lifting his arm up in a chopping motion. First his hand came down with one finger pointing out, then two, then a clenched fist and the shouted command—"Go! . . . go! . . . go!"

Immediately, Santiago jumped out of the door, pulling himself through with his arms and pushing with his legs. A few seconds later, Reyes and Falcon pulled themselves through the door and pushed away from the plane. All three men dropped away into the darkness and were instantly swallowed up by the night.

Assuming a good modified frog position, Santiago fell through the sky in a stable drop. His legs were bent up at the knees and his hands were on either side of his head with his arms bent at the elbows. The air whistled past his ears and the changing pressure made his eardrums pop. It seemed that only a few seconds passed before he entered the top layer of the clouds.

The impact with the cloud gave Santiago the sensation of hitting a solid surface. The water droplets that made up the cloud were not solid enough to affect his fall at all, but the sudden darkness on entering the cloud was startling.

Moving his head only slightly, Santiago could make out the glowing lightstick attached to his altimeter. He had to turn his head more than he liked to in order to see the lightstick through the night-vision goggles, but his experience and expertise gave him the ability to maintain a stable position in spite of the movement.

When he had opened his hand after exiting the plane, Santiago had let go of the ribbon he was holding. Now he could see the streamer of cloth as it fluttered up from his hand. The moisture in the cloud built up on the single lens of his night-vision goggles, blocking his view of the altimeter. As he carefully reached and wiped off the goggles with his hand, Santiago suddenly saw that the ribbon was fluttering directly in front of his face. The streamer was extended from his left hand straight across to his right side. Without the indicator as he fell through the clouds,

Santiago would have never known he was tilting—
outside of the wind, there was no sensation of him even
falling. Turning his body, he straightened his position
and continued to fall through the cloud.

The darkness inside the cloud seemed to become
even blacker. Suddenly, Santiago found himself breaking through and underneath the clouds. The altimeter
on his wrist read just below 4,000 feet and the city of
San Diego spread out below him.

An instant later, the bulky figures of Reyes and Falcon broke through the clouds less than a hundred feet
from where Santiago was falling. The ballooned
drogue chute streamed behind the tandem jumpers,
both men maintaining a modified frog position, Falcon
having his feet sticking up between Reyes's spread
legs.

Looking down, Santiago could see that they were
dropping almost directly above the huge L-shaped federal office building just to the northeast of their target.
Through his night-vision goggles, each man could see
the brilliant pulsing of the infrared beacon on top of
their target. As they dropped to 3,500 feet, Santiago
and Reyes opened their main canopies.

Both Ram-air canopies streamed out from their container, pulled by the small pilot chutes the jumpers had
released. The dark cloth canopies trailed from the pilot
chutes like long tails as they slipped through the air.
The individual cells bulged from the pressure of the air
that was rammed by the momentum of the fall into the
leading edges of the canopies. The inflating cells
curved the cloth of the canopies into flat rectangular

wings, wings that could be controlled and flown through the air like a plane.

Holding on to the toggle line controls, the jumpers steered for the top of the tall building off to their left. The night-vision goggles were no longer needed because of the bright lights illuminating the top of the building. Automatic high-light cutoff controls turned down the power of the goggles, protecting both the image tubes, and the eyes of the wearer. Watching the flag on top of the flagpole told Santiago the direction and approximate speed of the wind below them. Correcting their approach by pulling on the toggles, Santiago and Reyes turned their canopies and tracked to the wind.

Now the jumpers silently slipped through the air toward their target.

———

Watching Pena run around the circumference of the exercise area made Stevens realize even more that smoking was a bad habit for him or anyone else. He knew that he should quit, it wasn't as though he didn't hear that advice from just about everyone. For right now, these midnight-to-eight shifts were real killers. Coming up as he was to the last few hours of a shift, he found that a cigarette helped keep him awake. And even if they were watching just one prisoner right now, staying alert in this kind of job was a good thing.

Turning his back to the wind, Stevens reached into his jacket pocket and pulled out a pack of cigarettes along with his Zippo lighter. Tapping the pack against his finger, he popped up one of the slim white cylinders and drew it out with his lips. Flipping open the lighter, he thumbed it into flame. Tilting his head down, Stevens cupped his hands around his face and lit the cigarette.

"You know, those things will kill you," Pena said as he trotted by.

"Yeah," Stevens said, "well, just keep running. You'll stay warmer that way."

Damn, even the inmates were harassing him about smoking. Fuck it. With his eyes closed, he drew in a lungful of the rich, fragrant smoke. Turning his face back up, Stevens blew out the tobacco smoke in a large, white cloud.

"What the hell," he thought. Suddenly, there was a sparkling red line within the cloud of smoke. The line darted about and then disappeared as the smoke was blown away by the wind. Looking down, he could now see that there was a red dot bouncing around his chest. The cigarette hanging forgotten between his fingers, his eyes were drawn up into the sky where the red light had come from. Stevens raised his hand to shield his eyes from the glare of the lights around the exercise yard and saw a red light with a suddenly flashing faint white light below it. Before he had time to more than wonder, the sledgehammer blows of the 9mm bullets striking his chest slammed him backward against the fencing.

The frangible copper bullets tore into his chest and shattered into hundreds of copper fragments. The shockwave of the impacts and the ripping fragments shattered his heart and shredded his lungs. The shock of the wounds was so overwhelming, there was no pain, only a heavy pressure on his chest as the bright copper taste of blood filled his mouth. Through his fading eyesight and astonishment, Stevens's last thought on earth was that he saw the dark wings of an angel coming down toward him. And then he saw nothing at all.

Chapter Three

In the tandem rider position, strapped to Santiago, Falcon swept the rooftop with the muzzle of his submachine gun. His MP5K-PDW had a long suppressor screwed on to the muzzle. The beam from the laser sight above the suppressor was plainly visible to Falcon through his night-vision goggles. To reduce the already-compact size of the MP5K-PDW, Falcon had removed the folding stock and fitted the weapon with a receiver cap that had a mounting point for a sling. The sling was attached to the weapon by a spring clip, and looped around Falcon's upper chest and left shoulder as he rode in front of Reyes on the Sigma tandem parachute system. With the MP5K-PDW pushed out against the resistance of the sling, Falcon was able to accurately aim the stubby weapon with the aid of the laser sight.

The two men had practiced their combined approach to a targeted landing zone for weeks out in the desert of northern Sonora, Mexico, less than fifty miles southeast of Nogales. That was where Santiago had them practicing to break Pena from the federal lockup in San Diego. Falcon still had bruises on his chest and legs from the practice tandem jumps that hadn't gone well. The MP5K-PDW submachine gun had been carried in the case strapped to his chest. He had pulled it out during the approach to the rooftop.

Loaded, the submachine gun seemed to be nearly as wide as it was long, due to the 100-round Beta C-Mag drum magazine that was attached to it. The two drums stuck out from either side of the weapon, each loaded with fifty rounds of Engel Ballistic Research's Sky Marshal frangible 9mm ammunition. The special powdered copper/nylon matrix hollowpoint bullets would shatter if they hit a hard target, minimizing the danger of a ricochet. But they would rip deeply into the soft tissue of a human body, as Stevens had suddenly found out.

A long silver sound suppressor was attached to the threaded muzzle of the MP5K-PDW. That was the source of the white flashing light that Stevens had seen next to the laser sight of the weapon. The suppressor had lessened the sound of the shots so much that the wind covered what little was left of the noise. The cracking zip sound of the high-velocity 9mm frangible bullets, breaking the sound barrier at the muzzle of the suppressor as they fired at 1,700 feet per second, wasn't even recognizable as a gunshot. No sound of gunfire even reached the rooftop, or the city streets far below.

Sweeping the area of the roof in front of him, Falcon couldn't see any further targets. He only had a few seconds to look over the area as Reyes brought the tandem parachute rig in for a landing. One moment, the street-lights were visible more than a hundred feet below them. Then the fence line swept by only a few feet under their feet as the tandem jumpers came in on the roof.

The incessant landing practice demanded by Santiago proved its value as both men moved in smooth unison dropping down to the rooftop. While still holding up his MP5K-PDW, Falcon lifted his legs, bending them at the hip and knee, so he was in a sitting position. With Falcon's legs out of the way, Reyes spread his feet out to help cushion the impact of landing.

Pulling down on both of the steering toggles, Reyes flared the canopy, causing it to stall and lose much of its forward momentum. The stalled parachute dropped the tandem jumpers almost straight down from a height of less than six feet. The wall of the machinery structure was coming up to them just as Reyes's feet touched down on the rooftop.

Immediately releasing the left-hand toggle, Reyes and Falcon twisted to the left as Reyes's legs took up the pressure of hitting the roof. Both men fell on their sides, rolling with the impact. The turning motion twisted the suspension lines together, and helped collapse the huge Icarus canopy before the wind could catch it and drag the jumpers into the fence or back up into the air and off the roof entirely.

With the canopy collapsed, Reyes reached to the toggles and pulled the quick-release catches that held Falcon to him. Rolling away, Falcon quickly scrambled to his feet, putting his back up to the nearest wall and sweeping the rooftop with the muzzle of his MP5K-PDW.

Reyes had his hands full gathering up his parachute canopy and lines into a bundle. He wasn't acting to recover the chute for another use, just to get it out of the way of Santiago who was coming in for a landing a few seconds later. It was Santiago who was bringing in the means of escape for them all.

With the AN/PVS-7B night-vision goggles pushed up onto his helmet, Santiago came in fast and low, pulling his steering toggles down at what looked like the very last moment. With the toggles pulled very low, the black PD-193 canopy of his parachute seemed to almost hit an invisible wall in the air. The ex-SEAL's feet hit the ground in unison, trotting forward to match his last bit of forward speed. Turning hard and bending forward at the waist as he released his right-hand toggle, Santiago collapsed his chute, quickly reducing it to a pile of cloth fluttering in the breeze.

Standing almost directly under the men as they flew in over the building's east wall, Pena just stared for a moment in admiration and awe. He had been a skydiver himself for years, but this was a demonstration of daring and skill rarely seen by anyone. Even in the military, jumping into a cloud-covered night sky and landing on an area the size of a rooftop would be considered something extraordinary. To do it into a crowded city with no special beacons showing on the landing zone wouldn't even be considered possible, let alone practical. And here three men had done it for him.

As Santiago was gathering up his parachute canopy and shedding his Vector 3 M-series harness, Pena walked up to him. In spite of his wearing a bright orange prisoner's garb, his approach to Santiago caused a reaction Pena did not expect.

In a fast, smooth motion, Santiago dropped his harness and pulled out his Glock 19 pistol from its Omega VI holster on his thigh before the whole rig hit the rooftop. Pena's eyes were pulled to the parachute rig as it fell, when he looked back up, he was staring down the muzzle of a pistol not a dozen feet from his face. Instantly, he realized he was looking at a man who was more used to dealing out death than even Pena himself was. For only a second, there was a view of what could have been fear in Pena's eyes—then the look was gone.

"You are Santiago?" Pena said after a moment.

"No names please," Santiago said. "But you were possibly expecting someone else?"

"No, of course," Pena said, "but my lawyer only told me that you would be coming to release me, not how you would enter the building."

"He didn't have a need to know," Santiago said, "besides, he didn't want to know. He did what he was paid for and took almost no risk for it, that was enough for him."

"But how are we going to get out of this building?"

"We already are outside of the building," Santiago said. "The trick now is to get down from here."

"You brought rappelling ropes and equipment?" Pena said as he looked at the cloth bags strapped to Santiago.

"Too far and too slow," Santiago said. "Besides, rappelling wouldn't get us away from the building fast enough. I was told you were an experienced skydiver, Jefe. It's time for your first BASE jump."

The use of the "chief" honorific softened the lack of respect Pena noticed in Santiago's tone. But the man was something of a legend in the very select circles of the men who made their living running tons of narcotics into the United States. He could be excused because of the pressure of the moment. But a BASE jump (Building, Antenna, Span [bridge], and Earth)?

"Time," Santiago called out.

"Thirty seconds," Falcon said from across the rooftop.

Falcon and Reyes were over by the cattle chute gate. As Falcon looked to Santiago for a signal, the leader of the breakout nodded his head.

With a short, snarling burst of fire, Falcon blasted the locking mechanism from the gate. The frangible 9mm projectiles from the EBR Air Marshal ammunition smashed into the lock. In spite of each bullet only weighing eighty-five grains, their power was evident as the steel lock broke into pieces. After they had delivered their energy against the lock, the frangible powdered copper and nylon bullets broke into dust from the impact. Reyes jerked open the door and the two men entered the fenced corridor.

At the far end of the cattle chute, past the elevator door, was a second gate. Again, Falcon's submachine gun spit out 9mm projectiles at a rate of 900 rounds per minute. The sound of the burst was reduced to a stuttering thudding sound by the stainless-steel suppressor screwed to the muzzle. A half-dozen bullets removed the second lock from the equation, and the gate was open.

On the far side of the gate was a ladder leading up to the top of the machinery structure. As Santiago stripped off the cloth bags he had strapped to his legs, he looked to Pena.

"Is there anyone else up here?" he asked.

"There's a second guard," Pena said. "He's the one who normally escorts me up here but I haven't seen him since we got up here."

"Two!" Santiago called out.

Falcon looked at Santiago and nodded. With Falcon leading the way, his MP5K-PDW pointing forward, Reyes and Falcon went up the ladder to the roof of the machinery structure. No one was visible during a quick look around, so both men approached the guard shelter. With his Glock in his hand, Reyes made ready to open the door to the guard shelter. Falcon held his submachine gun at the ready and nodded. Reyes pulled the door open and Falcon sprayed the inside of the shelter as soon as it was exposed.

The bullets ripped across the small area, shattering the windows and tearing up a small control panel.

"Don't kill him!" Pena shouted. He was just coming up the ladder. Right behind Pena was Santiago, the handles to the bags he had carried on the jump slung over his shoulder.

Just as he was about to sweep the other side of the small shelter, Falcon held his fire and raised the muzzle of his weapon. With the stuttering sound of the suppressed submachine gun gone, the tinkle of falling glass could be heard along with a high-pitched sobbing. Pena walked up to the shelter. Looking in, he saw Sergeant Munson scrabbling around against the wall, crying and refusing to look at who was standing at the door. After a moment, Pena could make out the words Munson was saying.

"No one was supposed to be killed," he kept repeating in a high-pitched whine. "No one was supposed to be killed. There wasn't supposed to be any shooting."

"Munson!" Pena said.

"No, no, no," Munson cried as he put up his hands, thrusting them out toward Pena. "Don't let him kill me. Please, don't let him kill me. I did what I was told."

"Don't worry, Munson," Pena said in a calm voice, "I won't let him kill you. You did what you were supposed to."

"That's right," Munson said as he finally looked at Pena. "I did what I was supposed to. Stevens wasn't supposed to be here."

"No, he wasn't," Pena said, as he gestured to Falcon to give him the submachine gun.

Falcon looked to Santiago, who was opening up his bags and pulling bundles of equipment out. Santiago looked up for a moment and nodded.

"We don't have time for this," he said.

Quickly unsnapping the MP5K-PDW from the sling he had looped around his shoulder, Falcon handed the stubby weapon to Pena.

"And don't be afraid," Pena said quietly to Munson as he took the weapon from Falcon. "But we must make it look good, as if you had no part in this whatsoever."

"Uh, okay," Munson said with his voice still shaky.

"But you really shouldn't have spoken badly about my brother," Pena said and he pulled up the submachine gun.

Before Munson could do anything more than stare with bulging eyes at the weapon, Pena pulled the trigger. The frangible 9mm projectiles tore into the prostrate guard, shoving him across the floor of the small shelter. The power of the rounds almost exploded the man's chest, the cloth blowing into tatters as blood and tissue sprayed across the area.

"Time!" Santiago called out.

"One minute," answered Falcon as he looked at his watch. Pena handed him back his weapon and Falcon clipped it back into his sling.

The situation at the guard shelter seemed to be under control, so while the men were talking, and Munson was dying, Reyes had turned back to his job. Along one of the poles supporting the fence on the west wall, Reyes was cutting free the chain-link mesh. Using a short pair of bolt cutters he had pulled from the pouch on his left thigh, Reyes had cut free the fencing as high as he could reach. Now, he was doing the same thing along the bottom of the fencing, where it was wired to a pipe running around the edge of the wall.

While Reyes was opening a hole in the fence, Falcon was standing guard, watching across the area of the rooftop with his MP5K-PDW in his hands.

"Here, put these on," Santiago said as he handed

Pena a set of boots. They were the same kind of Han Way Fly 2000 boots that the rest of the team were wearing. "We can't afford you breaking an ankle when you land wearing those sneakers you have on."

Stripping off the cheap canvas and rubber sneakers all the prisoners wore, Pena pulled on the boots and laced them up tight. When he looked up, Santiago was holding out a set of protective Centurion pads. The velcro straps that held the pads were quickly secured around Pena's elbows and knees.

"Thirty seconds," Falcon said.

By this time, Reyes had finished cutting free the fence flap and had pulled it back—securing it in place with a loose piece of wire. Now he was opening up a container that had two pieces of rope tied around it. As he pulled them out, the contents of the container could now be seen to be another parachute rig. As Reyes began to put on his harness, Santiago was holding an identical rig up in front of Pena.

"Now this," Santiago said as he started to help Pena into his rig.

The parachute systems were Vertigo Warlock containers and harnesses, each container being packed with a specially rigged Dagger 277 canopy. Only Falcon's rig was different, his Warlock container held a Dagger 222 canopy. The systems were specially made for BASE jumping, the low-altitude parachute jumping from buildings, antennas, spans (bridges), and earth (cliffs). Each man strapped into his own harness. Since he was standing guard, Falcon was the last man to don his rig.

"Okay," Santiago said. "These are static-line opening rigs. You don't have anything to concern yourself with about opening the canopy. You jump out and take up a good free-fall position. Don't look down, don't look to either side. Keep your head up and look at the horizon.

"You have to fall free for a couple of seconds to build up enough speed to open the canopy properly. Once she pops, you steer across the street. There's a good-sized patch of grass and bushes just fifty to sixty meters to the southwest. An easy drop. Steer the canopy with the toggles and keep away from the building. People do this all the time for fun."

"You consider this fun?" Pena asked.

"Oh, this is a blast," Santiago said. "You can tell me how much you liked it when we're on the ground. Any questions?"

"Where's the reserve?" Pena said as he looked down at his rig.

"There isn't one," Santiago said, "and you wouldn't have time to use it anyway. Once you land, there will be a gray van waiting on the street, right next to the south end of the grass patch. The van will have the name 'Princesa' on its side."

"Princesa?" Pena said, "why Princesa?"

"It's the name of the other part of this ride," Santiago said. "Now, once you get to the ground, don't try anything fancy. Just do a standard parachute landing fall (PLF). A regular PLF, understand? Don't try to land standing up, just roll with it."

Santiago handed Pena the last item from the gear bag, a black Pro-Tec helmet.

"Ready?" he asked as Pena secured the helmet to his head.

Pena looked up at Santiago and a wide smile crossed his face.

"After you, please."

Stepping up to the hole in the fence, Santiago wrapped the wire coming out from the pack of his parachute container to the steel pole the fence had been attached to. Snapping the flat metal clip to the wire, he turned to the edge of the wall. Leaping forward with his arms spread and his elbows bent, Santiago dropped from sight.

Falling almost a third of the way to the ground, Santiago dropped for over a second before the wire stopped playing out from the container on his back. With his head tilted up, the ex-SEAL held a perfect, stable modified-frog free-fall position as he dropped to the street below. The static line wire pulled open the container on his back and drew out the parachute canopy inside. The canopy streamed out from the container, trailing its suspension lines behind it. As the air rushed into the cells of the canopy, the 277 square feet of F-111 cloth bulged and took shape.

Less than sixty feet from the ground, Santiago's fall slowed and he took control of the parachute. Pulling on the toggles, he turned the canopy and started gliding across the street. He reached the patch of grass and missed the low bushes. The area was very dark, only the light from a few streetlamps reached into the shadows. The fall of the parachute canopies was silent and the early hour and cold had kept anyone from being around. It was only a few minutes before six o'clock in the morning. Traffic hadn't even really started yet in the city.

Looking up, Santiago could see a second parachute falling to the ground, following roughly the same path he had. The cloth of the canopies was black and it was like watching a giant bat glide across the dark sky. The man hanging below the parachute landed with a grunt as he hit the ground with his feet held tightly together, knees bent, and body relaxed.

Falling in a controlled roll to his legs, side, and shoulder, Pena completed a PLF, spreading out the impact of his landing over the length of his body. As Santiago dropped his rig and went over to Pena, Reyes jumped off the roof in the same manner as the first two men. Then it was Falcon's turn.

With his weapon dangling from its sling, Falcon attached his static line to the same pole the other three men had. The wires from their parachutes were now hanging down along the side of the building, all but invisible in the dark. Turning to make one last look across the roof, Falcon swept the area with the muzzle of his weapon. Satisfied everything was clear, he turned and leaped from the wall. Only he was standing too close to the pole and the jagged edges of the fence wire still attached to it.

As Falcon leapt, the sharp end of a wire brushed against his pant leg and dug into the cloth. The tough Nomex of the flight suit resisted the pull of the wire and refused to tear at first. Then, the sharp edge of the wire cut through the cloth and Falcon's leg was free. But by then it was far too late.

The small man might have survived the pull on his pant leg throwing him off balance. But Falcon made the final mistake of looking down at what had caught him. With his head turned down, he wasn't in a stable free-fall position. He tumbled forward and continued his fall. The wire of the static line kept paying out as Falcon fell, but as he dropped, he began to turn over.

Within the first second of his fall, Falcon was too terrified to even make a sound. As he dropped, the canopy was pulled out by the static line, only it didn't inflate from the air pressure pushing against it. Instead, the black cloth wrapped around Falcon as he dropped and kept turning. It covered him like a shroud as he hurtled to the ground. The only final mercy that Falcon had was the fact that it took less than four seconds for him to fall the twelve stories to the ground.

The small, squeaking scream that finally made it out of Falcon's mouth was cut short at his impact with the hard concrete of the sidewalk. The thud was flat, dull, and final. Falcon was moving at more than fifty miles an hour when he hit the ground, the impact more than enough to instantly kill him in spite of the protective clothing and equipment he was wearing. The MP5K-PDW submachine gun that he had been carrying and practiced with so much was driven deeply into his chest by the impact—smashing his sternum and ribs, and crushing his heart.

Chapter Four

Across the street, Santiago and Pena witnessed Falcon's final seconds of life. Reyes hit the ground lightly and remained on his feet. Turning, he collapsed his canopy, and heard the sound of Falcon's impact with the ground.

The loss of a man on a mission was something that just happened. Santiago had made certain that no piece of equipment, clothing, weapon, or ammunition, could be traced to him. He had paid top dollar to have the gear all sent to multiple cut-outs in order to confuse the trail to him or to Pena's organization. Where possible, labels had been removed and serial numbers cut out. Not one of the men were carrying anything that could identify them personally. And there were no witnesses to their action.

"Come," Santiago said. "There's nothing to do for him. The van is right here."

Parked under a small tree not twenty meters away

was a very sorry-looking van. Dented and beaten, the rear bumper of the van was tilted and looked to be held on with wire. The entire machine didn't appear to be capable of making it two blocks, let alone making a getaway from what was essentially a prison break. But the muffled sound of a well-tuned powerful engine rumbled out as it was fed some gas. The tires looked dirty and scuffed, but the treads were almost brand new. The men hastily gathered up their parachute canopies and dashed to the vehicle.

Pulling open the back doors of the van, Santiago waved Pena into the van and climbed in after him. Stepping into the van, Reyes pulled the door shut behind him. There wasn't a sound or any lights coming on in the building just across the street from where they sat.

"Go," Santiago said.

In the front seat of the van, Jago Diaz shifted the transmission into drive and pulled away from the curb. He drove south down State Street, quickly, but not fast enough to draw any attention. The beat-up outside of the van was nothing but a cover for the very well maintained machine inside. Reaching the corner at G Street, Diaz turned right and headed toward the waterfront less than a kilometer away.

While Diaz drove them toward the water, the men in the back of the van began stripping off their harnesses, equipment, and protective gear. Reyes pulled up a barracks bag and opened it. After passing out bundles of clothing to Santiago and Pena, Reyes opened a bundle for himself and began to change clothes.

"If you can't strip out of those jail clothes fast, we'll cut them off," Santiago said as he handed Pena a bundle.

For a mad few minutes, the three men almost rolled around the back of the van, pulling items of clothing on and off. When the van finally reached the waterfront area off Harbor Street, it wasn't two commandos and a prisoner who climbed out of the back of the van. Instead, it was the rough-clothed workingmen who manned the fishing boats—the same kind of boats that were tied up to the commercial pier in the Tuna Harbor right next to them.

Leaning back inside the van, Santiago flipped the cover back on a haversack lying on the floor of the vehicle. Choosing one of several small green cylinders inside the haversack, he lifted up the one with a tag on it that said 15. Pulling the ring of the M60 fuse igniter, he lit off the delay to the incendiary charge in the haversack. In fifteen minutes, the two AN-M14 TH3 incendiary grenades would ignite. The more than three pounds of thermate in the two grenades combined would burn at 4,000 degrees Fahrenheit, spraying molten iron as a byproduct. It would be only seconds later that the five-gallon container of gasoline under the haversack would burst into flame and completely consume the van, the equipment, and parachutes left inside it. It would be a spectacular fire.

Coming out of the van, Santiago pulled back the sleeve of his left arm and looked at his watch. Pressing some buttons on his Casio G-Shock watch, Santiago looked up at the men around him.

"We're running nearly five minutes ahead of schedule," Santiago said.

"This is a problem?" Pena asked.

"Not really," Santiago said, "besides, it gives us a moment to grab a cup of coffee."

"Coffee?" Pena said in astonishment. "You want coffee? Now?"

"What I want is for you to be seen for just a second by a witness," Santiago said as he handed Pena a ten dollar bill. Pointing to a small coffee shop next to the docks, he told the stunned man:

"Cream, two sugars please. We'll wait here."

Not completely understanding the situation, but trusting the man who had saved him from a probable death sentence, Pena went to get the coffee.

It was just ten minutes later that four apparently commercial fishermen walked up the dock to where the nearly fifty-year-old thirty-six-foot trawler *Princesa* lay tied to her moorings. Lights were on in the cabin of the salmon trawler and the sound of an engine could be heard rumbling softly. The men walked past another fisherman standing on the dock near a thirty-three-foot trawler that was tied up.

"Going out today?" the man said as he turned to the four walking on the dock.

"Yup," Santiago said. "Going to try our hand at some channel rockfish."

"Well, you're sure going to have to catch a bunch of them to pay for the gasoline that engine uses," the fisherman said. "I can't see why you don't change over to a diesel, it's a lot safer. Cheaper, too."

"No argument from me," Santiago said as the rest of his men walked past him. "But the skipper says we'll get a new engine the next time this one needs an overhaul."

"Well, good luck."

"Thanks."

Walking over to the *Princesa*, Santiago followed the others and climbed aboard.

"Let's go," he said to the man standing at the wheel.

"Let go forward," Captain Naldo Flores said as he leaned out the port to his left, "let go aft."

Standing up on the dock, Diaz removed the last restraining line from the dock bollard and tossed it to Reyes up on deck. Then he jumped aboard. Reyes quickly joined Santiago and Pena in a small cabin aft of the wheelhouse. Going into the wheelhouse, Diaz took up a station in the back of the compartment. Where he could watch Captain Flores at the wheel.

Captain Flores was more than capable of taking the boat out on his own. He gunned the engines as he backed away from the docks and turned the bow of the *Princesa* south to the opening in the breakwater that led out to San Diego Bay.

"I can't believe you intend to make our escape in this old tub," Pena said. "She's so old that the wood in her hull is rotting."

"Not quite," Santiago said. "The important parts of this boat are sound and dependable. And she was chosen in part just because of that wooden hull you mentioned."

"Still, I can't see escaping in this slow pig," Pena said.

"Oh, we won't get away in her," Santiago said. "But this is a good boat for you to die on."

Pena stared at the man standing in front of him. This made no sense, who would go to all of this trouble just to kill him. It would have been easier just to let the American legal system have its way with him.

"Relax," Santiago said, as if he knew what Pena was thinking. "If we wanted to kill you, you would have never gotten off of that building. Those very high-priced drug lawyers you hired all said the same thing. Even if we broke you out and got you back into Mexico, you would be a hunted man. The U.S. government could bring enough pressure to bear on Mexico that they would have to do something about you, no matter who you had control of. Or, you could end up with a price on your head so high that some bounty hunter might get lucky and take you down."

"Oh, a price on my head," Pena said as the shock he had originally felt changed into anger, "as has worked so well for the Americans against Osama bin Laden? They're offering what, five million for his head?"

"Instead of thinking about bin Laden," Santiago said calmly, "you would do better to think about Saddam Hussein. Or even more to the point, his two sons—his two dead sons."

That thought sobered Pena quickly. He had not gotten where he was by acting irrationally. He well knew the value of money as a tool to make men do things they would never consider otherwise. The anger in Pena's face gave way to thoughtful consideration of the situation as Santiago watched the men. Now he continued his explanation of what led up to his complex plan.

"As far as the lawyers on either side of the border are concerned, you have to give the Mexican government some kind of reasonable excuse not to hunt you down. You have influence over a lot of very powerful people in Mexico City as well as all over the countryside. All they need is a reason, some kind of plausible deniability they can use to ignore any American requests. The very best one is to give some evidence of your death during this escape."

"And how do you plan to pull off this magic feat?" Pena asked. He was more than impressed with what Santiago had accomplished up to that point. It would be very interesting to see what else the man had up his sleeve.

The trawler had moved well out of the Tuna Harbor and was heading northwest, out toward the main channel of the bay. The fat-hulled boat was moving steadily, but still hadn't reached her maximum cruising speed of only ten knots. Even with her engines going all out, the boat could only do eleven knots. Eleven knots, little more than twelve miles an hour, was not a great speed for a getaway. But a slow trawler didn't draw much attention at a major seaport city.

Captain Flores was well aware that the hard-looking men who had hired his fishing boat weren't interested in commercial fishing. But the fishing had been poor and he couldn't afford to pass up the money they had offered. He had almost balked at giving the men the keys to his boat weeks earlier, but another handful of dollars had convinced him. Besides, one of the few things that was paid up to date was his insurance on the *Princesa*.

The money he had received made for a good Christmas for him and his family, the first they had seen in a few years. He had ignored the large packages that he noticed around the deck and in the compartments. It was much harder to ignore the new bulkhead that cut the main hold in half. The only easy thing was to concentrate on maintaining the course and speed he was to follow. That, and ignoring the eyes of the man who was watching his back.

The bearded man who had been in the group that came aboard acted like he was used to being in charge. But it was the taller man, the one the other two deferred to, the one with the hard cold eyes, he was in command. That much was obvious for anyone who had worked with groups of men before. Flores would be glad when this job was over and he could go back to just working the sea.

As the men Captain Flores was thinking about discussed their plans, the incendiary charge back in the van ignited. The boat was too far away for him to be able to hear the explosion of the gasoline container, and then the blast from the fuel tank of the van. But Captain Flores could see the glow of the fire come in through the starboard side of the wheelhouse. He knew that whatever the trouble was behind them, it had something to do with the men he had on board.

Just a moment before Flores saw the light from the fire, Santiago had looked at his watch. The timer he had set at the van had reached zero. Stepping out onto the deck, he could see the fire in the parking lot almost three-quarters of a kilometer behind them. It wouldn't take long for the authorities to realize that the *Princesa* had something to do with the fire—not with the name of the boat painted on the side of the van.

"Time to move," Santiago said as he ducked his head back into the cabin. "Things are going to start happening fast now. Reyes, you're going to have to take up Falcon's station. Pena, come below with me."

Without a word, Reyes stepped out of the cabin and headed to the stern of the boat. He crouched down behind a long crate, one of the boxes Captain Flores had noticed as now being on board.

Going over to the hatch above the central hold, Santiago lifted up what was obviously a very new steel cover. In spite of being heavily made, the hatch cover raised easily on its counterbalancing springs. There was a ladder attached to the forward bulkhead of the hold and Santiago used it to climb down into the center of the boat. Pena followed him down into the smelly darkness.

The hold Santiago and Pena were standing in stank of old fish and sawdust. Boxes of equipment lay around the hold, some of which were very familiar to Pena. There were crates of hand grenades, M26A1 fragmentation grenades according to the markings on the boxes. A long cardboard box with a side-mounted handle and webbed strapping around it had markings that said it held five M72A2 LAW rockets. There were metal ammunition cans, unmarked cardboard boxes, and a long, low mound of something on the deck of the hold, something covered with a black tarp.

"There's enough material in here to raid the Federal Building and fight our way out," Pena said as he looked around.

"That's what it's supposed to look like," Santiago said. "Now help me with this tarp."

Both men unlashed the tarp and pulled it back from four long, bulky bags. The bags were so cold that they seemed to suck the heat right out of the air. Pena suddenly felt a lot colder as he realized just what the bags were.

"Those are bodies?" he said.

"Can't have a really convincing death without a body," Santiago said. "Now help me get these out of the bags."

Bending down, Santiago pulled an Emerson Commander knife from his right side pocket. Thumbing open the curved black blade of the Commander, Santiago turned the blade edge-up and used it to slice open the bags. As he moved to the next bag, next to him, Pena began pulling the cloth cover off the body.

Wherever Santiago had come up with the bodies, the original occupants had died hard. The flesh was cold to the touch, but not frozen. The bodies were bent and mangled, as if they had been in some kind of a wreck. One body that was Pena's size was missing its entire face, the whole front of the head and jaw had been torn away. Even as hard as he was, Pena could feel the gorge rise up in his throat at the sight.

"But how will they ever mistake these bodies for us?" Pena said to take his mind off of what he was handling.

"They won't really," Santiago said as he stood up. "There won't be enough of them left to recognize." He flipped a tarp up that was covering a smaller mound next to the bodies. It was two green cloth haversacks. The rectangular bags were about a foot long and slightly thicker than they were wide. Several coils of green fuse lay on top of the bags with an M60 fuse igniter attached to the end of each coil.

Fascinated, Pena leaned forward to look at the explosives.

"C-4?" he asked.

"Forty pounds worth of it," Santiago said.

"But if the bodies are blown apart by the explosions," Pena said, "won't they just run DNA tests?"

"Yes, but they don't have to find a body, or even parts of it if the explosion is big enough," Santiago said. "Just a sample of blood would be enough to limit their search once it was identified."

Before Pena could straighten up from where he was examining the explosives, Santiago's right hand suddenly darted out. As fast as a snake's forked tongue, the hand seemed to just pass over Pena's arm, the blade of the Commander in that hand leaving a bright, red line growing on the arm as it passed.

As Pena gasped and spun away, Santiago tossed an old-fashioned orange kapok life jacket to him.

"Press that over the wound," Santiago said. "Get it good and bloody. Then I'll give you a waterproof bandage for it."

Without a word, Pena rubbed the bloody slash with the cloth cover of the life jacket. In front of him was a man who considered all of the details, and accepted what had to be done. Santiago was valuable, and dangerous.

There was the sudden sound of heavy gunfire from the deck almost directly over their heads. The noise was the knocking thunder of a light machine gun being fired from the stern deck of the *Princesa*.

"Sounds like the party has started," Santiago said.

Taking the bloody life jacket from Pena, Santiago handed the man a plastic bag with a four-inch Bloodstopper dressing in it.

"Here," he said, "put this on, then gear up."

With his foot, Santiago pushed a heavy duffle bag across the deck to Pena. Leaving the other man standing there, Santiago went back up the ladder and out onto the deck. He tossed the bloody life jacket to the deck as he headed to where Reyes was at the stern of the boat.

As he had suspected, the sheriff's cruiser from the Embarcadero Marina Park just south of the Tuna Harbor, had come after the *Princesa*. Having opened up the long case on the stern deck, Reyes had pulled up a loaded M60 machine gun and sent a long burst of 7.62mm slugs dancing across the water toward the sheriff's boat. The flashing light on top of the cabin cruiser shattered as the streaking bullets slashed through it.

When Santiago came up next to Reyes, the sheriff's boat had already turned back and was heading toward shore at a high rate of speed.

"Next will be the Coast Guard," Santiago said as he reached into the box.

Pulling on a lanyard line that went down into the engine compartment, Santiago fired several igniters buried in oil-soaked cotton waste. Smoke quickly began billowing up from behind the boat. Picking up a folding stock AKMS-47 from the box, Santiago turned to the wheelhouse where Captain Flores was looking back at the men with wide eyes.

"We will never be taken alive!" Santiago said as he brandished the AK.

Flores was beginning to look panic-stricken. To emphasize Santiago's point, and help push Flores to the breaking point, Diaz pulled a Smith & Wesson Model 36 revolver from his pocket. The small five-shot revolver was loaded with Federal 125-grain .38 Special hollowpoints. The weapon sounded like a small cannon in the confines of the wheelhouse as Diaz fired it up into the overhead.

Deciding that he had had just about enough of these madmen, Flores darted out of the wheelhouse and made a dive over the side of the boat. He had no way of knowing that if he had frozen in place with fear, Diaz had orders to throw him over the side. The plan was to have a witness to some of the actions on the fishing boat, and Flores was that witness. Later, he would tell the authorities that he had expected to feel the impact of bullets across his back at any moment. He could see that smoke was pouring out of the engine compartment and smell the burning oil. Hot brass or whatever from the men's weapons must have started a fire.

Stepping forward to the controls, Diaz took hold of the wheel and kept the boat moving along its original heading. Santiago and Reyes went into the hold leaving Diaz the only man up on the upper decks. The most important job Diaz had now was to keep watch. Timing was going to be tight.

In a short time, Diaz could see the bright orange and white markings on a Coast Guard boat as it came out of the station to starboard. The *Princesa* was just passing the end of North Island and the main Navy air base there. Instead of trying to make a run for the open sea, Diaz cut back on the throttle, killing the engines. Leaving the controls, he abandoned the wheelhouse and climbed down into the hold. The heavy steel cover on the hatch shut with a thud as Diaz pulled it down and dogged it tight.

Chapter Five

Lieutenant Commander Foxbury on board the Coast Guard *Island*-class patrol craft *North* felt that whoever it was on board the trawler, they had made a serious mistake in their seamanship. The boat was wallowing in the water, smoke pouring from her stern. These were probably the hardcases who had just made the daring jailbreak that was on all of the police frequencies in the area. At least two officers were down in the Federal Building and there was one sheriff's deputy on the radio who was uninjured but badly shocked. He had been the first to come under fire from the boat. The men on board the trawler appeared to be heavily armed, but the 25mm Mark 38 cannon on the forward mount of the *North* would make short work of the wooden-hulled boat if the terrorists offered much in the way of resistance. Foxbury was not going to take any chances with the safety of his men.

"Chief Cushing," Foxbury said, "go forward and make sure the Mark 38 is ready for action."

Before Chief Cushing could acknowledge the order, 500 meters in front of the patrol craft, the smoking hull of the trawler vanished in a shattering explosion. An instant later, a roiling orange-red ball of burning gasoline blossomed into the early dawn sky. The shock of the blast could be felt in the superstructure of the *North* as the pressure wave struck the craft a second later.

"Jesus Christ and all of the saints," Chief Cushing said as he looked at where the fishing trawler had just been obliterated. Bits and pieces of wreckage were raining down from the sky, making small splashes where they hit the waters of the bay. The time to hurry was past now, even for the Coast Guard. There could be no survivors of such a blast, no matter how tough and daring those men might have been.

———

The sun was up and burning off the cloud layers above San Diego a few hours later as Ensign Rawlings stood next to the helm of the twenty-five-foot homeland security response boat as it approached another civilian craft tied up to a mooring ball near the Grape Street Pier #1, south of the Coast Guard station. This was going to be the fifth boat the ensign had approached since he had been sent out to look for witnesses to the action that morning. The fifty-foot custom catamaran he was approaching was a beautiful motor-sailer. The single tall mast holding furled sails as the boat rode against her mooring line. The Coast Guard craft was coming in from the stern of the catamaran, moving to approach between the twin hulls that gave that class of boat her name.

Before Ensign Rawlings could even hail the big catamaran, a man in a white windbreaker walked out onto the forward deck. Chief Boatswain's Mate Majors at the controls of the Coast Guard boat cut the two 250-horsepower Honda outboards driving the small boat as the man on deck caught a tossed line. Seaman Watson held the bright orange foam floatation collar of the Coast Guard boat away from the catamaran as they came up to a boarding ladder, hanging next to a secured Zodiak F-450 inflatable boat.

"Permission to come aboard," Ensign Rawlings said as he took the extended hand offered by the man on deck.

"Permission granted," the man said. "I'm Captain Wellings. Welcome aboard the *Freedom*. What can I do to help the Coast Guard today?"

"Thanks, Captain Wellings," Rawlings said. "We're looking for any witnesses to the explosion out in the bay this morning."

"That was quite a blast," Wellings said. "Knocked us around and put the boat's owner and his wife right out of their bed. They just came down from Orange County last night. But no one saw anything. That's Samuel Green and his wife and daughter right here in the main salon if you would like to ask them yourself."

Looking forward, Rawlings could see several people sitting around a large table in the main salon of the boat. The older-looking man was leaning back in his seat, a cup in his hand. The heavy blue bathrobe he was wearing framed his smooth-shaven face and short black hair shot with gray. A mature red-haired woman sitting to the man's right was wearing a matching bathrobe. The bulky robe wasn't able to mask what looked like a spectacular figure on the redhead.

The much younger blonde wearing very stylish blue and white sportswear looked like almost any other Southern California college girl, one who came from a well-to-do family. The very pretty girl smiled brightly and waved to the young officer, who was suddenly very concious of his appearance in his waterproof, insulated coveralls.

"No, that won't be necessary," Rawlings said.

"Just what was that explosion this morning anyway?"

"A boat caught fire and there was a fuel explosion," Rawlings said. "They're searching for evidence at the site right now."

"We're planning to go out and do some whale watching to the south over the weekend, Ensign," Wellings said. "The grays are migrating south and the sightings have been pretty good off Point Loma. Is there anything about the incident this morning that would interfere with that?"

"No," Rawlings said. "Just give a wide berth to the anchored boats in the channel. And remember, don't disturb the whales directly. You can't take a boat within a hundred-yards of them and I would advise that you run on sail as much as you can—the whales don't like the sound of engines."

"Not a problem," Wellings said with a wide smile. "Thanks, Ensign."

Standing on the rear deck of the *Freedom*, Garcia

Santiago, aka "Captain Wellings," watched the Coast Guard boat push away from the catamaran and move off to head to the next craft moored some distance away. He turned and headed back into the salon where Pena sat rubbing his hand across his freshly shaved chin. A fast application of makeup by the redheaded woman had masked the lighter pallor of the skin under his beard.

"I must say, a busy morning," Pena said.

"Nothing wrong with a jump and underwater swim before breakfast," Santiago said. "It's a great way to start the day back in the SEAL Teams."

"But I imagine you used to go over the side of the boat," Pena said, "not down through her hull."

"No, but now the Coast Guard are witnesses to the fact that no one got off that boat before she blew," Santiago said. "So as far as anyone knows, everyone who was aboard is now dead. They'll search hard enough. But there won't be anything to find but pieces. And 'Mr. Green' and his family are free to spend a leisurely weekend following the migration of the Pacific gray whales to their calving grounds off the coast of Mexico. Maybe even stop off at a port or two while south of the border."

"I must say your choice in boat camouflage is admirable," Pena said as he looked to the ladies on either side of him. The pretty blond girl was much older than she looked. Her young teenage looks were why she had been reasonably successful in a variety of adult entertainment venues. Her redheaded "mother" had also been in the entertainment business, running a call-girl operation, one of Pena's other business interests.

"I thought you might like some companionship after your long separation," Santiago said. "And they did manage to run that young ensign off fast enough."

"You may cast off whenever you are ready, Captain," Pena said. "I shall begin my new life by dealing with those who ended my old one soon enough."

The cold look on the drug lord's face promised a short life to those he felt had wronged him.

Chapter Six

The sun shone down from the clear blue of the Southern Arizona sky. It was going to be a real hot day, thought Ted Reaper as he drove along at the wheel of his rented Saturn sedan. But it's a dry heat, and he smiled at the thought. The upper nineties was still hot, no matter what the humidity was.

Back in Michigan the past June, it had been unseasonably cold, and the spring rains had been heavy. Some bright sun and heat would feel pretty good for a while. Reaper had spent a lot of time in the West during his time in the SEAL Teams, setting up training with various agencies, learning what facilities were available. He really liked the area and was looking forward to some downtime with old friends, and doing just a little bit of business to keep things moving and play with some new tools.

Traveling southeast out of Tucson on Highway 10, Reaper was just passing the Saguaro National Park to his north. That still gave him about sixty miles to go before he reached Sierra Vista. From there he would head out to the Dogbone Ranch southeast of town.

The beauty of the desert appealed greatly to Reaper. It had a wild, untamable quality that seemed able to ignore a lot of man's encroachment. The sand went on for miles, covered by rough brush, cactus, and rocks. A short distance to the right of the road, Reaper could see some dust devils moving across the ground. The miniature tornadoes of dust and grit popped up and cut across the desert. One of the tall, tan, twisters was passing through a parking lot and some people were going to be very unhappy about their car being sand-blasted.

His mind went back to the problems he was having with money, cars, and everything only twelve months earlier. It had been a long year for Reaper. Any financial problems he had were pretty much gone, but his family life was flushed down the head as well. Just over a year before, his wife Mary and son Ricky had been kidnapped by a drug gang that wanted him to furnish weapons for them. The weapons were intended to help supply a Mideast terrorist cell in the U.S.

It was only through the skills Reaper had learned as a SEAL that he was able to get his family back and prevent a major terrorist incident. But even those skills wouldn't have been enough without the help given to him by a close Teammate and old friends from the Special Operations community. His Teammate Bear had died in the action against the terrorists, and Reaper missed him every day.

Bear hadn't been the only one to pay the bill for Reaper's actions. He had just paid the most of any of them. Reaper's marriage had been on rocky ground before the incident. Afterward, he wasn't able to argue against Mary's feelings that she and their son would be better off away from him and his past at least for the time being. Reluctantly, Reaper had agreed to a divorce. Now Mary was living with Ricky in another state.

Damn, Reaper thought, it wasn't as though he was still in the Navy and deploying with the Teams. But he still wasn't able to make a go of both his career and his family life. He had to agree that Mary was right. She and Ricky were safer not being with him, at least not while he was now working as a consultant and contractor for the Department of Homeland Security.

That was just about the only thing that had worked out for the better from Reaper's involvement in the terrorist incident. Retired SEAL Rear Admiral Alan Straker had left the Teams and taken up a position with the Department of Homeland Security. It was because of Admiral Straker's intervention that Reaper wasn't in prison or worse. The admiral had made all of the legal problems go away. Otherwise, the list of charges applied to a group of ex-military personnel using a variety of illegal weapons against foreign nationals within the territories of the United States would have been fairly long. Normally, the U.S. government did not look kindly on its citizens taking the law into their own hands.

It hadn't hurt at all that Reaper and his people also

received the rewards the State Department had been offering for the elimination of several of the terrorists on their most wanted list. The $2.5 million in cash they had recovered from drug dealers also stayed with Reaper's group, Straker hadn't asked about it, and the information wasn't volunteered. The cash was divided equally among all of the guys, and Reaper felt they had more than earned it. These men had helped him get his family back, safe and unhurt.

The most astonishing thing Reaper and his group had received was the full use of an island in northern Lake Michigan as their base. The place had a huge mansion on it, shooting ranges, boat docks, an airstrip, machine shop, boats, even an airplane. And Reaper's people had it as their base of operations.

The island had been paid for—big time. Ted "Bear" Parnell had also checked out while covering the withdrawal of Reaper and his family. It was easy to understand that Bear preferred going that way instead of dying of the cancer that was eating him up inside. Reaper felt he owed it to Bear's memory to keep "the Four Horsemen," a term Bear used, as the registered name of their security consulting company. The base on South Wolverine Island had become the company headquarters.

As far as Reaper could tell, a Horsemen operation was one that Straker couldn't palm off on any other unit. That might not be exactly fair as the Horsemen hadn't even been called out for a hot operation yet. But to Reaper, the situation felt that way. The Horsemen were going to work in the United States and be one

way to get around the Posse Comitatus Act that prevented U.S. military units from acting as a direct part
of civilian law enforcement.

The new headquarters did not come without some
strings attached. In order to receive all of the largess
from the government, and avoid a lot of criminal prosecution, they had to agree to conduct operations as
needed, the missions to be directed from Admiral
Straker's office alone. So now Reaper and his merry
band were contractors for the U.S. government, a nice
little euphemism for mercenary.

Reflections on the past year occupied Reaper's mind
as he headed down the road. He was almost surprised
when he realized that he was approaching Sierra Vista.
Soon he was turning off the main road and heading up
the half-mile-long dirt road leading to the main compound of the ranch. The wire fence that went around
the 175-acre property extended from either side of a
tall set of poles supporting a crossbeam. Hanging from
the beam was a big wooden sign in the shape of a bone.
Dogbone Ranch was spelled out in big letters burned
into the wood.

This was going to be what he needed. Instead of
spending time organizing the Horsemen or training,
Reaper would spend some downtime with a friend far
away from anything. It would be the first vacation he
had taken in a very long time.

The dirt road leading up to the main house was dusty
and winding. It went around the base of a number of
small hills and crossed several dry wash gullies that
would be rushing, destructive waterways once the rains

came. But right now, the area was dry. Dust blew through the scattered undergrowth.

A few hundred yards away to his right, Reaper could see tall, full trees, bright green and heavy with leaves. The trees and the grassland around them bordered the San Pedro River, a riparian national conservation area. The thorns, mesquite, and mostly brown sands only a short distance from the trees starkly illustrated the value of water in the area.

The road ended at a long brick wall surrounding the main buildings of the ranch. A wrought-iron gate penetrated the south wall without a latch or lock anywhere on its face. Next to the gate was a small sign reading DOGS ON PREMISES.

"That's an understatement," Reaper said out loud as he reached out the window. Punching a six-digit number into the keypad on the pole next to the driveway unlatched the gate and powered it open. The electronic gate was only the first layer of security for the compound. Reaper knew that the second layer was going to be a hell of a lot more intimidating to any stranger.

Beyond the gate, the end of the road widened into a large, gravel parking area. There was a long, low building along the north side of the area, the three wide garage doors giving a good idea of what was held under the roof. Neat spaces of crushed red stone, raked and smoothed around a few scattered desert plants, bordered the parking place and the low adobe wall surrounding the house. Through an arched opening in the wall, Reaper could see green grass spreading out in the shade of several trees.

As he pulled up to the edge of the parking space, two huge black thunderbolts rushed from inside the adobe wall and stopped on either side of his car.

The two large, black-and-mahogany rottweilers barked only a little, but their loud voices clearly announced the arrival of the vehicle. It was obvious, as they stood at each door of the car, that they were in control of the situation no matter what any passengers of the vehicle might think. Anyone who didn't know the dogs would be more than a little intimidated by the mere appearance of the two powerful animals.

The rottweilers were relatively quiet, but the big brown-and-black German shepherd standing in the shade of the trees inside the adobe wall made more than enough noise to make up for them. The rottweilers kept watching Reaper intently, intelligence shining in their brown eyes. Reaper wasn't intimidated by the animals, but he was very respectful of them.

"Major, shut up," came a loud voice from inside the house, "you know him."

"Yeah," called out Reaper as he opened the car door, "but does he like me? And what about his friends here?"

"He's not the one you have to worry about," said the man who stepped out of the house and into the walled patio, "it's that big dummy next to you who'll knock you over just saying hello."

"Grunt?" Reaper said as he held out the back of his hand for the rottweiler to sniff. "Is that you? Damn, you're a big dog now."

"Well, it's been almost two years since you saw him

last. They do grow when you keep feeding them."

Jerry "Cowboy" Hausmann walked up to Reaper and wrapped his arms around him in a big, masculine hug.

"Good to see you, Ted," Hausmann said. "Glad you could manage to find your way back. Looks like Grunt remembers you, Sarge, too. Got some cold beer on tap inside, if I can force one on you."

"You may be able to twist my arm," Reaper said as he vigorously rubbed Grunt's big head. The short tail of the rottweiler was wagging so quickly it looked as if it would break the sound barrier. Sarge, the other rott, had seen that Hausmann was happy to see the man in front of him, and that was good enough for the dog. He came up to Reaper for his share of attention. The German shepherd had gone back to lying down on the grass in the shade of the tree.

"What's with Major?" Reaper asked as they walked through the yard and up to the house.

"Just getting a bit old, is all," Hausmann said, "just like the rest of us. His arthritis slows him down a bit now. Anyone comes into the yard, all he does is ask for their license and registration—lets his deputies do the heavy lifting."

Stepping through the arched entrance to the patio, Reaper followed Hausmann into the adobe-style house. The inside of the building was light, airy, and comfortably cool. The center of the room was dominated by a large pool table. Surrounding the table was a leather couch and well-padded leather chairs. A bar with four stools in front of it was on the opposite side of the room from the door.

As Reaper was standing at the door, a big chunk of dog waddled into the room and shoved itself up against his legs. The massive, heavily wrinkled face looked up at him as the heavily muscled body sat right down on his feet.

"Jarhead!" Reaper said as he bent over. "Still waddling around I see."

As Reaper scratched the fawn-and-white English bulldog on the back, the animal practically convulsed with pleasure. Behind the bar, Hausmann opened a small freezer.

"Just don't fall for his begging bit," Hausmann said. "If I really starved him as much as he acts, he wouldn't weigh nearly sixty pounds."

Jarhead looked up at Reaper with a wide bulldog smile as his tongue came out and the dog started panting. The comedy of the big lump of a dog made Reaper laugh as he stood back up and went over to join Hausmann. The bulldog decided that rolling over on his back and doing the happy-doggy wiggle on a rug was the best way to continue his personal pleasure.

With a grin on his face, Reaper took a seat at the bar, and looked around at the definitely masculine Western-style decor of the room. Filled gunbelts hung next to framed Western artworks. And there was more than one Stetson hat and set of horns hanging from the walls. Past experience with Hausmann and his habits told Reaper to expect that every one of the weapons in the room was loaded—from the single-action Colts to the Winchester and Sharps rifles hanging in scabbards or on racks.

It wasn't that Hausmann was paranoid. He just believed that tools should be kept ready for use. Besides, anyone invited into the house was an adult and usually a long-time professional with weapons.

"Still roughing it out here in the sticks, I see," Reaper said.

"Hey, us heartless attorneys have to hide out somewhere," Hausmann said as he handed Reaper a mug of beer. "Might as well suffer in style."

The first cold Corona in an icy mug went down well. The Western barbecue that Hausmann pulled out of the kitchen oven went well with another beer and some small talk between old friends. Afterward, both men went outside to the swimming pool to enjoy some coffee and cigars and to treat the dogs to some bones Hausmann had specially ordered for them from the same place he had gotten the barbecue.

Taking their treats and spreading out, each of the dogs lay down to enjoy a big bone from dinner. In the cool of the evening, even Jarhead was outside being sociable. It was startling to Reaper to hear the loud crunching and snapping sounds as the two rottweilers actually chewed up the bones.

Bullfrogs from the river nearby were putting their own sounds out to compete with all of the birds in the area. There was even the buzz of hummingbirds slipping up to the flowers growing around the patio. As the stars came out and the evening darkened, a huge full moon rose to shine down from the east. The peaceful surroundings helped the two men open the conversation to more serious subjects.

"So where's Colonel?" Reaper said, asking about the other German shepherd he remembered Hausmann having. "He wasn't that old, was he?"

"No, he wasn't too old," Hausmann said with some heat in his voice. "There's a bitch we call the snake lover who owns the property just south of mine. She's trying to buy up all of the riparian land around here whenever it goes up for sale, which isn't very often. The government is trying to buy every acre it can but she's got some kind of pull with the local politicos and manages to pick up her share of it.

"She runs some kind of organic food company south of here, has a big ranch and warehousing just a mile or so from the border. It must be successful, she has too much money available for her crackpot schemes. She's trying to make it illegal to harm a rattlesnake anywhere around here, has some kind of thing for the poisonous bastards. At any rate, I found Colonel down by the river about six months ago. He'd been poisoned and I swear that bitch was the only person who could have done it. She hated my dogs, said they scared all of the local animals."

"You didn't take her to court?" Reaper asked.

"Not enough evidence to prosecute. Or at least that's what the sheriff said. I would sue her myself except that I've been wrapped up in a criminal case for the last several months and haven't had a minute free. Well, paybacks are a bitch."

Leaning back in his chair, Hausmann took a long drag on his cigar.

"I was really sorry to hear about you and Mary," Hausmann said, changing the subject.

"Well, we did give it a good try," Reaper said after a long pull from his beer. "We just finally had to admit that we just weren't going to work out well. We had to finally call it quits before we tore each other apart, and made Ricky's life completely miserable. I think she's happy now teaching school. And Ricky's developing a good set of friends. I see them as much as I can and they both know that I'll always be there for them should they need anything at all."

There was a flash of sadness that went through Reaper's eyes. Most of the men who had served in the Teams kept their emotions solidly in check, their feelings to themselves. It wasn't that they didn't feel happiness, or sadness, anger, joy, or sorrow. In fact, they felt all of these emotions and more, and they were felt more strongly than the average person experienced them.

SEALs lived on the edge. Even just conducting their training was dangerous. Operators had died over the years without there being an enemy in sight. Emotions could get in the way when a man had to concentrate on his job. They could trip you up during an operation, cause you to fail to achieve your objectives, get you killed. So Reaper didn't show his feelings very much at all. It was an old habit that was hard to get rid of, if he ever could.

Noticing the flash of sadness that passed over his friend, Hausmann kept quiet for a moment.

"Yeah, I understand," Hausmann said finally. Changing the subject, he went on. "So, what's this I hear on the grapevine that your company is doing contract work for the government?"

"Nothing special yet," Reaper said. "Doing more work on a consultant basis than anything else. Checking out the new toys, seeing what looks good."

"Anything over in the sandbox or the rockpile?"

"No, nothing for us in Iraq or Afghanistan. There's quite a lot of contract work over there now. Especially in Iraq. A lot of guys are right in the thick of it."

"So what finally brought you back to my happy home?" Hausmann said. "Checking up on your investment?"

"Hardly," Reaper said, "I had business up in Phoenix. Diamondback Tactical has a new vehicle, what they call their Prowler RTV. We're thinking about getting a couple."

"RTV?" asked Hausmann.

"Rugged terrain vehicle."

"I wouldn't mind seeing one of those."

"You will," Reaper said with a laugh, "they're shipping a pair of them down here. Probably arrive tomorrow. I thought you could help me out and put them through their paces."

Hausmann's eyes lit up like a kid looking forward to Christmas.

"Hey, cool," he said, "we can run them out through the foothills of the Mule Mountains. That's just on the far side of the training area."

Reaper knew very well that Hausmann had been working with several retired SEALs to build up a training site in the Arizona desert. The ranch was only about twelve miles from the border with Mexico and interaction with the local units of the Border Patrol was common. While with the active Teams, Reaper had cross-trained with the Border Patrol a number of times. They were an excellent source of information and skills on desert work, observation posts, and tracking.

The group Hausmann was with had leased a huge section of desert, a square mile of sand, rocks, and brush, to build up into a training area. The training area began about a quarter mile past a branch of railroad tracks belonging to the San Pedro Northwestern, on the far side of the San Pedro River just east of the house. The Four Horsemen company had invested in the buildup of the training site. They had more than enough cash available and Reaper knew that a desert training area would prove very useful.

"Speaking of your training area," Reaper said, "how are the range facilities coming along?"

"The first stage of building is complete right now," Hausmann said. "We've got all of the berms in and the backstops built up for three shooting lanes. The shooting-house is going in later this year so we can run close-quarter combat. The berms are already up for that so there's kind of a fourth lane you can shoot 360 degrees around a central firing point. Why, you need some trigger time?"

"I wouldn't mind it," Reaper said. "I stopped in at GG&G in Tucson on my way down here. It's why I was so late in finally showing up. They tricked out my M4A1 for M2, and I waited for them to finish up."

"They build great rigs," Hausmann said. "I take it you haven't had a chance to try it out yet?"

"Not really," Reaper said with a laugh. "I didn't want to be too late for the barbecue. The technicians up at GG&G put the whole thing together for me and boresighted the sights, but I didn't have a chance to live-fire it."

"Well," Hausmann said as he looked at his watch, "it's getting pretty close to midnight. You up for a ride in the country?"

"Now?" Reaper said.

"Seems like a good time to try out a night-vision sight," Hausmann said. "We'll take the short route and ride cross-country. Still know how to get on a horse?"

"It's been a while," Reaper said, "but I don't think I'll fall off."

Chapter Seven

Within twenty minutes, the area was cleaned up and two of Hausmann's three horses saddled. While Reaper was unlocking his Kalispel aluminum weapons case in the poolroom, Hausmann came in from the garage with two large metal ammunition boxes.

"I figured you'd probably need some ammunition since you flew in," Hausmann said. "Need any magazines?"

"The ammunition would be appreciated," Reaper agreed. "I brought my rifle and pistol, but that was about it. Even locked up my Emerson in the gun case. I do have some magazines, at least enough to zero the gun in."

Opening up the case, Reaper pulled out his Colt model 927 M4A1 carbine. The long, ribbed flat top of the carbine held the PVS-14 night-vision monocular just above the receiver with the Aimpoint Comp M2 sight in front of it. Looking through the light magnification tube of the PVS-14 allowed the user to see in anything but complete darkness. With the Comp M2 mounted the way it was on the FIRE rail, the red dot inside the sight could still be seen through the PVS-14.

There were three thirty-round magazines for the M4A1 inside the case, along with a customized Springfield Armory M1911A1, holster, pouch, and magazines for the pistol. The M1911A1 .45 automatic had been customized by Reaper himself, installing a Wilson stainless-steel barrel, beaver tail grip safety and Ed Brown national match trigger, as well as fitting all the internal parts for maximum accuracy and reliability.

While Reaper thumbed rounds from the ammunition cans into the magazines of both weapons, Hausmann went into the weapons room of the house, just up the hall from the poolroom, and opened up the gun vault. He chose a Custom Firearms Inc. M1911A1 in a Blade Tech formed kydex belt holster already on a 1¼-inch wide leather belt. On the left side of the belt was a Blade Tech combo pouch holding a spare magazine for the M1911A1 as well as a SureFire 9Z tactical flashlight. Heading back to the poolroom, Hausmann was adjusting the belt around his waist as Reaper was finishing loading up his magazines.

One of the magazines to the carbine was slipped inside a buttstock mag pouch that was attached to the left side of the collapsible stock on the M4A1. The other two magazines were locked together with a Mag-Grip dual magazine holder. With one of the magazines locked into the weapon, the second was right alongside ready for a quick reload.

"You always keep the second magazine on the left side of the weapon?" Hausmann asked.

Picking up the M4A1, Reaper clipped the snap shackle on his Chalker sling to the Ambi-Egg attachment plate at the front of his carbine's stock.

"Yeah," Reaper said, "made it a habit. That's the fastest way I've found to see if the reload's been used or not."

Rotating the carbine so that the muzzle was up by his left shoulder, Reaper secured it in place with a Chalker Hi-Port weapons catch. Now the weapon hung from both of Reaper's shoulders, secured in place by the shackle and Hi-Port catch. All he had to do was flip the Velcro tab of the Hi-Port catch open with the thumb of his left hand and the carbine would immediately be free to use.

Picking up his pistol, Reaper pressed it into the formed plastic of his Fobus Model C21 paddle holster. The large oval piece on the back of the holster, the paddle that gave it its name, slipped over his belt to rest on the inside of his pants over his right hip. A Fobus double magazine pouch of the same design and material went onto his belt at his left hip. Sticking up slightly from Reaper's right front pocket was the pommel end of his Emerson CQC-7 knife with the Wave. The hooklike Wave on the folding knife's blade would pull it open against the back edge of the pocket when it was drawn.

In his khaki 5.11 long-sleeved tactical shirt and his 5.11 range pants tucked into camel tan-colored Bates Durashock model 129 boots, Reaper looked to be ready for just about anything but a nighttime horseback ride.

"This your normal outfit for a night out in Detroit?" Hausmann asked with a grin.

Smiling back, Reaper thought about an evening the year before when he had dressed much as he was now just for a night in downtown Detroit.

"Well," he said. "I know just how cold it gets here at night so I figured the long sleeves would be good."

"You've got that right," Hausmann said as he headed for the door. "But what are you going to do when the batteries run out on all of that cool sighting gear you have there?"

"That's why the folding rear sight," Reaper said. "Besides, this new model vertical foregrip from GG&G has spare batteries for the sights in it."

"Today's military runs on batteries," Hausmann said as both men walked back to the barn. "The Energizer bunny would be so proud."

The barn with the horse stalls was to the east of the house, behind the patio with the swimming pool and the concrete flat of the basketball court. A fenced-in paddock was to the right of the barn, and Reaper could see that there were two horses in it, a black and a roan. Both horses were harnessed up with saddles and bridles ready.

"Vixen, the roan, she's yours," Hausmann said. "She's a real good ride for someone who hasn't been in the saddle for a while. The stallion's Eagle and he's a bit of a knucklehead so I'll ride him."

Taking up the reins, the two men walked the horses to the far side of the paddock where it faced the river and the tree line. Opening the gate, Hausmann let

Reaper through and handed him the reins to Eagle while he secured the gate again. Then they walked down to the other fence, part of the wall that surrounded the compound, and repeated the procedure. Once up on the bank of the river, Hausmann put his foot in the stirrup and mounted up onto Eagle.

Competently, but not quite as smoothly, Reaper mounted into the saddle on Vixen and settled in with a squeak of leather.

"Oh, this has been a while," Reaper said.

"Don't worry, it'll all come back to you," Hausmann said. "And you can be sure your thighs will remind you about your ride tomorrow morning."

Though the trees overhead cut back on the moonlight, it was still a bright enough night to see all the way down to the river. The frogs were only quiet long enough for the two horses to pass before building up their normal level of night noise again. Down by the river, the horses paused to drink while Hausmann explained how they would cross the river.

"It took nearly twenty loads of rock," Hausmann said, "but we managed to build up an easy fording area right here."

Hausmann pointed to where the path they were on met the river's edge.

"You don't have to worry about where we're going or how to get there," he said. "This is the same ride I take just about every morning. I rotate through the horses and exercise them just after sunup. This is just a little early for them, is all."

Crossing the river, they went up over the bank on the

other side and were soon following a railroad line. There was still heavy brush growth close by the river, but the trees were much fewer in number and not nearly so tall and lush. Riding along the rails, the men were about a hundred yards from the house when Hausmann pointed to a trail leading back down to the river.

"There's a single-line rope bridge across the river at the bottom of that trail," Hausmann said. "It's the only way across without getting your feet wet for miles."

The river and the rail line curved off to the east, coming close enough together that the larger trees were growing up near the rails. The men hadn't ridden another fifty yards up against the tree line before both horses suddenly stopped. Vixen had pricked up her ears and swiveled them forward, raising her head in the process. Eagle was pulling his head up and did not appear to want to take another step. Raising his right hand, Hausmann closed it into a fist—the silent signal to stop, not the sort of thing Reaper expected to see that night.

Pulling hard on the reins, Hausmann had Eagle under control as he sidled him up to Reaper. Leaning over, Hausmann whispered:

"Looks like we have company up ahead. Probably illegals coming up from Mexico and heading . . ."

He never finished the sentence as suddenly there was a long burst of fire from a suppressed weapon coming at them from just past the curve. It was only the fact that both men were bending down to whisper, and that most shooters aim too high at night, that kept both Reaper and Hausmann from being hit in that first burst.

As the bullets went by, Eagle tried to break away from Hausmann's control. With the whites of his eyes shining in the dark, Eagle twisted to the side and down the embankment to the river. The panicking horse smashed Hausmann into a low-hanging branch, knocking the man back and out of his saddle.

Pulling hard on his own reins to keep Vixen from following the stallion into panic, Reaper fought to maintain control of the horse. Seeing Hausmann get knocked from the saddle, Reaper had to move quickly to get to his friend. Pulling his feet from the stirrups, Reaper jumped from the saddle, his right hand on the pistol grip of his M4A1.

Hitting the ground in a roll, Reaper quickly got to his feet and remained in a crouch. The incoming gunfire had stopped, but Reaper could hear bodies carefully moving through the undergrowth. Snapping off the Chalker Hi-Port catch, Reaper swung his M4A1 into firing position. Snapping switches with his left hand, he turned on the PVS-14 night-vision monocular and the Aimpoint Comp M2 reflex sight as his right hand thumbed the safety selector switch to the full automatic position. Now he could see in the dark, probably better than whoever it was facing them. And they probably weren't expecting to be facing an armed and highly trained ex-Navy SEAL.

With the M4A1 solidly against his shoulder, Reaper moved up to where he had seen Hausmann fall into the underbrush. In the sparkling screen of the PVS-14,

Reaper could see the world in tones of green and shadow. There was movement in the brush ahead as Reaper saw armed men moving toward them. The men were armed with at least one suppressed submachine gun, and two of them were carrying what looked like heavy rifles, possibly German G3s, to Reaper. If this was a bunch of illegals just crossing the border, they were pretty damned heavily armed.

Moving forward, Reaper came to where Hausmann was lying on the ground. The man had a deep gash on his forehead and was moving weakly. Before Reaper could pick his friend up and get him out of there, he had to slow up the approaching men.

Taking careful aim, Reaper placed the red dot in the middle of the chest of one of the men. Squeezing the trigger, the night was split with the sound and flash of the fourteen-inch-barreled weapon as Reaper sent a three-round burst at his target.

The man Reaper had been firing at dove into the underbrush. But he was moving too well for Reaper to have hit him with his first burst. The damned sights may have been off. Tracking the weapon around, Reaper sent several short bursts of fire across the bend in the rails, strafing the area with high-speed M855 5.56mm projectiles.

He didn't have enough ammunition with him to be lavish with such fire. But Reaper knew that the only way to break an ambush was to go right through it with as much firepower as you could bring to bear. The trouble was, he didn't have all that much firepower.

Deciding on a course of action, Reaper dumped the

rest of his magazine in a long burst of fire across the area. Crashing in the brush and the sudden booming roar of several 7.62mm rifles firing on full automatic told Reaper that he had gotten the men's attention. The bullets snapped by overhead, screaming through the trees and knocking leaves down onto Reaper's head.

Quickly Reaper pulled his empty magazine from the M4A1 and immediately inserted the fully loaded one that was attached to it. Slapping the bolt release sent the bolt carrier forward, stripping off the first round in the magazine and loading the weapon. That gave him twenty-eight rounds at the ready with one round in the chamber and twenty-seven in the magazine. It wasn't a lot, but it would have to do.

Bending down, he picked up Hausmann and slung him over his left shoulder. He would do his best to pull out with his friend, there wasn't any possible way he would leave him behind. But right now, John Wayne and the cavalry coming in would be a very welcome sight.

There was a sudden thundering noise coming up behind Reaper. Before he could even swing his weapon around, two deadly black shadows charged past him as Sarge and Grunt arrived on the scene. The rottweilers were just black shapes in the dark of the night as they silently ran forward. No barking, no growls, only muscular power and shining white teeth. In spite of his situation, Reaper suddenly felt a little sorry for the ambushers in the brush.

High-pitched terrified screams rang out from the woods, along with a roaring growl as the rottweilers moved in for the attack. Reaper had never heard a dog make a sound like that. It wasn't a growl or a bark. If anything, it sounded like the deep-throated roar of a lion. Gunfire lashed out in all directions, but there were no answering yelps to indicate a dog was hit.

Taking advantage of the situation, Reaper started heading back toward the compound with Hausmann across his back. It was obvious to the ex-SEAL that the dogs could take care of themselves very well. Hausmann was hurt, probably a concussion at the very least. And Reaper had to get him to a hospital.

Coming to the path that led down to the rope bridge, Reaper passed up on it to cross at the ford. Hausmann was starting to move around more and Reaper didn't want to risk crossing a V-shaped rope bridge with a possibly struggling man on his back.

Moving down the bank to the water, Reaper heard the thudding noise that indicated the approach of the two dogs. Up ahead, Major and Jarhead were barking madly and running up and down the fence. The two rottweilers must have jumped over the fence, Reaper thought just as the two dogs appeared from out of the darkness.

Neither animal looked hurt, but the glistening shine from their short, broad muzzles told Reaper the story. Someone, or a group of someones, had learned first-hand that night just how powerful a rottweiler's bite could be. He wondered if there were some bodies back in the brush to be found by the sheriff after Reaper called the incident in.

Chapter Eight

When Hausmann opened his eyes the next morning, the first thing he did was put his hands over them and groan.

"Jesus," he said, "just what the hell did we do last night? Tie one on and end up drinking mouthwash?"

"Nope, just a couple of beers," Reaper's voice said from the other side of Hausmann's hands. "But the party later with the neighbors did get interesting."

Putting his hands down and slowly opening his eyes at the light, Hausmann realized that he was in a hospital room. That explained the antiseptic smell. He saw Reaper step over to the window and draw the curtains against the bright sun outside.

"The doctor figured you would have a hell of a headache this morning," Reaper said as he looked at his friend. "Other than that, you should be fine."

"You mean that shit that hit the fan last night happened?" Hausmann said. "All I really remember is Eagle bolting and a whole bunch of pain. That, and a lot of noise. Then things pretty much went away."

A nurse came into the room and interrupted the conversation.

"Well, Mr. Hausmann, you look much better today than you did last night when your friend brought you in," the nurse said as she started examining her patient. She touched a bandage on Hausmann's head, causing the man to wince with pain.

"Hey, watch that," Hausmann complained. "That hurts."

"You cracked your skull against a tree and you're lucky it only hurts," the nurse said. "Now if I can finish my examination, Dr. Terry will come in here and decide whether to release you or not."

Reaper decided this was one battle he didn't want to witness and he left the room just as a doctor in green scrubs came through the door.

"Oh, Mr. Reaper," Dr. Terry said as she almost bumped into Reaper. "You're still here? I thought you had left last night."

"I did," Reaper said. "Came back an hour ago."

"Well, I think you'll be able to take your friend home as soon as he's up and dressed. Just let me take a look at him."

"That'll be great, Doctor," Reaper said. "I think I'll go grab a cup of coffee in the lounge."

Not particularly wanting to listen to his friend, or watch the doctor shine a light in Hausmann's eyes, Reaper retreated from the room and headed down the hall. The small hospital had a comfortable lounge on the same floor as the room where Hausmann had spent the night. For Reaper, the idea of lying in bed for a while held real appeal. He'd been up all night dealing with the aftermath of the incident at the ranch, collecting two loose horses, and cleaning up a bloody pair of rottweilers.

Reaper was about halfway through his second paper cup of coffee when Hausmann came down the hall, accompanied by Dr. Terry. Hausmann was tucking in his shirt and looked up as they approached Reaper.

"Just make sure he takes it easy for a few days," Dr. Terry told Reaper. "He can take that bandage off tomorrow. Try not to get it wet.

"You were lucky you didn't break any bones, and the CAT scans showed that your skull and spine are all intact," the doctor said as she turned to Hausmann. "You do have a concussion, so take it easy for a few days." She shot a glance at Reaper, then back to Hausmann. "That means stay off the horses, stay out of the sun and away from loud noises, and I don't advise washing the pain meds down with a beer."

As the doctor walked away, Hausmann looked at Reaper.

"What did you tell her last night in the emergency room?" he said. "That doctor acts like she thinks I'm some kind of idiot."

"Just the truth," Reaper said as the two men walked out the door. "That you hit your head on a tree while out riding in the moonlight."

"Oh, thanks a whole lot," Hausmann said.

On the drive back to the ranch, Reaper brought

Hausmann up to speed on what had happened the evening before, and the strange situation since then.

"I don't know what the hell you did to the local cops to piss them off so much," Reaper said as he drove the car, "but that sheriff's deputy who finally showed up at the ranch last night acted as if I had made the whole thing up to cover a drunken horse-riding accident.

"He finally went out and spent a few minutes half-assed looking around the area by the river and the railroad tracks. That was enough for him to come to the brilliant conclusion that there wasn't any evidence of a crime that he could find. To top his little visit off, he went on about it being against the law for a civilian to use force to apprehend or detain any illegals. We were supposed to call the authorities instead.

"Damn, if this is how your local sheriff acts, I'm not calling them for anything. I had the definite impression that if I had told him that the dogs had broken up that ambush, he would have impounded them to be checked for rabies!"

"I'm sorry you went through that, Reaper," Hausmann said. "It doesn't surprise me very much though. I'm pretty much on the locals' shit list for the time being."

"What the hell did you do?" Reaper asked, "Knock up the sheriff's daughter?"

"No," Hausmann said with a small smile. "That would have at least been something kept private. No, I made the mistake of defending an innocent man against a trumped-up murder charge. The only problem was, the man who was killed was a very well liked

Border Patrol officer. The whole thing was covered in all of the local papers and the news. Was a nationwide story for a few days."

"So if the guy didn't do it," Reaper said, "what's the beef with you getting him off?"

"As far as the local law enforcement community was concerned," Hausmann said. "They had their man. The Border Patrol officer was a longtime veteran of the force named Victor Langstrom. He was visiting an old buddy of his who had left the Patrol years back to go over to the DEA. There's not a lot of love lost between the Border Patrol and the DEA, at least not among the officers in the field. They do the dirty work, tracking illegals and manning observation posts out in the desert all night. When they make a drug bust, especially a really big one, the DEA swoops in and scoops up the bad guys and they take the lion's share of the credit. It keeps their all-important seizure rates up and that's the bottom line with the people in Washington."

"Same shit, different day," Reaper said. "It sounds like the old bullshit about body counts back in Vietnam. Just keep the numbers up and ignore the real hard targets."

"Pretty much," Hausmann agreed, "but the drug wars around here are different than most people back East expect. A group of mules packing a load of pot or cocaine is about all that's ever taken. Sometimes the loads can be pretty big. But the real important targets are the leaders of the cartels. With all of their money and the influence it buys, the Mexican government does damned little to bust them. The drug trafficking trade is probably the biggest cash business there is south of the border. The poverty down there is staggering. That's why it's easy to hire some mules to take the risks moving the product across the border to the people here. Offer a guy a couple of hundred bucks to carry a package, more money than he would normally see in six months, and he's not going to ask a lot of questions."

"So the business is worth big bucks and the bosses are hard to target," Reaper said.

"Yeah," Hausmann said. "They seem to be immune from prosecution most of the time, or at least real hard to nail down with enough evidence for a conviction. Over the last year or so, they've been thinning out their own ranks. There's been a regular shooting war south of the border, north of it, too, but to a much smaller extent. Big shakeups in the cartels."

"So that's what the man you defended was involved in?" Reaper said.

"No, not at all," Hausmann said. "Sam Duran, his name's Salim but everyone calls him Sam. He was one of the good guys. Used to be a Border Patrol officer himself back in the day. Worked for the State Department before that. Then he transferred over to the DEA, thought he could make a bigger difference there. Was a hell of an undercover agent and made multimillion-dollar arrests. Personally took down tons of coke, heroin, and pot. But he never forgot what it was like to be an officer on the ground. When a cop, sheriff's department, or the Border Patrol made a bust, he saw to it they kept the credit. It didn't exactly endear him to his superiors, but he never seemed to care about that."

"So how did he get charged with killing an officer?"

"That was the strange thing," Hausmann said, "and it was why I took the case in the first place. He retired last year after he had to kill a man during a big king-pin's takedown—some young guy he had known while undercover. Bothered him so much he took an early re-tirement. So it didn't make any sense that he would get in a fight and kill an old friend he had known for years—but that's what the investigators said.

"You have to know that when a fellow officer goes down, every Border Patrol man for miles comes in to help on the investigation. They turned over every rock and pebble between Texas and the California state line. Didn't find a damned thing. The only thing that did turn up was a gun in the man's backyard. Didn't have any fingerprints on it, and the serial number was cut off, but ballistics matched it up to the bullet that killed Langstrom.

"It was nothing but circumstantial evidence, and weak evidence at that. The case should never have even gone to an indictment. But the pressure was on to come up with a perp, and the federal prosecutor in charge wanted to make a name for himself. So he painted a picture of a corrupt ex-undercover DEA agent who killed an old friend who was going to expose him."

"Expose him?" Reaper said. "Expose what?"

"Oh, Sam's got money," Hausmann said, "and plenty of it. But he inherited it from his old man. The Duran ranch was a big place when it was a running concern. But Sam lives out there alone now, he's the only member of the family still alive. You live alone, have money, and used to be involved in the drug business, even as an undercover agent, that's enough for ignorant people who are just looking to take a man down."

"So you got him off?" Reaper asked as they pulled into the long driveway on the Dogbone Ranch.

"Wasn't that big a deal," Hausmann said, "except to Sam, of course. The motive was weak to the point of being nonexistent. No prints on the murder weapon, no eyewitnesses, no forensic evidence at all that I was ever shown. And some tracking of foreign bank accounts that were never shown to have had a direct, personal attachment to Duran.

"Like I said, the case should have never gone anywhere and I got it dismissed. But that means there's an open murder of a fellow officer still on the books. There's no suspects, the trail is cold and all of the extra manpower on the job have gone back to their posts. Sam is guilty in the court of public opinion, that's all. But that's enough for some people. And that's why the local law-enforcement community does not think highly of someone who got a cop killer off."

"And what the hell are those?" Hausmann asked as they went through the electric gate.

"Those are the Prowler RTVs from Diamondback Tactical. Came down this morning. They just unloaded and parked them. We can put them in the garage later."

"Damn," Hausmann exclaimed, "they look like some pretty stripped-down, mean-ass dune buggies."

"That's pretty much what they are," Reaper said.

"Only they're a hell of a lot tougher than a dune buggy. And they really stand out in the accessory department—passenger side seats, roll bars, places you can strap just about anything on board. Oh, and there's gun mounts."

"Cool," said Hausmann. "Can we play with them?"

"We have to hold off on playing with them for a bit," said Reaper. "Right now we have to deal with the welcoming committee."

Though Major was the only one barking, the rottweilers were letting their exuberance show as they bounded up to the car. The muscular dogs were bouncing into the air as they demonstrated their pleasure at seeing the car and Hausmann back home. The joy of the dogs was at having their "pack" once more complete. This made their world a steady, understandable thing in dog terms.

Still walking a bit stiffly, but with his full bushy tail wagging, Major had given up the shade of the tree to come up to the car. Even Jarhead, bringing up the rear of the procession, panting, bouncing, and drooling came outside to meet them. The thick-bodied bulldog had no real tail to wag, so he settled for just wiggling his butt back and forth.

"Dogs, you gotta love them," Hausmann said as he turned to Reaper. "They really let you know that you're welcomed."

"And what do they do when you're not welcome?" Reaper said.

"If you're not a threat?" Hausmann said. "One of the rotts pees on your leg, that's pretty much it."

Stepping into the house, the parade of men and happy dogs moved into the cool interior of the tile floor and adobe walls. Passing through the hallway from the poolroom, the men went into the main part of the house where Hausmann immediately headed for one of the sofas in the living room. The living room, dining room, and kitchen being all along one wall of the house, Reaper turned and headed for the kitchen. Calling over his shoulder, "Want a cup of coffee? That stuff in the hospital was pretty bad, little better than instant."

"Coffee?" said Hausmann. "All these looks and he can cook, too."

"Well, somebody has to," said Reaper, walking back from the kitchen carrying two cups of coffee. "The kitchen is spotless, do you have someone come in or just not use it much?"

"Yes," Hausmann said, "to both. I have a cleaning lady come in twice a week. That, and I don't cook much."

"I noticed there wasn't much in the way of food in the house," Reaper said.

"Lots of takeout."

"So, where do we go from here?" Reaper said as he sat down after handing Hausmann his cup of coffee.

"What do you mean?" said Hausmann.

"Well, just who the hell were those guys last night?" asked Reaper.

"No idea," said Hausmann. "They shouldn't have been illegals. Not even coyotes guarding drug mules carry suppressed submachine guns."

"They had a lot more than that," Reaper said. "What

sounded like big-bore rifles, too. Sounded like G3s or something like them. And there was a bunch of them, four at least. If it weren't for the dogs. . . ."

Just then, the subjects of Reaper's comments came thundering through the living room, rapidly closing the gap between the two rottweilers and the bulldog they were chasing. Catching up to Jarhead, Grunt clamped his jaws down on the sleeve of the jacket streaming along behind the bulldog. As the rott leaned back in a playful tug-of-war, Jarhead spun around and then just plunked his butt down on the floor. No matter how strong he was, the rottweiler was not going to pull anything from the English bulldog's jaws. The two dogs were demonstrating the meeting of an irresistible force against an immovable object. The thing that was going to give up first was the fabric of the denim jacket between the two of them.

"Jarhead! Grunt!" Hausmann shouted as the cloth started to rip. "Drop that! Damn, Reaper, is that yours?"

"Never saw it before," said Reaper.

Reluctantly, Jarhead let go of his end of the jacket.

"Grunt . . ." Hausmann said warningly. The young rottweiler tilted his head down and dropped the jacket on the floor.

"Where the hell did they get that?" Hausmann said as Reaper stood and picked up the jacket off the floor.

"My guess?" Reaper said. "This is from our friends last night. There's blood all over the sleeve. Whoever was wearing it is hurting bad today."

Holding the torn and filthy jacket out at arm's

length, Reaper turned it around to examine it. Blood spatters stained the faded blue denim fabric. Long rents in the sleeves gave mute indications of just where the blood had come from.

Going through the pockets, Reaper pulled out a folded page of torn newspaper. Unfolding the page, Reaper saw that he was holding a Spanish-language newspaper story with a large picture above the text. The photo was of Hausmann and Sam Duran coming out of the courthouse after Duran's trial. Notes along the margins were hurriedly and faintly scrawled, but careful examination showed them to be addresses—Hausmann's and Duran's home addresses.

"Who were they, a hit team?" Hausmann asked.

"A hit team with a Spanish-language newspaper?" replied Reaper. "Did you piss off some drug lord? Not get his people off?"

"I don't take drug cases," said Hausmann. "There's something hot going on south of the border. Lots of shooting going on; bodies stacking up like cord wood, but nothing to involve me."

"Damn," Hausmann said as he picked up the telephone from the coffee table in front of him. "I wonder if they tried going after Duran as well?"

Dialing the phone, Hausmann held a handset up to his ear for a long moment. Finally, there was an answer. Walking into the kitchen, Reaper missed the conversation, but it was a short one. When he walked back into the room, Hausmann had hung up the phone but was staring at it as if it were going to bite him.

"So?" Reaper said.

"Sam's dead," Hausmann said in a dull voice. "That wasn't him on the line, it was the sheriff's deputy who's at the crime scene. Duran was ambushed in his car when he came home last night. It wasn't until this morning when his hired hand arrived that anyone even knew about it.

"His car is ripped to shit, he never had much of a chance at all. He went down with his .45 in his hand, but never got a shot off. They're calling it a drug hit and basically writing it off. This is bullshit! Sam Duran never took a dishonest dollar in his life, and he hated drug dealers. Now whoever killed him is going to get away with it. All the sheriff's office thinks is that the drug community is cleaning up its own."

"Then there's not a hell of a lot we can do for Duran directly," Reaper said. "The best thing for us to do is track down whoever those fuckers were last night. I don't think there's much of a question that they were part of the hit that went down on Duran. It looks to me like our next step should be to check out where that firefight was last night. The sheriff's deputy didn't find anything, but he was only searching for a little while. I don't think he looked around all that carefully. Could be there's something out there worth finding. Is your head up for a ride?"

"For Sam? You bet your ass I am. Just not that damned horse again," Hausmann said as he put his hand up to his temple.

"No problem," said Reaper. "Remember, we've got wheels."

Chapter Nine

As far as the world was concerned, Placido Pena died during his escape attempt from an American jail. That was the official opinion of the government of Mexico. There was no body—at least no complete or intact body ever found of any of the men who were on board the escape boat when it blew up in San Diego Bay. And no swimmers could have slipped through the Coast Guard and police cordon that surrounded the area soon after the blast.

Of the bits and pieces of bodies that had been found, none matched that of Pena. DNA testing determined that a sample of blood found among the floating wreckage and debris did match Pena's sample on record. Not a single witness could be found that ever saw him get off the boat. The U.S. government reluctantly came to the conclusion that he had been killed in the explosion of a heavy weapons cache, the explosion caused by a fire started from the gunfire of the escape conspirators.

The only complete body that was ever found was that of one of the jumpers when he impacted the sidewalk outside of the Federal Building. Even that body was of little use, the Mexican government refusing full disclosure of the identity of the man, citing national security issues. By meting out the death penalty to himself, Pena had escaped federal justice in the United States.

For Pena himself, he agreed with the general opinion that he had died, and that he had to make sure that the body was never found. Once again, Santiago had proven his value by arranging a number of appointments for Pena with some of the contacts he had developed over the years. Pena spent weeks in medical clinics, clinics that specialized in cosmetic surgery. His face, his hair, his entire demeanor changed along with the drastic shifts in his life. Now, Pena considered himself reborn. And he would build his new life on the remains of the old one.

The midwife for Pena's new life was Garcia Santiago. Since the time of the high-risk escape from U.S. federal custody, Santiago had done nothing but continue to prove himself more and more trustworthy to Pena. When Pena went under the knife of the plastic surgeons, Santiago was in the operating room to watch over him. With the armed ex-SEAL standing guard, Pena knew that he wouldn't "accidentally" die from the anesthetic—as Amado Carrillo Fuentes, another Mexican drug lord, had in 1997. The last person Pena saw as the sedatives took effect was Santiago, and he was the first person the new man saw the moment he opened his eyes again.

High full cheekbones helped outline a narrower chin, patrician nose, and thinner eyebrows. Short silver hair replaced black and the beard remained gone. After the bandages were removed, the man who looked back at Pena from the mirror was unrecognizable. But behind the contacts that now gave him black eyes, was the dark soul of a ruthless killer.

The new face did not come without cost, there was pain involved even with a rebirth. The thin surgical scars that covered his face faded in the weeks following the surgery. But the signs of the work did not go away completely. When Pena became angry, when he flew into a rage, his face flushed and the scars stood out in stark contrast to his normally olive skin. Instead of being a reasonably handsome man who appeared to have European ancestry, when angry Pena would wear a mask of scars, a network of painful tracings that followed the lines of the surgeon's knife.

The baptism of pain and scars that gave Pena his new face also helped him come up with his new name. His brother, Turi, was gone and Pena had no other blood relatives. So his name joined that of his brother in death. The person who would become the new leader of the Mexican drug cartels would be Eduardo Masque. He would lead his men as a priest leads his flock. His word would be law, so he would be much more than a simple priest, he would be a Cardinal, Cardenal Muerte, and his benediction would be death. To his enemies, he would quickly become known as the Red Death.

For over a year, Masque stripped out the leadership of the drug families in Northern Mexico, securing his position as undisputed leader. Without warning, a new force among the drug lords had come out of nowhere and swept through their ranks like a brushfire. In a business known for sudden violent death, the blood-bath leading to the Cardenal Muerte cartel's rise to power shocked even the most hardened criminals.

Securing an initial base of power was simple, Masque went back to the fractured Pena crime family and secured it under his control. The new army Masque used to conduct his takeover came from Santiago's sources. The ex-SEAL and mercenary recruited a unique group of professional gunmen, mercenaries, to make up the ranks of Masque's attack squads, hard men for whom fighting and violent death was a common factor of life. For himself, Masque took to wearing a red balaclava mask when he went out on some of the more delicate, and bloody, operations. The drug lords never knew the identity of the man who was killing so many of them.

The deaths of the drug lords started with the lieutenants in the Pena family, who had tried to fill in the power vacuum left by Placido and Turi's deaths. Knowing every hideout, safehouse, ranchero, and hacienda in his old network, as well as the strengths and weaknesses of each location and person, gave Masque's people a great advantage. The information allowed the killers working for the Cardenal Muerte cartel to reach an incredible level of efficiency in eliminating all opposition. Those who resisted Masque died, suddenly and violently. Those who accepted his leadership found a place at the table of a new drug cartel.

And the drugs flowed into the United States. Heroin and cocaine, marijuana and amphetamines, crack and new formulations of old vices, they all were products that the Muerte cartel sent on north. The red ink imprint of a stylized skull found on the packages of cocaine and heroin smuggled into the U.S. were quickly becoming a favorite among street users. Eduardo Masque knew that good product meant good sales, and he made certain that his drug labs used the most up-to-date techniques and materials. The income surging into the coffers of the Muerte cartel illustrated the business logic of that philosophy.

The all-encompassing drive that forced Masque into eliminating all of his competition was that of revenge. He wanted revenge on the people who had arrested him, those who had placed him in a situation where he was on trial for his life, and those who had killed the brother of Placido Pena. One person was the primary focus of Masque's hatred—the undercover agent of the U.S. Drug Enforcement Agency who had infiltrated his organization and set up Pena's arrest. That arrest triggered the gun battle that had killed Turi Pena.

The tool that Eduardo Masque was using to obtain the information he wanted was the carrot and stick, threats and money. What he wanted more than anything was the real name of the undercover DEA agent who had infiltrated his organization and betrayed his personal trust. That was the man who had killed his brother, shooting him when Turi swung around with a submachine gun in each hand.

Money was easy to come by with the tons of drugs that were being sent into the United States. Eventually, the price for any information could be reached. Computer hackers penetrated databases, highly placed informants were located, unscrupulous lawyers found ways around the law, and corrupt officials on both sides of the border were found who would willingly sell anyone's soul for enough money or the promise of power.

The name of the undercover informant who had penetrated the Pena cartel was Sabino Duran. He had retired from the DEA during the Pena trial and had moved to a family ranch in southeastern Arizona. The Arizona/Mexican border was an active area of smuggling, both illegal migrants and drugs passed through the more than 350 miles of border between Southern Arizona and the state of Sonora in Northern Mexico. Masque relocated to a large ranch in Northern Sonora in order to be near both a major hub of his business, and the primary target of his personal revenge.

The mercenaries available to Masque had the drawback of sometimes being too ready to use violence to solve any problem. A pair of the men had been discovered while conducting a surveillance of Duran's ranch. True to form, they killed the man who had found them. When the mercenaries immediately reported back to Santiago, Masque sought to turn the situation to his advantage.

Duran would be destroyed by the very same people he used to work for. He could be broken and humiliated, punished by the government he had dedicated his life to. The man who had been killed was an old acquaintance of Duran's, a veteran Border Patrol agent. By planting evidence, Masque would have the man framed for the murder of his friend. It was the actions of a competent attorney that had terminated Duran's indictment for murder, and earned the man the attention of Masque's hatred. Masque had placed a half-million dollar bounty on Duran's head the day after the charges were dropped. For the lawyer who had gotten him off, Masque offered one-hundred thousand dollars.

Hatred was also what Masque felt for the American people, their legal system, and their government. He wanted to see it all destroyed. And if he couldn't bring down the system, he would make it hurt. Masque wasn't so blinded by hate that he couldn't see how nearly impossible it would be to bring down the government of the United States. But he did know that he could hurt it a lot, and that there were people all around the world who wanted to do the same thing. They would be tools to aid him in his revenge.

A wide number of people were on the payroll of the Muerte cartel and all of them had something in common, they wanted more money. The commandante of the local military zone had been corrupted by the easy flow of dollars from the drug business long before Masque had arrived on the scene. As long as his bite of the profits stayed steady, General Ricardo Martinez couldn't have cared less who was in charge of the drug cartel that paid him. His passion was for the glow of gold, no matter where it came from.

When word of Masque's bounty offer reached his ears, General Martinez was more than happy to assign a special squad of his very best men to gather that windfall for him. His elite unit was a group of airborne infantry, paratroopers, among the toughest and most ruthless men under his command. General Martinez had a career military man's opinion of the mercenaries the Muerte cartel had been employing—he despised them.

The disciplined soldiers that General Martinez had at his disposal had been guards and escorts for drug shipments before. The lieutenant in charge of the unit had worked closely with Felix Zapatista, the drug lord who had been working the Sonora/Arizona border before Masque arrived on the scene. The soldiers under the direction of their officer had crossed the border and gone well into the United States before returning. They were experienced, and knew how to keep their mouths shut.

Martinez knew that proving himself a valuable asset was a good way to make certain that the money kept coming. And it couldn't be a bad thing to be on the good side of the leader of one of the largest and fastest growing drug cartels in Mexico.

The plan was a relatively simple one. The men would cross the border along one of the most secure drug routes that Zapatista knew. They would use staging areas that were well known to them as forward bases. They would first lay an ambush for Duran at his ranch. If that proved successful, they would do the same for the lawyer. If Duran proved too difficult a target to reach, the lawyer would be used as bait to get to him.

As a backup plan, the soldiers would observe the lawyer's ranch prior to capturing the man at his home. Once he was in their hands, General Martinez knew that his men would be able to persuade the lawyer to ask his client out to the ranch to talk over a legal problem. That would insure that both Duran and the lawyer were eliminated. That had been the plan—only it hadn't worked out as expected.

The military men had failed—badly. Duran was dead, but the lawyer had proved a much more difficult target. The men had returned across the border in a shambles, beaten, bloody, and hurt. One of the men would probably lose his arm while several others would be badly scarred for the rest of their lives. The pain and suffering of the men meant nothing to the Muerte cartel, and to Eduardo Masque in particular. Taking those kinds of risks were what they were paid for. What enraged Masque when he learned about it, was their failure to complete their mission, to eliminate both of their targets. And in the process, they had possibly exposed one of his newest and most valuable assets.

"Who were these failures?" Masque said as he threw a heavy crystal tumbler of whiskey into the fireplace of his hacienda. "They come back beaten and bloody and all they can tell me is that they were set on by a pack of attack dogs and U.S. troops? I want no more of these soldiers General Martinez considers so elite. You have the best of your mercenaries carry out the job."

"Jefe," Santiago said, "if you keep ordering killings on the other side of the border, the authorities will respond—they won't be able to afford not to. When you had that officer killed, every Border Patrol agent for hundreds of miles came down to help in the investigation. The border was closed for weeks, nothing could move. It cost us millions of dollars in lost revenue. With our new clients paying to use our routes into the States, we can't afford that kind of heat coming down on us."

"Fine," Masque said as he stalked the room, "then you order your men to clean up the mess that general has made of things. I want the men who conducted this fiasco eliminated. Sterilize everything, everyone who had a hand in that operation is to be gone. Make them disappear into the desert. You can spare General Martinez and our contact in the States. But Martinez is to know that we consider him expendable. Exactly the same thing can happen to him at any time. The only danger we face right now is from the incompetence of the people we have around us, not from the Americans."

"Most of the population of the States are sheep," Santiago said. "They do what they are told if it doesn't interfere with their daily lives or their pleasures. They don't want to take risks of any kind. But don't make the mistake of underestimating them. If the flock feels that they are in danger, the sheep will start bleating. They will tell their government to do something about the situation.

"The present administration will not just sit on its

hands and make empty threats. Saddam Hussein and the Taliban thought the U.S. was nothing but a paper tiger and wouldn't act. They found out they were very wrong. There are some very capable people in the States who could do us very serious harm."

"I understand your concern, but you are mistaken," Masque said as he continued to pace the room. "The American people won't do anything to us. They practically pay us to kill them. In fact, in a way they do pay us to kill them, or at least put them out of their misery. The U.S. has an insatiable demand for the products we send them. Marijuana, cocaine, heroin—it doesn't matter what we send, they want more. And if they want something new, we'll get that for them, too.

"The war against drugs is an unwinnable joke. Law enforcement, the DEA, the U.S. government, even the Mexican government, they all know that as long as there's a demand for drugs, the people will keep their hands tied. The high-and-mighty want cocaine, the inner city wants crack, street addicts want heroin, and the college kids want pot along with everything else. We supply their needs and they give us money. With that money comes power, enough power to buy the protection of governments from governments."

"Down in Colombia not too long ago," Santiago said, "Pablo Escobar thought the same thing. That money was power and with enough of it, no one could come after you. He was wrong and now he's dead."

"Escobar?" Masque said. "Pablo Escobar was an uneducated peon suffering from delusions. He didn't want to simply control the Colombian cocaine trade, he wanted to control the entire country of Colombia. He rubbed shoulders with that thug Noriega and thought himself a world leader. That slum-raised peon wanted the poor people to worship him and the rich to fear him. He was nothing but a terrorist. That's why he was hunted down and killed.

"No one knows who exactly is in charge of the Cardenal Muerte cartel. It's why I've never let my face be seen except by people who were about to die. That's my protection. And I'm not interested in taking over a country, I want to destroy one, help it rot from the inside. If there are others who hate the Americans and want my help to attack them, I can give it. Terrorists are tools I can make use of. Besides, what are the Yankees going to do? Kill me? They already did that once, there won't be a second time.

"I'll use their own vices to supply the means to destroy them. It's simple business. The crack smokers don't like the crash that comes ten minutes after their high? Then we'll sell them moonrocks, crack mixed with heroin. Their bodies will still crash, only it won't hurt as much. With our own laboratories, we'll produce the drugs ourselves, use our own distribution networks for sales, and eliminate the middle man. That makes for even more money coming in to us, and eliminates a possible infiltration route for DEA agents.

"The Americans want to die stoned out of their minds? Fine, I'll help them with their wish. And they can pay me for the privilege. The U.S. tried to kill me once, now I'll help kill them. Those actions you are so concerned about, what the American military has done in Iraq and Afghanistan. Those have made the Americans a lot of enemies in the world—enemies who also have money. I can have my revenge and make a profit at the same time.

"The other drug cartels have been afraid to take any of the terrorists' money and help them. They fear that will risk their precious bottom line, their drug profits. Now that I'm in charge, I say what is the bottom line. Besides, if the U.S. becomes more oppressive of its own people in trying to defend against terrorists, that will just push up the demand for our products. This situation will work for us."

Not agreeing with the man who paid him so well, Santiago simply sat there in the spacious room and considered the situation.

"Using our pipelines to help funnel in terrorist finances is one thing," Santiago said. "We can profit from that and the threat to us is minimal. But further involvement such as you have been considering, that's what is really dangerous."

Eduardo Masque merely smiled softly at Santiago's concern. The look in his eyes glinted with a hint of madness.

"Another of our Middle-Eastern friends is due to arrive tomorrow," Masque said. "He's bringing with him another package to be taken into the United States. I want you to escort him across the border, after suitable security precautions are taken of course."

Chapter Ten

As the two men headed out to the parking area, Hausmann stopped at a side door in the short hallway that
led from the living room to the poolroom.

"I don't think I'll travel quite as lightly as I did last
night," Hausmann said as he opened the door. "Something with a little more range and power than a pistol or
carbine sounds good."

The room past the door was a compact but well
equipped exercise area. Dominating the center of the
room was a universal weight machine with its various
stations for different resistance exercises. For those
workouts done better with free weights, there were
racks of weights lined up along the outside wall, just on
the other side of a large bench. On the opposite wall
was both an elliptical trainer and a treadmill for cardio-
vascular work.

The left-hand wall of the room was completely covered with floor-to-ceiling mirrors. As Reaper watched,

Hausmann went over to the mirrored wall and pressed hard on a seam between two panels. There was a soft click and two of the panels unlatched and swung outward, revealing a pair of large safe doors with a combination lock dial on the right-hand door.

A fast series of spins of the combination dial allowed Hausmann to unlock the doors and pull them both open. Inside the safe was a long rack of rifles and shoulder arms along the back wall. The doors were each covered with pegboards holding a variety of handguns and holsters. Several shelves along the top of the safe had stacks of magazines and different boxes of ammunition across their length.

"Got enough guns?" Reaper asked.

"You mean there's such a thing as enough guns?" Hausmann said. "What an astonishing concept. Must come from all of that city living you've been doing back East. These are just what I have to make do with for a while. Besides, this is just the household supply. The rest of the hardware is in the armory at the back of the garage."

Pulling a Springfield M1A Super Match rifle from the rack, Hausmann pulled the breech open on the big military-style weapon. He reached up to the top shelf and took down a pair of magazines for the rifle. Each gray parkerised steel feed device held twenty rounds of 7.62×51mm ammunition. Slipping one of the magazines into a pouch on the stock of the big rifle, he locked the other into place in the magazine well in front of the trigger guard. An older-model 8-power Leupold telescopic sight was set along the top of the weapon's receiver in a secure three-point mount.

Leaning the now loaded rifle back into its slot in the rack, Hausmann pulled his belt rig down from the left-hand door. The leather belt still held his Custom Firearms Inc. M1911A1 in its Blade Tech kydex holster. Reaching up to the ammunition shelf again, Hausmann took down a second kydex magazine holder, this one having two full eight-round stainless-steel magazines, the same style as Reaper was using, slipped into its pockets.

"Well," Hausmann said as he attached the second pouch to his belt, "at least you didn't have to clean it."

"I'm just glad I remembered the combination to the gun safe," Reaper said as he leaned against the frame of the door.

Buckling the belt around his waist, Hausmann picked up the M1A and slung it from his shoulder. Shutting the safe doors, he rotated the locking lever and spun the combination dial. With the mirror panels shut, the space went back to looking like nothing more than an exercise room.

Passing through the poolroom on their way out of the house, Reaper stopped and picked up his M4A1 carbine and M1911A1 from the open Kalispel aluminum gun case sitting across the couch. Reaper had already cleaned the weapon and reloaded his magazines after firing it the night before. Since they were going to be riding in the close confines of the Prowler RTVs, Reaper had decided against carrying his M1911A1 in his Fobus C21 belt holster. The hidden inside pockets of his 5.11 tactical shirt were too small to carry the full-sized M1911A1. So he had put on his 5.11 tactical vest.

The multipocket 5.11 tactical vest looked like just another sleeveless sportsman's or camera vest. But underneath the first layer of cloth was a hidden pocket on both sides of the vest, pockets that were lined with the pile material of Velcro. A holster that was lined with the nylon Velcro hook material held the M1911A1 securely inside the hidden left-hand carry compartment of the 5.11 vest. In the right-hand compartment, Reaper had secured the Velcro-sided double magazine pouch. Now the ex-SEAL was well armed with his customized Springfield Armory M1911A1 along with twenty-four rounds of high velocity .45 hollowpoints in three magazines. Two spare thirty-round magazines to the M4A1 were in pockets on the outside of the vest, in addition to the pair of magazines already locked into the weapon.

The two men headed outside to where the Prowler RTVs were parked. Both vehicles were relatively small, barely more than five feet tall. And each was less than eight feet long. A normal man could stand behind a Prowler and grab either side of the just over four-foot-wide vehicle.

The body of the Prowlers were made of formed steel tubing with expanded metal grids along the sides and across the front and back areas. Only the middle of the vehicles had a seat, with the rough travel capability of the RTVs indicated by the five-point safety harness on the operator's seats.

"Damn," Hausmann said as they walked around the two vehicles, "these things do look like stripped-down dune buggies, only smaller. Either that, or four-wheeler bikes on steroids."

"They are a lot smaller than most all-terrain vehicles," Reaper agreed. "But that helps them be a lot more maneuverable. Their center of gravity is a foot-and-a-half lower than most ATVs, and that makes them stable as hell on the run as well. These things are not modified off-road vehicles. They were purpose-built to protect the operator in military operations. They are just about the most rugged thing out there on wheels. They're a big improvement even on the fast attack vehicles (FAVs) the Teams were using just last year in Afghanistan. You can secure your rifle in that set of rubber-covered hooks in front of the operator's compartment."

Hausmann slipped his M1A rifle into the cradle made by the two hooks Reaper pointed out. The weapon's mount was on the two roll cage supports on either side of the front of the Prowler. Two flat elastic straps slipped over the rifle and held it low, keeping it from blocking any of the operator's sight line, but ready for quick withdrawal and immediate use. Over at the other Prowler, Reaper was securing his M4A1 in the same weapon's mount.

"It does look like the driver is just about completely surrounded by metal when he sits inside this thing," Hausmann said as he climbed into one of the Prowlers.

"So far, just about all of the Special Operation units and most of the services have been trying them out," Reaper said. "There hasn't been an operator injury in a vehicle accident with one yet. So buckle up that harness and try not to be the first one ever hurt, okay?"

As Hausmann slipped the safety harness over his shoulders he noticed that both vehicles were just about the same, but that the one Reaper was climbing into had what looked like vertical wings on either side of the padded roll cage. The extensions had black cloth pads strung up inside their tubular frameworks.

"And just what the hell are those wings for?" Hausmann asked.

"Those are the side passenger racks," Reaper said. "They're jump seats so that you can take two more people on board besides the operator. Only thing is that they have to sit on that unpadded metal grid instead of a seat. There's even a swing-arm gun mount here on the left side that'll accept an M249 Squad Automatic Weapon or a 7.62mm M240 machine gun if you want. The arm can be locked in place or rotated to give a 360-degree field of fire around the vehicle. They drive pretty much like a car. There's an automatic transmission, two or four-wheel drive, and standard driver's controls."

"Geeze, Reaper," Hausmann said, "I don't want to buy the damned thing. That gun mount does make me wish I had a nice big belt-fed machine gun to go in it. Something useful you know, just in case we find any of those bastards who ambushed us. Of course, with the way my head feels, I think I'd prefer an Abrams tank rather than this Prowler ATV thing."

"That's an RTV," Reaper said, "a rugged terrain vehicle. Not an all-terrain vehicle. And these Prowler's have an advantage over any tank made."

"Yeah?" said Hausmann, "and what's that?"

"They're smaller, and lighter," Reaper said with a

grin, "they get a hell of a lot better mileage—and they're here."

With that, Reaper started up the 660 cc engine on his Prowler and fed it the gas. The wide rubber tires threw gravel as the agile little RTV darted forward. Spinning in a tight circle, Reaper pulled his vehicle up to the electronic gate and punched his code into the keypad. The gate opened and Reaper sped up the road.

Firing up his own Prowler, Hausmann took off after Reaper, passing through the gate well before it began its closing cycle. The two tan-colored vehicles hugged each curve and turn in the road, the heavy-duty suspension holding the RTVs steady as their deeply ridged run-flat tires tore through the gravel and dust.

"It's your ranch," Reaper shouted as Hausmann pulled alongside of him, "you know the way best. I'll follow your lead."

With a shouted "Okay," Hausmann turned off the roadway and headed north to drive around the wall surrounding the ranch house compound. Driving around the grove of trees that lined the north wall of the compound, Hausmann headed down to the river and the ford there. The water over the ford was shallow enough for the two vehicles to cross, but the roll cage of the Prowlers offered little in way of protection.

The roll cages were strong, but very open. Both men slowed their vehicles down as they splashed into the river. The all-terrain tires of the Prowlers threw up foaming waves of water, but both men managed to get across the river without being too badly soaked.

Once up the opposite bank, Hausmann again led off.

Following the path they had ridden only the night before, the two men quickly came up to the railroad tracks and soon passed the path leading down to the rope bridge. As the rails and path they were on started to turn, Hausmann stopped his Prowler. Reaper pulled up and stopped alongside his friend.

"This is about as far as I remember going," Hausmann said.

"Looks about right to me," said Reaper. "The ambush came from that brush just past the curve. You can see the hoofmarks of the horses and dog tracks in the dirt over there."

As Hausmann looked down to where Reaper was pointing, he could see the marks of shod hoofs pressed down into the dust. On either side of the hoofprints were the widely spaced padmarks made from the feet of two large, running dogs. Getting out of the Prowlers, both men took their long guns from the racks before walking over to the marks in the dirt. Crouching down, they followed the marks with their eyes as far as they could see.

"That's where your horse turned and headed into the trees," Reaper said as he pointed to a scuffed area in the dirt.

"So they fired on us from beyond that turn," Hausmann said, nodding toward the area ahead.

Getting up, the men slowly walked along the path. Within just a few feet, they came to a point on the path where both sets of hoofprints had turned back. Only the footprints of the dogs could be seen for a few steps before they turned off into the brush on either side of the path.

Twenty feet farther on, the two men were just at the edge of the brush growing heavily along the river side of the path. All around could be seen the shining cases of fired cartridge brass. The shells were mixed and scattered over a wide area. Both short-pistol caliber as well as much larger rifle brass shone and winked from where the sun struck them scattered around the area.

"Damn," Hausmann said, "looks like somebody fought a small war around here."

"Someone did," Reaper said, "and it looks like the guys with the guns lost."

Pointing to the leaves of a bush, Reaper indicated the dark brown stains of dried blood. After finding the first few splashes among the leaves, both men started to see bloodstains scattered all around the area. Whoever had ambushed them, had either shot at and hit each other in the dark, or the two rottweilers had created some serious carnage the night before. By the amount of brass Reaper could see, there had to have been at least two men armed with submachine guns and as many or more men carrying G3 or HK-91 rifles.

"Take a look at the brass," Reaper said as he picked up a mixed handful of the very familiar caliber rifle and pistol cartridge cases.

Along the sides of the 9×19 millimeter and 7.62×51mm cases were multiple thin black marks running about half the length of the brass. The marks were spaced out evenly all around the circumference of the cases.

"All of this ammunition looks like it was fired from either a Heckler and Koch submachine gun or rifle,"

Reaper said. "Those are the only weapons I know of with the fluted chambers that mark up cases like this when they're fired. What drug runner wants to carry a heavy battle rifle like a G3 or HK-91?"

"None that I know of," Hausmann said, "but both the G3 and the MP5 are issue weapons in the Mexican military.

Hausmann closely examined a handful of the fired cartridges.

"Here's something really interesting," he said. "Look at the headstamps on these cases. This stuff is practically fresh from the arsenal."

Around the bottom of each cartridge case were letters and numbers surrounding the central primer. They identified both who had made the rounds and when they had been manufactured. The letters on the base of the cartridge were FNM while the numbers were 03.

"FNM," Reaper said. "That's Mexican isn't it?"

"Yup," Hausmann agreed. "Mexican military. And it's usually in short enough supply that they don't sell it on the surplus market. Besides, that 03 means it was made just last year."

"So," Reaper said, "we have new-issue military ammunition having been fired in weapons known to be used by Mexican forces. Sounds a lot like a bunch of stolen hardware in the wrong hands south of the border."

"More likely a rogue bunch of Mexican soldiers," Hausmann said. "Mexican military forces don't get paid all that well. But they don't commonly sell their guns or ammunition on the black market. Instead, they rent them out complete with operators. More than a few soldiers have supplemented their incomes by hiring out to guard drug shipments across the border. There's commanders of units who hire their men out as private security forces to the drug lords. And they've been coming across the border for years. More than one Border Patrol unit has come under fire from guns in the hands of the Mexican military all along the border."

"And now it looks like they're coming after you," Reaper said. "We're going to need some help on this one."

"Local law enforcement can't do a damned thing about them," Hausmann said. "Even the Mexican military has the average sheriff's car badly outgunned. Before a SWAT or U.S. military unit can be called in, they cut back across the border and the government denies the incident. The feds haven't been able to do anything about the problem diplomatically. And the U.S. government sure as hell isn't going to authorize an armed invasion of Mexico. And that's about what it would take."

"Who said anything about authorized?" Reaper said. "But let's see where these blood trails lead before we go charging across the border."

There were some areas in the brush where the ground was torn up and the leaves were heavily spattered with blood. These obviously were the spots where the dogs had grabbed hold of individual gunmen. Fired brass, especially 9mm brass, was all around the area. Dozens of rounds had been fired in all directions. It looked like it was only the darkness of the night and the black coats of the dogs that had saved them from being shot and killed.

As far as either man could tell from the volume of blood all around, the gunmen may have accidentally shot each other in the confusion. Even though the gunmen wouldn't have shown either of them mercy, neither Reaper or Hausmann cared to think about what it must have been like for the gunmen when the slashing teeth and powerful jaws of the rottweilers had come up from the black of the night.

The trails of blood spatter and bootprints in the dirt and gravel headed south along the pathway on the riverbank. This was the direction Reaper and Hausmann traveled as they followed the trail. The two men had their rifles in their hands as they left the Prowlers behind them.

Both Reaper and Hausmann had some experience following a trail and reading signs in the dirt. Their skills were strained trying to figure out just how many gunmen had been facing them at the ambush. At least one man had been bleeding heavily, and the prints looked as if he had been carried by one of the other men in the group. One set of prints ran straight in the dirt while another walking right alongside had long scuff marks from both feet. Others stepped into the prints of the men who had walked in front of them, confusing just how many sets of footprints there were.

Finally, the footprints all stopped just a few hundred yards farther away from where the ambush had taken place, in a small clearing in the brush, where the heavily cross-hatched tracks of several all-terrain vehicles began. The tread marks were too close together to be from a jeep or other full-sized vehicle, but they were spaced too far apart to be from a four-wheeled bike or the like. What was obvious was that the gunmen had climbed aboard vehicles and were well out of the area.

"We need someone with better tracking skills than you or I have," Reaper said, "if we're going to follow this track from the RTVs and make any time."

"I know just the guy," Hausmann said. "He's a Border Patrol agent who's probably one of the best trackers in the area."

"I thought you said you were on the shit list for every law enforcement department around here," Reaper said, "especially the Border Patrol."

"That's pretty much the case," Hausmann agreed. "But the man I'm thinking of used to be a close friend of both Sam Duran and Victor Langstrom. He never thought Sam was guilty of killing Langstrom, refused to even consider the idea. He's about the last friend I still have on the Border Patrol. He may not want to come right out to the house though. He still has to work with all of his fellow officers and they don't quite share his opinion of me. But now with Sam having been murdered, I'll bet he'll help us if anyone will.

"Let's get back to the house and give him a call. We can meet him up in Tombstone and ask if he can help us here."

"Sounds like a good idea to me," Reaper said. "You look like this sun is about to beat you into the ground anyway."

"I will admit I've had better days out here," Hausmann agreed.

Chapter Eleven

The finger slowly slipped through the white stones piled inside the black dish. The stones rustled and rang faintly as they brushed against each other and the dark porcelain.

"Amazing," Masque said, "they look like little more than bright pebbles. They show no color, shine a little like lead at best, and even feel a little oily to the touch. Yet they are considered so valuable that even today men, women, and children are held as slaves and die to dig them from the clay of the earth. More still give up their lives in order to try and own them. There is so much death around these tiny rocks that I understand they're called Blood Stones."

"We do not use such a loaded term for them," Youssef Daumudi said from where the Arab sat in an upholstered leather chair. "They are simply a valuable commodity. Much like that white powder you move across the border in such huge amounts. Only these uncut and unpolished stones are much less bulky than cash—paper money, and vastly lighter than the gold we have more traditionally used. Each of those green-pea-sized "pebbles," as you call them, is roughly a carat in size. They are worth about $500 U.S. each, some more, some less. That small mound of stones there you could hold in the palm of your hand, barely more than a few ounces in weight, is worth about $150,000 U.S."

"What you have there is only about three hundred carats' worth of diamonds," Ammand Humzan, the other Arab in the room, said. "They are in a raw, un-polished state, but as such they are much easier for us to move from place to place. It is only when they are cut and faceted that their true beauty shows through."

"Of course for our cause," Daumudi said, "a great deal of their beauty is in their ability to refill our finances. The Americans and their investigative pro-grams have seriously depleted our available funds in the United States. Even our traditional hawalas, the centuries-old banking system of our people, have been breached and stripped of their funds by the Americans and their Operation Green Quest.

"The American people could never even use a hawala system of their own. It is a bank based on trust and honor. There is none of the paper trail that is so popular with Western law-enforcement agencies. Gold has been the preferred medium of exchange in the past, but the weight of that metal has eliminated it from practical use. A carrier could move perhaps eighty pounds of gold in a specially made vest, but that's only about half a million dollars' worth. Cash would be useful, but it has its drawbacks as well."

"Yes," said Masque, "I've run into that problem a number of times in my own business. The North Americans can be so astonished when they stop a shipment and find it's money instead of drugs. There have been occasions when we've had to move pallet loads of cash all bundled up in plastic, to try and launder it into useful funds."

"So you understand our problem," Humzan said. "Laundering funds has become more and more difficult with the increasing investigations going on within the United States. It is only the incessant internal squabbling among the different law enforcement agencies in the U.S. that finally forced the U.S. Customs people to end Green Quest only a year ago when they became part of their department of Homeland Security. But the damage done by that operation as well as other unforeseen difficulties have forced us to seek other means to move operational funds into the United States. That is what has finally brought us to you."

"The results of our previous dealings with you have proven very satisfactory," Daumudi said. "So we have decided to expand our business considerably."

"I still feel that working more closely together would be to our mutual benefit," Masque said. "After all, I have exposed some of my most valuable routes into the United States to your people. And now you ask me to show you even more. Trust should be a two-way proposition, gentlemen."

"You should understand," Humzan said, "that there

are relatively few of us available to conduct operations inside the United States. Though our numbers are small in comparison to our brothers elsewhere in the world, our determination and faith make our power great. But, we cannot afford a loss of our faithful by exposing them unnecessarily."

"It is completely understandable," Masque said, "that there are some things you feel you must keep secret for security's sake, of course. But my people are concerned with our security as well as yours. My security chief there," Masque nodded to where Santiago was standing on the other side of the room, "has proven himself more than competent at setting up a security force, as well as developing an intelligence arm inside the United States.

"It was through the observations of this intelligence force that we were able to learn about such places as the Mysteri Jewelers."

Pausing for a moment, Masque was impressed with the impassive look the two Arab terrorists maintained on their faces as he mentioned the name. Only a narrowing of the eyes on Daumudi's face gave any outward sign of recognizing the name.

"That is a chain of wholesale and retail diamond merchants," Masque said, "or so I understand. Their retail stores are in so many major cities: Washington, D.C., New York, Miami, Houston, Los Angeles, and where was it? Oh, yes, Las Vegas, Nevada."

"Enough!" Daumudi almost exploded. "It is obvious that you must have had our people followed. One of our men was almost exposed when he tried to make a contact in Las Vegas. Was it your people who put him at risk?"

"That isn't something I was aware of," Masque said as he looked pointedly at Santiago. "None of your people were endangered by anyone working for me. If they were and I find out about it, they will not be working for me, or anyone else, much longer."

The ex-SEAL remained standing in a relaxed position near the door into the room. His arms were crossed, and his hand only inches away from the 9mm Glock 18C select-fire machine pistol sheathed in his shoulder holster. The selector switch of the weapon was set to full automatic fire and it was loaded with a nineteen-round magazine. If the situation went against him, Santiago knew that he could sweep the room with a single long burst from the machine pistol before reloading with one of the extralong thirty-one-round magazines hanging down from the holder on the opposite side of his holster. Firing at 1,200 rounds per minute, the pistol would put out a spray of nineteen rounds in under a second.

Using such a small automatic weapon correctly took a lot of training and discipline, something Santiago was willing to commit to its use. The sudden firepower of the machine pistol could help keep his options open if things went bad. He had grown used to Masque's fits of temper, though he was still very careful about them.

"But I wouldn't worry about your men being easily found out," Masque continued. "The U.S. government doesn't even know that they are in the country, what they are doing, where they are going, or even what they look like. On the other hand, my men have those facts, and more, at their disposal. You shouldn't be concerned about any mistakes on our part. The people we have in our employ are among the very best available—or so I've been assured."

From where he was standing by the door, Santiago relaxed just a little as he listened to Masque's calmer words. Though less concerned about the situation at least for the moment, Santiago kept his arms crossed and his right hand within a short reach of his weapon.

The negotiations between the drug lord and the al-Qaeda representatives had been going on for some weeks. Though the Arabs had presented themselves as being from another organization, Santiago's research and Masque's own style of diplomacy had forced the men to admit their true affiliations. With Masque's own great hatred of the United States, the fact that the two Arabs had close ties with al-Qaeda were actually points in their favor as far as he was concerned.

The terrorists had been making use of Masque's smuggling routes to move people and materiel into the United States for over a month. So far, the numbers of people had been small and they were easy to hide among a group of illegal workers crossing into the States. The amount of baggage the terrorists had been carrying along with them hadn't been very great either, little more than a tiny bag or two of raw diamonds and some currency.

Now the terrorists wanted to take a much larger quantity of diamonds across the border—five million dollars' worth. The package was less than four-and-a-half pounds of stones and would fit inside a large purse, or even a standard shoebox with lots of room to spare. That package was going to be carried across the border by a high-ranking terrorist operative. But the al-Qaeda were less than satisfied with the smuggling routes that they had been allowed to use up until then. Now they wanted access to the most secure route Masque had available. And the drug lord wasn't sure he wanted to risk exposing one of his major assets just yet. So Masque was playing for time with the terrorists while he made his decision. Santiago only hoped that Masque realized just how dangerous a game he was playing and exactly who the people were that he was leading along.

Both the terrorists and Masque had intimated that there was an even bigger and much more important package coming up that had to go through the pipeline. Whatever this item was, Masque was keeping Santiago in the dark about precisely what was being discussed. In spite of the trust that supposedly existed between the two men, when Masque started keeping secrets from his chief of security, it was time to question the relationship.

Not knowing all the facts of a situation made Santiago very uneasy. He had stayed alive as long as he had in a very cutthroat business by knowing as much about a situation as he could, and planning accordingly. Santiago knew very well the value of timing, and how important it was to be able to just cut his losses and run. Those familiar alarm bells were ringing faintly in the back of his head. This would be a good time to make sure that his private avenues of escape were open and ready.

Those were actions Santiago had to do during his own private time. At the present time, paying close attention to what was being said between his boss and the terrorists was what was most important.

"I know you have been using other routes to get some of your people across the border," Masque said. "You have a woman agent, from South Africa by way of London, I believe, who has been crossing fairly regularly into the United States across the Rio Grande River into Texas."

This time, the hard stares were from both of the Arabs in the room as Masque again showed that he knew another of their secrets.

"Please, gentlemen," Masque said, "there is no need to be shocked. None of my people followed her. You think we are a single-product business? That everything I do is involved with the drug trade? My cartel uses our contacts within the government to supply the majority of illegal documents all along the border. Your agent simply used one of my sources and it was brought to my attention."

Though he had no way of knowing it, Masque had now come very close to death in his dealings with the two al-Qaeda men. The woman he was speaking of was one of the highest level al-Qaeda operatives working between Mexico and the United States. Faridari Achmed Goolharm had been establishing the lines of communications between cells in the United States for years. She had crossed the border hundreds of times, and she would have to be warned that at least part of her cover was blown. But that was for a later time. Dealing with this drug lord and getting their materials across the border undetected was of the utmost priority to Daumudi and Humzan. Besides, they were unarmed in the presence of the drug lord, and his guard dog standing at the doorway was obviously on the alert. It would be better to appease this criminal drug merchant and make use of his facilities. He could always be dealt with in a satisfactory manner later, after their mission was accomplished.

Masque had continued talking while his fate was decided by the two Arabs sitting in front of him. He was oblivious to their intent stares and just carried on with his view of the situation.

"The gentleman who used to control this part of the Mexican border met with a very unfortunate end when he refused to join with my organization," Masque said. "Felix Zapatista thought he was invincible after he had eluded a nineteen-month-long investigation of his drug smuggling into the United States. He thought his techniques made him better than anyone else when it came to moving product across the border since the Americans had only broken his pipeline a few times in more than ten years.

"His secret was simple really, he liked tunnels. The Rio Grande River acts as a natural barrier against tunnels along the border in Texas. And the lack of facilities, cities and towns and such, along the border on the U.S. side in New Mexico made tunnels impractical on that part of the border. But here along the Arizona border, they proved very successful indeed. It was his downfall that he felt it unnecessary to share his good fortune with his peers. That problem has been eliminated and the facilities are now in my hands.

"So we have been running both immigrant workers who could afford our fees and drug mules through our tunnels. There are a few along the California border, but the Americans have become more sophisticated in finding them. Here, not even their ground-penetrating radar and seismic tests can find our best tunnels. Our most secure route into the States is a geological rarity. Something that may never be found again. And you want us to risk our most valuable asset for your people?"

"During our first jihad against the Soviet invaders of Afghanistan," Humzan said, "our mujahideen well learned the value of caves and tunnels. We could only survive in some areas and drive the invaders from our land by using the vast network of underground passages that Allah, All Praise be on His Name, put there for our use. We could move for miles under such cover, and you say there is something like that available for us here?"

"It is a combination of natural and man-made tunnels that we have used to move very large loads across the border," Masque said. "And it is completely undetectable to the Americans."

"Your reluctance to tell us about such a commodity is understandable," Daumudi said. "But even though you will be risking such a rarity, we will be risking our lives and mission. We will do nothing that will put our actions at risk before we can act against the Americans, and that includes exposing your tunnel or any part of your organization."

"I understand this and respect your position," Masque said. "To demonstrate my own good faith to you, I will assign my very best man, my most trusted lieutenant, to guide you across the border tonight. You can see how a part of our operation works and just how valuable it can be to your own actions. But you will follow my lieutenant's instructions to the letter. It is no small trust I am putting in you having all of this shown to you.

"It would be very valuable for you to remember that I am the only one who is taking product across the border now who is even willing to help you. None of the smaller dealers will risk exposing their smuggling routes no matter how much you offer them. In the words of our shared enemy—we're the only game in town."

Chapter Twelve

No matter how beat up the men were, there were things that had to be done on the ranch before they could go on to Tombstone and meet with the Border Patrol agent. Hausmann and Reaper made sure both the horses and the dogs were fed and watered. The horses were rotated out of their stalls into the exercise yard, the area mucked out, and all of the things done that couldn't be ignored. Navy SEALs and Mexican gunmen didn't impress a bunch of hungry horses and dogs.

The drive along Route 80 passed a lot of open, desert terrain. There were long spaces between any form of home, spaces filled with creosote bushes, mesquite, and a variety of cactus. As the two men approached the town, they passed the Tombstone Hills off on their left. To the right of the road, Reaper saw a chain-link fenced area surrounding a flat field and three arched silver Quonset hut shelters.

"Just what is that?" Reaper said from the driver's seat.

"That is the luxurious, ultramodern Tombstone Municipal Airfield," Hausmann said. "There's a graded airstrip down in the draw past those shelters there. That's about it, no control tower, radio, radar, gas pumps, or anything else really."

"Who uses it?" Reaper said. "Drug runners?"

"I don't think even dopers use this field," Hausmann said. "This really is the middle of nowhere. Besides, it's a long drive to anywhere and outsiders kind of stand out during the off season at Tombstone."

"The off season?" Reaper said.

"Pretty much the summer around here," Hausmann said. "The tourists don't like the heat that much. And tourism is just about the major industry here in Tombstone."

The town in question was coming up as the two men were talking. There was a substantial residential area built up around the central core of historic buildings. Several blocks of downtown Tombstone were closed off to motor traffic, so Reaper parked his car under the shade of one of the trees lining Allen Street, the main street. Except for the vehicles that could be seen several blocks away down the street, the central area of Tombstone in the middle of the day didn't appear to have changed all that much from over a hundred years ago.

The place where they were meeting Pat Manors, the Border Patrol agent, was just across the street from where Reaper had parked the car. As he looked toward the central part of historical Tombstone, Reaper asked:

"And just where is the O.K. Corral anyway?

"Right there across the street," Hausmann said

pointing. "That's it behind that fence. That's why they call this restaurant the O.K. Cafe, it's not thirty yards from the corral."

There were several tables outside the cafe and sitting at one of them in the shade of a tree was a young man wearing a white Stetson hat and dark sunglasses. He stood up as Hausmann and Reaper approached. He was about medium height and slender, wearing denim jeans and a light-colored shirt.

"Hey, Pat," Hausmann said as he extended his hand, "good to see you again."

"Same here, Cowboy," Manors said using Hausmann's nickname. "So this is your SEAL buddy? A long way from water, guy."

"Ted Reaper," Reaper said as he shook hands with Manors. "As long as there's ice to cool the beer, I'm close enough to water."

Small talk continued as the men sat down and took a look through the menus. When the waitress came out to take their orders, Reaper passed on the famous O.K. buffalo burger and just went with a standard hamburger and fries. He felt he had probably done the right thing when Hausmann and Manors both ordered the same.

"Nah," Hausmann said, "I just like their hamburgers."

"Their breakfasts are pretty darn good, too," Manors said.

They continued to talk about nothing very important until their food had arrived and they ate. There were no other customers at the sidewalk tables and few pedestrians were walking past. The trio had sufficient privacy to talk about more serious subjects while they were leaning over their coffee. Manors sat quietly listening while Hausmann brought him up to speed on the situation. Reaper filled in the detail about what happened the night before, after Hausmann had been injured.

"So you had a run-in with some kind of armed coyotes the other night?" Manors said.

"Not quite a run-in," Hausmann said, "more of an out-and-out ambush. And these guys weren't like any coyotes I ever heard of. They weren't guiding a bunch of illegals through the desert, or escorting some drug mules. They were moving in to set up an ambush—specifically for me. And the evidence looks like this might be the same bunch who hit Sam Duran last night."

"I sure wouldn't mind nailing the bastards who took Sam down," Manors said. "You know the department is writing it off as a drug hit? They figure it was either a falling out among thieves, or a payback for all of the trouble that came down on the border after Langstrom was killed."

"There's not much question the men we're after were at least involved in Sam's murder," Hausmann said, "they were carrying his address as well as mine."

"And they had a newspaper picture showing both Hausmann and Duran," Reaper said as he pulled the clipping from his shirt pocket. "This thing had all the earmarks of a military ambush, including the use of only military weapons and ammunition."

"Sounds like you folks ran into some Mexican military types working for the wrong side," Manors said. "That isn't all that new, I'm afraid. Rogue Mexican military units have been renting out troops as drug escort guards for years now. It's really bad along some parts of the border."

"This hasn't been something that's made the press very much," Reaper said. "And there has been almost nothing reported about it in DEA and intelligence reports about the border."

"No one back in D.C. wants to make this a major diplomatic incident," Majors said. "Most of the time, any reports about Mexican military units crossing over into the United States seem to get squashed long before anyone important reads them. And the DEA doesn't want to rock the boat by demanding any action. And they sure as heck don't saddle up and ride out into the desert where they could meet these guys face-to-face."

"There doesn't seem to be a lot of love lost between the DEA and the men on the ground in the Border Patrol," Reaper said.

"The DEA? For the most part we hate them," Manors said. "I don't know any agents who like them at all. It seems that they mess with us every chance they get. I'll give you an example. The DEA is supposed to have all of this intel available to them. A Border Patrol agent, a close friend of mine, was driving down the road and saw this horse trailer heading on down the way. He couldn't put his finger on it, but something about the trailer just didn't seem right to him.

"Something just wasn't hitting him right about that trailer, and then he finally figured it out. So he pulled over the trailer and went up to talk to the driver. Now, the driver was just sitting there, he had a ball cap on, mustache, looked like he lived in the local area. That was just the wrong combination, this guy should not be driving this truck.

"When my friend asked the driver if he minded if he looked in the trailer, then the guy got nervous and a little belligerent. So he took the guy out of the truck and cuffed him. In the trailer was 3,800 pounds of marijuana, a whole trailer load, one of the biggest ones we ever had.

"So here's this Border Patrol agent, just doing what he's doing, going by a hunch—and he really did take it seriously, he's a good agent. The DEA comes in and they wanted to claim the load."

"So there's no love lost between the Border Patrol and the DEA?" Reaper said.

"I will tell you," Manors said, "and any Border Patrol agent will say the same thing, a huge percentage of the DEA's local narcotics seizures are ours. If I was to just pull a number out of my hat, I would say that 80 percent of their numbers belong to us. We do the seizing, and they get the numbers.

"There was a time when a group of us walked more than 350 pounds of marijuana out of the desert. It took something like ten hours to get all of it out. There was no way to get anything on wheels in there and we didn't have a helicopter to fly it out. So we packed it out on our backs.

"After we got in, it was put in the station. All of us were pretty dusty and dirty, but we took the time to take a bunch of hoo-rah pictures standing around the seizure. Then the DEA came down and got out of their air-conditioned trucks. One DEA agent was here, and another in the back. It looked like they were setting up some protective detail for some super-important person, at our station.

"And they were all wearing their little fag-bags right up front, the fanny packs that go around the waist. Those things just aren't cool out here. They denote you as someone who just doesn't know any better, and around here that means FBI or DEA.

"And they took the marijuana, claimed it for their own right there in our station. And we hadn't even cleaned up yet after packing it in on our backs. That one pissed off a bunch of us. So you could say there isn't the best working relationship between most of the agents in the Border Patrol and the DEA.

"But Sam Duran was never like that," Hausmann said. "He never became the kind of bureaucrat who looked at just the numbers over the people. That's why the higher-ups in the DEA always had a case of the ass against him."

"I never heard about his career problems in the DEA," Manors said, "but you're right about things being a hell of a lot different with how he operated. Duran always made sure that the men who did the work got the credit. It didn't make him the most popular man with the bean counters back in D.C. Those guys just live to count the numbers, that's all that means anything to them. Bigger numbers for their agencies meant more money coming their way.

"No, none of the DEA supervisors were very happy with Sam not making sure that their agency got the credit for all of the seizures that it could. But he was so good at working undercover and pulling in the big busts that they couldn't do anything to him. His seizure and conviction rates were so high just because of his own work that he didn't need to steal anything from any of us just to puff himself up. He wasn't afraid to get his hands dirty, knew the area up and down the border as well as anyone, and could ride a horse without falling off—not something a hell of a lot of DEA agents can do. When Sam Duran retired last year, he was on the books as one of the most successful agents of all time down in Mexico.

"Then he came out here, back where he grew up on the ranch. Victor Langstrom knew him back in the days when they were kids together climbing around the hills along the border. They both could speak Spanish like a native, that was one of the things that made them both so successful at what they did. But a whole lot of people could never get past Duran's background as a DEA agent.

"Some of that was just because of what I told you with the DEA doing what they do. Other law enforcement agents, and quite a few prosecutors, just can't believe that a man can be as successful an undercover agent as Duran was without some dirt rubbing off on him.

"Victor Langstrom was my mentor. I loved that man like a father. No one wants to nail his killer more than I do. But he personally vouched for Sam Duran and that was good enough for me. That case they had against Sam never did make any sense to me. And I don't blame you," Manors said as he nodded at Hausmann, "for it falling apart."

As he leaned back in his seat, Hausmann looked down at his coffee cup in quiet silence for a moment.

"It strikes me," Hausmann said, "that if anyone was willing to go through all of the trouble that it took to try and frame a man like Sam Duran, they would still have a serious case of the ass against him after he slipped out of their trap. They killed a federal agent, a Border Patrol agent, and that brought all kinds of hell down on the border."

"I know for a fact," Manors said, "that every Border Patrol agent for a hundred miles in any direction showed up here. It was when they couldn't find any other suspects that they came down so hard on Sam Duran."

"Then those same people," Reaper said, looking pointedly at Hausmann, "would probably be seriously pissed off at whoever it was that wrecked their frame-up of Duran."

"My thoughts exactly," Hausmann agreed.

"Sounds like you two are thinking along the same lines," Manors said. "Do you have a plan together yet? And just what part did you have me playing in it?"

"Just to use some of your skills, really," Reaper said. "Hausmann told me that you were one of the best trackers he knows."

"I don't know about being the best," Manors said, "but I've had my share of practice. Illegals don't just walk along the roads around here."

"Well," Reaper said, "it's not exactly people we need you to help track."

Filling Manors in on what they had found earlier

that afternoon, Reaper and Hausmann told him about the footprints and the blood trail ending at the tire tracks.

"And you figure those vehicles were some kind of dune buggies or ATVs?" Manors asked.

"They definitely had four tires," Reaper said. "So they weren't some kind of dirt bikes."

"The tire tracks had very deep tread marks," Hausmann said. "They could have been dune buggies. Why? Is that important?"

"It could be," Manors said. "Dirt bikes would be a lot easier to take across the desert and still stay hidden. And crossing the border with them would be easier as well. But injured men would have a real hard time riding one, especially across country.

"Dune buggies and ATVs are a lot bigger than bikes. That makes them a heck of a lot harder to hide when you cross the open desert, even at night. And Border Patrol agents are keeping a careful eye out for cross-country vehicles this close to the border. Your place is what, twelve miles from the border?"

"Almost thirteen miles as the crow flies," Hausmann said.

"That's a heck of a long way to travel in any kind of ATV," Manors said, "especially if you're traveling at night and trying to hide. That means no lights and a real familiarity with the area. There's also several roads they would have to cross between your ranch and the border. Roads mean fences on either side so cutting through them would make another obstacle to slow them up, plus it would make an obvious trail to anyone just driving along the road. ATVs and dune buggies are pretty big, so there are relatively few places they could cross over with something that size. And they aren't big enough to do a drive-through."

"A drive-through?" Reaper asked.

"Yeah, those used to happen all of the time," Manors said. "They became pretty common after 9/11, that's when we lost a lot of agents transferring over to other agencies. In a typical drive-through, the Mexican drug cartels would run two to three vehicles right through the fence, just bust right through. We're talking new GM 2002 Suburbans, white ones with antennas on them. That way they would look like customs vehicles. Most of them were stolen from Phoenix and other places, so the expense wasn't too bad for the cartels.

"They would have their own scouts out, looking for us watching for them. I can tell you right now that they have their own sensors on our side of the border. I've been told that the cartels have hired Mexican Special Forces soldiers who have been trained in our military schools to go in and find our bugs and map them. Then they would put in their own sensors.

"When they're pushing hard drugs, cocaine and such, on a run, they would have as many as fifteen or twenty scouts along the highway. They had their own codes they would use on their cell phones to stay in touch.

"But the drivers of the vehicles weren't anything like the kind of people you're talking about. These guys were all kinds of hopped up on drugs, speed usually. They would drive right through our spike strips along the road. But they usually can't cross the border both ways. A drive-through is a one-pass deal to bring drugs across."

"So you don't think the guys we ran into came from Mexico?" Reaper said.

"I didn't say that," Manors said. "But I do think they would have to have help on this side of the border to appear and disappear the way you said they did. It would have to be something a lot more organized than your usual coyote running a bunch of illegal migrant workers along the river."

"So," Hausmann said, "do you think you can help us follow those tracks we found?"

"I don't see why not," Manors said. "It's not like I'm doing anything else right now. Seems that my CO and I have had a bit of a disagreement on the outcome of a certain case a short while back. Now I'm on administrative leave pending the results of a board of inquiry—something about charges of insubordination and whatnot. I'm still a Border Patrol agent, but that may change in the near future. Looks like I won't have a career or a pension to worry about for much longer, so I would be glad to help you.

"Besides," Manors said as a nasty smile spread across his face, "it sounds like whoever is chasing you just may be a good lead to Langstrom's killers—those are some people I would surely like to meet under the right circumstances."

Chapter Thirteen

Early that evening Reaper was sitting at the table in the dining room at the ranch, going over topographical maps of the area. He intended to be as familiar as he could be with the place before they went out that night. From where they were lying on the floor, the rottweilers suddenly alerted, both dogs sitting up and turning their heads in the direction of the gate. Getting up, both big black dogs silently trotted off to the pool room. Still lying on the floor, Jarhead lifted his massive head and cocked it, listening for something.

The sudden noise of the rotts' barking told Reaper that someone was at the gate. Before he could get up from where he was sitting, Hausmann was already on his way to quiet the dogs down and let the person in. A few minutes later, Hausmann came back into the main area of the house with Pat Manors walking along behind him. Poking their broad muzzles at the new arrival, both dogs' short stub tails wagging violently, the rottweilers intended that Manors was going to give them their share of attention.

Dressed in a set of khaki pants and workshirt, Manors had his duty belt secured around his waist. On the belt was a Beretta 92-F 9mm pistol secured in a Bianchi Model 99A holster at his right side. On the left side of his belt, Manors had a double magazine pouch for the Beretta hanging behind a SureFire Z2 combat light slipped into a tactical holster.

Slung from his shoulder, Manors was carrying a 12-gauge Benelli M3 Super 90 pump/auto shotgun set up with a pistol-grip stock and ghost ring sights. The fore end of the shotgun was a SureFire 6V tactical weapon light with a built-in flashlight sticking forward underneath the barrel. On the left side of the shotgun's receiver was a Tac-Star sidesaddle shell holder with six black-cased rounds of ammunition slipped into the slots.

The white Stetson he had been wearing at the O.K. Cafe that afternoon was set firmly on his head. Shining on the breast of his shirt was the badge of a Border Patrol agent. Manors looked the picture of a modern Western police officer and Reaper figured that this was just the man's normal appearance.

"Looks like you're about ready to take on anything we could run into out there," Reaper said.

"No need going out unprepared," Manors said. "Those folks you ran into last night are probably long gone, but they may have some friends still hanging around."

"We'll have to lock the dogs in tonight," Hausmann said as he walked into the room behind Manors. "I don't particularly want them following us on this trip. Besides, there's no way of telling how far we'll have to travel."

"So we'll take the Prowlers?" Reaper said.

"Those buggies out in the yard?" Manors said. "That sounds good to me, depending on how far we have to go. They look open enough that you could spot sign from them easily enough."

"These are small vehicles we're going to be following," Reaper said as he got up from the table. "They should leave a trail obvious enough that we won't have to work too hard to follow it."

"So you just asked me to the party for my pretty face," Manors said with a grin. "Or could it be that you need a Border Patrol agent who can go onto private property to follow a trail and not get charged with trespassing?"

"Oh, I suppose it could be something like that," Hausmann said.

"I kinda figured that," Manors said. "Nice to know I'm wanted for a skill."

It wasn't long before all of the banter was over and the men were heading south to follow the trail of the ambushers. Instead of taking both Prowlers, Reaper had decided on all three men going on one vehicle, Reaper doing the driving and Hausmann and Manors riding on the outside passenger seats. Reaper had his M4A1 secured in the carrying rack that fit horizontally in front of the driver's position. Both Manors and Hausmann had slung their long guns across their chests.

Before leaving, Reaper had passed out black TC2002 helmets that Diamondback Tactical had sent along with the vehicles. The helmets were the side-cut models so the wearer's ears would be exposed and they wouldn't interfere with hearing. Since they were armored to level 3A ballistic protection, they would stop most handgun bullets and quite a few rifle projectiles. Manors reluctantly left his Stetson in the pickup he had driven into the ranch compound and slipped the helmet over his head.

With Reaper in the driver's seat, Hausmann was in the right-side rider seat, little more than a padded back rest and a flat space on the rear fender right over the back wheel. From his position on the side rider seat on the left side of the vehicle, Manors was able to closely examine the ground in front of the vehicle in the glare of the twin headlights.

Night had fallen and the moon was already up. Reaper had wondered if it wouldn't have been better to wait until the next day to try and follow the trail in the light. Manors said he could follow a trail well enough at night and didn't want to wait another day. When they came up to the ambush site, Manors called for a halt while he got out and took a close look at the ground and the tracks that Hausmann pointed out.

"These things were anything but new vehicles," Manors said as he shone the light from his SureFire 6V light across the ground. By laying the beam from the light down and shining it across the surface of the ground, rather than pointing it straight down, the shadows cast inside of the tire tracks were starkly outlined. They were even more obvious than they would have been with the sun directly overhead.

"What do you mean?" Reaper asked as he bent down over the tracks.

"Drug runners use just about anything that suits their purpose," Manors said. "But they tend to steal newer vehicles for their runs across the border. These tracks aren't like anything I've ever seen them use. The spacing of the wheels is too wide for any ATV that I know. And the scalloped edges of the tires look like something the military would use more than a civilian dune buggy.

"See these marks," Manors said as he pointed to the tracks, "the treads are deep, but the tires that made them are notched and chipped in places. One tire has a big divot cut out of one tread that makes it as distinctive as a fingerprint. And all of these tracks are from worn tires, on what looks like two vehicles."

"So you can follow them?" Hausmann asked.

"Heck, these are easy for right now," Manors said. "As long as the buggies that made them stay on sand or gravel, we can follow them to the far end of South America."

Getting back into the Prowler, the three men started to follow the trail of the two ATVs back along the high ground between the railroad tracks and the riverbank. Manors well demonstrated his skill at tracking, even from the side seat of the Prowler.

As they followed the trail, Manors would sometimes signal Reaper to stop. The Border Patrol agent would then get off the Prowler and crouch down on the ground, shining his SureFire light across the sand and gravel. The shadows and highlights of the tire marks told him what he wanted to know. Climbing back onto the side seat of the Prowler, Manors would then point out the direction in which he wanted Reaper to drive.

The three men drove along slowly for about a half mile, weaving slightly across the top of the ridge but staying on the river side of the railroad tracks. The trail turned suddenly to the right and down the bank to the river. From where he was sitting, Reaper could plainly see the tracks of two wheeled vehicles sunk into the side of the riverbank.

Stopping the Prowler at the edge of the water, Reaper turned to the Border Patrol agent. But Manors wasn't looking at the same set of tire tracks Reaper was. Instead, he was looking closely at a second set of tracks only a few yards away down the riverbank.

Climbing out of the side seat, Manors went over to the second set of tracks and squatted down to look at them. Only the gurgle of the water flowing by and the croaking of frogs could be heard. Some of the bigger bullfrogs were loud enough to be heard hundreds of yards away. But none of that noise affected Manors as he looked at the trails. Knowing he would just get in the way of the skilled tracker, Reaper kept a 360-degree watch around the Prowler.

Getting off the vehicle, Hausmann stepped to the river's edge and squatted down to look at the flowing water. When Manors walked back to the Prowler, Hausmann got up and stood with him next to Reaper. Everyone spoke in very quiet voices, little more than whispers.

"There's a second set of tracks from those same two ATVs," Manors said. "Only these two are going up the bank from the river. This is where they crossed both coming and going."

"Pretty poor opsec [operational security]," Reaper said.

"I don't think they had much of a choice," Hausmann said. "The river is pretty low right now but there are still damned few places you can cross it with any kind of vehicle. Someone dumped a lot of rocks into the bed here to make a fording spot, just like I did up at my place."

"So how deep is it?" Reaper asked.

"Looks like a foot or more," Hausmann said. "Can this thing cross that?"

"She's fitted with the snorkeling attachment," Reaper said. "We can cross water up to thirty inches deep without flooding out. No need to take a chance on what the bottom is like. I'll take her across and you guys follow on foot once I'm on the other side."

"No," Manors said. "It's better if I go across first and scout the trail. That way you won't tear up the trail if you land in the same spot as they did."

"Go for it," Reaper agreed.

Slipping into the water with his Benelli held up, Manors slowly walked across the river. With his M14 in his hands, Hausmann kept watch along the other bank, the bright moonlight making it fairly easy to see. At the controls of the Prowler, Reaper watched as the water crept up Manor's legs as he walked along the river bottom. At no time did the water go over Manor's knees, so Reaper knew he would have no trouble taking the vehicle across.

Once Manors was on the other side of the river, he

bent over to carefully examine the ground. The occasional gleam of the flashlight was all Reaper saw. Straightening up, Manors turned and waved to Reaper to bring the Prowler across. Slowly entering the water, the light rugged terrain vehicle easily crossed the river. The smooth banks on either side of the river made entering and exiting the water simple. The water flowing through the open sides of the driver's compartment drained away as Reaper took the Prowler up the opposite bank and stopped.

Hausmann then crossed the river with nothing more happening than his feet getting wet. Once they were all together again, Reaper leaned in close to Hausmann and whispered:

"Just where are we?"

"This is the edge of one of Valentine Dupree's places," Hausmann said. "That's the snake lover I was telling you about. She has a barn and some buildings near here, but there's no one living on the place."

"Sounds like the place to look," Manors said.

While Manors and Hausmann walked up to the crest of the riverbank, Reaper carefully drove the Prowler up the incline. The bank wasn't so steep that he felt that the tough little vehicle would have any trouble with it, but you didn't take chances when you didn't have to.

Pulling up under some trees, Reaper parked the Prowler and pulled his M4A1 from the weapons rack. Moving over to where Hausmann and Manors were both kneeling at the edge of the tree line, Reaper approached them in a low crouch. His compact Carl Zeiss

7×30mm binoculars to his eyes, Hausmann was looking out across an open area to a cluster of buildings a few hundred feet away.

Just past the trees, about ten feet in front of where the men were kneeling, was a long fence. The line of four rows of barbed wire stopped at a wide gate and then continued on the other side to run on out of sight. Pointing, Manors indicated where the tire tracks they had been following went up to the gate, and continued on the other side.

"No movement, lights, or any sign that anyone's there," Hausmann said as he handed the binoculars to Reaper.

Looking out across the field, Reaper could plainly see two long pole buildings with corrugated sheet metal roofs and open sides. There was a relatively small shed, about the size of a one-car garage, to the north of the pole buildings. A wide metal-sided barn with a concrete apron extending out ten feet past its wide door was just north of the smaller shed. The bulk of the big barn, which looked to be more than forty feet wide and a hundred feet long, dominated the area. More than a hundred feet farther to the west were parked three long semi trailers.

None of the windows that lined the side of the barn showed any lights. There wasn't a sound beyond that made by the water behind the men and the critters that lived along it. If there was anyone at the buildings, the only way the men would know for sure would be to go up and look for themselves. Which is exactly what Reaper intended to do.

"I want to see just what's in that barn," Reaper whispered to the others. "You can stay here or go with me."

"Didn't get all dressed up just to miss the party," Hausmann said.

Reaper smiled at this. Both men were wearing exactly the same black 5.11 tactical pants and shirts, with a 5.11 tactical vest over the shirt to carry their equipment and ammunition. With the vests on, they had enough weapons and ammunition to feel comfortable and not look like a trio of commandos out on an assault—as long as they took off the black TC2002 side-cut helmets they had on.

"If those tracks are from illegals," Manors said, "or even worse, narco-militarists, it's my duty to check it out."

"Okay," Reaper said. "I'll go to the gate and cross over, you two cover me. Then you follow on my signal. Hausmann, you keep cover with that rifle and come over last."

With answering nods from the other two men, Reaper moved out in a crouch. He darted over to the steel-tube gate and knelt down to see just how it was secured. A heavy Ingersol lock looped through a length of welded steel chain held the gate shut. It was an expensive lock to just close off a ranch gate. And the shiny surface of the lock and the chain told Reaper that neither had been exposed to the elements for very long.

The fence itself was four strands of barbed wire strung between steel posts set about fifteen feet apart. That style of fence would keep livestock from passing through, but it wouldn't even slow Reaper down.

With his M4A1 secured across his chest in the hi port position on his Chalker sling, Reaper stood by the fence post the gate was chained to. Setting the sole of his Bates boot on the second strand of wire, very close to the post, Reaper just stood on that leg and swung up and over the fence.

Once crouched down low on the inside of the fence line, Reaper watched and listened for any sign that his incursion had been spotted.

A full minute passed without any noise or light. There wasn't even a dog running around the area of the buildings. With his M4A1 held out level in his right hand, Reaper signaled for Manors and Hausmann to come across the fence.

Both men stepped over the fence in the same manner that Reaper had. Never turning around, Reaper kept watch as the men moved up to crouch down next to him. Reaper knew that both Hausmann and Manors were skilled enough to move with him, but the ex-SEAL kept his actions simple and straightforward. Rushing from the cover of one set of scrub brush to another, the men crossed the open area in a bounding overwatch style of travel.

One man would move ahead and take cover while the others watched over him. Then he would wave the others forward and maintain watch while the other two went ahead past him. Only a few minutes passed before the men had reached the area of the buildings and started their search.

The two pole buildings had fully open sides and there were only a few tarp-covered piles under the metal roof. None of the piles were large enough to hide any sort of four-wheeled vehicle, so the three men passed them by with only a cursory search. They went on to the smaller enclosed shed.

The men hadn't trained together, but both Hausmann and Manors knew the basics of a building-to-building search. With Reaper in the lead, they all moved quickly and quietly to either side of the door that led to the interior of the smaller shed. The building was only about ten feet square with a single door and two windows on each wall. The walls were plywood nailed to supports and the roof simply corrugated metal.

With Hausmann behind him and watching out the way they had come, Reaper looked over to where Manors stood on the far side of the door. Nodding to him, Reaper reached out with his left hand and softly tried to turn the knob on the door. The door wasn't locked and the knob turned easily.

Looking over to Manors, Reaper pointed to himself and then extended his left thumb and swung it to the left. Pointing at Manors, Reaper then gave the same thumbs-up signal to the right. Comprehending the message that Reaper would move to the left while he was to go to the right, Manors nodded his understanding.

Giving a thumbs-up signal to Manors, Reaper then turned to the door. His M4A1 was held in both hands, muzzle down with the stock up against his shoulder. Manors held his Benelli in the same ready position.

With a single deep breath, Reaper pushed the door open and immediately rushed into the building. Darting to the side, Reaper stood with his back about a foot away from the wall, the muzzle of his M4A1 up and sweeping the room. "Cutting the pie," Reaper cleared the left side of the single room in the building while Manors came through the door and moved to the right.

Looking through the PVS-14 night-vision monocular mounted to the rail of his M4A1, Reaper could see the interior of the room in shades of green and black. The red dot of the Aimpoint Comp M2 sight in front of the PVS-14 indicated exactly where Reaper's round would strike if he pulled the trigger of the weapon. Earlier that afternoon, Reaper had gone behind the garage at Hausmann's ranch and checked the zero on his weapon's sight, firing into a target he had set out at a carefully measured distance. Now, Reaper knew exactly where his weapon would hit if he fired it.

No movement showed in the sparkling green field of the PVS-14. Three sets of double bunks lined the walls of the building, along with a table and chairs in the center of the room. A cupboard and bottled-gas stove made up the rest of the room's furnishings. It was an unoccupied bunkhouse and nothing more.

All of this information Reaper took in with his eyes in scant seconds from his entering the room. He said "Clear" in a quiet but firm voice. From the other side of the room, Reaper heard Manors say "clear" in the same way that he had. Their voices were loud enough that Hausmann could hear them both through the open door, but they wouldn't carry much farther, even in the still night air.

A quick search of the building turned up nothing of interest, not even any personal belongings. Within a minute of having entered the bunkhouse, both Reaper and Manors were back outside with Hausmann. Now they would be taking down the biggest target, the steel barn only twenty feet away to the north.

Weapons up and ready, Manors and Hausmann crossed over to the barn at Reaper's signal. The muzzle of his M4A1 pointed slightly down in a safe ready position, Reaper kept watch while the other two men set up at an open window in the side of the barn.

Seeing that the other two men were ready, and that there hadn't been any sign of their being spotted, Reaper rushed over to the side of the barn. As they had been moving around the building compound, the men had seen that there were four long compound windows on the sides of the barn, but only three doors. Two of the doors were large, overhead rolling doors that would make the devil's own noise if they raised them. Next to one of the overhead doors was a smaller steel door with an obvious lock and hasp on it. The whole structure was set on a cast concrete slab. There wasn't any quiet way into the barn except through the window.

Hausmann and Manors had their backs turned away from the window to watch in opposite directions. Lifting up his M4, Reaper looked through his PVS-14 into the dark interior of the barn. Even the incredible fifty-thousand-time magnification of available light through the PVS-14 was not enough to show much in the way of details inside of the barn. About eight feet from the open window was the wall of an enclosure, and that was all that Reaper could see.

Turning back to Hausmann and Manors, Reaper

pointed to Hausmann's M14 and then to his own boots. Nodding that he knew what Reaper wanted, Hausmann held out the buttstock of the rifle to Manors. Letting his Benelli hang from its sling, Manors took up the buttstock of the M14 and braced himself. With a nod to Hausmann, Reaper set his left boot on the middle of the M14 and stepped up into the window. Sitting on the edge of the window, only about five feet above the ground, Reaper swung his legs over the sill and dropped into the dark interior of the barn.

His booted feet hit a sandy floor with a very muffled thud. For some reason, the enclosure that Reaper had landed in had a floor completely covered with sand scattered deeply over the concrete slab. With the M4A1 at his shoulder, Reaper could see the walls of the enclosure more clearly now through the PVS-14. The walls were smooth plywood and extended up about five feet from the floor. There was a door that Reaper could make out only a few steps away.

As he moved forward, Reaper noticed a distinctive musty stink in the air. It was more than the smell of the sand dust he had kicked up. And a sudden sound in the darkness behind him told Reaper exactly what that smell was. The sound was the dry, buzzing crackling made by the specially formed horny scales found on the end of a rattlesnake's tail. Somewhere in the dark behind Reaper, there was a pissed-off rattlesnake warning him—and the snake didn't need light in order to successfully strike the SEAL standing right in front of him.

Chapter Fourteen

As Reaper froze in position, the noise of the rattlesnake behind him grew louder. It would be only moments before the snake would zero in on the SEAL's body heat. It didn't need to see him in order to strike, the snake could aim itself very well with nothing more than the heat sensors on the inside of its mouth and with its forked tongue. The rattlesnake's rattle was loud enough that both Hausmann and Manors could clearly hear it on their side of the open window.

Realizing that they had a much greater danger to deal with at that moment, Manors abandoned light discipline and slipped his left hand into the window. Pressing down onto the base switch of his tactical light, Manors illuminated the enclosure with a brilliant white blaze.

The disk of light from Manors's SureFire darted across the floor for only a moment before it centered on the coiled form of a large snake on the sandy floor.

The huge rattlesnake was coiled in a classic pose, its tail raised and twitching while the broad, triangular head sat up at the end of a neck drawn back into a sharp S-curve. The snake would strike out by straightening the *S* of its neck, and by the size of the thing, it would have no trouble reaching Reaper's leg just two feet away.

Looking down and back over his left shoulder, Reaper could see the reptilian threat coiled behind him. The chances were low that he would swing around with his M4A1 and shoot the snake before it could sink a fang into him. Even though they hadn't seen anyone in the compound, the sound of firing could bring in anything nearby to discover the three intruders.

The big rattlesnake held enough venom in one bite to put Reaper into a world of hurt, if not kill him, before his friends could get him to a hospital. He had to do something, but his options looked very limited. Then Reaper heard Hausmann quietly call out his name.

Lifting up his eyes from the threat on the floor, Reaper could see that Hausmann was slowly extending the barrel of his M14 to where the SEAL was standing. Realizing what Hausmann was trying to do, Reaper decided to take the chance he was being offered.

Moving with infinite care, Reaper let go of his M4A1 with his left hand, and slowly raised it to reach out for the rifle extended toward him. The buzzing of the rattlesnake didn't change as Reaper reached for the muzzle of the M14. His fingers closing around the prongs of the long flash hider on the rifle, the edges of the front sight digging into his palm, Reaper took a solid grip on the end of the weapon. He drew the gun back from Hausmann, each movement seeming to take an eternity.

Finally, Reaper felt the entire weight of the big rifle twisting down from the grip of his left hand. Even the very strong ex-SEAL was under a severe strain holding the heavy weapon in such an unnatural extended position. But it wasn't for very long that Reaper had to hold the M14 out at almost arm's length.

Sensing something, the snake suddenly increased the volume of its rattle. It was now or never. Swinging the rifle down toward the poisonous head of the reptile, Reaper took his chance and smashed down hard with the steel buttplate of the M14.

With a crash, the steel bottom of the rifle drove down onto the head of the rattlesnake. Before the reptile could strike out, its head was crushed down into the sand. Turning to face his deadly little opponent, Reaper bore down on the M14, grinding and crushing the head of the snake into the sand as its body thrashed about. Finally, the death throes of the reptile slowed as its body accepted the fact that its brain was destroyed.

Facing a deadly reptile was something new in Reaper's experience. His heart was beating like a triphammer, the pulse thudding in his ears. For a moment, Reaper wasn't trying to kill the snake by pushing down on the M14, he was trying to hold himself up. As he breathed rapidly through his nose, Reaper brought himself back down. In what felt like a long time, but was actually only seconds, he calmed.

Now able to continue with the task at hand, Reaper lifted the butt of the M14 and looked down at the huge reptile. The slowly twisting body of the snake had to be over five feet long, probably more like six feet long. The most important aspect of the rattlesnake at that moment was the fact that it was dead. Reaper lifted the M14 up and extended it back out to the window where Hausmann and Manors were standing.

Signaling Manors to come into the building through the window, Reaper turned back to the inside door of the snake enclosure. After first taking a fast look around into the corners with his SureFire flashlight to make sure there weren't any other slithering night guards on duty, Manors climbed in through the window. After the recent bout with the snake, Hausmann had no problems with remaining outside on watch.

The enclosure was about eight by twelve feet in size, the floor covered with several inches of sand and a scattering of small piles of rocks. The plywood walls were five feet high with a row of heavy wire fencing stapled in around the top edge. The inward-leaning wire mesh looked as if it was able to prevent the escape of even a larger snake than the one Reaper had just killed.

The door had a standard interior doorknob and lock plate. The whole enclosure had a professional look about it and had taken some thought to design. But the layout of a big snake cage wasn't of interest to Reaper at that moment—the contents of the big barn were. With his M4A1 up to his shoulder, Reaper reached out with his left hand and turned the knob. The door opened easily and no sudden lights came on inside the building. Both Reaper and Manors were able to see over the wall of the enclosure, but taking extra care in this kind of situation had been instilled into Reaper over years of training.

What was inside the cavernous interior of the barn was just a lot of nothing. No vehicles, trailers, or much of anything caught the men's eyes. All Reaper could see through the PVS-14 was a row of enclosures down either side of the huge building, and that was all. Waving Manors in, Reaper still swept the interior with the muzzle of his M4A1. The caution of the big SEAL was contagious and Manors also kept his Benelli up to his shoulder while the two men quickly moved through the enormous structure.

All that they found was a number of tools and supplies, both for ranching and the care of vehicles. The tools were nothing out of the ordinary, but Reaper examined each corner and enclosure with care before turning to Manors.

"Okay," Reaper whispered, "go ahead and use your light, but be careful with it. See if you can spot anything that will tell us what happened to the ATVs."

Not about to accidentally sweep his brilliant flashlight beam across one of the windows, Manors nodded and turned to one of the big roll-up doors at the end of the building. While Manors began his search, Reaper started looking more closely at what was around the inside of the barn. All he found were empty cloth grain sacks, rakes, shovels, wrenches, hammers, and the like.

Next to the roll-up door at the south end of the barn

was a small desk, the kind that was used by dispatchers and such. Inside the desk, Reaper only found shipping forms, most of them blank. Hanging on the side of the desk was a clipboard with more forms, only these were filled out.

All of the forms were for the same company, Heart Green Foods. There was the outline of a large green-colored heart symbol at the top of the form, right above the block letters spelling out the company name. Below that, in smaller letters, were the words NATURAL ORGANIC FOODS OF THE WEST.

What the hell is that, Reaper thought to himself, cactus fruits? Any free-range chickens out here would be eaten by the coyotes.

Flipping through the forms, Reaper just read lines of various produce and other food products, and the locations the material was sent to. All of the locations were inside of Arizona proper except for one. That form, just below the top of the stack, was for a delivery made to Las Vegas, Nevada.

Now this whole situation was making even less sense. He and Hausmann had been ambushed by some Mexican military types working for an organic food company? That was a little too weird for consideration.

A small trash can next to the desk yielded nothing more than an old map tossed among the papers and trash. The papers showed nothing, most being just damaged shipping forms. There were some old paper bags from a fast-food outlet, the bags having been in the can for a long time by the looks and smell of them. Reaper was just unfolding the map and seeing that it covered the southwestern states of the U.S. when he heard Manors call him.

"Reaper," Manors said softly, "come here."

Turning, Reaper could see that Manors was bent down near the ground. His Benelli was slung out of the way on his back and he was shining his light down onto the ground, shielding most of the lens with his left hand.

Stuffing the folded map into the inside pocket of his 5.11 tactical vest, Reaper picked up the clipboard once more. On impulse, he pulled the Las Vegas shipping form from the stack he had been reading off the clipboard and stuffed it into the same pocket as the map. Going over to where Manors was examining the ground, Reaper leaned in close and looked down at what was being illuminated with the slivers of light from between Manors's fingers.

There were a number of tire tracks in the dust on the concrete floor. Reaper couldn't make much sense of them, but to Manors, they were like an open book.

"Look," Manors said, indicating with the light, "these are the same ATV tracks we've been following. Only now there's two sets of tracks—one coming in, and an earlier one going out. See how the tread marks coming in cross over the tread marks going out? The V's of the treads first point out, then they point in. The tracks on top were made last."

Reaper nodded his head.

"Well," Manors said. "Right here, both sets of tracks disappear completely. I don't mean they were brushed away. I mean they were never made, the ATVs never crossed the concrete."

"What do you think happened?" Reaper said, keeping his own thoughts to himself for the moment.

"The ATVs drove up a ramp and into a trailer," Manors said with assurance. "There's the line across the dust where the ramp was laid down from the back of a trailer.

"And over here," Manors took a few steps to the side, "are the tire marks from a dual-axle. Four sets of tires, two close to each other, on either side of the trailer. And the tires on the right side are pretty worn. On the left side there, one of the tires wore out-of-balance. So it has scalloped edges. These tracks are distinctive as hell. You find me a trailer, and I can tell you if its tires made these tracks.

"And here's the clincher," Manors said as he moved back over to the ATV tread marks. Shining his light down, Reaper could then see small dark flecks in the dust.

"Those are blood splashes," Manors said. "Somebody got on this trailer leaking from a wound, probably through a bandage by the small size of the drops. There's all kinds of boot prints all over the ground here."

"What are those bright blue bits there?" Reaper said as he squatted down and pointed with his left hand, his right maintaining a hold on his M4.

"Don't know," Manors said, "looks familiar though. There's some of the same stuff in some of the boot tracks. And there's a bunch of it in the ATV tracks where they first appear in the dust. Must have popped off the tires or underbodies when they hit the end of the ramp."

Taking the shipping form from his inside vest pocket, Reaper quickly folded it several times. Pulling out his Emerson CQB-7 knife, the wave feature on the back of the blade unfolding it as he drew it from his pants pocket, Reaper slipped the blade tip underneath some of the blue material, scooping up the material and the surrounding dust. Dumping the dust and blue bits into the paper, Reaper folded it several times to seal the sample in.

"Hey," Manors said, "you have to leave that. That's evidence at a crime scene."

"Evidence of what?" Reaper said as he folded his Emerson and put it back in the pocket of his 5.11 pants. "This isn't exactly a legal search. Nothing we find right now can be used as real evidence against anyone. Besides, there's plenty of this stuff still on the ground."

Realizing the big SEAL was right, Manors stood and looked around the barn and changed the subject.

"Each one of these enclosures," Manors said, "is made to keep in snakes. And they're under every window."

"Kind of a natural burglar alarm, I guess," Reaper said, "you just listen for the screams of whoever broke in. Grab that empty bag there, we're getting out the same way we came in, less the scaly welcoming committee."

Going back to the enclosure, Reaper took the cloth bag from Manors before waving him on through to the window. Then he backed away from the door after closing it. As he backed up, Reaper brushed the cloth bag across the sand, obliterating the footsteps the men had made coming in and going out.

Suppressing a momentary shudder, Reaper picked up the rattlesnake that had almost bitten him and stuffed it into the bag. Then he kicked sand over the blood from the dead snake and brushed it over with the bag. Finally back at the window, Reaper handed the bag out to Hausmann.

"Here, a present for you," Reaper said. "Take it with you to the river. I don't want it found around here."

Then Reaper climbed back out the window. Pulling the red quick release on his Chalker sling, Reaper dropped the M4A1 free of the brass shackle in the center of his chest. Leaning back into the barn, Reaper used the butt end of his M4A1 to obliterate the last of his footprints.

The covering of their trail that the men had done wasn't intended to fool a real tracker. But with no obvious sign of their having been in the area, there would be no reason for anyone to search for the harder-to-find footprints outside of the window.

Now Reaper could understand the big green heart symbol on the trailers he saw only a few dozen yards away. The stacks of old pallets, grown brush, and junk around the trailers showed that they hadn't been moved for some time. None of those had been used to hide and transport the ATVs.

Moving around to the big roll-up doors, Reaper and Hausmann maintained watch while Manors examined the ground just off the concrete apron extending from the barn. He found the signs he'd expected. There were two sets of tracks for the ATVs coming in and out of the rear door of the barn, the door pointing toward the river. All that he could find near the other door were the tire marks of a tractor-trailer rig, a rig with worn tires on the rear axle of the trailer.

The men had learned just about all they could from their covert visit to the facility. Now it was time to withdraw and examine their options. Leaving the way they had come in, the three men worked at obliterating the signs of their passage. Bringing up the rear and walking backward as much as he could, Hausmann brushed at their footsteps with the cloth bag holding the dead snake.

When they reached the gate, the men climbed back over, leaving little sign of their passage into the compound. Once more Reaper noted the big expensive lock securing the chain holding the gate closed. With there being so little in the way of valuable materials in the compound, why was there such a lock when all you had to do was jump the fence as they had? Then again, anyone trying to break into the barn would find the way in very easy—and what was waiting for them on the inside very deadly.

Taking the Prowler back across the river, the men once more took their seats for the ride back to the Dog-bone Ranch. The dogs announced the arrival of the trio back at the garage. As they climbed off the Prowler, Hausmann pulled off his helmet and ran his fingers through his hair. When he looked at his friend, Reaper was surprised to see that Hausmann still had the cloth grain sack in his hand, and the bulge at the bottom of the bag showed that it still held the snake carcass.

"What in the hell are you doing still hanging on to

that dead snake?" Reaper said. "You going to give it to the dogs?"

"Nope," Hausmann said with a grin, "they can have the leftovers if there are any."

"What does that mean?" Reaper said.

"This is a Western Diamondback, a nice big one, too," Hausmann said. "I'm going to clean it, skin it, cook it, and eat it. Might even get the skin tanned and make a belt or something out of it. It's damned near big enough to make a pair of shoes, maybe boots even."

"You have got to be kidding," Manors said.

"Not a bit," Hausmann said. "The dried-up loser hippie bitch that owns that place killed my dog. I know it and there's nothing I can do about it. Well, I'm going to eat her damned snake. Besides, rattler is good, especially grilled over mesquite with barbecue sauce. It tastes like chicken—dark meat at that. I like it."

"Didn't think you could cook," Reaper said.

"Hey, I can grill like a madman," Hausmann said.

"Well," Reaper said, "I believe the madman part."

Chapter Fifteen

The Cristal Hacienda had once been a shining example of richness in the northern Sonora desert. With the end of the optical-grade crystals that could be found in its mine, the hacienda fell on hard times. Picked up cheaply by the Zapatista cartel when they moved into the area, the hacienda saw some improvements made to its fading splendor. But Felix Zapatista had the taste of a peasant and a thug at best.

When the hacienda was taken over by Eduardo Masque, he saw to it that the garish colors and tastes of the Zapatista cartel were eliminated. A large main manor house was built of modern materials and classic Spanish lines. The thousands of square feet of living space in the sprawling six-bedroom building were used by Masque, his guests, and his most trusted lieutenant.

Across the walled courtyard of the hacienda was another building, this one much smaller than the main house and only consisting of four bedrooms. On the

south side of the hacienda was a long garage with living quarters for the staff of the hacienda as well as for
the bulk of Masque's men. The nine mercenaries
brought in by their captain, Garcia Santiago, lived in
the four-bedroom home along with their sergeant,
Miguel Rodriguez. Santiago stayed in the main house
with Masque.

Though he didn't like going into the main house of
the hacienda, Rodriguez did so when he had to meet
with Santiago to discuss his plans for the mercenaries.
These meetings took place in a small office just off of
Santiago's quarters, to the left of the main entrance to
the building.

"How many men do you want me to bring with us
tonight, Capitan?" Sergeant Rodriguez said.

"In addition to you and me?" Santiago said, "four
should be enough, Sargento. Two to escort our guests
and two to maintain watch. Shoulder weapons and side
arms. The Arabs are supplying their own vehicle and
driver on the other side and carrying their own materiel,
so we won't need any manpower to move anything."

"I don't like these Arab terrorists, Capitan," Garcia
said. "They are not to be trusted at all. Even while they
pay for our services, they look down their noses at us.
In spite of what they do, they think they're better than
anyone, that we're all infidels and unbelievers, unwor-
thy of being in their presence. I think that all of their
plans against the United States is just going to bring
the wrath of President Bush down on us."

"We are not paid to think," Santiago said, "only to
act. But privately, Miguel, I agree with you. They are

dangerous and we must be ready to move on when the time comes. This has been a rich time for us, but all good things must come to an end."

Before Sergeant Rodriguez could answer, there was a knock at the door to the office. Without waiting for an answer, Youssef Daumudi opened the unlocked door and stepped into the room.

"It is my understanding that you will be escorting Humzan and myself this evening?" Daumudi said, ignoring the glare of Rodriguez at the rudeness to his officer.

"Yes," Santiago said, "that is what my sergeant and I were just discussing."

"We are ready to leave now," Daumudi said. "Humzan does not wish to miss the meeting with our confederates on the other side of the border."

"Humzan?" Santiago said. "So you are not going to be making the trip?"

"I will be accompanying you to make sure that everything is in order," Daumudi said. "If the route is as secure as you say it is, then I will be coming back to make further preparations for our next trip. For now, that is all you need to know."

"Get the men ready, Sergeant," Santiago said, turning to Rodriguez. He could see that the big sergeant was becoming seriously angry with the attitude of the Arab terrorist and wanted him out of the office before something was said, or done.

"Yes, Capitan," Rodriguez said, and he walked past Daumudi who had to move quickly out of the doorway to keep from being jostled.

"Your sergeant forgets his place," Daumudi said.

"His place, as you put it," Santiago said, "is at my side. Which is where he has been for over eight years now. I trust him completely."

Leaving the suggestion that he did not trust Daumudi unsaid, Santiago simply waited for the other man to continue the conversation. Instead of saying a word, Daumudi turned and left the office as rudely as he had arrived.

It was the early hours of the morning when two Silverado Suburbans pulled out of the garage and up to the front of the main house at the hacienda. Standing on the large round porch of the house were Eduardo Masque, Garcia Santiago, and the two al-Qaeda members, Youssef Daumudi and Ammand Humzan.

"I still do not see the need for this very late hour," Daumudi said.

"You understand that we must maintain the security of our facility," Masque said. "This time of the night there is very little traffic on the U.S. side of the border. We have also arranged for a number of coyotes to move groups of people into the United States at a number of sites some distance from here. The U.S. Border Patrol will be very distracted by the activity.

"The coyotes have orders to allow a large number of their people to fall into the hands of the Border Patrol. The agents will have their hands full for some time tonight and won't be able to set up the roadblocks or even to man the watchtowers around this part of the border. It would have been simpler for us to supply the transportation for you on the U.S. side . . ."

"No," Daumudi said, "you have done very well so far, but we have our own network to depend on in the United States. If things tonight go as you have assured us they will, our business will expand considerably. And you will be liberally rewarded."

"The enemy of my enemy is my friend," Masque said. "And if you need my assistance to help bring down the United States and its corrupt people, you have but to ask. Most of the requests you have made have already been completed, the rest will be done within twenty-four hours."

The requests Masque had mentioned were a surprise to Santiago. And he was not a man to like surprises. Masque had been letting his hatred of the United States blind his business sense, as well as his trust in his best lieutenant. Santiago was going to have to maintain appearances for the time being while making preparations of his own.

Stepping up to the trailing Suburban, Santiago opened the rear driver's-side door with a flourish, bowing slightly to Daumudi as he walked up to the door. Stiffly ignoring Santiago, Daumudi first set the satchel he was carrying into the vehicle then climbed into the SUV himself.

Going around to the other side of the Suburban, Ammand Humzan entered the rear passenger area of the SUV under the glaring eyes of Miguel Rodriguez. Standing right next to the front door of the vehicle, Rodriguez made certain that the front seat would only be taken by Santiago.

Standing around the leading Suburban were some of

the hard-faced mercenaries that made up Santiago's team. Most of the rest of the men were back in the barracks. Only the back of the head of the driver sitting at the wheel of the first Suburban could be seen. The man at the wheel of the trailing SUV maintained his grip on the wheel and didn't bother watching the men on the porch of the main house.

The two men standing on the outside of the lead vehicle were both armed with vicious-looking 5.56mm Galil SAR short assault rifles. Their combat harnesses held pouches of spare magazines and pistol holsters at their hips. The finish on the weapons was a little worn from use, but all of the guns were spotless and looked to be in perfect operating condition.

Over his shoulder, Rodriguez had a 9mm Uzi submachine gun, that weapon also showing hard use and careful maintenance. For himself, Santiago was only wearing his shoulder holster and his Glock Model 18C machine pistol.

The sidearm was for appearances. Santiago knew that there was a Galil MAR micro assault rifle, the stock folded and a thirty-five-round magazine locked into place, underneath the front seat of the suburban. Next to the deadly little assault rifle was a shoulder bag containing six spare magazines. He also knew that the more attention you paid to the details, the less you would be surprised as developments occurred.

When Santiago climbed into the trailing Suburban, Rodriguez quickly moved to the same place in the front vehicle. When the doors slammed shut on both vehicles, the heavy, solid thunk of their closing was the only clue to the fact that both Suburbans were heavily armored. They were effectively light tanks, only missing an upper turret with a cannon to be the equivalent of a WWII scout tank.

The small convoy moved out of the hacienda's gate while under the watchful gaze of the two mercenaries standing guard. Normally, the mercenaries were exempt from such duties, but Masque only wanted his best shown to the Arabs. The powered gate closed behind the last vehicle and their red taillights disappeared behind the heavy doors.

The trip taken by the Suburbans was a short one. Less than half a mile away from the hacienda, on the side of a small hill, was the mouth of its namesake, the Crystal mine. The machinery and most of the buildings around the mine shaft were crumbling with decay. Only the front of the mine and the heavy timbers framing it looked well maintained. A wide steel gate inside the mouth of the mine powered open at the touch of a remote control. The vehicles drove directly into the wide opening of the mine.

Both Suburbans fit well inside the mouth of the mine with room to spare. Getting out of the rear vehicle, it didn't take long for Daumudi to comment on the situation.

"I do not see why it was necessary to take two vehicles to cross from the estate to this entrance," Daumudi said.

"It was simply a courtesy extended to you by Masque," Santiago said. "And the simple fact is that no one can see inside the tinted windows of these vehicles. Anyone watching would only be able to say they saw two vehicles come in, and later they will see those same vehicles leave. But they will not be able to say how many people were in them at any time."

"Your caution and attention to detail is commendable," Daumudi said. "But we have yet to see this vaunted secure route you have into the United States."

"This is the entry to that route," Santiago said as he turned and started to walk deeper into the mine.

All of the mercenaries climbed out of the Suburbans. Now it could be seen that the drivers of the two vehicles were armed the same as the two guards. The Arabs ignored the display of firepower around them as they followed Santiago down the tunnel.

A few hundred feet from the mouth of the mine, Santiago stopped and pointed to the mouth of a side tunnel. A stack of boxes and crates could be seen just inside the entrance to the tunnel.

"That is some of the ordnance, weapons, and supplies you have asked us to receive and store for you," Santiago said. "They are also ready when you want them. Shall we go on or would you like to inspect the stores?"

"That will not be necessary," Daumudi said, "we should be making our crossing now."

"The trip will not take long," Santiago said.

The group quickly came to a large, open elevator cage. The elevator rode in a shaft that had a string of bare bulbs running down along one corner of it. The bulbs showed the openings of a number of side shafts inside the mine, but in spite of the lights, the bottom of the shaft couldn't be seen.

Once everyone was in the elevator, Rodriguez pulled the overhead gate down and then worked the controls. With a slight lurch, the cage began to move down, lowered on cables controlled from an electric winch.

The cage traveled down several hundred feet before Rodriguez moved the control to the stop position. One of the other mercenaries lifted the gate at the back of the elevator cage and the group moved out into a wide, well-lit tunnel. Directly in front of them were four open ore cars and a small engine. Three of the cars had been fitted with passenger seats. The last car in the small train was filled with a large box with a closed lid. The lid had a large handle on its front, as well as a lock hasp and two latches.

"This is the box we were told to bring down into the mine," Santiago said. "Only my men worked on moving it. They said it was too heavy for them to get it here in one piece. So they brought it down here in two sections and bolted it together."

"It looks satisfactory," Daumudi said. "But why is the car holding it not attached to the rest of the train?"

"I wasn't told what it was for," Santiago said, "only to get it down here. It is only a matter of a moment to hook it to the train, but our speed is cut down noticeably when we pull it. We left it off for the time being to eliminate the excess strain on the engine."

The men all climbed into the ore cars and Rodriguez got into the seat of the engine. The boxy engine was nothing more than an electric donkey, its motor driving geared wheels with power from a large collection of lead-acid batteries. Unhooking a charging cable from the top of the battery box, Rodriguez turned on the power and moved the speed control forward. Smoothly and with little noise, the engine started pulling the small train into the earth.

More strings of bare bulbs illuminated the walls of the mine as they slipped past. The tunnel seemed to go on forever with only the passing support timbers showing besides the rock. Then, the rock walls suddenly changed. They were much rougher with sharp edges to the cuts that removed the rock. Then the walls suddenly ended as the train entered a huge cavern.

The line of lights continued on alongside the tracks laid on the floor of the cavern. A small trestle ran from the mouth of the mine tunnel down to the floor of the cavern. The train stopped at a signal from Santiago as it reached the bottom of the trestle. In spite of themselves, the two Arabs were looking around open-mouthed at the interior of the cavern.

"Impressive, isn't it?" Santiago said. "It was discovered quite by accident a number of years ago by a professor who was trying to trace some kind of bat that makes its home down here. After an earthquake, the bats no longer came in and out of the mine every night. Some nights they didn't come out at all, others they did. When he came in to investigate that peculiar behavior, he found where the wall of the mine shaft had collapsed, exposing this series of caverns."

Though they were listening to Santiago's words, Daumudi and Humzan were looking about at the gleaming points of the stalactites extending down from the ceiling, some of them touching the tips of the stalagmites that stretched up from the floor to meet them. With the engine stopped, there was no sound in the great open cavern except for the dripping of water and the sound of the men's breathing.

"It was that professor's poor fortune for Felix Zapatista to learn about his discovery. The Zapatista cartel had dug dozens of tunnels underneath the border. But they were only a few dozen feet at most below the surface. A number of them have been found over the years, especially when the authorities used sensing equipment and earth-penetrating radar.

"But this cave is huge and natural. It is too deep to show up on most types of scans. Zapatista had it excavated and improved. And he installed this electric train. Over several years, he's moved tons of cocaine and marijuana through here."

"It is truly beautiful," Daumudi said. "You leave these lights on all the time?"

"It is much easier to notice a burned-out bulb or break in the lines when we leave them on all the time," Santiago said. "That way we notice when they go dark before we need to turn them on for a trip."

"Where does this cave come out?" Humzan asked.

"You shall see," Santiago said. He signaled to Rodriguez and the small train started back up on its way.

The group of cars moved more than a mile along the floor of the cavern before the Arabs began noticing a terrible smell in the still air. The mercenaries all ignored the stench. They well knew what it was.

"There is a charnel pit over there," Santiago said pointing to a black opening in the floor a short distance away. "It was first used by Zapatista to get rid of the bodies of the Indians he used to build his tunnel and lay the rails. There were some recent additions to the bodies of some people who had used this tunnel without permission. We ran out of lime to spread over the bodies is all."

"Security for this tunnel has been breached?" Daumudi said.

"No," Santiago said, "you can be sure all of the leaks have been plugged. Only my men and I work the train system now. Zapatista had trusted others who are no longer a problem."

The train continued down the track, pulling a lingering trace of the stench of decaying flesh along with it. Finally coming to another small trestle, the train began moving up as well as ahead. The mouth of another tunnel loomed in the cavern wall. As the train was swallowed by the tunnel mouth, Santiago turned to the Arabs.

"Welcome to the United States," he said.

Chapter Sixteen

Once back at the ranch house, Reaper, Manors, and Hausmann took off their 5.11 tactical vests and laid their weapons down alongside them on one of the couches in the poolroom. Sitting down at the bar, Reaper took out the map, paper, and sample of material he had picked up in the barn. Pouring the dust and blue material into a clean ashtray, Reaper poked about in the stuff with the point of his Emerson CQB-7 knife.

Having stepped out of the room, and been followed by the rottweilers and bulldog, Hausmann went into the house proper. Coming back a few minutes later, he was holding a small book and a powerful hand magnifier loupe. Handing the magnifier to Reaper, Hausmann stepped behind the bar and drew three mugs of cold beer from the tap. Passing out the beer, he leaned down on the bar top with both elbows.

"So, Sherlock," Hausmann said, "made any sense of the clues yet?"

"Geology isn't exactly my field," Reaper said as he held up the ashtray and examined the material through the magnifier. He set down the ashtray and the loupe and picked up his beer.

"This stuff looks like some kind of rock chips or flakes," Reaper said, indicating the ashtray. "It sure isn't any bits of paint, no matter how blue it is."

"Let me take a look," Hausmann said.

Pushing the magnifier and ashtray across the bar top, Reaper lifted his beer mug to his lips and took a long pull. Having watched the little exchange between the two men, Manors continued sitting at the end of the bar, quietly drinking his beer.

Grunt, the youngest of the rottweilers, shoved his big head up underneath the Border Patrol agent's left arm. Flipping up the arm with his muzzle, Grunt pointed out his opinion that the arm in question would be put to much better use rubbing his head rather than just being there. Manors started to scratch behind the big dog's ears as he watched the other men.

Lifting up the ashtray, Hausmann held it close to his eyes while standing over a lamp at the end of the bar. Through the magnifier, he could see that the chips of material were sharp-edged fragments, far too thick to be paint flakes. They looked like shattered pieces from much larger crystals.

Setting the magnifier and sample down, Hausmann started flipping through the pages of the small hardcover book he had opened on the bar.

"So, Watson," Reaper said, "is the game afoot?"

"So you've read Doyle," Hausmann said. "Well, I

don't know about the game, but I think I know what this blue stuff is."

"Hey," Reaper said, "you really do know geology!"

"I wouldn't exactly say that," Hausmann said. "More of a practical working knowledge. When I was a kid, I wanted to strike it rich finding a gold mine in the mountains. Never did find that big strike, though, or a little one for that matter. But I did learn something important."

"What's that?" said Manors, his interest peaking at the conversation.

"That a smart man doesn't necessarily know everything," Hausmann said. "Or even knows a lot. A smart man does recognize when he doesn't know something, but he knows how to look it up."

Pushing the open book across the bar to Reaper, Hausmann turned it around at the same time so the big SEAL could see the page it was turned to.

"According to the *Field Guide to Rocks and Minerals*," Hausmann said, "this stuff is azurite. Basically copper carbonate. Here's the text," Hausmann said as he pointed to the book, "and there's a color picture on plate ten. This might be an old copy of the field guide, but I don't think the rocks have changed very much."

"That's where I know that stuff from," Manors said. "They have all kinds of crystals of azurite and malachite on display over in Bisbee at the Mining and Historical Museum. The building the museum is in used to be the office of the Copper Queen Consolidated Mining Company years ago."

"Bisbee?" Reaper said looking up from the book. "Isn't that near here?"

"About fifteen miles southeast of here," Hausmann said. "There's still some active mines around there. And a lot of old ones. A bunch of old copper mines."

"So these ATVs could have come from Bisbee?" Reaper said. "Why would they come from there?"

"I can't think of a reason," Manors said. "Bisbee isn't right on the border. It's about eight miles north of Naco, and that is on the border. Lots of illegals and drug runners break through the border around Naco. There's a sister town with the same name just across the border on the Mexican side."

"That doesn't seem to show any really strong connection between Bisbee and our ATV tracks," Reaper said. "Why would they come from there? It would make a hell of a lot more sense if they came from Naco or some place right on the border itself. Are there any mines around Naco? Any right up close to the border?"

"There are played-out mines all around the countryside here," Hausmann said. "Copper, lead, tin, manganese, uranium, zinc, even gold and silver have all been taken out of the ground in Arizona. Copper, silver, and tin have all been mined a lot in the local area."

"Any way to tell where this particular azurite came from?" Reaper said. "That could narrow the search area down for us."

"Maybe by a laboratory analysis," Hausmann said. "But I don't know how we would get a criminal lab . . . Hey, wait a minute. The Blue Star!"

"You're right," Manors said. "The Blue Star, that fits perfectly."

"Okay," Reaper said, "anyone want to tell me what the Blue Star is?"

"It's a closed mine," Manors said. "A copper mine they shut down back in the seventies I think."

"And this mine fits our bill?" Reaper asked. "It's down by the border?"

"Less than half a mile from the border," Hausmann said. "But that's not the big deal about it. It's right next to the Heart Ranch. She doesn't own the mine, but Valentine Dupree leased the land the mine is on just a few years ago. She claims to be setting up a sanctuary for the endangered Arizona ridged-nosed rattlesnake and the Yaquia black-headed snake. She's an absolute loon about snakes, especially rattlesnakes—so no one goes anywhere near her place.

"She runs an organic food company down there that always struck me as just barely holding on. There's just not much of a market for that stuff around here. There's something of a market in some of the bigger cities, especially over in Taos, New Mexico. But she always seems to have enough money to keep going. It wouldn't surprise me at all if she's into selling drugs along with her nuts and twigs. Pot would be something she would think shouldn't be illegal, or at least that the laws don't apply to her."

"Sounds like just the kind of person we should go see," Reaper said. "Maybe just to take a look at her snake sanctuary. Manors, you'd say one of those semi trailers we saw down near that barn could have left the tracks we saw inside the building?"

"Easily," Manors said.

Reaching out to where he had set down the old road map, Reaper picked up the creased piece of paper. Carefully unfolding it, he turned it out along its most heavily worn folds. One section of the map was much dirtier than the others, and the paper folded easily to put the dirty section uppermost.

"That's kind of interesting," Hausmann said.

"What is?" Reaper said.

"That part of the map shows the country around here and down to the border. That X-like mark there down near the bottom is the Blue Star mine."

"I think it's time to saddle up again," Reaper said.

The other men just nodded and moved to where they had left their gear.

Their weapons and vests back on, all three men went out to where they had left the Prowler.

"Isn't that going to be a hell of a long ride in that thing?" Hausmann said. "Going to stand out a bit, too, isn't it?"

"Got a better idea?" Reaper said.

"How about the best of both worlds," Hausmann said as he tapped on a key pad next to the garage door.

The left-end door of the three hinged up, exposing the interior of the garage. In front of the men was a large dark gray truck, the chrome fittings gleaming in the moonlight.

"I think this will take care of us," Hausmann said.

"Looks big enough," Reaper said. "How's it fitted out?"

"She's a 2003 Chevy Silverado 1500 regular cab half-ton pickup," Hausmann said. "It's got four-wheel drive and an 8.1-foot-long Fleetside long box bed. So it will carry your Prowler easily enough. That thing's only about what, seven feet long?"

"Ninety inches," Reaper said. "That's seven and a half feet."

"Okay," Hausmann said. "Still, she'll carry it with a little room to spare. And I got the biggest engine they had available for that year, the 5.3 liter V-8. That's 300 horsepower, enough to move us, the Prowler, and our gear right on down the road. We just cover it up with a tarp and it won't even stand out around here."

"Someday," Reaper said, "I have to introduce you to a partner of mine back in Detroit. Keith Deckert is a gear head and I think the both of you would get along fine."

With the use of a couple of eight-foot-long planks and some care, the Prowler was driven up into the bed of the Chevy pickup. The rear gate had to be removed for the operation, but it had been designed for that so there wasn't any problem. There was room on either side of the Prowler for the planks to be laid into the bed of the truck. It took a big tarp to cover up the relatively tall RTV. Once covered, the truck looked like it was just hauling another piece of ranch or farm machinery.

With the Prowler ready to go, Hausmann headed back into the garage to enter the armory at the rear of the building. This was a cinder-block room with a poured-concrete roof and floor. The entrance to the room was closed off by a steel door with a combination lock dial.

Spinning the dial quickly and rotating the locking

lever, Hausmann pulled the vault door open and quickly stepped inside the room. He punched a numeric code into the keypad to the right of the door, shutting off the alarm system as well as disarming the CS tear gas disperser in the ceiling. With the room safe to enter, Hausmann told Reaper and Manors to "come on in."

The center of the room was dominated by two very impressive weapons—a three-inch "six-pounder" 1855 Napoleonic muzzle-loading cannon and a Model 1874 .45–70 Gatling gun. The brass-barreled cannon was on a short wheeled carriage, while the six-barreled Gatling gun was mounted on a brass and wood tripod. The wood of the weapons had a deep walnut color, the brass was polished to a high gloss.

"Those things antiques?" Reaper said, indicating the two weapons.

"No," Hausmann said as he opened a cabinet on the far side of the room. "They're both reproductions. They work, though. The cannon has a steel bore inside a cast-brass body. Loud as hell on the Fourth of July. Takes forever to polish them, though."

Reaper just shook his head as he and Manors looked at the racks of weapons that lined the walls. There was a wide variety of hardware, from antiques to ultramodern, flintlocks to rifles, swords, spears, even a couple of bows. Stacked up below the racks were cardboard and wooden boxes, most with orange warning stickers on them indicating that they were full of ammunition. There were also a number of odd-sized green-painted wood boxes Reaper recognized as those used in the older Army to store ordnance. For the moment, he had no desire to know what was in them.

As Reaper and Manors looked about the room, Hausmann pulled a desert-camouflage pattern backpack from the cabinet he was rummaging in. The pack was a Spec-Ops brand T.H.E., Tactical Holds Everything, model. With the pack hanging partially opened from his left arm, Hausmann was pulling some materials from a drawer lower in the cabinet. He stuffed a pair of Steiner Military/Marine 10×50 binoculars into the bag.

Turning to Reaper, Hausmann said, "Why don't you go into the dojo and pull a couple of bottles of water out of the fridge?"

The dojo was the workout room on the other side of the armory. Beyond that room was the machine shop and another roll-up door leading to the area behind the garage. As Hausmann filled his pack, Reaper took his suggestion and went to get the water.

Along with the binoculars, Hausmann put a Bushnell Trophy Compact twenty-to-fifty-power 50mm spotting scope into the pack. The powerful telescope with its wide objective lens came with a small folding tripod. When Reaper returned a moment later, Hausmann took the three one-liter bottles of water from him and put them into the bottom outside pocket of the Spec-Op's pack.

"That everything you want to take?" Reaper asked with a smile. Personally, he thought the optical equipment was a good idea but wanted to needle his friend a bit.

"Yup," Hausmann said.

"You're sure now?"

"Any way we can mount the Gatling on the Prowler?"

"No," Reaper said. "I think we're done now."

A little humor could lighten a moment. Reaper just shook his head at Hausmann's attempt at it. After securing the door to the armory, the men all headed back out to the truck. Firing up the truck's engine, Hausmann spun the wheels as he pressed down on the gas, sending gravel flying as they took off out of the parking area.

There were not a lot of different routes down to the location of the Heart Ranch or the Blue Star mine. Taking a side road off State Route 92, the men traveled for several miles without seeing another vehicle or even the lights of a house. They were just about as far south in Arizona as you could get without being in Mexico. Finally, Hausmann pulled the truck over to the side of the road at a locked gate that closed the road just before it reached a sharp curve.

"Well, this is something new," Hausmann said. "I don't remember this gate ever being here."

"So just where are we?" Reaper said.

"Just about there," Hausmann said, "the road to the ranch is on the left just past that curve. The ranch house is only a few hundred feet from the road inside a stand of trees. About a quarter mile past that on the right is the road leading to the mine."

"How far is the mine from the main road?" Reaper asked.

"Maybe a couple hundred yards," Hausmann said. "It's just on the other side of that ridge line on the right there. You can't really see anything of the mine itself from the road."

"You know," Manors said, "there's a branch of the San Pedro, a stream really, we passed there about a half mile back that runs below the far side of that ridge. We could probably drive that little Prowler right alongside the bank almost up to the mine if we stayed quiet enough."

"Oh, we can be really quiet," Reaper said. "Let's head back to that stream."

Once at the stream, Reaper could see that the fence line that had been running on either side of the road stopped before it reached the water. The bridge wasn't much more than a couple of culverts under the roadway. A flash flood after a heavy rain would be a completely different situation. The junk that moved along in a flood was probably what had torn down the fence line.

The pickup was able to traverse the rough ground along the side of the road and up the streambed without much trouble. Stopping the pickup after it was well out of sight of the road, the men got out and unloaded the Prowler. The same planks they had used to load the small vehicles aboard had been stuck into the bed of the truck to be used at that time. With the planks and the Prowler's own motors, one man could have loaded or unloaded them. As a final detail to make sure that everyone could find the keys to the pickup, Hausmann put them under the gas cap cover.

Reaching into one of the upper pockets of his 5.11 vest, Reaper pulled out an odd-looking clip and attached it to a plate on the front of his TC2002 helmet. Dismounting his PVS-14 night-vision monocular from his M4A1, Reaper snapped it onto the clip he had attached to his helmet. Tilting the monocular down put it in front of Reaper's right eye. Now he could look through it and see well enough in the dark to drive the Prowler without using the headlights. For Hausmann and Manors, it would just be a spooky ride in the dark.

With the two men back in their side seats, the Prowler moved out into the dark. The rough terrain was no obstacle for the little vehicle, though the riders got tossed around a bit. They had traveled close to half a mile to the south when Reaper stopped the Prowler at the edge of a four-strand barbed wire fence. Off to the left was a sign hanging on the upper wire of the fence. The sign read:

HEART REPTILE SANCTUARY

NO TRESPASSING

"Cut it," Reaper said to Hausmann.

Getting off the Prowler, Hausmann pulled a black Gerber Model 600 needle-nose multiplier from the upper left pocket of his 5.11 vest. Snapping his hand down hard, he slipped the pliers head down out of the handles where they locked into place. The cutting jaws of the pliers easily severed the tough barbed wire.

Having held the wire just next to one of the supporting posts Hausmann cut it between his hand and the post. With his hand holding the loose end of the wire, he was able to keep down the noise of going through the fence. Lowering the wire, he went through all four strands and then waved the Prowler forward. Collapsing the multiplier, Hausmann slipped it back into the pocket of his vest as he climbed back into the side seat of the Prowler.

The three men and their vehicle hadn't traveled more than a quarter of a mile before Hausmann slapped Reaper on the shoulder. They had been approaching the top of the ridge line when Reaper brought the little vehicle to a stop and they all climbed out. Getting down first on all fours and finally crawling on their bellies the last few yards, the trio slowly came up to the top of the ridge and looked down the other side.

They had hit the target almost perfectly because Reaper had been able to see a glow through his monocular as they had come up to the ridge. Only a couple of hundred yards from them was the small building surrounding the mouth of the Blue Star mine. It wasn't much, but the lighting around the building was still a hell of a lot to see at a supposedly abandoned mine. So was the big truck backed up against the front of the building.

Chapter Seventeen

The rock walls of the mine tunnel closed in on the small train as it moved along the tracks. The clicking of the wheels as they passed over the joints in the rails could be clearly heard as it echoed off the walls.

"This part of the mine tunnel was flooded years ago when they cut into an underground stream," Santiago said for the benefit of Daumudi and Humzan. "It blocked the tunnel and they finally abandoned the mine. The same tremors that opened the cavern wall back at the Crystal mine changed the flow of the water. It used to go down that hole back in the cavern floor. Now, that underground stream has just disappeared."

As hardened as they were, the two al-Qaeda terrorists suppressed a shudder when they thought of the horrible smell that came up from that black hole in the ground behind them. Wherever that water had gone, it no longer washed the hole clean.

"The professor found that this was the other exit the

bats used," Santiago said. "During the day, parts of the cavern are full of them. At night, they're out hunting. This tunnel also had to be improved when the rails were installed and that trestle built."

The train continued up an incline for hundreds of yards. To the Arabs, it seemed as though they had been moving through the tunnel for miles in the amount of time it took them to travel the 1,800 foot length of the tunnel. Rodriguez slowed the train engine as it approached an open-sided elevator in the middle of the tunnel. The tracks continued through the elevator and extended down the tunnel on the other side.

The train rolled over the tracks and stopped on the other side.

"Normally, if we're moving a load," Santiago said. "We would unhook the last car and lift it up on the elevator. We have vehicles in the upper tunnel that can pull the cars much more efficiently than the mules they used in this mine more than a hundred years ago. Once the cage returned, the engine would push a car into it and the process would be repeated. When all the cars were back, the train would be reassembled and the engine would just push them back to the other mine. Simple enough."

In spite of their blank expressions, the two terrorists were greatly impressed with what they had seen. It was obvious that Masque could deliver on what he had promised as far as crossing under the border went. What else could be done was yet to be seen.

The elevator platform was easily big enough to hold all of the men at once. Long gates were pulled down from overhead to close off the edges of the platform. When Rodriguez moved the controls, the platform began to smoothly rise up to and through the ceiling of the tunnel. As the edge of the rock went past the platform, the solid walls of the shaft seemed to close in on the elevator.

In spite of the relative size of the elevator, this was the kind of place that would bring out even a well-buried hint of claustrophobia in a person. Both of the al-Qaeda terrorists had spent a lot of time in the caves of Afghanistan, but even they felt the psychic weight of the millions of tons of rock pressing down on them from above.

As the elevator came level with an upper tunnel, Rodriguez moved the controls and stopped it. Latches swung down that met sockets in the tunnel floor and the rails in the elevator perfectly matched the ends of rails that continued on down the tunnel.

"This is the main tunnel of the original copper mine." Santiago said. "Years of ore cars moving along the floor have paved it with crushed copper minerals. This is the area where the lights are turned on only when we need them. It wouldn't do to have an abandoned mine show lights to anyone going by."

"People can simply travel past this mine?" Humzan said. "We were told it was a secure site."

"It is a secure site," Santiago said. "We control the surrounding area and use vehicles that have a solid cover for being here. But we cannot control the overhead travel of a plane or helicopter.

"In fact, insisting on using your own vehicle to

transport your man to his destination is taking an unnecessary chance. We have a good system in place and it would have been much better if you had taken advantage of it. It worked well enough when your man crossed the border by another route last week. He was taken by one of our trucks all the way to Las Vegas."

"We will consider using it again in the future," Daumudi said. "For the time being, it is better if we use our own devices in this country. You say we are actually in the United States right now?"

"A little less than half a mile north of the border, actually," Santiago said. "This is one of the longest tunnels of its kind in the world."

"The rail system is indeed worthwhile," Daumudi said, "but Allah in his all-powerful wisdom and mercy saw fit to supply us with tunnels and caves that went on for dozens of kilometers in the mountains of Afghanistan. Now, just what are these?"

The group had continued walking up the tunnel as they were speaking. Turning a corner, they had come on to a pair of dark green John Deere 6×4 Gator utility vehicles. The short, flat vehicles looked a little like shrunken military Humvees, the replacements for the jeep, but they acted more like ATVs in their ability to move over rough terrain.

"We use them to move the loaded cars from the elevator to the mouth of the tunnel," Santiago said. "They are called Trail Gators. Something like the model being used by the U.S. military. We have found them quite useful for moving about the area and maintaining security as well."

"Whoever was using them last seems to have run into a bit of difficulty," Humzan said as he noted the dried blood in the open-back beds of both Gators.

"That was a mistake," Santiago said. "It will not happen again. You may have noticed the individuals who caused those stains back in the cavern."

"Individuals?" Daumudi said. "We saw no one."

"Perhaps I should have said smelled them," Santiago said with a smile.

Daumudi ignored the answer.

A large truck had been backed up close to the mine's entrance. The green outline of a stylized heart symbol took up most of the roll-up door on the rear of the truck.

"What is this truck?" Daumudi said. "And why is it here?"

"Your confederates in this country have not yet arrived," Santiago said. "This truck is backup transportation in case something has happened to your people. Masque wanted to be certain that all options were available to you if needed."

Opening the satchel he hadn't let out of his hands once during the entire trip, Humzan reached in and removed a cellular phone. It was just a generic prepaid phone, one of a large purchase of such phones that had been made by al-Qaeda operatives in the U.S. more than a year earlier. The phones were almost impossible to trace. This particular one would be used for the present operation only and then discarded.

Dialing a number, Humzan listened and then spoke into the phone in a flurry of Arabic. The conversation was a short one as Humzan snapped the phone shut and returned it to his satchel.

"Our people were slightly delayed in their trip here," Humzan said. "They estimate that they will be arriving here within the next half hour."

"Very well," Santiago said. Turning to the man who had been the driver of the lead Suburban, he called out in Spanish, telling him to take one of the Gators and go wait at the front gate. The man went back to the Gator and started its engine. As he drove past, Santiago handed him a single large key. The man continued on his way out of the mine, moving slowly to ease past the truck by the entrance. He quickly disappeared into the darkness beyond.

"We keep the gate locked, of course," Santiago said, "especially at this time of night. During the day, our trucks can simply blend in with the normal traffic flow. They are such a recognized part of the local community that they are rarely if ever stopped by the regular authorities or the Border Patrol.

"We have built-in compartments at the front of the truck beds that can hold a number of men or large amount of materiel comfortably. Even if you knew what you were looking for, the compartments would be very hard to detect. You would have to cut your way into it from behind the cab of the truck. That is not something that the U.S. law-enforcement community is likely to do."

As the men looked out into the desert a few minutes later, they saw the headlights of a vehicle come up the road toward them.

"Ah, our brothers have arrived," Daumudi said.

After looking intently at the oncoming lights, Santiago suddenly turned to his men.

"Take these men back into the mine," he said.

"What?" Daumudi said. "These men are our brothers in struggle, our fellow mujahideen."

"Not unless they drive Lincoln Navigators," Santiago said. "I know who this is and I don't want her seeing you. So don't argue with me, just go, now!"

"We do not hide from women . . ." Humzan started to say.

"I said now!" Santiago commanded.

The two Arabs decided against arguing further. This was Santiago's area of knowledge and not theirs. Humzan thought about the Soviet Stechkin APS machine pistol he had in the satchel next to the bags of diamonds. The big weapon held twenty rounds of 9mm Makarov ammunition in its magazine and was capable of full-automatic fire. At a cyclic rate of 750 rounds per minute, the Stechkin would empty its magazine in a little over a second and a half. If Santiago was trying some form of scheme to steal the diamonds or turn Humzan and Daumudi over to the Americans, Humzan would make sure most of that first magazine went into Santiago himself.

The weapon Humzan had hidden away wasn't necessary. Either of the heavily armed mercenaries would have kept him from ever drawing it against their captain. The huge green Lincoln Navigator SUV pulled up next to the truck in a swirl of dust and spray of gravel. The driver's door swung open and a tall, thin, blond woman stepped out.

As she stormed up to him it was obvious that the woman knew Santiago. And her attitude demonstrated that she was more than used to having her own way.

"What is this?" Valentine Dupree shouted. "This is the second time inside of a week that there's been activity at this mine that I haven't been told about. How can this be kept a secret if people are coming and going every night? I would have never allowed this to happen . . ."

"Be silent!" Santiago shouted at the woman, cutting her off in midtirade. "Do not presume to speak to me in such a manner. I will have you cut off at the knees. Is that perfectly understood?"

Obviously, it was not understood, but it was shocking. Dupree was not used to being talked to in this manner. Normally, she was the one who just bowled people over with her pushy manner and rude behavior. She just stood there stunned for a moment with her eyes wide and staring—the whites showing in a big circle. For a moment, her mouth just gaped like a beached fish trying to breathe air.

"You cannot speak to me in such a manner!" she started to say as she tried to recover her composure. "This is my property and you will do as I say."

"I think you have a dangerously inaccurate view of the situation," Santiago said in a low voice. "We have allowed you to make a profit selling what we have delivered to you. In no way does this put you in charge of anything at all. You may run your business as long as it is convenient to us. But do not think for a minute that we wouldn't get rid of you like a snuffed-out match if it served our purpose.

"You may think you are some kind of political do-gooder in this country, selling your organic trash and protecting the slithering little animals. To me, you are just another burned-out ex-hippie drug dealer selling pot—nothing more. It would be very unwise for you to consider yourself above the situation. We can always get another front person to run this ranch."

Before Dupree said a word, two of Santiago's men stepped forward, both holding their Galil SARs in a threatening posture. She knew that at a single word from their commander, she would be cut down in a hail of fire and bullets. The woman was of course against any civilian ownership of vile assault weapons in the United States, or any guns for that matter. As she looked at the two very deadly appearing men and the lethal hardware in their hands, she sincerely wished that there were hundreds of armed neighbors behind her at that very moment.

For the first time, she realized just what kind of people she was dealing with. These were not the sort of men who would be swayed with stupid phrases and repeated platitudes. And there was no question that they couldn't be intimidated by her personality. She was lost in a quagmire of her own making and sunk in it up to her neck.

"But, but," she sputtered, "there can't be all of this traffic here at night. People will notice the coming and going. First there was that unscheduled truck that left here last week, then the men taking the truck a few nights ago. Now this. They will wonder just what is going on and the authorities will start asking questions."

"Then you will have to give them answers they can understand," Santiago said in a much softer voice. He had intimidated the woman and set her in her place, now it was important not to cause her to panic. People did stupid things when they panicked, and he didn't have the time or desire to deal with the results.

"You do not have to worry about the truck being taken out tonight," Santiago said, "there will be no further exposure of the mine, our operations, or your company's connection with them. Now, we have people coming here right now. It would be better if they didn't see you. That way we can protect you and your valuable contribution to our organization."

As Santiago was talking to Dupree, he was gently guiding her back to her SUV. She put up no resistance as he pulled open the door to the Navigator and held it for her.

"Please," Dupree said, "we must be careful about all of this."

"We certainly shall be," Santiago said, and he shut the door.

As the big SUV turned around and headed back the way it had come, Daumudi and Humzan came up from their concealment in the back of the tunnel.

"That woman is a danger to our operation," Daumudi said. "She is a weak link in your chain of security."

Watching the luxury SUV reach the road and head back to the Heart ranch, Santiago heard the comments and knew the al-Qaeda terrorist was right. But he wasn't going to let him have the satisfaction of knowing that.

"We have been running this operation for a year now," Santiago said as he turned to Daumudi, "you do not need to concern yourself with its security. I would think that what you have seen so far would amply demonstrate that we are well able to seal off any security leaks when we deem it necessary."

The two men looked at each other for a moment before Santiago broke the tense silence. He turned and walked to the front of the truck to watch for the car that was due at any moment. Daumudi knew that the man was dangerous, but then again, so was he. And he knew for a certainty that he could allow nothing to threaten the upcoming operation.

All of the expensive transportation of people and materials across the border had been in preparation for what would take place over the next few days. A specialist and his very valuable cargo was due in within a day. Once again al-Qaeda would strike at the very heart of the United States—and uproar and destruction of the vaunted U.S. people, their government, and their economy, would make the glorious World Trade Center and Pentagon attacks seem as healthful as a walk in the garden. Allah be praised.

It was less than fifteen minutes later that the silver Jeep Wrangler turned and came up the road to the mine entrance. Driving the Wrangler was Paul Stebbins, an ex-political-science major who was disillusioned with the United States and how he felt the U.S. was pushing its corruption of democracy onto the rest of the world. Having taken up the Islamic faith, Stebbins, whose new Muslim name was Mustafa Ibraham, was doing what he could to help with the overthrow of the U.S. government and an establishment of an Islamic world state.

Daumudi and his fellow al-Qaeda fighters found Stebbins a useful tool, one that could be discarded without a second thought. Stebbins was not truly trusted by the organization. Ali Issa, who rode with Stebbins, watched the man carefully. He had orders to eliminate Stebbins at his first misstep.

With Humzan ready to get in the Wrangler and continue with his journey, there was nothing more to do at this point. Daumudi and Humzan embraced and kissed each other on the cheeks. Then Humzan climbed into the backseat of the Wrangler, his ever-present satchel clutched securely in his hand.

While the dusty Wrangler moved back to the road, Santiago and his men waited for the driver of the Gator to come back after the gate was secured. With his return, they headed back into the mine, the cavern, and Mexico at the other end.

Chapter Eighteen

While Hausmann dug out his spotting scope to set it up, Reaper took out the compact Carl Zeiss 7×30mm binoculars he had borrowed from Hausmann while they were still in the truck. Looking over the area in front of him, he could make out the sign on the truck identifying it as one of the fleet belonging to Heart Green Foods.

Having gotten the Bushnell spotting scope set up and focused on the area of the mine entrance, Hausmann once more rummaged in his Spec-Ops T.H.E. pack and pulled out the pair of binoculars he had placed there earlier. Handing the binoculars to Manors, Hausmann settled in behind the spotting scope and adjusted its focus.

The observation post the men had set up was just under the cover of a heavy stand of creosote bushes. If they were careful, and they would be, none of the men would be able to be seen from even a few feet away. They all were experienced in the bush and their skills showed it.

The three men could clearly see the front of the mine, and the activity that was starting up there. At first, it was merely the movement of some shadows. Then a John Deere Gator rolled out of the mine and headed down the road. A few men followed from the mine and watched the Gator move off. Observing from the crest of the ridge, Reaper, Hausmann, and Manors knew that they had each probably just seen one of the ATVs that had made the tracks along the railroad and in the barn.

The men standing around the truck didn't look like they had stayed in the mine since the night before. All of them appeared to be heavily armed. The distinctive lines of the Israeli Galil rifle, with its long, curved thirty-five-round magazine and tubular folding butt-stock, was familiar to all of them. Both Reaper and Hausmann knew that the fired ammunition they had found at the ambush site had come from weapons that certainly weren't Galils, so who were these people? For Reaper at least, that question was partially answered in just a few moments.

As the men watched, another vehicle shone its head-lights onto the road leading up to the mine. While Hausmann and Manors turned their optics on the new-comer, Reaper's eyes were riveted on the front of the mine and the man who stood there.

"God damn," Reaper cursed quietly and he gritted his teeth.

"What?" Hausmann whispered. "That just looks like Dupree's Lincoln Navigator."

"Not that," Reaper hissed through his clenched

teeth. "I know that bastard down by the truck."

"Who?" Hausmann said. "The one with the shoulder holster giving the orders?"

"That's him," Reaper said. "That motherfucker is Garcia Santiago. He deserted from Team Four back in 1990, right after Panama. He was going to be charged with stealing Team funds and drug dealing. I was going to be one of the witnesses against him. I never expected to see him in the United States again."

"So what is he doing here?" Manors said.

"I don't know," Reaper said, "but I'm sure of two things. One, that whatever he's doing, it can't be good. And two, that I will find out what it is."

The men lay still and watched the exchange between Dupree and Santiago. There wasn't much question that the woman went from being aggressive to very meek and more than a little scared. If this was the tough broad who had killed Hausmann's dog, she was finding out that she was at best a pup among a pack of wolves. The exchange didn't go on for very long before she was back in her SUV and heading for the safety of her ranch. Nothing happened for a few minutes and the trio returned to their observations.

"Somehow," Hausmann said quietly, "I don't think she's running off to call the sheriff."

"Not that a county sheriff would have much of a chance against these hardcases," Manors said. "They would eat a deputy up before he ever got out of the cruiser. And who in the hell are those Arab types down there?"

"I've got a feeling we're going to find out before

long," Reaper said. "Here comes another vehicle."

The Jeep Wrangler drove up to the mine entrance and the occupants got out. Whatever the conversation was, it was short. One of the two Arabs, and Reaper was sure that's what they were after watching them embrace—a very Middle-Eastern action—got in the Wrangler and drove off.

"I couldn't make it out through these glasses," Reaper said. "Either of you two get the license plate number?"

"I couldn't read it," Manors said, "but those colors make it a Nevada plate to me."

Having pulled a small notebook and pencil from his vest pocket, Hausmann was leaning close to the paper and writing in the light of the brilliant desert moon.

"I got a partial," he said, looking up from the notebook. "And you're right, it's a Nevada plate. That's a hell of a long drive from here. It's about five hundred miles from Tucson to Vegas."

"Make sure you note down the make and model of that vehicle as well," Reaper said.

"I'll put out a call for the Patrol to keep an eye out for it," Manors said.

"No, you won't," Reaper said firmly. "We'll keep watch for the time being. I have some people in Washington I'll contact who can bring a hell of a lot more heat down on a target than the Border Patrol can. This information could lead to some very big fish."

"You had better know some very good people," Manors said. "I may be on administrative leave, but I'm still a sworn officer of the law. My duty is to report what I've seen."

"Believe me," Reaper said, "the people I know are very, very good."

"I've never cared for this secret squirrel stuff," Manors said as he settled back down to the ground.

"That ATV is coming back," Hausmann said.

As the men watched and noted the activity, the Gator returned from the road and went back into the mine entrance. All of the men were out of sight now. A few minutes after they had disappeared, the lights shining out from the mouth of the mine went black.

Continuing to watch for another twenty minutes, Reaper and his partners could see no more activity in the area. Outside of the truck being parked where it was, the place had taken on the appearance of an abandoned mine.

"Think we should investigate it a little more closely?" Hausmann said.

"Not the way we're armed," Reaper said. "Those men down there were handling their weapons like professionals. And if Santiago is just half the pro he used to be, they're some of the best he could find. We would be outnumbered and outgunned, big-time. Besides, I think they're gone for the night."

As they watched the area, Reaper's observation seemed to be right. There was no movement and no lights showing at the mine or out on the part of the road they could see. The mine entrance was completely out of sight of the road, but Reaper figured that the truck that was parked there would be gone in the morning.

Packing up their limited gear, the men carefully slipped back from the ridge and returned to the fence in the Prowler. Pulling up some slack in the wire, Hausmann and Reaper held the ends in place while Manors twisted them together with a Victorinox Swiss Tool Reaper pulled from his vest pocket. The folding pliers secured the loose ends together firmly. It would have taken a close examination to see that the wires had ever been cut in the first place.

The ride back to the truck in the Prowler was conducted in silence. Each man kept his thoughts on what he had seen to himself. It wasn't until they were in the truck and returning to the ranch that they all started to relax a little. With that relaxation came questions.

"Just who is this Santiago guy you saw anyway?" Hausmann said from behind the wheel of the pickup. "You really sounded like you had a case of the ass against him."

"He's not someone we talked about much back in the Teams," Reaper said after a long silence. "A good operator gone bad. I knew him back in Four when we were gearing up for Panama. I was really fresh in the Teams then, it was only my second deployment with a platoon. Basically, I looked up to the guy as a real operator, someone I wanted to be like. Figured I could learn a lot from him. Glad I didn't learn the wrong things."

"What happened?" Manors said from where he sat between Reaper and Hausmann.

"You still got any cigars in here?" Reaper asked.

"There's a cigar case and cutter in the glove compartment," Hausmann said. "Matches, too."

Opening the glove compartment, Reaper found the

long, slender cigar case with a cutter held in a side pocket. Removing one of the Baccarat Churchills in the case, Reaper clipped off the end. Opening the passenger window a few inches, Reaper used one of the big wooden kitchen matches held in a medicine bottle he found in the glove box. Once he had the cigar burning to his satisfaction, he drew on it for a moment, then started to talk.

"We went down to Panama as part of Task Force White," Reaper said. "We were broken up into different task units. You probably heard of Task Unit Papa. That was the three-platoon force that went in to take down Noriega's private jet at the Paitilla Airfield. They ended up in a meat grinder, completed the mission, but at the biggest single loss to a SEAL Team from enemy fire since the Vietnam War.

"My group was Task Unit Foxtrot. We were a smaller detachment working as part of the main unit. Santiago was our leading petty officer and would move from place to place. He spoke Spanish like a native, not a big surprise since he had a Latino mother and an American father. So he would run field interrogations as prisoners were taken. It was supposed to give us a shot at gathering immediate intelligence as to just where Noriega was.

"The mission for Task Unit Foxtrot was to secure the approaches to the Panama Canal from the Pacific side. The day after the airfield was taken down, Foxtrot captured a couple of Noriega's personal yachts along with about eighteen Panamanians and a bunch of guns and ammunition. There were several packs of other items seized in that capture that I never saw the inside of. But supposedly a couple of them had a bunch of money and documents."

Stopping for a moment, Reaper continued to look out the window at the desert night. The passing bushes and plants were painted with a silver light from the moon shining down. It was a peaceful, beautiful scene—very different from the one that was playing in Reaper's mind. He drew on his cigar and the others waited for him to continue the story in his own good time.

"Santiago went through the packs and read some of the documents," Reaper said. "Then he took one of the officers who had been captured into a cabin to interrogate him in private. I remember asking him if he wanted me to back him up during that interrogation, just keep an eye on the officer. But he said no and just took the guy inside.

"I never did find out what they had talked about. Santiago came out a while later and said the guy didn't have anything for us—that they were just guards who were supposed to keep Noriega's boats ready for him and secure the materials.

"For the rest of the week, Santiago kept disappearing into Panama, trying to develop intel was all he told me. I had no way of knowing just what he was doing, things were pretty busy for us off and on. By the second of January, everything was pretty much over and our unit was disbanded. We were sent to Little Creek but Santiago and a couple of others stayed back to work with the Intelligence people. I never saw him again.

"About a week later at Team Four, some Naval Criminal Investigation Service [NCIS] officers came down from D.C. and questioned a bunch of us, me in particular. Seems that those packs full of money or whatever never did get turned in. As far as Santiago went, he never came back from Panama. He deserted down there before they could find him. Went over the fence into South America. The last I heard, he was working as a mercenary for the drug cartels in Colombia."

"So he's wanted in the United States?" Manors said.

"You could say that," Reaper said. "He's wanted big-time by the Navy for desertion, and there's a few questions NCIS would like to ask him about the stories that he had made contact with Noriega's drug-running buddies in Panama. Helped them get out of the country during the chaos after Operation Just Cause. They were probably his introduction to the drug cartels.

"He was really hounded by the Navy and especially the NCIS people. It looked to us like they wanted to make an example of him. After all, we had gone into Panama in part to stop the drug traffic in the country, not add to it with one of our own. NCIS, DEA, the FBI, they all got on Santiago's case. Staked out his family, friends, Teammates, everyone who ever knew him or even just heard about him. The story was that the stress of the investigation caused his father to have a stroke and die. And Santiago never made it to the funeral, or even to say goodbye to his dad in the hospital. Both places were covered by so many agents that they outnumbered the people who belonged there.

"I really used to respect that man," Reaper said quietly, "considered him my sea daddy at Team Four. That crap he pulled left my career under a shadow for over a year. I finally transferred to SEAL Team One over on the West Coast. Took a while to get past that little experience."

Hausmann knew that a sea daddy was the older operator who took a young SEAL under his wing so to speak, and showed him just what it took to be a real SEAL operator. It was a relationship that could be closer than family. Manors didn't really know the significance of the term, but he could see that it meant a lot to Reaper.

"And now he's back," Reaper said. "Maybe this time I'll get some answers."

It was very early in the morning when the men got back to the Dogbone Ranch. It even took the dogs a moment to all wake up and start barking as they arrived. The gear was all taken down and cleaned up, the Prowler unloaded, cleaned, and refueled. Weapons were wiped down and racked. Once all the chores were taken care of, a couple of beers were passed around and the men sat drinking quietly. Reaper went up to the second floor of the house, where Hausmann had his office.

Sitting at the computer, Reaper went online while Hausmann and Manors took care of the dogs and the rest of the livestock. Not having a secure line meant Reaper had to go through some long procedures to get the information he had to the right people in D.C. It was early morning in Washington, but Reaper still didn't want to try and make any direct phone calls just yet. He still wanted to think a little about what he would say, especially considering that he would be talking to another SEAL.

The wheels were now in motion. The information that he and his friends had developed on the situation in Southern Arizona was sketchy at best. But he had the feeling at the back of his mind that this was a really important situation that had to be addressed by the right people. The actions of that sheriff's deputy the night before had told Reaper that the local law enforcement might have a hard time dealing with exactly who, and what, was going on.

Besides the professional considerations, there were personal ones he had to think about. This was not just an enemy who was very good, this was someone he had known closely at one time. And Santiago had known him as well. Reaper would want the best people he could find to help him on this one, and he knew just who they were and how much he could trust them.

After careful thought, Reaper went back online and sent out some additional email. This was more of a warning order to his friends back in Michigan. There might be a very hot time coming up in the desert of Arizona, and they were cordially invited to the party. This was going to be a BYOB—bring your own booze—affair and he would let them know just what party favors they should get together.

The sun was just starting to lighten the sky to the east as Reaper signed off on the computer. Hausmann had already hit the sack after telling Manors to grab one of the guest rooms. Heading to his own room, Reaper stripped off his 5.11 tactical shirt and pants.

Changing to a fresh pair of 5.11 Academy shorts, he pulled on a well-worn T-shirt and tied on his running shoes.

The cold early morning air felt good as Reaper started off on a run. The exercise would help clear his head for the work that he would have to do that day. He needed to get some sleep, but that could come later. Right now, the peace of the desert beckoned to him and he heard his shoes hit the sand and gravel in a rhythmic crunching beat.

The peaceful image would have been a lot more complete if he hadn't also felt the bounce of the M1911A1 pistol at his right rear hip. The weight of the weapon had a comforting feel of its own as he continued on his run.

Chapter Nineteen

Though SEALs are trained to be able to go long periods without sleep, that doesn't mean they want to. Reaper well knew the value of being rested, and that was something he was going to have to make time for.

After he came in refreshed from his run and had eaten breakfast, Reaper decided that getting some sleep was a priority. It had been an all-night operation the evening before and Reaper knew that things promised to only get busier. Grabbing some rest while he could, he crashed in his room and was sound asleep within a minute of his head hitting the pillow.

It was close to noon when Reaper awoke. The house was silent as he headed downstairs. The dogs were there and greeted him enthusiastically, but no one else was around. A note in the kitchen told him that Manors had gone home and would be back that afternoon. Hausmann had to go in to nearby Sierra Vista to deal with the disposition of Duran and the care of his estate.

He would also be back as soon as he could.

Going into Hausmann's office and logging on to the computer, Reaper started downloading the information that came in as a result of some of his earlier requests. At Homeland Security in Washington, Straker had been very interested in what Reaper had spotted at the mine. Not only was the appearance of the Arabs a serious development, the Santiago presence held personal importance. Straker had been a SEAL himself, and Santiago's story was known to every SEAL in the community. The chance to bring in one of their own who had gone bad greatly appealed to the retired admiral.

Attacking the pile of information that had come in, Reaper noted that it was a good thing that Hausmann had a high-speed connection as he was downloading hundreds of megabytes of information and photographs.

Not having taken full advantage of the facilities of the Department of Homeland Security before, Reaper was surprised at the volume of information that was made available to him. This was more information, and was supplied in greater detail, than he usually worked with even when he was an active-duty SEAL. All of the Intelligence services and law enforcement had been tapped for what they could bring to the table. The picture of just what may have been happening along the Arizona border was filling out rapidly.

The partial license plate and vehicle description Reaper had sent in had borne fruit. A Jeep Wrangler was registered to a Michael Sanskrit of Las Vegas. What had proved more interesting than knowing the owner was the record of a traffic ticket issued on the vehicle only a few days earlier. The driver who had been ticketed for speeding used a license under the name of Paul Stebbins. Sanskrit had no police record and nothing had come up under his name. The name of Stebbins brought up a police record, an FBI file, and even a Secret Service notation.

Apparently Stebbins had been a student who found his calling not between the pages of books, but as a protester. He had a wide number of minor infractions in his police record, most of them involving trespass and making a public nuisance. It was after 9/11 that Stebbins had increased his enthusiasm as a protester, claiming that the U.S. was unjustly accusing Osama bin Laden and al-Qaeda of having a hand in the destruction of the World Trade Center buildings.

The Secret Service notation on Stebbins regarded an incident during the visit of President George W. Bush to New York and ground zero shortly after 9/11. Some New Yorkers—in particular a group of construction workers—had taken offense at a protest sign carried by Stebbins, and had removed both him and the offending sign from the area. The notation listed the results of the police investigation, and that no assault charges were pending against the workers as no one admitted to witnessing the incident. The fact that Stebbins had still been on probation resulting from a trespassing charge months earlier had also weighed in on the disposition of the case.

This guy is not exactly the sharpest knife in the drawer, Reaper thought. The report didn't list what the protest sign had said, but that was a time in New York when it wouldn't take much to get a punch in the face from a construction worker, or damned near anyone else for that matter. Stebbins sounded like just the kind of guy that a terrorist group would use for cannon fodder; a disposable worker who would act as a cutout, eliminated after his useful time was over.

After the New York incident, Stebbins had moved out West and taken up residence in Las Vegas. The report listed his employment record and the release given to him by the probation department. The address of Stebbins's employer brought a smile to Reaper's face. He had a much more direct source of information regarding this particular employer.

Using a number from a card in his wallet, Reaper called Las Vegas. As he had suspected for that time of day, only a machine answered the phone. Leaving a message, Reaper hung up and went back to the task at hand.

Even with the cable hookup, it took some time to download the huge photo files that had been sent. These were almost real-time satellite images of the immediate area of the border and were more than worth the wait. Hausmann's computer laser printer was working overtime to crank out the pictures and files Reaper fed into it.

In spite of the work he was doing, Reaper found a moment to smile about the situation. Not much longer than a year before, he had barely used a computer. Now he was finding it an indispensable tool for gathering intelligence and transferring information.

Finally, Reaper started reading through the message that had come directly from Admiral Straker's desk. There wasn't going to be any time for smiles or pleasant thoughts after Reaper got through reading the admiral's message. Working with a scratch pad and pencil, Reaper went over a simple plan of action. Revising, scratching out, and writing over, he came up with the outline of what and who he needed to help him.

Once more getting on the phone, Reaper dialed a long distance number from memory. This conversation was a long and involved one. When he finally hung up the phone, Reaper knew he had committed himself to a major course of action. When Hausmann returned home a few hours later, he found Reaper in the dining room with maps, photos, and printouts scattered all around him.

Before Hausmann said a word, Reaper held out a sheaf of papers to him.

"Take a look through these," he said, "tell me if anyone looks familiar."

A little puzzled, Hausmann took the papers and began flipping through them. He saw the faces of a variety of men, all generally the same, and all looking as if they were of Latino or Middle-Eastern descent. As he went through the pictures, one in particular caught his eye.

"Hey," Hausmann said, "this guy here, he's the same one that we saw last night. Yeah, he's the one who hugged the other guy before he left in the jeep. Just who in the hell is he anyway?"

"Same guy as I picked," Reaper said as he took the papers back. "I thought you might have gotten a better look at him through that spotting scope. There are people in D.C. who are very interested to know that he's in the area along the U.S. border."

"People in D.C.?" Hausmann said. "I thought you were out of the service, that all you did now was consulting and training. This sounds pretty damned official to me."

Taking a deep breath, Reaper blew it out through pursed lips.

"Okay, I guess you have a pretty good need-to-know now," Reaper said. "I don't really work as a consultant for the government. There's a small group of us who work as kind of a contract security service for the Department of Homeland Security. We get support and direction from a director at Homeland Security, but we only have a very limited official standing. Strings get pulled and legal problems go away and, as you can see, the intelligence we have access to is pretty impressive."

"So you're a mercenary for Homeland Security?" Hausmann said. "You came down here on some kind of mission?"

"Hell, no, I didn't come here on any mission," Reaper said. "I came down here to hang out a little with you on the first vacation trip I've had in years. All of this crap just came up—lucky me. My vacation just became work, in as official a way as it gets for me. As far as being a mercenary—I do get paid, and pretty damned well, but I work for Homeland Security, not some foreign military.

"This wonderful gentleman," Reaper said as he picked up another sheaf of papers, "is Youssef Daumudi. He's the reason a bunch of intel people are jumping through hoops for me. He's a higher-up in the food chain of al-Qaeda leadership. This guy is Osama's go-to man for building sophisticated bombs and making them go boom at the right time and in the right place. This clown being spotted right on our doorstep during an election year is not a good thing at all.

"Daumudi was a chemical-engineering student in Germany when he decided to go jihad and joined with bin Laden. His hand has been found in a number of attacks against U.S. interests, but he's been keeping a low profile for the last few years

"Two years ago, he was spotted in Afghanistan, but he disappeared before our Special Forces could move into the area and grab him. The year before, he was spotted in Iraq, attending a meeting with some of Saddam's scientists, the ones he had working on his weapons of mass destruction program. Daumudi had made a particular point to spend a lot of time with Dr. Emil Ammad. Ammad disappeared from Iraq before the invasion took place and hasn't been seen since."

"Who's Dr. Ammad?" Hausmann asked as he picked up the paper that had Daumudi's information on it. "Was he that other Arab? The one who drove off."

"He wasn't that other guy," Reaper said. "They sent me pictures and information on Ammad and his description doesn't fit that guy last night at all. Ammad was one of Saddam's nuclear scientists. He worked on

Hussein's radiological bomb project in the 1980s. That's the proper name for what the news services call a dirty bomb. It's not a nuclear explosion, but it spreads radioactive material all over the blast site. If he couldn't get a real atomic bomb, Saddam was going to settle for one that just poisoned the area for a couple of thousand years.

"The Iraqis built and tested some radiological bombs back around 1987. But Saddam killed the project for military use before the Gulf War started. In the 1980s, he was probably looking for something he could use against the Iranians. A dirty bomb is a crappy military weapon and he probably wanted a bigger bang for his buck. It does make a hell of a terrorist weapon, though. And you would need a nuclear scientist and a bomb maker to crank one out without killing yourself.

"So D.C. wants this Daumudi character badly. Everything we've come up with points to Daumudi having hooked up with a major drug cartel in Mexico. That puts a known terrorist in bed with people who commonly smuggle material and people across the border. That's a bad mix by anyone's standards and it only gets worse."

"Worse?" Hausmann said. "How's that? It sounds bad enough all by itself."

"The people at Homeland Security have access to sources of intelligence that you or I are only used to seeing in the movies at best," Reaper said. "They've sent me photos taken by some of the new KH-Improved Crystal spy satellites. Those are the new, upgraded Keyhole birds. This stuff is amazing, take a look for yourself."

Picking up some of the photo printouts he had scattered on the table, Reaper handed them over to Hausmann. The detail in the pictures was incredible—they appeared to have been shot from an overhead aircraft, not a satellite orbiting out in space.

Most of the photos covered an overlapping area around the Blue Star mine. There were also shots of another mine entrance that Hausmann wasn't familiar with. Still other photos had a very strange color scheme in their layouts. In those pictures, the entrances to the mines stood out in high contrast to the surrounding desert.

"Jesus," Hausmann said. "These pictures were taken by our own spy satellites? Over our own country?"

"Things are a little different in the spy game now," Reaper said. "Our intelligence agencies have been paying a lot more attention to our own borders rather than just those of other countries. There's always been satellites overhead, orbiting above the United States, both ours and Russian birds. They're always looking down at something.

"The thing was that the folks in the intelligence community who analyze these pictures didn't know where to look, or just what to pay attention to. Our information told them that. The importance of this Daumudi character was enough for the folks at the National Security Agency to download some shots from a satellite passing right over the area we were looking at last night. The bird was overhead within a hour of us being out there in the woods. That's not a small bit of luck and these results show it."

"I'll say so," Hausmann said. "But I'm not so sure I like the idea of Big Brother looking over my shoulder in my own backyard. There's no question that these pictures are fantastic, though. I've never seen anything like them. You'd swear you can see individual rocks in these shots."

"You can," Reaper said. "And, by the way, that's classified. These shots were taken with a camera that has a resolution of about ten centimeters. That's about four inches. You could tell if a man had his hand open or was making a fist in that fine a picture. And you can see it from a couple of hundred miles up in space."

"Amazing," Hausmann said. "So what are these weird-looking shots?"

"Those are specialized infrared and radar images," Reaper said. "They confirm activity at both mines."

"Both mines?" Hausmann said. "Where's the other one?"

"In Mexico," Reaper said. "Not far at all from the border. These shots here," Reaper tapped a couple of the pictures with his finger, "are of a place called the Crystal mine in Sonora, Mexico. It's an old mine with a hell of a lot of activity around it for a place that's been shut down for the last half-century."

"The Crystal mine?" Hausmann said. "Never heard of it."

"No reason you should have," Reaper said. "It was closed down years before either of us were born. It used to supply optical-grade feldspar crystals to the

U.S. war effort during World War II. They made lenses for bombsights out of the crystals, so the place was considered of strategic importance.

"There's a lot of information about the place in the stack here. Old maps of the layout of the tunnels and everything. By the way, your printer is low on ink."

"There's more in the office closet."

"No," Reaper said with a grin, "not anymore there isn't."

"So," Hausmann said as he shuffled through the papers, "what are your people in Washington going to do about all of this?"

"Nothing much they can do," Reaper said. "At least not immediately. There's that little problem of Mexico being a sovereign country. We can't just send troops in, that would cause a diplomatic incident that no one in D.C. is willing to accept right now. And by the time the Mexican and U.S. authorities could agree on any course of action, Daumudi would be long gone.

"Even increasing the law-enforcement presence on our side of the border could warn off Daumudi and whoever he's working with. If he gets scared off, we could lose him until it was too late and he pulled off whatever operation he has in mind. If he took off, he would just set up his operation in another location."

"So what in the hell are they going to do about him?" Hausmann said.

"Not them," Reaper said, "me. I've already called people in to help, both with equipment and manpower. It has been strongly suggested by Homeland Security that I try to find out just what Daumudi's mission is, capture him if I can, and kill him if I can't grab him up. Anything happens to me or my people, and the government had no idea about what was happening, never heard of us. We're just private citizens acting on our own volition."

"Not just you," Hausmann said, "or the people you have coming in. You can count me in too. These bastards took a shot at me and killed a friend of mine as well. I owe them big-time."

"I kinda figured you'd feel that way," Reaper said.

"So what can I do right now?" Hausmann said.

"Not much, to tell you the truth," Reaper said. "The most important thing you can do is maintain a communications watch here at the ranch. I've got people coming in who'll use the number here to get in touch with us about their final arrival time. There's also probably going to be more intelligence coming in over the computer and you can download it as it comes in. And I want you to get Manors back in with us when you can. You can tell him as much as you feel you have to. I'll make sure things are square with his higher-ups."

"I don't think that's going to matter a hell of a lot with him," Hausmann said. "He never did give a hoot or a holler about what the boss thought of him, as long as he could do his job. But what are you going to do?"

"Me?" Reaper said. "I'm going to explore an old mine shaft."

Chapter Twenty

With Hausmann maintaining a communications watch on the phone and computer at the Dogbone Ranch, Reaper headed back to the Blue Star mine to conduct a more in-depth reconnaissance than they had done the night before. Heading in to do such a dangerous mission by himself wasn't exactly his choice. It wasn't bravado that sent the ex-SEAL to the mine, Reaper didn't have anything to prove to anyone, not after a career in the Teams.

The situation was simple enough. Time was in short supply, he had people coming in to conduct an op and a high-value target that could leave the area at any moment. Someone had to see just what was inside that mine, and he was the most qualified person on hand to do it.

During a career in the Navy SEAL Teams, the first thing an operator learns is the value of teamwork. Everyone works to the betterment of the group. That didn't mean a maximum single effort wasn't asked of an individual from time to time. Reaper knew that rule well, and it was what led him to be driving Hausmann's pickup truck back to the area of the Blue Star mine.

The fact that Reaper didn't have all of his tactical gear with him in Arizona had at least been partly dealt with by Hausmann. Digging around in Cowboy's own equipment, Reaper had been able to gear up properly for the reconnaissance he was facing.

The khaki-colored 5.11 tactical pants and shirt would blend in with the surrounding area well enough, so Reaper stuck with them. He added a new accessory to the tactical pants that 5.11 had sent him some weeks earlier. There was a pocket on the inside of each pant leg that accepted a pad to protect the knee. The seven-millimeter-thick neoprene pads that 5.11 had sent him slipped into the knee pockets and would protect those joints from the rocks and sharp corners he could expect to encounter in a mine.

Reaper was still using the 5.11 tactical vest to carry his spare ammunition and other equipment. His Emerson CQB-7 knife was still in his right front hip pocket, but Reaper had borrowed a sterile-model Gerber Silver Trident knife from Hausmann.

The sheath to the big fixed-blade knife was hanging behind Reaper's right hip. The Blackhawk airborne deluxe knife sheath that the knife had come in was a good one. There was a big pocket on the front of the black nylon sheath that held Reaper's Victorinox SwissTool firmly under a velcro flap. Reaper knew that he was going to have to go back through the barbed-wire fence they had seen the other night and wanted to have his folding pliers easily accessible.

Since the inside of the mine would be dark no matter what time of day it was, Reaper had taken his SureFire 9Z flashlight and put it in a SpecOps deluxe tactical light sheath that fit on his belt. The light sheath had a velcro flap that held the light in place. The top of the flap was flexible enough to be pressed in and activate the light inside it. The bright white beam from the flashlight would shine through a grommeted hole in the bottom of the sheath that was lined with a blue filter. Only a faint beam of blue light would leave the sheath, more than enough to see by to dark-acclimated eyes, but too dim to be seen by anyone looking from a distance.

Since the old SEAL rule of thumb for any critical piece of gear was "two is one, one is none," Reaper carried a spare tactical light in a pocket of his vest. Four spare lithium batteries were also in the vest. In a dark mine, a dependable light source would be worth a man's life.

By the looks of the satellite photos and maps of the area, Reaper might have to move underground for several miles to go from the Blue Star mine to the Crystal mine in Mexico. To get up and down in the mine's tunnels and shafts, he had brought a Blackhawk tactical rope bag that Hausmann used when he climbed around the Arizona mountains. The black nylon bag held the 165-foot length of olive drab New England Maxim climbing rope Reaper was carrying. The $7/16$-inch-thick nylon rope was still new and more than strong enough for any practical need that Reaper would have for it.

In the outside pocket of the rope bag, Reaper had put the CMC Rescue eight-link and some carabiners he would need to rappel with if necessary. Around his waist, he had already secured the CMC Rescue tactical rappelling harness.

Inside the hidden holster of his vest, Reaper had his M1911A1 pistol. For a primary weapon, he had accepted the loan from Hausmann of his registered, transferable MP5A3 submachine gun. Fitted with a Gemtech Raptor suppressor, the weapon was quiet, reasonably compact, and not something Reaper could legally borrow from Hausmann. Legal questions were the least of either man's worries right now and Reaper was glad to have the suppressed capability of the MP5A3 available to him for the recon. Four spare thirty-round magazines filled the long pockets of his vest with a single magazine locked into place in the receiver of the submachine gun.

With all of his gear and weapons, Reaper was not going to be able to pass himself off as a lost hiker if he was spotted during his recon. For the drive down to the mine area, he carried the bulk of the gear inside Hausmann's SpecOps T.H.E. pack. At least while he was in the pickup, he wouldn't stand out at all from the local traffic.

One thing he had added to the inside compartment of the pack was a Camelbak hydration bag full of water. The hose that let him drink from the hundred-ounce water bag slipped through a hole made for it on the top of the pack and was secured to the upper-left shoulder strap. Until he entered the mine itself, Reaper would be under the desert sun, not a place to be found without water available.

Traffic was very light in the area and Reaper had no trouble finding the stream they had followed the night before. Moving the Chevy pickup along the edge of the streambed, Reaper parked it in a group of trees and bushes that concealed it. In short order, he had the Prowler unloaded and was heading up toward the fence line.

The cutting jaws on his SwissTool folding pliers easily cut through the barbed-wire fence surrounding the reptile sanctuary. It would not have been a problem for Reaper to find the same section of fence that they had cut through the night before, but following the same line of infiltration on a sneak-and-peek twice in a row was just asking for trouble.

Not one to take chances when he didn't have to, Reaper took the Prowler through the new hole in the fence and secured the cut ends of the barbed wire behind him. The ground ahead was scattered with brush and rocks, but didn't look to be any problem for the tough little Prowler. The deep-treaded tires and heavy-duty suspension went across the hard-packed gravel and sand without difficulty. Reaper traveled slow and easy in order not to raise up a dust trail behind him.

It was early afternoon with broad daylight under a bright blue sky. The perforated metal covering the roll cage of the Prowler offered little in the way of shade as Reaper drove carefully along the side of the ridge line. The hot sun was probably also what was keeping the snakes that were supposed to be all over the sanctuary back under cover. Reaper didn't see any of the poisonous reptiles as he drove along, and he didn't mind at all. He'd had his fill of rattlesnakes the night before. Never seeing one again would be just fine with him.

Approaching one of several large clusters of creosote bushes, Reaper decided that this was about as close as he could bring the Prowler to the mine entrance without detection. The vehicle ran quietly, but there was no reason to push his luck at that moment, he might need all of it later. The rest of his approach would be done on foot. Hiding the rugged little vehicle from casual view, Reaper slung his pack on his back and secured his submachine gun to the shackle of his Chalker sling. Patting his hands around his body, Reaper did a quick touch-check on all of his equipment.

The mouth of the Blue Star mine was only a short quarter-mile hike away on the other side of the ridge. The terrain he was crossing was rough to walk, but not so much that it slowed him down at all. Reaper was glad of the tough cloth the 5.11 tactical pants were made of. No matter how carefully he moved, the brush and cactus seemed to reach out for him with their thorns and spines. He had earlier turned down the sleeves of his shirt to help protect his arms from the nasty plant life. The Kevlar and leather Hatch SOG-L Operator gloves he had over his hands kept the bulk of the thorns out of his skin. In spite of the extra warmth of the gloves and long sleeves, he was glad he had them on as he crouched down low to approach the crest of the ridge.

The hot sun beat down on the black DSC/Cobra logo baseball cap Reaper had picked up back at Diamondback Tactical. He took frequent sips of water from the drinking tube of his water bag. Getting dehydrated out in the open desert was easy and could be as lethal as a bullet. Reaper was not going to make the mistake of not taking in enough water.

Crawling over the top of the ridge, Reaper started his final approach to the mine. Raising his head next to some brush, he scanned the area around him as well as the mouth of the mine only a few hundred feet away. There was no visible activity at all. Even the truck that had been there the night before was nowhere in sight.

The time had come to get up close to the mine. With his MP5 in the ready position, the GemTech Raptor suppressor secured in place over the muzzle, Reaper slipped up to the wooden shedlike structure that surrounded the actual entrance to the mine.

Standing so that his back was almost against the gray, weathered boards, Reaper held still and listened. Even in the bright daylight, your ears could warn you about things well before your eyes ever saw them. His SEAL training and experience had taught Reaper that rule well. So he stopped and just listened.

There was no other noise in the immediate area except for the sound of his own breathing. In spite of the loudness of his own breath in his ears, Reaper knew that sound couldn't be heard more than a foot away from him. There was the rustling of a light breeze blowing across the desert and nothing else. Even the sounds of traffic on the main road was muted by distance.

After a full minute had passed, Reaper had still heard nothing out of the ordinary. Moving along the wooden wall, but not touching it, Reaper slipped past the piles of rubble and scrap from the mine. Unidentifiable bits of abandoned machinery, piles of dried-out old timbers, and a twisting, coiling, mass of rusted cable was all around Reaper as he covered the last ten feet between himself and the opening to the mine. When he looked around the corner of the shack, a wide steel gate, chained and padlocked shut, was the first thing he saw.

There hadn't been a gate visible the night before. Not even a sign of one. But here it was, blocking his way, and there was nothing he could do about it. Whoever had moved the truck had probably closed the gate behind them.

There wasn't space enough to go around the gate and into the mine. Even climbing over it couldn't be done, the gate extended all the way up to the low ceiling of the shack. The gate wasn't across the mouth of the mine itself, only the front of the shack was closed off. That was something Reaper could work with.

Moving back along the outside wall of the shack, Reaper found a low door that had been padlocked shut. This door was locked, but the lock was old and rusted. There wasn't any way he was going to open that lock with the tools he had at hand, but the hasp the lock was secured to, that was another matter.

Kneeling down, Reaper took his SwissTool out of

the pocket of the knife sheath. The Victorinox engineers who had designed the tool had put a lot of thought into what was included with the folding tool along with the pliers. There were screwdrivers, cutters, knife blades, a file, hacksaw, and a thick, blunt prybar tip. Unfolding the prybar tip and locking it into place, Reaper slipped the chamfered edge of the tool back behind the lock hasp.

When the nails began to pull out of the old wood, they screeched and groaned. A squirt of water from his Camelbak drinking tube, and the water wetted down the wood enough to eliminate much of the noise. Folding the SwissTool and putting it away, Reaper took out his broad-bladed Gerber Silver Trident knife. The thick, strong blade went behind the lock hasp and levered the whole mechanism out of the way. Now, Reaper used the tip of the knife to pry open the edge of the three-foot-square door.

The dry wood cracked and splintered under his onslaught, but the door opened for the first time in decades. The way into the Blue Star mine was now open for Reaper's exploration. He slipped the knife back into its sheath and snapped the thumb break strap to secure it in place. Crawling through the low door, Reaper made his way into the mine.

The mouth of the Blue Star faced southwest, so a good deal of afternoon light came streaming in through the barred gate. Kneeling in the sunlight, Reaper picked up a handful of the crushed rocks and gravel that made up the floor of the mine. Holding the handful up to his eyes, he could plainly see the glinting of smashed blue azurite crystals in the rubble. Dropping the grit and brushing his hand on his thigh, Reaper knew that this was indeed the mine that the ambushers had come from.

The sunlight brightly lit the front portion of the mine, and grew gradually darker as Reaper went farther down the main tunnel. The tunnel was fairly wide at this part, enough so that carts and horses or mules could have passed each other and not crowded men on either side. As the tunnel turned to follow the original ore vein, the light faded quickly.

As Reaper turned the corner of the tunnel, he came across the two John Deere Trail Gator utility vehicles. The small six-wheeled transports were immediately familiar to him. The U.S. Army had been using a modification of the Gator, called the M-Gator, since late 1999. He had seen footage of the M-Gator in use during Operation Anaconda in Afghanistan.

Even in the dim light, Reaper could see that these were most likely the two vehicles whose tracks they followed into the barn the night before. With the aid of his flashlight, Reaper removed all doubt about the identity of the two transports. The deep cargo boxes on the back of both Gators had dark stains in them. The stains were almost black, even in the bright light of the SureFire. They were dried blood—and there was a lot of it. The dogs had done some serious damage when they had come to the rescue of Hausmann and Reaper during the ambush.

The brilliant white beam from the SureFire tactical light had clearly illuminated the bloodstains. But the light had also been dazzlingly brilliant to Reaper's eyes. He stood by the Gators for several minutes with his eyes closed, listening to the dark and giving his eyes a chance to readjust to the dim light of the tunnel.

Putting the flashlight back into the upper right pocket of his vest, Reaper decided that he was going to stop using white light for a while. The SureFire tactical lights were great illuminators, but the brightness of the beam took too long to recover from after using it in the dark. He would be using the SpecOps light sheath instead. The blue-green shine-thru-bottom feature would give him enough illumination to see by without blinding himself with his own light. The SureFire 6V fore-end weapon light that Hausmann had fitted to his MP5A3 would do very well if Reaper needed white light for aiming a weapon or lighting up a target.

The rails that ran down the center of the mine tunnel stood out as two straight lines in the dust. Kneeling down, Reaper could see that the rails were shiny and smooth on the top and inside surfaces. The outside surfaces of the steel rails were rusty and rough. The rails had been used regularly, and recently, too.

Moving through a dark mine can be an experience, even for a combat experienced SEAL. Reaper had no backup at hand, no Teammate he could depend on to watch his back. He shook off the momentary chill that ran through him, blamed it on the coolness of the tunnel, and concentrated on the task at hand. He had moved several hundred feet into the main tunnel from the mouth of the mine and there was no end in sight. When he stopped and listened every few feet, Reaper couldn't hear anything that told him what was ahead. But he did feel a strange breeze flowing up against his neck. The air was moving into the mine from the mouth of the tunnel. There had to be further openings in the darkness ahead.

The light from the mouth of the tunnel was nearly gone as something loomed up from the darkness ahead. As Reaper approached, the confusing mass before him started to come together and make sense. It was the support structure for a mine elevator. A small cagelike door had been drawn down to cover the opening to the shaft, it would keep the unwary from stepping off into nothing.

The elevator cage itself was missing. The rails that ran across the floor simply ended in black nothingness, and then continued on the other side of the elevator shaft. The open mouth of the shaft yawned in front of him as Reaper stepped closer. Suddenly he was very wary of booby traps, tripwires, or electronic warning devices. He saw nothing as he leaned out over the shaft. Then, as he looked down, he could see something. It was light! Far below him there was light shining into the elevator shaft. And the breeze that he felt faintly blowing against him was now flowing down into the shaft. There was no question but that he would have to descend into the lower levels of the mine.

Chapter Twenty-one

With his SureFire light in the SpecOps light sheath, Reaper looked around the open mouth of the elevator shaft. The light far below was visible, even fairly bright, but it did nothing to show the details of the deep shaft. There were greased and well-maintained cables running up the center of the shaft. They went up over a pulley system and down to the side where they wrapped around the drum of a winch.

The fact that the cables were obviously cared for was just another piece of data to add to the evidence that the mine was far from abandoned. As Reaper further examined the elevator shaft, he saw that there were I-beams running vertically along each corner and extending down to the bottom of the shaft. The central channel of the beams were smeared with grease and had shiny marks in the steel. That told Reaper that they were used to guide the platform as it rode up and down the shaft.

The greased cables and I-beams were useless in

helping Reaper climb down the shaft. The cables were far too greasy and slippery to allow him any kind of sure grip. And the I-beams were also too slick for him to climb down them with toe and hand jam-holds. He also didn't want to rappel down the open hole, not that he couldn't. But using the rope that he had brought with him meant a long, slow climb back up that same rope when he returned. There wasn't a chance in hell that he was going to try to bring the elevator platform up to his level and use it.

He had just about decided on rappelling down when Reaper spotted a ladder built into the side of the elevator shaft. The ladder was nothing more than a long series of forged iron staples driven into the rock walls of the shaft. But they extended down into the darkness as far as Reaper's light would reach. He could faintly see the rungs of the ladder reappear from the gloom far below.

Snugging up his MP5, Reaper slipped the hi-port weapons-catch around the front of the submachine gun and held it diagonally across his chest with the Raptor suppressor up near his left shoulder. Getting on the ladder involved lying on his belly and slipping his legs over the side of the shaft. Reaper didn't allow himself to think about the long drop if he slipped from the ladder. Instead he concentrated on just getting his feet properly in place on the damned thing.

When the soles of his boots hit the rungs of the ladder, Reaper slipped backward and let his weight press down on one of the rungs. The old iron staple held solidly in place. Taking his next step, Reaper began his long descent into the depths of the mine.

The ladder passed several more tunnels as Reaper descended. But the level that held the most interest for him was the lit one far below. The steps seemed to go on forever as he climbed down into the lightless hole. Having reattached his light sheath to his belt, Reaper was enveloped in darkness as he stepped farther and farther down, each step taken by feel alone.

In spite of their apparent age, the simple iron steps remained strong. For safety, Reaper only let go with one of his hands after his foot was firmly on the next lower step. In a steady rhythm, he continued just concentrating on each step. If he let his imagination run away with him, it would seem as if Reaper was climbing down a great chimney into the furnaces of Hell itself. He shook off his momentary morbid thought and went back to concentrating on the task at hand.

Finally, after what seemed an eternity of steps, Reaper went past the upper framework of the elevator platform and stepped onto the solid wood-plank floor. The rails that he had seen on the floor of the main tunnel were duplicated on the floor of the elevator cage, and they matched up with more rails extending far off down the long tunnel in front of him.

This is weird as hell, Reaper thought. The entire tunnel was illuminated by a string of electric lights attached to the ceiling. The lights were bare bulbs in sockets, but they appeared to go on forever. The end of the string wasn't in sight, they just dipped down and looked as if they disappeared into the floor.

The lightbulbs were small low-wattage ones that probably needed little maintenance. In the darkness of the tunnel, they were bright enough to show everything. There was another section of the tunnel that continued on behind Reaper. It was on the far side of the elevator platform and also had a set of rails running along it. In spite of his urge to follow the lit tunnel, Reaper went back through the elevator to check on the other tunnel.

It didn't take long to see that the rails along the floor on the other tunnel were corroded and covered with dust. But a short section near the elevator shaft had no dirt on the rails and showed the shiny marks of recent usage. There wasn't much question of which direction he had to take. Releasing the MP5 from the hi-port weapons catch, Reaper held it in the ready position and started to move on down the lit tunnel.

Whoever had placed these lights was supplying the electricity from some other source than the power grid aboveground, Reaper thought. The lines the bulbs hung from ran along the ceiling of the tunnel but stopped at the elevator shaft. Power had to be coming from the far end.

The tunnel was a long sonofabitch, Reaper decided, as he moved down its length. He'd covered more than a quarter of a mile by his pace count, and there still wasn't an end in sight. The tunnel was gradually sloping down, which explained why the lights had seemed to disappear in the distance when he first looked down the long tube in the earth.

There was nothing on the walls of the tunnel but the evenly spaced support beams. The tunnel rock was solid, there were no signs of cracks in the rock that made up the walls and ceiling. No rubble covered the floor of the rails that ran along it. There wasn't a sound except for the crunch of Reaper's boots in the gravel on the floor.

He could hear the pounding of his heart in his ears and the sound of his breath moving in and out of his nose. But other than that, Reaper could have been buried alive for all of the activity that was going on around him. That was a frightening thought and he pushed it out of his mind as he moved ahead.

He came to a point where the walls of the tunnel took on a different texture. As the tunnel sloped downward, the walls were no longer as rough as they had been. It was as if water had scrubbed at them over years. As if he had passed a line, the tunnel walls suddenly became very rough. The chips in the rock were sharp-edged and looked fairly recent, much more recent than any other work Reaper had seen since leaving the elevator shaft. The rails on the tunnel floor looked almost new, with very little corrosion on the outside of the steel. Then, the tunnel ended.

It was astonishing. The mine tunnel had suddenly opened up to a huge cavern. There he could hear the sound of dripping water, and the echoes gave the impression of a vast underground chamber. The rails continued down a small wooden trestle. Instead of climbing down the timbers, Reaper stepped off the side of the tunnel mouth and down the pile of scree and broken rock that made up the slope of the cavern wall.

The cavern smelled of wet rock and water. There was an underlying stink, kind of a sweetish rotten smell, in the air that Reaper recognized. It was the smell of death, of decomposing human flesh; something that once smelled, as Reaper had on the battlefields of

Bosnia, could never be forgotten completely. Someone had died in the cavern, and the body hadn't left the area.

In the cavern, the lights were held up on poles that ran along the rails as they extended down to the cavern floor and off into the distance. The ground was smooth and an easy walk, so Reaper made good time moving in the direction of the rails. Even though he was paying close attention to where he was going, the SEAL's eyes kept being drawn to one natural wonder after another in the huge underground arena.

As a kid, Reaper had watched the Jules Verne movie, *Journey to the Center of the Earth*. The surrounding stalactites and stalagmites in the cavern as he could see them, reminded him of that old film. He certainly didn't expect to run into any dinosaurs like in that movie, but the long cones of the growths down from the ceiling and up from the floor did resemble long, sharp fangs lining a gigantic mouth.

Reaper could see why the lights were left on. Anyone who came into the cavern without the chain of illumination would be lost in an instant. Whatever kind of train it was that followed those rails probably had headlights, and bright ones. But the long line of lights along the rails gave reassurance that that was the way out. Or the way in as Reaper looked at it.

The ground he was walking on was rock worn smooth by running water. But there was no water anymore. The area was dry. It looked as though the original waterway had traveled along and then ended in a black sinkhole Reaper was coming up to. Whatever it was, that hole was where the horrible smell was coming from. Taking out his light, Reaper stepped up to the mouth of the hole while holding his breath. The brilliant white light illuminated a scene straight out of a nightmare.

The hole bottomed out and curved off to the side about thirty feet down from where Reaper was standing. Lining the bottom of the hole were bodies—dozens of them. On top of the pile were recent corpses that suggested to Reaper that he didn't have to look for the men who had ambushed him. The ambushers had used military weapons, and there were signs that these bodies may have been military men at one time.

Bloated and blackening, several of the bodies in military fatigues had ripped and torn wounds on their stiffened arms. They had died hard, that much stood out. One arm stuck up with a hand clenched into a claw—as if the owner had been trying to reach whatever it was that had killed him.

The other bodies were little more than skeletons. Whoever had made the mass grave had a lot to answer for. It was something Reaper had seen before. Only the details were different; he'd seen man's inhumanity on battlefields all around the world. And like those times before, the sight filled him with a resolve to bring those responsible to justice, if not legal justice, then a more biblical kind.

With a cold rage deep within him, Reaper continued to follow the rails and line of lights. He wasn't looking at the natural beauty that was all around him anymore. He had allowed himself to be distracted by the amazing appearance of the cavern, and the sight of the bodies brought him back down to earth. He didn't like to think that an ex-SEAL gone bad could have anything to do with such a horror. But he had seen Santiago come out of the very same mine, and it would be impossible to travel along that path without noticing the heavy stench of death.

His pace count told Reaper that he had covered nearly a mile and a half across the floor of the cavern, leaving the death pit well behind him. The place was a natural wonder as the light bounced and refracted off of crystals embedded in the walls. The long cavern had probably been cut out of the rock by an underground tributary of what became the San Pedro River on the surface. But the whole thing was pretty much dry now.

Speculation about what had formed the cavern would wait for a later time. Certain that he was still moving in a southerly direction, Reaper figured that he was a mile or more on the Mexican side of the border. The place was a perfect smuggler's route—too far underground for detection from above. The hundreds of feet of rock and earth between the top of the cave and the surface above made certain that accidental discovery was just about impossible. The site was not a common drug runner's tunnel that could be found by accident or casual observation. The thing was a really sophisticated major asset someone had put some real money and work into.

The small rail line at that point started to go up another small wood trestle. Like the trestle far behind him, this one went up the wall and into another tunnel. The rock walls were too rough and unstable for Reaper to risk climbing them when he didn't have to. By stepping on the ties between the rails, he cautiously walked up the trestle and made his way into the new tunnel.

That part of the tunnel was not smoothly cut by water action like a part of the Blue Star had been. Instead, the walls were rough and cracked, broken where the rock had been blasted and torn out. It was obviously a newly cut tunnel and the rails disappeared down the length of it.

Reaper's senses remained at a peak level as he walked hundreds of feet down the tunnel. This was a rougher-cut mine, not nearly as uniform or carefully made as the Blue Star was. The support timbers along the walls and across the ceiling were often just logs, some with the bark still hanging from them in tatters. Others were new wooden posts, their wood still gleaming a little in the light.

There was almost no cover in the tunnel at all. It was like walking down a huge sewer pipe. Reaper felt terribly exposed as he walked along the rails. If he had stretched out his arms, he could have touched both sides of the tunnel at the same time. The ceiling ran along scant inches over his head. He had to duck several times to miss an overhead support and exposed lightbulbs.

As he wondered just how long the tunnel could be, Reaper spotted twin reflections up ahead. The lights were the reflections from the headlights of the engine. Reaper didn't know it yet, but he had found the train.

Crouching down against the wall of the tunnel, Reaper once again trusted his ears as he became still and listened. There wasn't a sound to be heard. No movement drew his eye and nothing appeared in front of him. If he had been spotted by anyone up ahead, they were incredibly disciplined and were not making a sound.

The trip through the tunnels and cavern had already gone on for hours. Everything he had discovered so far wouldn't mean a thing if he didn't get back to tell anyone about it. But it was obvious that there was a lot more just ahead and he needed to check it out before heading back.

With the muzzle of his suppressed MP5 trained on the area in front of him, Reaper moved toward the train. It appeared to be a simple affair made out of several ore cars and a battery-powered engine. A thick cable ran from one wall to the engine where it was attached through a heavy industrial socket and plug. That pretty well established that the train was electrically powered. Keeping the batteries of the engine charged was probably another reason the electricity was kept on in the mine.

Only the last car in the small train was different from the others. That ore car held what looked like a large metal-reinforced footlocker or steamer trunk. The lid wasn't locked or even latched, but when Reaper tried to open it with one hand, it wouldn't move.

Surprised at the weight of the lid, Reaper needed to use both hands to lift it up. Looking under the lid, Reaper could see that the trunk was empty. What had made the lid so heavy was that it, and the rest of the trunk, was lined with lead sheet. There was a thick layer of gray lead metal on every interior surface of the container. Lowering the lid, Reaper wondered just what the hell such a heavy box would be for.

Turning from the train, Reaper saw there was another elevator shaft behind it. Only this time, he was standing at the bottom of the shaft and looking up at the floor of the elevator cage far above him. Like the last elevator shaft, there was a ladder going up its side. Except that, instead of being made of iron steps, it was built of wood boards nailed across upright beams— and all of the wood looked old, dry, and brittle.

There wasn't much choice of routes if Reaper wanted to see what was up above. With extreme care, he started climbing the wooden ladder. It looked like there was plenty of space up above to get past the floor of the elevator. The only trouble was climbing the weak old ladder up that high in order to be sure.

Several of the ladder's steps creaked and gave a bit as Reaper put his weight on them. Each time it happened, he froze in place, hanging on to the ladder with one hand and on the pistol grip of his MP5 with the other. No face appeared up above to check out the noise, and Reaper again took hold of the ladder and continued his climb. Finally, he reached the uppermost tunnel of the mine.

This area was as well lit as the lower tunnel had been. Crawling up past the elevator floor, Reaper stayed in a low crouch as he moved through the passage. This was a much larger and more heavily used tunnel than the one far below that he had come in through. Up ahead a few dozen yards the passage curved and he could see the light coming in what was probably the entrance to the mine. As he watched, the light suddenly dimmed.

Whether it was the shadow of a passing cloud or an incoming truck, Reaper neither knew nor cared. He immediately moved to take cover in a small side tunnel a short distance away. Ducking into the side passage, he crouched down behind a large pile of crates that filled the center of the area.

The last thing he wanted was to get in a firefight with some random guard. It wasn't that Reaper worried about himself. His faith in his skills with the weapons at hand prevented that. If it came to a silent kill of a single person, Reaper knew he could use the Silver Trident blade and take the person out. But then he would have to deal with the body. Carrying it back to that death pit back in the cavern was possible, but not very practical. And there would still be the problem of a missing guard to point out that something was wrong at the mine.

These were the thoughts that went through Reaper's mind as he crouched in the dark. With his MP5 up and aimed at the mouth of the side passage, Reaper waited for possible discovery. Outside of the beating of his own heart, he didn't hear a sound. There were no shouts of discovery, no thud and crunch of running feet. After several very long minutes had passed, Reaper could see that the light in the mine had brightened and nothing else was happening.

Relaxing for a second, Reaper took a deep breath and blew it out. That had been a sharp moment of stress and he needed to make his heart slow down. It was a good thing he kept in shape through constant exercise, the walk and climbs of this recon had really started taking some of his energy away.

As he looked about, Reaper started to wonder about all of the boxes and crates that were stacked up in the side passage. There was something disturbingly familiar about a number of them. Taking his light sheath and light from his belt, he pressed down on the back of the sheath to turn the light on. What he saw startled him more than when he had first seen the cavern.

Box after box of ammunition, weapons, and explosives were stacked up in the tunnel. Right in front of his face, the familiar-looking shapes turned out to be wire-bound wooden packing boxes. Each box had big block letters printed on it in black ink: 20 CHARGE, DEMOLITION, M118. That was forty pounds of C-4 plastic explosive in half-pound sheets.

There were crates of hand grenades, both American M33 fragmentation grenades as well as Soviet RGD-5 grenades. The contents of the tunnel were a mixture of American and ex-Soviet ordnance. The labels on some of the boxes were printed in English, the others in Cyrillic, and still more a mixture of the two languages.

The markings on a stack of boxes said that the contents were AKMS-47 rifles, ten of them to a case along with magazines and accessories. There were thousands of rounds of ammunition in sealed metal cans. Cases of PG-7v rockets for the RPG-7v launchers, with several boxes of the launchers as well. There was even a case of RPG-18 antitank weapons, the Russian version of the American M72 LAW, light antitank weapon, series. Deeper in the tunnel on the far end of the pile, was a stack of long green-painted metal boxes, each over four feet long and about a foot square.

The sight of those long boxes raised the hair on the back of Reaper's neck. He had seen them before and knew what a threat they were. Each case held an Igla-1 9K310 missile launcher, the NATO code name was SAM-16 Gimlet, a newer Russian shoulder-fired heat-seeking antiaircraft missile. Recognizing the markings after seeing similar boxes in Bosnia, Reaper knew that these weapons were a very serious threat to U.S. airlines and even low-flying military aircraft.

There was no way immediately at hand for Reaper to destroy the missile launchers. Even with the cases full of explosives, he had no reasonable time-delay that would allow him to get to some kind of safety before everything blew. In spite of what might be done by SEALs in the movies, Reaper wasn't about to try to blow up the missiles, along with several hundred pounds of high explosives, with a four-second delay hand grenade from one of the boxes. All he would manage to do with one would be to kill himself, maybe blow the missiles, and certainly warn anyone around that they had been discovered.

No, it was time to withdraw and tell what he had seen—and to do it quickly.

Chapter Twenty-two

The morning after Humzan's crossing, Daumudi got up, washed, did his morning prayers, and then immediately started making a series of phone calls. Most of the communications he made over his cell phone, but there were several he conducted on the land-line phone in the main house of the hacienda.

When asked if there was anything he needed, Daumudi answered the question with rude, stony silence. Feeling in a magnanimous mood, Masque didn't press the question with the terrorist leader. For his part, Santiago thought that the odd mood swings of his boss were becoming more and more pronounced. The man swung between calm and rage on what seemed like almost an hourly basis now.

By early afternoon, a very strange vehicle showed up at the gate to the hacienda. When called up by the gate guard over his radio, Santiago's first impulse was to have the thing turned away. The vehicle was a huge tanker truck, old, dented, and rusty in a variety of places. The big tank on the back of the truck said AGUA on both sides in chipped black paint. It was a water tanker truck.

No one had told Santiago to expect a water truck at the hacienda. The arrival didn't make sense. The water storage cisterns at the hacienda were full and the deep drilled well was producing large amounts of pure, clean water. So the truck was an unnecessary delivery, something that automatically set off all of the alarms in Santiago's head and fully raised his suspicions.

Before Santiago could issue the orders to send the truck away, Daumudi came out into the central courtyard, all excited about the arrival. He was followed by an equally smiling Masque.

"Quickly," Masque called out, "open the gate and let him in, the truck is expected."

Surprises were something Santiago hated passionately. Gritting his teeth for a moment, Santiago smiled at Masque before he lifted the radio to his mouth and issued the orders.

The big steel gates were unlocked and swung open. The big tanker rolled into the central courtyard of the hacienda. It was a hard-used British Foden 8×4 tanker truck. Originally, it had been designed to carry 22,500 liters of fuel in its long tank. The tanker was over ten meters long and almost filled the center courtyard. There wasn't room enough for it to be able to turn around. It would have to be backed up to go out the gate. That was something Santiago wanted to see as soon as possible.

The passenger-side door of the cab opened and an older man stepped out and down to the ground. He stretched slowly and then his frowning face smiled slightly as he saw Daumudi approaching him. The old man had white hair and Middle-Eastern features. He was slight of build and could have been any older college professor of history or antiquities.

The man who stepped out from behind the steering wheel of the truck was another story entirely. He was massively built and carried himself like a bull gorilla checking out his territory. The driver wore his black hair cut close to the skull, like a frizzy cap. And he had a huge hooked nose that dominated his face. His chest was so wide that his muscular arms couldn't hang down straight to his sides. Instead, they stuck out from his body at a slight angle. If there was a definite form for an old Turkish wrestler and leg-breaker, this guy was it.

The big man looked around the hacienda with poorly concealed arrogance. The older man was warmly greeted by Daumudi, who embraced him and kissed him on both cheeks. Masque merely stood nearby smiling while the other men spoke to each other rapidly in Arabic. Catching Santiago's eye, the big man glowered at him with an obvious challenge in his look.

Masque was being introduced to the newcomer. By Daumudi's smile, Santiago knew that something between them all was working out to the terrorist's satisfaction. That wasn't necessarily a good thing in Santiago's opinion. Finally, Santiago was called over from where he was standing with his arms crossed.

"I would like you both to meet my security chief and most trusted lieutenant, Garcia Santiago," Masque said. "Santiago, this is Dr. Emil Ammad and his bodyguard Abu Hydar."

"Pleased to meet you both," Santiago said as he reached out his hand. Shaking hands with Dr. Ammad was less than pleasant. The man had a soft, moist grip that reminded Santiago of the skin of a particularly unpleasant dead fish. Shaking hands with Hydar was everything he expected from a big, dumb muscleman who appeared to think only with his fists.

When Hydar took Santiago's offered hand, he immediately tried to nonchalantly crush it in his grip. Tensing his hand with his own not inconsiderable strength, Santiago kept smiling and simply waited. Unhappy and frowning at the loss of reaction, Hydar finally dropped the other's hand.

The last thing that Santiago wanted to do was hold his hand while still in front of the hulking bodyguard. He turned to Masque and ignored the throbbing.

"What shall we do with the tanker truck?" Santiago asked. "It has to be moved, it is completely blocking the garage."

"Just place it against one of the outer walls then," Masque said. "And place a guard, no, make that two guards, to watch it twenty-four hours a day until further notice. That should be satisfactory, gentlemen?"

Astonished but not letting his surprise show, Santiago watched as Masque was asking the terrorist's and the old man's permission to move the truck! When the two men gruffly nodded, Santiago called over one of his men.

"No," Dr. Ammad said sharply, "Hydar will move it. Just show him where it has to go and make sure the guards are posted."

Things were becoming more and more unusual at the hacienda as far as Santiago was concerned. The doctor and his bodyguard were now arguing in rapid-fire Arabic. Ignoring the two men, Santiago called to Rodriguez who was standing nearby.

"Rodriguez," Santiago said, "this vehicle will be stored close to the hacienda. See to it that men are assigned to keep it under a twenty-four-hour guard, two men to a shift."

"Yes, sir," Rodriguez said as he snapped to attention. Turning smartly, he began barking orders to the men standing nearby.

Normally the mercenaries were much more relaxed in their military mannerisms. The experienced sergeant could see that his leader was not happy with the present situation. Some sharp military snap could help ease things or impress the strangers.

If the Arabs were impressed, they didn't show it at all. For himself, Masque loved the military aspects of his mercenaries. It made him feel like a true leader of men in the greatest traditions of Mexico.

Dr. Ammad and Hydar had finished their discussion and Hydar appeared to have lost. With the argument over, the sullen bodyguard climbed back into the truck and fired up the big diesel engine.

Even moving the truck could not go smoothly, it

seemed. Though he couldn't swear to it, Santiago suspected that the bodyguard intentionally tried to hit him with the truck as he was backing it up. This was ridiculous. It was like two grade school children trying to fight in a playground. Santiago simply wasn't going to play anymore.

Inside the hacienda's main house, Santiago walked in to see Masque, Daumudi, and Dr. Ammad sitting in the sunken living room. The doctor was talking, apparently about the house or something like it.

"Yes, yes," Dr. Ammad said. "It is a nice home. Not like what Saddam put us up in during the good days back home. But it is nice enough. Better than where I've been."

"That villa was the best home that Nueva Casas Grandes could offer," Daumudi said. "It was a decadent example of Western living and corruption. Made for American tourists."

"The only reason it was chosen was because of the deep pool it had," Dr. Ammad said. "It was for storage of the material and nothing else."

Hydar chose that moment to walk into the house. He shouldered past Santiago to go up to Dr. Ammad and report. The short burst of Arabic was answered with just a nod.

"Everything seems satisfactory," Dr. Ammad said. "At least the security meets with Hydar's approval."

"The best news I've heard all day," Santiago said as he walked into the room. "We shall strive to continue to earn his approval. So, Doctor, what materials would you need to store in a pool? A tanker full of fish perhaps?"

"He should know," Masque said. "He is in charge of my security. Santiago does his job best if he's aware of the risk. I've found him to be completely trustworthy and would put my life in his hands. In fact, I have done just that a number of times."

Now Santiago's curiosity was really piqued. The use of the term *risk* immediately activated his personal survival instincts and set them to a high level.

"Very well," Dr. Ammad said, "if you feel it is necessary for the safety of the material. What we have in the truck are four shielded containers of radioactive isotopes, particularly powerful ones. There are three containers of Cesium-137 and one of Cobalt-60. The Cesium-137 is packaged in small Lucite rods while the Cobalt-60 is in stainless-steel pencils about forty-five centimeters long and eight millimeters in diameter. There are several thousand curies of radioactive material there. It may be more simple for you to think of it as more than thirty kilograms of radioactive powder."

"It isn't the kind of thing that a nuclear bomb can be made of," Masque said with a hint of laughter in his voice. "At least not what the rest of the world considers a nuclear weapon."

"No, that isn't what the material is intended for," Dr. Ammad said.

"It will be used to make a series of radiological bombs," Daumudi said. "What the Western press calls a dirty bomb."

"Yes," Masque said. "It is all very amusing. The Americans, indeed the world, seem to be absolutely terrified of the idea of a dirty bomb. Even the suspicion of such a thing being in a subway or in a skyscraper can cause panic. There was even a television show about such a device. American Public Television made a program where they showed the effects of a dirty bomb in the Washington, D.C., subway system.

"The people were screaming when they learned of such a thing being detonated. And the device in the show was only a firecracker. Literally, a firecracker with a pinch of radioactive powder in it. And there are kilos of it here!"

"But what can such a device do?" Santiago said. His voice was not giving him away. Though he appeared calm on the outside, on the inside, his mind was racing over the possibilities—and none of them were good. He needed to stall for time in which to think.

"There is little in the way of practical data to work from," Dr. Ammad said. "We tested several types of devices in Iraq for use against the Iranians. Technically they were successful, but none of the bombs satisfied President Hussein. The isotopes we have came from Iraq and other sources prior to the illegal invasion of Iraq by American forces."

"And they invaded Afghanistan as well," Daumudi said. "Another offense in the eyes of Allah, All Praise be upon his Name."

"*Allah akbar,*" Hydar grunted.

"There is some hard data from an accidental isotope spill in South America," Dr. Ammad continued. "In 1987, scavengers in Brazil stole a radiation source that contained Cesium-137. They were breaking into an old medical clinic and didn't know what they had. When they broke open the container of the source, they split up about twenty grams of material among several people. The results were that fourteen people received overexposures to radiation and 249 were contaminated. Four died from the radiation and more than 110,000 people have ended up requiring regular monitoring for the rest of their lives. Cleaning up the contamination filled 125,000 drums and 1,4760 boxes. Eighty-five houses had to be destroyed."

"And that was twenty grams!" Masque said almost giggling. "Only twenty!"

"But why the water?" Santiago said. "Why a tanker truck?"

"The water acts as a moderator for the radiation," Dr. Ammad said. "It helps shield it from American spy satellites. It was brought up by boat to the coastal city of Guaymas in the Gulf of California. There we placed it in the water truck for transport to Nueva Casas Grandes. There it stayed in the bottom of a swimming pool until I received the call from Daumudi early this morning," he nodded in the terrorist's direction. "The same truck was used to bring it here.

"The boxes are shielded, of course. But the additional water moderator makes it even safer to move the material. The Americans have detectors all along their borders and at every border crossing, port facility, and airport. I have been assured that you have a secure route of getting it into the U.S. From there, Daumudi and I can use the munitions you have received for us to completely disrupt the American elections. The entire world will see what can be done in spite of all of the Americans' efforts."

"I assure you, Doctor," Masque said. "We have a most secure and positive route to get you into the United States. We have changed the timetable a bit to help ensure your security and the safety of the shipment.

"We will be crossing during the day. That will allow us to use the business trucks that have proven very capable of moving our drug shipments without detection. They blend in perfectly with the normal traffic throughout the area. I will personally lead you across the border myself. Santiago will assign his very best men to accompany me."

That was not going to be the best thing the men had ever heard, Santiago thought. The assumption that Masque would just order them around was something they had lived with, he was paying very well—which was always of primary concern to a mercenary. Protecting their paymaster was something they would accept. Working with these terrorists was another thing entirely.

"I'm afraid that Hydar will allow very few armed men to be with both me and the shipment," Dr. Ammad said. "He is very concerned with my safety and the success of our mission."

"That will not be a problem," Masque said. "Only Santiago himself and his trusted sergeant as driver will take you to the crossing. I would be honored if you would allow me to personally take the means of the Americans' destruction to the crossing point."

"I think that is agreeable," Daumudi said. "Don't you agree, Dr. Ammad?"

"Yes," Dr. Ammad said, "I think that is a satisfactory arrangement. As long as the materials always stay in our sight."

"That is easily accomplished," Masque said. "We will simply drive in front of you."

This is madness, Santiago thought to himself. Smuggling radioactive isotopes to be used against U.S. cities? Drugs were one thing, but this? There was no affection in Santiago's heart for the country that had hounded him since Panama. But he knew that the American government would spend years hunting down everyone involved in such a terrorist incident.

The U.S. had invaded Afghanistan and Iraq. Didn't Masque realize that? The leader of a drug cartel taking part in such an attack on the U.S. would just be signing his own death warrant. No place on earth would be safe for such a person—or the men who had worked for him. And that included Santiago personally!

While he maintained a calm outward appearance, Santiago was coming to a very serious decision. It was time for him to leave Masque's employ. The money had been good, but now the risks far outweighed the value. He would have to make arrangements immediately.

The ex-SEAL looked at the bulky presence of Hydar across the room. The bodyguard scowled at the slight smile that was on Santiago's face.

Chapter Twenty-three

It was late in the afternoon when Reaper finally pulled into the parking area of the Dogbone Ranch. He was dusty, dirty, stank, and knew that he would barely have time for a shower. The dogs didn't care how he looked, they enthusiastically greeted him as he stepped down from the truck. Considering how torn up some of those corpses in the cavern had been, Reaper had a lot of respect for the power contained in the jaws of the two rottweilers. He was very glad they gave him the reception they did as the two big dogs bounced and jumped around him, wagging their stub tails.

Once inside the ranch house, Reaper saw that Hausmann was sitting at the kitchen table surrounded by an even higher pile of papers than earlier. There were stacks of documents and printouts all around him with a cordless phone on top of the largest pile of papers.

"Damn, Reaper," Hausmann said, "I was starting to worry about you. This lone-hero crap really wears on the folks waiting back home. Find anything interesting?"

"That's the understatement of the decade," Reaper said. "Before we go into any of that, did my people check in?"

"Yeah," Hausmann said as he picked up a pad of paper and checked his notes. "Max Warrick called in from the Albuquerque airport a little while ago. Said that he and Mackenzie were refueling and that their ETA in Tombstone was 2000 hours. Pat Manors called in and he'll be here within the hour."

"Great," Reaper said, the relief showing in his face, "my guys will be bringing in the bulk of the gear we'll need to hit this place. We've got to move as fast as we can. I figure tomorrow night at the latest."

"Tomorrow night?" Hausmann said. "That's moving pretty damned fast. Just what did you find this afternoon, anyway?"

"I just hope it's moving fast enough going in tomorrow," Reaper said with concern in his voice. "I'd rather go in tonight, but there just isn't enough time to pull everyone and everything together."

Sitting down at the table, Reaper proceeded to tell Hausmann just what he had seen that afternoon. He spoke quickly and concisely, embellishing nothing but not leaving out any details either. Hausmann grimaced when Reaper described the pit full of bodies, but he didn't interrupt what the other was saying. The story took a while to tell. When Reaper was finished, he inhaled a deep breath and blew it out slowly. It had been a long, stressful afternoon, and the day was hardly over yet. He got up and walked into the kitchen.

For a moment, Hausmann just sat and looked at his friend rummaging in the refrigerator. It took a minute for everything Reaper had said to sink in and take hold.

"A cave?" Hausmann said finally. "You found a cave a couple of miles long?"

Straightening up from the refrigerator with a cold can of Pepsi in his hand, Reaper popped the top open and took a long drink.

"Not just a couple of miles long," Reaper said. "It's much longer than that. I only followed the tracks in it for about a mile and a half. The cave stretched out much farther. It went well past where the light could reach."

"Then you found the other mine?" Hausmann said.

"Just like the satellite pictures showed," Reaper said. "That underground railroad ends right in the middle of the Crystal mine in Mexico. There was activity at that other mine just like the infrared pictures showed. It sure as hell isn't abandoned by any stretch of the imagination."

"Son of a bitch," Hausmann said slowly. "They must have been running drugs under the border for years. I'll bet that bitch at the Heart ranch is involved with drugs up to her skinny ass. That company of hers was in financial trouble just a year or so ago. Then some kind of investor helped her out. I never did think that organic food business could make a go of things out here and turn any kind of a profit. I'll bet she's been moving pot and coke in those trucks of hers."

"Oh, that snake lady, as you call her, has to be involved," Reaper said as he sat at the table and took another drink, "involved up to her neck, I would think, going by that show we saw last night. But I don't believe that tunnel and the train system has been running for years. A lot of that installation looked pretty new. And I didn't see any drugs in either mine, though there's a hell of a lot of other stuff there we have to be worried about. That train setup can move a small truckload of freight past the border. And there's some really dangerous ordnance piled up in that mine tunnel."

"So why don't you call your Washington people about it and let them deal with things," Hausmann said. "They can send in the military."

"What I found won't change the situation," Reaper said. He got up and started pacing around the room while he spoke. "Washington will have the same problems moving that I was told about this morning. By the time they get something staged to go across the border, that tunnel would be empty. There's no way they could stockpile all of that stuff there without some cooperation with the local military. Even an airborne helicopter assault would take some time to get to the mine, and it would be on Mexican radar all the way.

"They would get a warning, Santiago was way too good not to make arrangements for something like that. They'd either bring the stuff through the tunnel, or more likely just move it and cross someplace else."

Ceasing his pacing for a moment, Reaper stood by the table looking down at the documents all across it. Anger started to well up in him as his face grew dark.

"Damn it," he said as he slapped the Pepsi can down on the table. "We can't make a mistake and let that stuff get away, not this close to the border. Those missiles alone could rip an airliner out of the sky. The rest of the weapons and munitions could keep a bunch of terrorist cells operating for weeks. No, Straker wanted me to deal with the problem down here if I could, and I think I can. He knows he can't order me to go, but he also knows that I will. So will my partners once I give them the details.

"You can count me in on this one," Hausmann said as he leaned back in his chair. He looked Reaper straight in the eye. "And don't argue about it. Those bastards killed a friend of mine, and they tried to kill me, too. If you think I'm good enough, I want to go with you."

Looking at his friend, Reaper knew that Hausmann meant every word that he had said. And he knew that Hausmann had tactical experience behind him, as a sworn police SWAT officer he had been on the sharp end more than once. Before that, he had spent a stint in the Army as an MP. He had experience and skills that would help and the determination to see things through to their end. Since he'd received his law degree, Hausmann was the only lawyer Reaper knew who habitually carried a cocked-and-locked M1911A1 under his suit jacket. His help would be welcome.

"Okay," Reaper said. "You're in, I hope you don't regret it."

"By the looks of this situation," Hausmann said, "you just may need a good lawyer along, anyway. I may have to brush up on my international law, though."

"Just don't take too long," Reaper said. "We have to move on this."

Before Hausmann could say a word, the intercom on

the wall behind him beeped for attention. Getting up from where he was sitting, Hausmann walked over to the unit. Leaning in to the speaker, Hausmann pressed one of the buttons on the panel.

"Yes," he said.

"It's Manors, Pat Manors," came out of the tinny-sounding speaker.

"Come on in," Hausmann said and he pushed a large red button on the panel. Outside, the electric gate opened to let Manors's truck in.

"Did you change the combination on the gate?" Reaper said.

"All but yours," Hausmann replied. "It seemed like the prudent thing to do."

The barking of the dogs cut into the conversation as Manors opened the door and walked into the house. Greeting everyone, he sat at the table and Reaper took him through the materials they had spread out. As Manors looked at the paperwork, Reaper went over what he had seen that afternoon, the Border Patrol agent was more than a little astonished at Reaper's discovery.

"A tunnel several miles long?" Manors said. "I've heard of tunnels that were dug under the border that were over a thousand feet long, but a couple of miles?"

"It's not just the tunnels of both mines," Reaper said as he got up and headed into the kitchen. "There's that huge cave connecting the two of them together."

"Even so," Manors said, "you're talking about one great big hole in the fence down here. Were there any other exits besides the two mine tunnels that you saw?"

"Nothing that I could see," Reaper said, pulling another Pepsi from the refrigerator. "I just followed the train tracks from one mine to the other. The cave is gigantic. You couldn't see either end with the lights that were down there. I would imagine that there are other openings to the surface, I just didn't see any. Parts of the cave floor were covered in bat shit, but there wasn't any bats, they had to get out somehow."

"There's small caves all around here," Hausmann said. "Some aren't much bigger than a coyote den, others are pretty deep. Every now and then, somebody stumbles across one with some old Indian artifacts in it that turn out to be a couple of hundred years old. But the only holes I've ever heard about that were big enough to lay tracks in were always mine tunnels, never a cave."

"That train track bit really stumps me," Reaper said as he sat down and opened his soft drink. "How in the hell could they have built all of this without ever being discovered? Those tunnels had to be dug out, trestles built, the bed graded, track laid. It was not a small job. Where did they get the materials? And just where would they come up with the manpower to do the job. Who were the workers?"

"Those are a few questions that may not be too hard to explain," Manors said. "As far as getting the rails goes, it sounds like pretty much a standard mine-car gauge. They could have just stripped the rails themselves from other parts of either mine. Some of those old tunnels go on for hundreds of yards."

"A thousand feet or more was my experience," Reaper said. "That's at least how long the tunnel was at the bottom of the Blue Star."

"The deepest part of that mine was supposed to have flooded out a long time back," Hausmann said getting up. "The story was that they hit water while following a vein. The whole mine didn't flood, though. They kept working the upper tunnels for years. You want a drink, Manors?"

"No, thanks," Manors said. "You know, as far as the workers go. The cartels have been using native Indian labor for the last twenty years or so. They grab up Indian workers from central and southern Mexico, basically just kidnap them. They move them across the country and put them to work on their opium poppy and marijuana plantations in the Sierra Madre Mountains well south of here.

"The Indians don't even know where they are most of the time. If one got away, he couldn't tell anyone where he came from. Most of them speak their own language and can't even understand Spanish. The cartels use them and either send them back or dump them someplace."

Standing in the kitchen, Hausmann held the cup of coffee he had poured for himself. He just stared at Manors for a moment.

"You're talking about kidnapping and slavery," Hausmann said.

"That's the way of the world south of the border," Manors said. "Whoever built that tunnel system probably used a bunch of those same Indians as slave labor. Then got rid of them. I'll bet they didn't see the light of day for weeks. Just stayed and worked in that hole."

"I don't think they ever left," Reaper said, as he remembered the older bodies and near skeletons that filled that pit back in the cave.

"Speaking of left," Hausmann said looking at the clock on the wall, "we'd better get moving if we want to be in Tombstone in time to meet your friends."

"Right," Reaper said. "I have to make a fast report to Washington. Then we can go."

Heading upstairs to Hausmann's office, Reaper logged on to the computer and started beating on the keyboard. After only a few minutes, he had sent a short but complete report on what he had found to Admiral Straker's office at the Department of Homeland Security. With the message sent, Reaper headed back down to the kitchen where Hausmann and Manors were waiting.

The three men headed out of the house. Reaper drove his own car while Hausmann and Manors took Hausmann's Chevy pickup. It was about a thirty-mile drive to the modest airport and both vehicles arrived at the gravel parking lot a little before eight o'clock. There was nothing to do and less to see as the men waited, each with his own thoughts. Before twenty minutes had passed, a lone aircraft could be seen approaching the airport runway from the northeast.

The fat-bodied, twin-tail boom plane was a Cessna Model 337 Skymaster. The plane had two propellers driving it through the air. One prop was at the front of the body, the other was acting as a pusher-prop spinning at the rear of the fuselage, between the two tail booms. There wasn't a tower or any facilities at the airport other than an orange wind sock blowing in the breeze.

The Cessna made one pass over the runway, then

turned around and came in for a landing. At Reaper's direction, Hausmann drove the truck down by the runway, near where the Cessna was going to finally stop.

As the Skymaster halted, the two propellers spun down and slowed as the engine noise quit. When the props had finally come to a stop, the cabin door directly under the wing opened up. A slightly built man, five feet, four inches tall, with thinning brown hair stepped out of the plane. From the other side of the aircraft, a taller, younger man with white hair emerged.

"Hey, boss," Max Warrick, the white-haired ex-Marine scout-sniper called out to Reaper. "You order takeout?"

On the other side of the Skymaster, Ben Mackenzie, the ex-Air Force parajumper and qualified pilot, was digging around in the back of the cabin for the wheel chocks to secure the plane. Together with Reaper and Enzo Caronti, who wasn't with them, the group made up the Four Horsemen. This was the first time in over a year that the group was seeing action together, and the first time they were operating under the "unofficial" blanket of authority of the Department of Homeland Security.

"Come on," Mackenzie said, "we've got to get the cargo pack unloaded while there's still light."

After introducing Manors and Hausmann to the others, all of the men set to work unloading some very heavy boxes and containers from the Skymaster. There was a fiberglass box that had been attached underneath the fuselage of the plane that held some heavy ammunition boxes as well as other packages and odd-shaped bags that Hausmann thought he recognized. For his part,

Manors just helped load the materials into the pickup truck, figuring he would be told what they were later.

Pulling other containers and bags from the back of the Skymaster, Warrick walked over to the truck holding one of several large gun cases. All of the men working together quickly emptied the plane of hundreds of pounds of equipment that was stowed in the back of the pickup truck and covered with a big tarp.

"Okay," Reaper said. "Hausmann, you and Manors take the truck back to the ranch. We'll meet you there later."

"Where are you going?" Hausmann asked.

"They're going to take the plane over to the Sierra Vista Municipal Airport," Reaper said. "It's the closest place we can secure it that has fuel facilities."

"Yeah, we sucked gas pretty heavily coming down here," Warrick said. "We have to refuel before we can head back."

"I'm going to head over there and pick them up," Reaper said. "We'll drive down to the ranch from there."

Mackenzie and Warrick were already climbing into the Skymaster as Reaper finished his explanation to Hausmann. As they fired up the twin props, the still-warm engines caught instantly and quickly ran up to speed. The boxy plane taxied around until it was facing back along the runway and soon was in the air and heading west.

The Sierra Vista Municipal Airport shared its runway with the Libby Air Force Base and was only a twenty-mile flight from Tombstone. But Reaper had to drive well over thirty miles to get from one base to the other. The Sierra Vista airport was a nice modern facility. And sharing its space with the Air Force made the location very secure. It was just the kind of place that was great for storing a plane, but Reaper and his friends wouldn't have wanted to unload their cargo there under all of those official eyes. There would have been too many questions that could come up that they just didn't have the time to answer.

During the drive to the Dogbone Ranch, Reaper gave Mackenzie and Warrick a full rundown on what had been happening during his vacation. The two men listened intently to the man they looked to as their team's leader. There had been no question that they would come when Reaper had called. Now they were learning just what the specifics for that call were.

Pulling into the ranch, Reaper saw that there was another car in the parking area, a dusty 2002 Mustang with Nevada license plates. Reaper had never seen the car before, but he had a really good idea who had been behind the steering wheel all the way from Nevada.

"Rick, Rick Column!" Reaper said as he walked into the house.

Sitting at the bar with a beer in his hand was the man Reaper had called that morning. An ex-Army Ranger, Richard Column ran security for a number of men's entertainment clubs in Las Vegas. Several branches of the clubs were in Phoenix, Arizona, where Column had been earlier that day.

"Damn," Reaper said with a wide smile on his face, "I thought you were just going to call me back."

"Hey," Column said, "I didn't get your message until

early this afternoon. I made some calls back to Vegas to confirm some things. You said in your message that you were here at Hausmann's, so I figured I would just come down when I had the answers to your question."

After everyone was introduced around and had picked up a beer, coffee, or soft drink according to their tastes, Reaper went over the situation that was going on in the area.

The smiles were gone now, Reaper was deadly serious and it showed.

"So that's it," Reaper said. "We have a group of drug runners who have hooked up with terrorists. And to make matters worse, there's an ex-SEAL who's gone over to the dark side working for them. The word from Washington is to shut down the drug runners' pipeline and take the terrorists out of the equation.

"They have some very bad news in the way of gear stored across the border. Weapons, explosives, RPGs, and shoulder-fired antiaircraft missiles. The missiles are SAM-16s, as close to state of the art as there is on the international arms market. I don't have to tell you what could happen if a terrorist cell in the United States got their hands on those."

"There's more," Hausmann said, "this message was waiting for you on the computer."

Handing Reaper the computer printout, Hausmann leaned down on the bar top to wait while the other man read the message. Reaper's reaction was what he thought it was going to be.

"So, things go from really bad to worse," Reaper said as he slapped the paper down on the table. Column jumped a bit, startled at Reaper's reaction.

"This is from Washington," Reaper said pointing at the paper. "That footlocker I found over in the other mine fits in with some intelligence reports that have been building up. The thought is that al-Qaeda is looking to build a dirty bomb and detonate it in the United States. They want to cause a disruption of our elections just like they did in Spain with that train bombing."

"A dirty bomb?" Column said.

"That's a radiological device," Mackenzie said. "A bomb with an explosive core packed inside a container of radioactive isotopes or waste. Just about the dirtiest bomb you can make. It doesn't make a nuclear explosion, but it can spread radioactive crap around for miles. Set one off of the right size and makeup in the right place, and you could contaminate a city the size of New York."

"Or Washington, D.C.," Reaper said. "And apparently, these guys may have the right stuff to build that bomb with. Some of the intelligence reports list the isotopes as having come from those underground radioactive storage sites they found in Iraq, only the materials were moved before the war started."

"So much for them not finding any weapons of mass destruction in Iraq," Manors said.

"A dirty bomb isn't really a weapon of mass destruction," Mackenzie said. "It is a hell of a terror weapon, though."

"The only part missing from the puzzle is how the terrorists are financing their operation," Reaper said. "We took down one of their hawala banks last year, and a big one at that. The State Department, Treasury, and Department of Homeland Security have been combining their efforts to shut down the rest of al-Qaeda's money supply in the U.S. But they must be getting their funding somehow."

"That brings up what you asked me about earlier today," Column said. "If I knew of anything unusual that had happened with this Paul Stebbins character, especially if any Middle Easterners were involved."

"What have you got?" Reaper said turning to Column. His blue-gray eyes bored intently into Column's.

Boy, am I glad he's my friend, Column thought. Looking into those eyes is like staring down a pair of gun barrels. He was suddenly worried that what he had to tell Reaper might not be important enough to bother him with.

"Could be nothing," Column said after a moment, "but it sure was weird. A couple of weeks ago, we had an incident at one of the clubs in Vegas. There was a couple of guys there, one of them was this Stebbins character. He'd brought an Arab with him into the club who obviously had never been in one before, but was playing the part of a big-time spender and trying to blend in. He was trying to blend in so hard that he stood out like a sore thumb.

"To make it short, he broke the rules and touched one of the girls. He didn't know and obviously was scared to death when the girl called security over. The guy looked like he was coming unglued trying to apologize and not make a bad scene worse. Stebbins just kind of stood there with his thumb up his ass not knowing whether to run or stand. The girl was yelling at these two that she was going to have the police come and throw them both out.

"The Arab offered a stone to the girl as an apology. She saw the guy was completely red-faced over the whole thing and was sweating with fear. So she took the rock and said everything was okay. She didn't really believe him when he told her it was a diamond. But she took it and those two were escorted out of the club. No one really thought anything of it and I wasn't told until I called up and asked about things today.

"You see, the girl took the stone in and had it checked. Damned if it wasn't exactly what that guy told her it was, an uncut diamond. It's worth a couple of grand, minimum. She didn't want to tell anyone after that so that she could keep the stone. When I asked my people about it this morning, the whole story came out. It sounded unusual enough to fit what you had asked about."

"Blood stones," Hausmann said.

"What?" Reaper said.

"Blood stones. That's what they call the diamonds that have been coming out of the African mines that any one of a dozen rebel factions are holding. They're turning into one of the underground currencies of the world. Small, light, and very valuable for their size. Reports have a lot more guerrilla and terrorist groups than just al-Qaeda using them all around the world."

"Underground is right," Reaper said. "In this case, it looks like the diamonds were taken out of one mine just to end up in another on the other side of the world."

Chapter Twenty-four

The next morning was an organized blur of activity for each of the men at the ranch. Hausmann had gone with Warrick to open up the vault at the back of the garage and go over all of the hardware. Things would be repacked as necessary to fit everything they wanted to take onto the Prowlers. In spite of the work at hand, Warrick was fascinated by Hausmann's weapons collection in the vault. He thought taking the Gatling gun would have been an interesting idea at least. Mounting it on the Prowler would make a great picture.

In the garage, Manors was going over the Prowlers themselves. Mackenzie had decided to go with Column up to Phoenix in case there was any trouble with Diamondback in his signing for the Four Horsemen company. And, with two men in the car, they could switch off driving to keep either one from getting too tired.

Back in the ranch house, Reaper was in the kitchen going over all of the information they had at hand.

Even more materials had arrived from Washington and an express courier was delivering some specialized equipment to Diamondback's offices for Reaper and his men. One of Admiral Straker's men was hand-carrying some sophisticated radiation detection gear on a red-eye flight from D.C. Homeland Security could call on the Air Force to fly their people wherever and whenever necessary without questions. Straker had exercised that authority for this operation.

In addition to the specific information on the operation, Reaper had informed Straker about the situation with Pat Manors. The Border Patrol, now renamed U.S. Customs and Border Protection, was the mobile, uniformed law enforcement arm of the Department of Homeland Security. Manors was the perfect officer to be on detached duty and working undercover for Admiral Straker's office. That was going to be the situation as it would be officially recorded. No matter what happened, at least Reaper was able to make sure that Manors didn't lose his job over his loyalty to a friend or working with the Four Horsemen.

There still weren't any hot radiation sources that could be detected by monitoring satellites over the Northern Sonora countryside of Mexico, or in Southern Arizona. If the isotopes for a dirty bomb were in those areas, they were well shielded from detection.

Straker was informed about the unusual situation regarding an Arab and uncut diamonds in a men's club in Las Vegas. He had told Reaper that he would immediately put law enforcement units on the job investigating that situation.

The description Reaper had been able to give on the single suspected al-Qaeda operative he had seen get in the jeep at the Blue Star mine had been a good one. Straker was certain that a surveillance operation could be conducted that could bring down the entire cell. In addition to identifying those terrorists, the active cell could lead to others in the country. At the very least, they would cut off another source of funds for al-Qaeda and other terrorist operations in the United States. And the lady at the Heart Ranch could expect a visit from the DEA, thanks to a warrant based on Reaper's observations.

Reaper's discoveries had helped give Straker a reason to reinforce the security of the southern border of the United States. Straker was already twisting the arms of other government services and agencies to have men and equipment assigned to the area. Predator unmanned aerial vehicles (UAV) were being assigned to overfly the Arizona border with Mexico. The UAVs would publicly be observing for illegal activity along the border with Mexico. They would also be outfitted with sensor arrays to allow them to detect even some shielded radioactive materials.

That was everything that could presently be done with the information they already had. Anything further would come about in part because of what Reaper and his people found. The Four Horsemen, with their leader, had already proven themselves a valuable asset to the people of the United States. Now, Reaper was concentrating on making sure he did everything he could to bring all of his men back home.

Arriving back at the ranch late in the morning, Mackenzie and Column returned from Glendale with a truckload of gear. The back of Hausmann's pickup was full of huge rectangular black nylon bags.

"Damn, Column," Reaper said. "I send you out to do some shopping and you come back with the whole damned store!"

"It's fun going out with someone else's credit card," Column said with a big grin on his face.

Each pair of tactical operations bags held a full operator's kit. Everything needed to fully outfit one man from the underwear out was in the kits. Boots, body armor, flight suits, gloves, knee and elbow pads, flashlights, spare batteries, a high-quality gas mask, a chemical/biological protection oversuit, individual medical kit, even sunscreen was included in the kits. The only major items missing were communications, weapons, ammunition, and munitions. There was even a SpecOps cold-weather clothing kit that included socks in the package—though the men didn't think they would be using the rest of the clothing from the cold-weather kits, at least not for this operation.

Everyone lent a hand in carrying the bags in from the truck. The gear was piled up in the poolroom, which was rapidly turning into the staging area for their operations. Diamondback Tactical had placed numbered tags on the cases to match them up with each other, and identify the contents as to size according to the list Column had supplied.

A welcome addition to the gear pile were the Garmin 120 radios and extra batteries that Column had brought.

In addition, he had picked up a tactical team rappelling kit to augment the equipment Reaper had used the day before. This kit made sure that both Reaper and Hausmann would have a full rappelling harness, rope, and rope bag for their part of the mission.

The last thing Mackenzie brought out was a large sealed box that had been hand-delivered to him by a courier. The man had been waiting in a rented car at Diamondback Tactical until Mackenzie showed up. Then he personally transferred the box and completed his mission. When Reaper cut the seals with his Emerson knife and opened the box, the contents were sobering.

Admiral Straker had sent them two AN/VDR-2 radiac instruments. These were lightweight survey meters and dosimeters. The pouches the devices came in could fit on a belt or on the back of an assault vest. The probes attached by a coiled wire to the meters would detect very low levels of radiation when properly set. Instructions came with the meters along with spare batteries and six more devices.

Each man in the room received one of the six AN/UDT-13 radiac sets that had been delivered by the courier. The sets were smaller than a paperback book and came adjusted to sound an audible alarm if there was a radiation source nearby. They would also keep a record of the radiation dose the user had received.

The idea of facing hard radiation was a scary one. Each of the men around the room had faced danger at multiple times in their lives. But normally, that danger was a man with a weapon that they could fight back against. Radiation was silent, unseen, and deadly. They were all from the generation that had lived through the nuclear menace of the Cold War. Now, they were very likely going to be facing a new version of that nuclear menace, one designed to poison and spoil, not blast suddenly to eternity.

"This makes it about as real as it gets guys," Reaper said as he laid the devices out on the kitchen table. "We have enough gear to carry as it stands. Washington wouldn't have sent this equipment if they didn't feel we had a real chance of finding something. Warrick, Mackenzie, and I are in this for the long haul, pretty much no matter what. Manors, Column, and Hausmann, you three are strictly volunteers. You can back out now and there won't be any hard feelings at all. Glowing in the dark is not something you signed on for."

The banter and joking the guys had been doing among themselves earlier was noticeably absent in the room. All of them had been given military training at one time or another regarding radiation exposure. It was an insidious poison that couldn't be seen. And it killed slowly and painfully. They looked at one another, no man knowing the others' thoughts but suspecting that they were all thinking about the same concerns. No one wanted to face the danger, but no one felt they could back away.

The answer Reaper received from everyone in the room was direct and straightforward. It was a quiet group of men who each reached out and picked up one of the devices. After glancing at the boxes, each man put the device into his shirt pocket. It was an eloquent answer to Reaper's question, in spite of the fact that not a word had been spoken.

The rest of the gear was broken out of the bags and Column and Manors started setting up their pouches and Predator Level 3a armored assault vests according to their own preferences. Hausmann headed back to the vault to finish up there before he began setting up his gear. There were ammunition boxes and magazines he wanted to pull out for the rest of the team to use.

After going over the gear and paperwork for a few minutes, Reaper headed out to the vault to lend Hausmann a hand. He found Hausmann and Warrick deep in conversation about some of the hardware that was in the room. They didn't even notice Reaper standing in the doorway, or at least Warrick gave no sign of seeing him. With a long rectangular box on the floor in front of him, Hausmann was standing with his back to the door.

"My dad was only seventeen years old when he fought with the Marines against the Japanese on Iwo Jima," Hausmann was saying. "He carried a hell of a weapon, literally, an M2A1 flamethrower. Said it was the best weapon the Marine foot soldier had to get the Japanese when they were dug into caves and emplacements. Just a couple of years ago, both the Army and the Navy were looking at resurrecting flamethrowers for use in Afghanistan against al-Qaeda and Taliban forces in caves. I think we can put one to good use on this operation."

"Yeah," Reaper said, stepping into the vault, "but a flamethrower is a heavy weapon to carry. And a bitch to maneuver with quickly, as well. I'm sure your dad told you that, too."

"Oh, he did," Hausmann said, turning to include Reaper in the conversation. "He told me that he hated dragging those twin fuel tanks and gas tank on his back. Made him feel like a big target waiting to go up like a barbecue. Which is why I'm not suggesting I bring one of those along. This is a different animal, though."

Flipping the latches on the long box on the floor, Hausmann opened the lid. Lying in the box was a strange-looking weapon, if it was a weapon. The device was black and made of some kind of plastic or fiber material. When Reaper crouched down and touched it, it was hard but didn't really feel solid. More than anything, the device looked like a six-inch-thick black tube folded over on itself in a hairpin bend, half of a gigantic paperclip. There was a cover over the squared-off ends of the tube. A shoulder strap was secured to buckles at both ends of the weapon.

"Okay, I give up," Reaper said. "What is it?"

"It's an M8 portable one-shot flamethrower," Hausmann said. "It's reloadable or you can throw it away. They were developed from a late–World War II design and were only issued for a short time to the Marine Corps and the Army in the 1950s and early 1960s.

"It doesn't have a pressure tank, there's a gas-generating cartridge that fires when you pull the trigger. At the same time an igniter cartridge fires for the load. The whole weapon is only about a yard long and less than a foot wide. Weighs twenty-six pounds loaded with two gallons of thickened gasoline. And it will throw that napalm out to between fifty-five and sixty-five meters range for four seconds.

"I've had fresh ignition and gas cartridges specially loaded for it by my friends at the All Custom Firearms shop in Sierra Vista. There's a can of the powder to make the napalm for it there in the box."

"And you want to take it along on the operation?" Reaper said.

"Like my dad said, best thing for fighting caves and tunnels," Hausmann said. "Besides, it doesn't weigh but a few pounds more than an M60 machine gun, and I carried one of them often enough."

"Yeah, but I'll bet your dad wasn't talking about using it against a cave he was standing in," Reaper said. "Bring it along, if you want. If it slows you down, we can always cache it somewhere."

"It won't slow me down," Hausmann said. "Besides, it doesn't look like a single-shot weapon, at least not to anyone looking at the working end."

"So," Reaper said.

"Even al-Qaeda won't willingly face a flame-thrower," Hausmann said. "That's damned near insane. Touch this baby off and after people see it fire, they can't throw down their weapons and put their hands up fast enough if you point it at them."

"You can't argue with that," Warrick said.

"No," Reaper said, "and I wouldn't argue with a torch myself. So get it ready, if you're going to carry it. We jock-up and load the gear for a noon launch at the latest. The temperature outside is already getting close to the nineties and it's going to be a hot day. Make sure your hydration containers are full and tell the others the same thing."

Reaper's "hot day" prediction was looking to be right on the money. Actually none of the four men were really suffering from the heat, but it was hot in Southern Arizona this year. The dry heat didn't feel very bad to Mackenzie or Warrick, they had just come down from Northern Michigan where the humidity could be the real killer when it got hot. But everyone had to be protected from the sun and heat. The only really good thing that Reaper could see from the weather was that the cloudless blue sky and scorching sun would keep most people indoors wherever possible. And it would make the normal Mexican siesta time between 1:00 and 4:00 P.M. even more popular. If they were lucky, they could literally catch the people sleeping down at the hacienda.

The gear was reduced to a single tactical accessory bag for each man. That, combined with all of the heavy weapons, ammunition, and the fact that both Prowlers were going, meant that they would have to take both available pickups. Manors's truck would be able to carry the Prowler that he was going to use. An additional advantage was that Manors had a radio in his truck that picked up the Border Patrol frequencies. That could help them as they approached the border crossing.

Weapons and equipment had been strapped to the front and rear decks of both Prowlers. The weapons carrier with Mackenzie, Warrick, and Column was going to be pretty heavily loaded since it also carried the

Mark 19, tripod, mount, and Warrick's rifles. So all but one of the heavy ammunition cans went on Manors's vehicle. The last belt of 40mm grenades and its can went with the gun to ensure that there was at least some ammunition always with it on the same vehicle.

The explosives and packs that Reaper and Hausmann would take with them were on the truck with the armed Prowler. Column would ride with them to the dropoff point near the Heart Ranch. For this insertion, Reaper and Hausmann would have to walk the whole way to the Blue Star mine. Remembering the incident in the barn, Reaper was hoping that the heat of the afternoon would keep the reptiles in the sanctuary under their rocks and in their dens.

Everyone had abandoned the flight suits that came with the operators kits and were wearing 5.11 khaki tactical shirts and trousers. If they were stopped by law enforcement, the khakis would look a lot more normal than sage flight suits. That might be enough to get them past a sheriff's deputy without him asking to look under the tarps covering the beds of the pickups. The Prowlers and all of the gear would be a little difficult to explain.

Finally, every magazine was loaded and slipped in a pouch, every piece of gear checked and rechecked. Warrick had tested the zero on all of his rifles before packing them for the insertion. The TTR-700 was so quiet it was hard to notice when he fired it. The Chandler M40A3 was a loud enough normal rifle. But the muzzle blast from the Barrett .50-caliber rifle was massive.

Warrick only fired three rounds to check the weapon, but the echoes of the shots rang out down the riverbed and across the desert. For each blast, the triangular muzzle break threw part of the propellant gases back and to the side. Anyone standing next to Warrick would have found themselves hit by the wave of sound and gas, as if they were slapped on the whole front of their body by a big wet towel. The noise drowned out the sound of the nearly six-inch-long spent cartridges flying out of the ejection port and bouncing on the gravel. The dogs jumped up and barked their disapproval with each roar of the powerful Barrett.

For his weapons, Reaper was armed with a much smaller and quieter selection than Warrick was using. He had his M4A1 and customized Springfield Armory M1911A1. Inside his shirt he had the suppressed Glock 26 with the Gemtech Aurora suppressor. Over the 5.11 tactical shirt, Reaper had on the Predator tactical-level 3A armored vest. The vest was covered with the ammunition and gear pouches he had attached to the MOLLE (modular lightweight load-carrying equipment) attachment points that lined the outside surface of the Predator.

The vest would stop most submachine gun and handgun projectiles. To increase the armor level to stop rifle-caliber bullets, Reaper inserted the Cercom-enhanced ballistic plate that came with the kit. Now at least his chest was protected from hits by 7.62 and 5.56mm ball rounds.

The four magazine pouches were filled with three thirty-round magazines each for his M4A1. The twenty-eight rounds in each magazine plus the one in the weapon gave him 364 rounds for the carbine. Three magazines for the M1911A1 gave him an additional twenty-four rounds of firepower. The pistol was in a Safariland tactical holster strapped to his thigh. One of the M183 demolition kits along with the AN/VDR-2 radiac instrument went into the three-day assault pack on his back. The additional rappelling gear went in the same bag except for the harness that Reaper strapped around his waist. Other gear was secured in pouches and pockets on his vest and in his pants.

The rest of the men outfitted themselves in much the same way as Reaper had. Hausmann was carrying his MP5A3 with a dozen thirty-round magazines in his pouches and his Gemtech Raptor in a pouch if he needed it later. Manors had laid aside his Benelli shotgun for one of the M4/M203A1 carbines that Mackenzie and Warrick had brought with them. Mackenzie was using the other M4/M203 combination. Column decided against carrying a shoulder weapon. Instead, he would use the M240B 7.62mm machine gun or the Mark 19 grenade launcher as his main weapon.

The last weapon to go in the back of the pickup was Hausmann's M8 flamethrower. The rest of the guys were impressed when he told them just what it was, and what it could do. None of them could think of a more horrible weapon to face in combat.

With their weapons secured in the backs of the trucks, the men climbed into the cabs. The only special preparation that had been done by any of them for a worst-case scenario was that Hausmann had contacted a friend of his to come and take care of his dogs and livestock if anything happened to him. Reaper and his men had made their final arrangements a long time before. Since Manors was an active law-enforcement officer, he faced the possibility of not going home every day.

For his final instructions, Column's were the simplest of all. He had no one to leave anything to, so the instructions he had standing in place were to give a hell of a party at the best of his clubs in order to send him on his way.

Chapter Twenty-five

Both trucks left the Dogbone Ranch and headed south together. The drive to the dropoff point was quiet. Each man rode in the crowded cabs of the two trucks keeping council with his own thoughts. The pickup with Mackenzie, Warrick, and Column on board pulled over to the side of the road and parked in a grove of trees. The truck was well concealed from any curious eyes that might pass on the road. With the other pickup safely hidden, Manors drove Reaper and Hausmann to their insertion point.

Instead of going in along the same road they had already used twice, Reaper had chosen a smaller, unpaved road that ran along the eastern border of the reptile sanctuary. The same stream that they had followed before crossed under the road they were on. Pulling off the road, Manors had no trouble driving the four-wheel-drive truck along the almost-dry streambed. Finally, he came to a bend in the stream that

Reaper pointed out; he had marked the spot on the overlay he had done for the satellite map.

"This is the spot," Reaper said, "drop us off here and turn the truck around. We won't go on until we're sure you can head back."

"Okay," Manors said. There wasn't very much more to say at that point.

Taking their packs and tactical bags from the bed of the pickup, Reaper and Hausmann geared up while Manors turned the truck around. It took a little maneuvering, but he soon had the truck pointed back in the direction they had come from. For the trip in, Manors had kept the truck in two-wheel drive. If he got stuck, then he could switch into four-wheel to get himself out.

The truck now had the best chance of getting back to the other men. For Reaper and Hausmann, this meant a great deal as the Prowlers on the truck were there as planned fire support and backup. If things completely went to hell, the Prowlers would be able to carry Reaper and Hausmann back to the border along with everyone else. It would be a rough ride, but a whole lot better than walking.

"Okay," Reaper said to Manors, "it's 1315 hours. You've got ninety minutes to get into position on the ridge line overlooking the hacienda. We're going to be in place at the mouth of the Crystal mine by 1445 hours and contact you by radio. If you don't hear from us by 1530 hours, you're free to move in on your own."

"Okay," Manors said, "good luck to you."

Snapping his M4A1 to the Chalker attachment point on his Predator vest, Reaper turned to start up the hillside to the fence line. Hausmann slipped the shoulder strap of the flamethrower over his head and across his shoulder. His MP5A3 was already attached to the shackle of his Chalker attachment and hung down from his chest. He moved out after Reaper. Sitting in the truck, Manors watched them climb up the hill and out of sight before he drove off.

The hot sun beat down on both men as they climbed up to the fence line around the sanctuary. Pulling out his SwissTool, Reaper unfolded it and cut through the wires of the fence while Hausmann stood watch. They were the only thing moving within sight. The spotless sky showed only the brilliant disk of the sun and nothing else. Not even a buzzard flew high overhead.

That was a good sign, or at least not a bad omen as far as Reaper was concerned. Now that they were both finally on the move, neither man had anything to say to the other as they went past the fence and headed up along the ridge line.

Using one of the scattered concentrations of creosote bushes for cover, Reaper slipped up to the edge of the ridge line and looked down toward the entrance to the Blue Star mine. Pulling out the binoculars he had borrowed from Hausmann back at the ranch, Reaper focused in on the area around the mine. No movement met his eyes. The place looked just as it had when he was there only twenty-four hours ago.

The headset of the Liberator special forces communications system Reaper had over his ears did not interfere with his hearing at all. Except for a slightly muffled tone to the sound, Reaper could hear everything there was around him through the electronics in the headset. As Hausmann crawled up alongside him, Reaper could hear the other man's breathing as he lay there and watched the front of the mine. Wordlessly, Reaper handed him the binoculars. As Hausmann examined the mine, Reaper looked out across the area below the ridge.

There was nothing to be seen. It was as if they were approaching a ghost town. Reaper knew well enough that it was when things looked the safest that you could get into real trouble. So he never let his guard down. But the clock was running and they could only hold their position and look for a short time. Tapping Hausmann on the shoulder, Reaper pointed to the mine.

"We're going to cross the ridge just a little ways up from here," he said in a soft tone. It didn't matter that no one was in sight or hearing. The habits of decades of special-operations experience did not go away for a single mission.

"We can cross down to the mine under pretty good cover over there," Reaper pointed. "I'll take point."

Nodding his understanding, Hausmann handed Reaper back the binoculars and slipped over to the other side of the ridge, away from sight of the mine.

The men moved in a low crouch, their weapons in their hands, as they moved across the back side of the ridge. When Reaper headed up to the top of the ridge, Hausmann closed in behind him. They walked in single file, crouching and finally crawling the last distance up to the ridge.

Once Reaper cleared the top of the ridge, he got

back up into a crouch. As Hausmann took up a kneeling position next to Reaper, he tapped the other man on the leg. Feeling Hausmann's ready signal, Reaper headed down across the ridge, moving low and fast with his M4A1 held at the ready in both hands.

Once he had gone about a hundred feet, Reaper stopped and took up a kneeling position. Waving his nonfiring hand in a forward motion, Reaper signaled Hausmann that it was his turn to move ahead. While Reaper held watch, Hausmann moved up to him and passed him, heading down toward the mine. About halfway between Reaper and the mine, Hausmann stopped and crouched down to cover Reaper's advance.

At Hausmann's wave, Reaper moved up and forward on the last jump of their leapfrog movement. He reached the dry old wood of the shack around the entrance of the mine, and knelt down with his weapon up and ready. Once more, Reaper stayed silent and still, listening for the sound that would tell him they had been discovered. The time stretched out as the long seconds passed slowly.

Reaper was by far the more experienced of the two men. For Hausmann, just kneeling there and watching Reaper stand still was more than hard, it was torture. When you were moving, it was easy to just think about the task at hand. Waiting drew the time out and you had to be careful not to let your mind wander and think about the things that could happen. That's how you got scared, thinking about what could happen. Watching Reaper was like seeing a predator, a great hunting wolf, moving in on its prey. For a moment, Hausmann felt like a small dog that had attached itself to the wrong pack. He almost had to physically shake his head to drive out the odd thoughts and feelings.

At the wordless count of sixty, Reaper signaled Hausmann to come up to the wall. The time had seemed an eternity to the man who had been kneeling on the side of the ridge, feeling exposed and alone while Reaper listened and watched. When Hausmann was once more at his side and squeezed his shoulder, Reaper went forward to the old door he had slipped through the day before.

The doorway looked to be undisturbed from when he had left it. Reaper could see the slender dry twig was in place. He had left the indicator leaning against the low door when he had come back through it the day before. Since it was still leaning up against the gray wood, Reaper could be fairly certain that the door had been undisturbed since he had last been here. The lock hasp was in place, but Reaper knew that the nails that had held it were in the brush behind him. It was an easy, and silent, matter to open the door and wave Hausmann through.

Then Reaper bent over and scuttled through the door. It was an uncomfortable but quiet way to gain access to the interior of the mine. Still secured across the front of the mine was the tall steel gate and impressive lock and chain.

Inside the Blue Star mine only Reaper had any knowledge of what they would see ahead of them. Walking silently next to Reaper, Hausmann looked into the beds of the Gator vehicles when Reaper pointed to them. Not a word was spoken as Hausmann looked at the black stains against the green paint.

As they approached the elevator shaft, Reaper pulled out his flashlight and pushed the back button. The brilliant beam illuminated the entire area around them. The white beam was shining on the elevator shaft, but the side light was more than enough to see the cable system going up over the pulleys at the top of the shaft and over to the winch at the side. Leaning out over the deep shaft, Hausmann could see the iron staples that made up the ladder driven into the rock.

Slipping his light back into his pocket, Reaper let the dazzle leave his eyes before going over to the ladder. Stepping out into the shaft, he slipped over the side and disappeared. Hausmann quickly followed.

The hundreds of steps took them deep down into the earth. Astonished to see that the shaft was actually growing lighter rather than darker, Hausmann looked down. As Reaper had been the day before, Hausmann was still surprised to see the lights, even though Reaper had told him about them. The mine took on an otherworldly appearance as they kept moving down into the light, past the rock walls and the interminable iron steps.

"Something else, isn't it," Reaper whispered as they both stood at the bottom of the ladder.

"Even though you described it," Hausmann said, "it's still incredible to actually see it for yourself."

"I know," Reaper said. "Come on, it gets even more amazing further on."

The two men moved quickly but cautiously down the tunnel. Knowing better than to question the other man's experience, Hausmann just followed Reaper's pace. Going at almost a jog, Reaper wanted to get out of the tunnel as soon as they could. In spite of not expecting anyone to come along from the southern end of the tunnel, Reaper still hated the trapped feeling the rock walls gave him.

When the tunnel moved downward to meet the cave, Reaper slowed to a walk. As they passed into the huge open area far underground, Reaper just stood on the trestle for a moment as Hausmann looked about them.

Hausmann thought the cave was as incredible as Reaper had. The natural beauty and majesty of the place filled him with awe. The lights along the tracks shone out across the vast area and reflected from a thousand points of crystal or water. Then, the faint stench of decay reached Hausmann's nose.

As they went forward, the stench grew stronger. Finally, Reaper stopped and pointed. The yawning black opening of the pit was just a short distance away. As Hausmann subconsciously started to walk toward the pit, Reaper reached out a hand.

Normally, Reaper never interfered with another partner's experience. It was up to each man to learn what he could about the world around him. That was something Reaper fully believed. But the sight of those bodies was something Reaper would see to his last day. It wasn't necessary that Hausmann also view that vision of hell.

"Don't," Reaper said softly.

Looking at his friend, Hausmann thought he knew the favor he was doing him. Nodding, he turned and the two men once again moved out across the cave floor. Under the hanging stalactites and around the growing cones of the stalagmites, they jogged along the route of the underground, very underground, railway.

———

After dropping Reaper and Hausmann off at their insertion site, Manors carefully drove back along the track he had made coming in. The trio waiting at the other truck had a map overlay on which Manors had marked the likely border crossing points. That map could get the guys into Mexico, but it would be a whole lot better if he took them across. And he couldn't do that if he got stuck or had a flat tire.

If the two Prowlers didn't get across the border and set up their fire support, Reaper and Hausmann would have to rely on the limited backup plan. The very least the two men could do would be to blow the mine entrance, denying its use to the drug cartels and the terrorists. At the same time, they would destroy the munitions and weapons stored there.

Nailing the drug cartel was of great appeal to Manors personally. He had been fighting the drug and people smugglers across the border for years. Taking out a powerful drug cartel and disrupting their operations was an accomplishment, one he wanted to be able to say he had a hand in. Of course if they broke up a terrorist operation at the same time, that would be icing on the cake even if it would probably classify things so much that he couldn't talk about them.

When Manors drove up in his truck, Mackenzie, Warrick, and Column all breathed an unconscious sigh of relief. The mission was a go and their teammates were on their way. Pulling his truck up to the side of the other, Manors leaned out his open window.

"Okay," Manors said. "Now it's our turn, follow me."

Having been standing by the open passenger door of the pickup, Warrick climbed back into the cab. There was more room in the cab of Manors's truck, so Column trotted over and climbed in with him.

The two Prowlers and piles of equipment in the back of the trucks made big mounds under the secured tarps. But none of the few drivers they passed on the road paid them the least amount of attention. Turning off of State Route 92 near Palominas, Manors started down some dirt roads that finally turned into little more than twin ruts in the gravel. They were about three miles from the Heart Ranch area when they started approaching a dry streambed that Manors was familiar with.

It was one of the crossing points Manors knew of closest to where Reapers and Hausmann had inserted. At that time of day, there shouldn't be any Border Patrol agents watching the area—if the schedule hadn't changed. He knew the men who normally patrolled the area and they didn't like it as a spot for daytime crossings. At night, things would be a different story. But Manors expected to be back long before that time came. And if he wasn't back by then, then he probably wouldn't be in a position to care one way or another.

There were several washes along the streambed that cut deeply into the banks. Pulling his truck up into one of the larger washes, Manors stopped and parked. The other truck had enough room to pull up alongside of Manors and stop. The wash was one of the best places they would have to hide the trucks and unload the gear. For just a second, Manors stopped with his hand on the door latch. Now was the last chance he had to turn back. But others were now depending on him. The decision had been made, and Manors opened his door and stepped out.

The Prowlers were quickly unloaded and checked over. If they were stopped, there wouldn't be a chance in hell of their explaining that they were just joyriding around the desert. No Border Patrol agent or sheriff's deputy would believe a line like that, not with all of the hardware they had on the Prowlers. The men strapped on their gear and weapons. Once they were all ready, Manors started out to lead the way.

The border itself in the area was a twin row of tall cyclone fence topped with razor wire. It was hard to climb and hard to cut through. Sensors in the wire would know if the wire was cut. And there were ground sensors scattered all around the desert as well. Manors knew the locations of the ground sensors, and he could bypass the fence alarms long enough for the two Prowlers to get through. Watching the coyotes over the years had taught him quite a few of their tricks. This was the first time he was actually putting them to active use.

The ground by the border itself was mostly flat and open to observation for a long way. There were well-maintained roads on both sides of the border so that law enforcement from either country could respond quickly. In the distance a few miles away, Manors knew there was a watchtower that they were in plain sight of. It wasn't supposed to be manned at that time, but things change.

They had to get through the fence quickly to cut down on the random chance that someone would see them. There could always be an odd aircraft flying overhead just sightseeing, or some real off-roaders running near the border. Mr. Murphy always picked his own time and place to slip up and screw with a plan. The trick was to cut back on leaving chances open for him to work.

Pulling up to the fence, Manors got out of his Prowler and pulled a small box from his pack. From the front of the vehicle, he took a pair of thirty-inch-long bolt cutters and a roll of wire. The second Prowler pulled up and Warrick climbed out. He went over to Manors's vehicle and got into the driver's seat. When Manors opened the fence he would have to go to the second wall and cut that one open as well. Warrick would follow Mackenzie through into Mexico to save time.

To speed up the penetration of the fence line, Column also got out of Mackenzie's Prowler and picked up another set of bolt cutters. Going up to the fence, he watched as Manors fiddled with the little box and hooked it up to the wires. Once the lights were on to

his satisfaction, Manors looked up at Column and nodded. The bolt cutters would make quick work of even
the tough, hardened wire of the fence. As Column
started cutting from the bottom of the fence up,
Manors took his cutters and started from the top down.
Soon, they had a wide flap of the fencing free and tied
it back on either side with the wire Manors had.

The second fence was also quickly penetrated. The
Mexican side of the border had very few sensors along
its length. But there was still the random Mexican border patrol to worry about. Not all of the sweat that was
pouring down the men's faces came from the heat of
the desert. When the two flaps were both up, Warrick
and Mackenzie barreled through with the Prowlers.
Before releasing the flaps, Manors recovered his little
box. They might need it again to cross back through
the fence line. For now, they had just conducted an
armed invasion of a sovereign country. That thought
went through Manors's mind as he tied the flaps of the
fence together quickly with his coil of wire.

Crossing over the Mexican desert, the two Prowlers
made very good time. There were few roads in the area
and that made for much less traffic than on the U.S.
side. They could drive along at speed and make up
some time. Even so, both Mackenzie and Manors were
careful in their choice of travel routes. If the vehicles
were to break down, they would all be in a world of
hurt, both the men on the Prowlers, and their partners
far down in the tunnels under the earth.

The only Mexican town of any size around them was
Naco, some ten miles to the east of their present loca-

tion. The bright screens of the Garmin Rino GPS loca-
tors and radios showed their locations in reference to
the roads and towns around them. That gave little detail
of their immediate surroundings showing on the
screens. Looming up ahead of them was a line of peaks
and ridges. From there, they would be looking down
on the Crystal mine and the hacienda.

It was a long thirty-minute drive for the two Prowlers
to cover the distance from where they cut through the
border to the side of the hill where they could see the
hacienda. They had slowed down to barely a crawl as
they approached the top of the ridge. Stopping near
some brush, Manors got out and slipped up to the top of
the ridge, crawling the last few feet on his belly. He
didn't need binoculars to see the mine and the hacienda
less than half a mile away. Looking to the west, he
could see the small saddle, a depression in the ridge,
where Reaper suggested they could set up the fire base.
They had hit the target almost dead on.

Slipping back to the vehicles, Manors quickly told
the others what he had seen. Getting back in his
Prowler, he pulled out ahead, again moving slowly so
he didn't raise a plume of dust. The saddle was an obvious landmark, and there was a large stand of brush
and cactus filling the center of it and spilling down to
either side.

Slowing the Prowlers near the brush, the two vehicles carefully approached the top of the ridge. In the
center of the saddle was a ravine cut by the intermittent
heavy rains that hit the area. That ravine would be
where they would set up the Mark 19 and park the

Prowlers. The dusty yellow-tan paint on the two vehicles was intended to blend them in with the desert sand. It was doing its designed job very well.

They were still inside of their schedule as the Prowlers came to a stop. The ravine opened up to a wide wedge at this point. There was a clear field of fire leading out to the west and east. The hacienda was about half a klick, 500 meters, off to their left. To the right, about 700 meters away according to Warrick's trained snipers eyes, was the opening of the mine.

With the Prowlers parked under the concealment of some tall brush, Warrick moved forward along the ground to find his preferred sniper's position. The rest of the team began unpacking and setting up the Mark 19 grenade launcher. The big gun was actually a machine gun that fired high-velocity 40mm grenades out to a range of 2,200 meters. It was a crew-served weapon, far too big for one man to move on his own. Unfolded, the tripod was almost as big as Mackenzie was tall.

Carrying the tripod forward, Column was moving in close to a fully bent-over position as he went past the cover of the brush. There was an open spot where he could set up the tripod and man the gun. The only real limiting factor was that it was about twenty feet from the Prowlers. That meant the heavy gun and ammunition boxes had to be brought forward. But at least the position was downslope of the vehicles. That meant that when the M240B machine gun was swung out and down the ravine, it would be firing well over his head when it opened up.

While Column was unfolding the tripod legs and stomping them firmly into the ground, Mackenzie brought up the M64 gun cradle. As they completed setting up the mount, Warrick kept a careful watch out over the countryside. He had set up his Chandler M40A3 rifle by laying it across his three-day assault pack. The ten-power Unertl sight on the M40A3 closely matched that on the Barrett .50-caliber gun, so Warrick could switch between them easily. Through the glass of the telescopic sight, he watched for movement at the hacienda as his teammates set up the grenade launcher. He would continue to watch while they worked.

The Mark 19 gun and its tripod mount made for a very heavy gun to be hand-carried and set up. Once Column had the gun locked onto the tripod, Manors brought up the first box of ammunition.

The steel ammunition box crunched into the gravel and twigs as Manors set it down. Flipping up the latches on both ends of the lid, Column opened the box as Manors went back for another. Once he had the end of the first belt locked into place in the feed tray of the Mark 19, Column quietly said: "Gun's up!"

That phrase told Warrick that he could now go back to the Prowler and bring up his Barrett. For a moment, Warrick hesitated over leaving his M40A3 lying in position. But he had to bring up the other weapon. As he was starting to rise, Manors crawled up beside the sniper. Dragging the black case of the Barrett behind him, Manors left it by Warrick, patted the man on the shoulder, and crawled back to the Prowlers.

Warrick looked at the black case for a moment and nodded his head. His opinion of Manors was already high enough because of the man's job, it had just climbed a few notches.

Warrick opened the case. The big gun lay nestled in cutouts cast in place for it in the case liner. Pulling out the big rifle, Warrick extended the bipod legs and set the rifle down. Reaching back into the case, he drew out the long upper receiver with the fluted barrel retracted into it and the Unertl scope secured to the rail across the top of it. He had just finished assembling the big gun when Manors called out softly:

"We have vehicles coming out of the hacienda, and they look like they're heading toward the mine."

Chapter Twenty-six

There was a dirt road running between the hacienda and the mine, and another that crossed it heading off to the south. Manors had watched the front gate of the hacienda open and a white Chevrolet Suburban SUV drive out with a second one right behind it. The two vehicles passed the road heading south and continued on toward the mine just over a kilometer away.

Warrick set the assembled but still unloaded Barrett down and immediately turned to his M40A3. He had the Suburban in his crosshairs in seconds.

"Targets up," Warrick said loudly enough that he could be heard back at the Prowlers.

Mackenzie had keyed the boom mike on his headset and was trying to contact Reaper and Hausmann at the mine.

"Death, this is Famine. You have incoming. I repeat, you have incoming."

Mackenzie repeated his warning call several times and heard nothing but static over the headset.

"Targets approaching the halfway point," Warrick said.

Mackenzie had a hard decision to make. If he let the vehicles through to the mine, whoever was in them could discover Reaper and Hausmann. But neither of the vehicles had posed an immediate threat to the men on the hill. They could be people on a picnic, or a bunch of armed drug smugglers. There was nothing else around anywhere that might appeal to a civilian, and the rest of that road only led to the mine.

"Take out the lead vehicle," Mackenzie said.

Leading the Suburban in the reticle of his sight, Warrick squeezed off a round. The M40A3 bucked as the sound of a shot rang out. Having aimed at the driver of the lead vehicle, Warrick had confidence that his shot would at least startle the man behind the dark tinted glass, if not kill him outright.

As he rode out the recoil and quickly brought his sight back onto the target, Warrick was astonished to see that nothing, absolutely nothing, appeared to have happened to the Suburban. Working the bolt of his M40A3, Warrick aimed and pulled the trigger a second time. The handloaded 190-grain Sierra hollow-point, boat-tailed match bullet zipped from the muzzle of the M40A3 at over 2,600 feet per second. Crossing the nearly 400 meters between the muzzle of the rifle and the target in just over half a second, the jacketed projectile smashed into the tinted glass of the driver's window, and spent its energy vainly against the thick, armored window behind it.

Seeing that Warrick was not having any effect on the large SUV, Mackenzie stepped over to the M240B mounted on the Prowler. Swinging the big gun around, he cocked the bolt back and fired off a long hammering burst at the lead SUV. As the 7.62mm projectiles smashed along the side of the Suburban, a number of them hit the long side window in the back, smashing the tinted glass and ripping it away. Everyone on the hillside could see the bright white stars that showed where the bullets had hit armor.

Pushing the M40A3 away from him, Warrick rolled over to where the Barrett sat on its bipod. Snatching up the back of the big gun, Warrick grabbed a magazine from the storage case that had a wide piece of tape around it. Inserting the magazine and locking it into place, he yanked back on the bolt handle, releasing the massive bolt to be driven forward by its springs, strip the top round from the magazine, and chamber it in the barrel of the weapon.

Swinging the big rifle around, Warrick could see that the lead Suburban was heading down into a low spot in the road, it would soon be out of his line of fire. Taking quick aim, he placed the crosshairs on the back of the SUV. He squeezed the trigger and the huge gun thundered in response.

The tape that Warrick had placed around the base of his magazines showed by touch and sight which ones were loaded with the Mark 211 ammunition. The projectile to the round was over two and a half inches long and carried a tungsten carbide penetrator. They were armor piercing and carried a small explosive and incendiary charge to boot. They were the nastiest thing you could put out of a rifle.

The tungsten carbide penetrator made quick work of smashing through the armor on the back of the Suburban. The three follow-on rounds that Warrick rapid-fired from the semiautomatic Barrett also punched through the back of the Suburban just as it dropped out of his sight. He watched the last round smash the back window to splinters as it hit.

The following vehicle was still an available target. The driver had put his vehicle into reverse and was backing up as quickly as he could. It wouldn't be enough to stop the prior Marine scout-sniper from taking him out. Swiveling the Barrett on its bipod, Warrick saw the window of the other Suburban fill his sight. He squeezed off the trigger and the thunder of the big .50 sounded out once more.

Sealed off from the world in his bubble of concentration, and with his ears protected by the electronics and mufflers in his Liberator headset, Warrick didn't hear the rounds snapping by overhead. But the rest of his teammates did. The blast of the Barrett kicked up more dust and debris than any of the other weapons the men had. That rising cloud of dust was enough of a target for whoever was in the hacienda to open fire at it with automatic weapons.

As the bullets snapped by, Mackenzie ducked down and made another decision.

"Open fire on the hacienda," he said. The occupants of the building had decided that shooting was okay. They would soon learn their mistake.

At the Mark 19, Column heard the command over the earphones of his headset. He cranked the cradle of the Mark 19 over on its tripod and pulled the trigger. The big gun thumped and rocked back as it fired. One high-explosive grenade headed downrange while another chambered up and fired. The slow knocking sound of the Mark 19 did not reflect the power of the weapon. The explosions of the grenades far downrange were a more realistic show of what it could do. Roof tiles of the hacienda shattered from the violent explosions. Thousands of steel fragments were joined by hundreds of red shards of broken clay tearing through the air as the M385 projectiles smashed into the buildings.

———

Far down in the mine, Reaper and Hausmann had finally reached the elevator shaft in the Crystal mine. This shaft had the shaky wooden ladder that led up to the floor of the elevator cage hundreds of feet above. It was not going to be an easy climb, and this time Reaper had a lot more equipment with him to add to his weight. Hausmann was even heavier—packing the flamethrower as well as a load equal to Reaper's. Using the elevator was still out of the question. Looking at Hausmann, Reaper smiled.

"No other way to go," he said, "start climbing."

"You needed a lawyer for this?" Hausmann said as he looked up.

"Only to say I wasn't crazy," Reaper said as he started to climb.

"Do let me know if you can find one who'll say that," Hausmann said.

The tension was barely broken by the banter between the men. The climb was nerve-wracking and Hausmann was more than glad that the plan called for them to seal the tunnel and bring down the mine. At least that would mean he wouldn't have to climb back down that damned ladder.

As Hausmann stepped up to another board, the old lumber his other foot was on finally snapped under the weight. His fall jerked to a stop as his hands clenched down on the boards they were holding. For a moment, Hausmann was hanging out over the drop, only being held up by his two hands and the dry, old boards they were gripping. As Reaper stopped his climb and started back down, Hausmann called out.

"No, I'm okay," he said softly in a hoarse voice, "keep going."

He had his feet back under him, both of them on separate rungs of the ladder. Just then, a long drink from his hydration pack sounded very good to Hausmann, but there was no way that he would let even one hand release the ladder in order to pull over the drinking tube to where he could reach it with his mouth. With a deep breath, he continued upward.

Climbing onto the elevator platform, Reaper reached down to his partner. He grabbed hold of the shoulder strap to the M8 flamethrower with one hand while the other held a strong grip of the lifting strap at the top of Hausmann's pack. With some of the weight off of him, Hausmann let go of the ladder with one hand long enough for Reaper to lift the flamethrower from his back and pull it up and onto the platform. Clambering up, Hausmann joined his partner on the flat boards of the elevator platform.

"Oh, that was way too much fun," he said as he pulled the drinking tube of his hydration pack into his mouth. Reaper just smiled as he watched Hausmann drinking.

"Welcome to Mexico," he said. "Don't drink the water."

That bad joke brought a weak grin to Hausmann's face. The two men stood up and moved off the elevator platform. As they walked down the tunnel, Reaper heard a noise coming in from the entrance to the mine. The rolling echo of thunder sounded faintly. Only it wasn't thunder, it was the sound of Warrick's .50-caliber sniper rifle.

As the two men ran forward, the shadows at the front of the mine resolved themselves into running bodies. One man came around the corner of the tunnel and looked straight at Reaper and Hausmann standing there. With a strangled cry in Spanish, he tried to raise the Galil SAR he had hanging at his side. Long before the mercenary could bring the weapon to bear, Reaper and Hausmann both opened fire.

The short blast of fire from Hausmann's MP5A3 was almost drowned out by the much louder roar from Reaper's M4A1. Both streams of projectiles slammed into the mercenary, driving him back against the tunnel wall where he hit, and slowly crumpled in a heap on the floor.

Stopping at the sound of the gunfire, Masque watched as one of his men was killed not fifteen feet from where he was standing. The other three men with him were heavily armed, but they were no match for the firepower that had come in and smashed the back of their armored Suburban. The threat ahead looked like one they could deal with, and they had the tools and skills to do that.

As Reaper and Hausmann crouched down at the sides of the tunnel, they began inching back to find cover. They were badly exposed. There was nothing more than the support timbers to take cover behind. Then there was a metallic tinking sound that made Reaper's blood run cold. He recognized the sound of a safety lever being released even before the green-painted ovoid came bouncing along the floor of the mine.

"Grenade!" he shouted as he grabbed Hausmann by the shoulder. Turning, the powerful SEAL almost threw the man toward the one side tunnel behind them. Then he too ran toward it.

Both men dove into the tunnel, hitting the floor with their weapons cradled in their arms, protecting them from the impact. They didn't have long to wait to see if the mine still had strong supports.

The roar of the exploding grenade echoed through the tunnel. For Reaper and Hausmann, it was like being inside a huge drum with a giant madman pounding on it. The sharp-edged steel fragments from the grenade spattered harmlessly across the rocks behind them. Pebbles and dust fell from where they had been shaken down from overhead. But besides the shattering of a dozen or so lightbulbs casting the mine into near darkness, little other damage had been done. That was not going to hold true for the eventual grenade that came into the small side room.

"Goddamn, that one was close," Hausmann said. "These guys are nuts using grenades in here."

Their bodies' reaction to the stress of combat had helped save both men. The headsets of the Liberator communications systems had saved both Reaper and Hausmann's hearing. But they were still shaking from the aftereffects of the shock wave as they got up from the floor. Enough of the lights had survived the explosion to illuminate the mine as the heavier dust and smoke settled.

"The next one could be a whole lot worse," Reaper said as he checked his weapon over for obvious damage, "nuts doesn't come close to describing these lunatics throwing grenades." When Hausmann looked at him questioningly, Reaper nodded at the boxes and crates that were stacked up nearby.

Reading the Cyrillic alphabet was not among Hausmann's skills, but he could recognize it. There were a few words on the wooden boxes from Czechoslovakia that he could read—SEMTEX. That was the name of the plastic explosive used by the old Iron Curtain states of the Soviet Union. The stuff was popular with terrorists all over the world.

Even if he hadn't been able to read part of the labels

on the Semtex cases, the crates marked: CHARGE DE-
MOLITION BLOCK M5A1 2½-LB COMP C-4 were very read-
able. And Reaper had said there were even more cases
of explosives in the tunnel. A grenade going off near
the boxes would literally bring the house down, or at
least cave in the mine. Either way, Reaper and Hausmann would be ground into the dust after they were
blown apart.

Slipping up to the corner where the side tunnel met
the mine, Reaper tried to get a look at just who and
what they were facing. Suddenly ducking his head
around the corner of the tunnel, Reaper was forced
back by the swarm of bullets chipping the rock face all
around him. He stuck the muzzle of his M4A1 around
the corner and fired off a long burst, emptying his magazine. Reaper had no real hope that the rounds would
hit anything, but they should help slow down the advance of the others.

He sat back down with a thump as the pack on his
back hit the wall behind him. Striking the magazine release of his M4A1, Reaper dumped his empty magazine. Pulling a full magazine from a pouch, he slapped
it into place in the magazine well. Hitting the bolt release on the left side of the weapon, Reaper completed
reloading the M4A1 as the bolt slid home with a metallic crack.

Crouching low, Reaper once more ducked around
the corner, barely exposing his face as he pointed his
weapon. The muzzle of the M4A1 flashed fire as he
sprayed rounds down the tunnel. There was a high-
pitched scream as one man near the mouth of the mine

threw up his hands and fell back. The Galil SAR in his hands fired in a single long burst as the dying man's finger convulsed on the trigger. Masque and the others with him had to duck back or face the danger of being hit from the wild spray of bullets. Reaper had just bought himself a moment's time as Masque and his men tried to regroup.

Only knowing that he had hit one of the gunmen facing them, Reaper ducked back into the side tunnel. Again, he reloaded his weapon, dumping the almost empty magazine for a fresh, full one.

"Shit," Reaper cursed, "these guys will just keep chipping away at us until one of them gets close enough to pitch a grenade in here."

"They want to meet Allah," Hausmann said, "let's arrange things for them."

As he spoke, Hausmann slipped the shoulder strap of the flamethrower from around his neck and across his chest. Slinging the weapon at his right side, Hausmann laid his MP5A3 down onto the floor of the tunnel. With the M8 ready to fire, Hausmann looked at Reaper.

"This thing could suck all of the air right out of here," Hausmann said. "Take us out along with the bad guys."

"Shit happens," Reaper said, "toast 'em."

The Galils in the mercenaries hands started to fire down the tunnel, alternating between one man and then the other. Under the cover of this spaced-out fire, they were trying to move forward, leapfrogging as one man lay down a field of fire and the other moved. Coming up behind them, Masque prepared to take out his opponents. He was certain that he could toss a pair of grenades just in front of the tunnel. That way their fragmentation would kill or badly wound the man who was shooting at him, but not detonate the explosives stacked farther back in the tunnel.

Projectiles chipped the rocks all around the mouth of the side tunnel on a constant basis. There wasn't a chance for Reaper to fire back. Careful of the incoming fire, Hausmann stood and stepped past Reaper. Snugged up against the side of the tunnel, he swung the M8 out away from him. Tripping the trigger, Hausmann stuck the front of the flamethrower out into the main tunnel at an angle. The ignition cartridge fired putting a small stream of sparks out in front of the weapon. At the same time, the pressure generating charge ignited. Pushed by the hot gases, a rubber ball was driven up the tubelike tank of the flamethrower, driving the thickened gasoline out of the nozzle, past the burning ignition cartridge.

With a terrifying roar, a black-edged stream of orange flame shot out of the end of the M8. The first impact of the stream was against the far wall of the tunnel at an angle where it splashed and bounced up toward the entrance. Twisting while the weapon was firing, Hausmann pushed it out farther into the main tunnel. Finally, Hausmann stepped all the way out into the tunnel with the roaring M8 now held tightly against his right hip. Not willing to allow his friend to face the enemy alone, Reaper stepped behind Hausmann and raised his M4A1. He didn't have to bother.

For four long seconds, two gallons of thickened gasoline streamed out of the end of the flamethrower. Moving only a little, Hausmann played the roaring stream of flame along the tunnel, up and down the walls. For those four seconds, the entrance area of the Crystal mine became the mouth of Hell.

Standing upright with two grenades in his hands, Eduardo Masque bore the brunt of the flamethrower's effect. So quickly that his brain couldn't even process the searing pain, Masque was killed; his hair flashed away in an instant. For a tiny moment of time, the scars on his face stood out in stark contrast to the skin around them. Then the flesh on his face and arms blackened and crisped. The final scream of rage his hate forced from his lungs was lost in the roar of the flames.

The corpse stood there encased in flames, even after the flamethrower had ceased functioning. The M8 was only a single-shot weapon, but what the one shot did was incredible. The front of the Crystal mine was a wall of flame.

The heat and gases of the burning fuel rushed out of the mine, away from where Reaper and Hausmann stood. The huge network of tunnels and caverns acted like a giant chimney. The top of that chimney was the mouth of the Crystal mine, and the flames were going out of it—saving Reaper and Hausmann.

There was still a danger in the tunnel besides the fire. In spite of the heat, the two M33 baseball grenades that Masque had been holding had not detonated. The corpse fell backward and thumped onto the ground. The impact popped the safety levers off both grenades. Again, Reaper shouted "Grenade!" only this time, Hausmann was already moving.

The explosions from the two grenades once more shook the tunnel. This time there was a rain of rocks and pebbles coming down from the ceiling. They had to move quickly to keep from being buried in the mine. But before they escaped, Reaper still had an important part of his mission to perform.

Getting up from the floor, he pulled his flashlight from its pouch. The rugged little light went on when he pressed the switch, the beam hazy as it flashed out through the dust. Swinging the pack from his back, he dumped the rest of the rocks and dirt that had piled up on it off onto the floor.

"Give me your explosives," Reaper said, "and watch the tunnel."

Hausmann pulled the pack off his back and handed it to Reaper. Shaking his head from the effects of the explosions, he moved to the mouth of the side tunnel and looked out into the gloom and dust. The rest of the lightbulbs had shattered, throwing the mine behind Hausmann into darkness. Only the glow of the bright sunlight outside, dimmed by all the dust in the air, illuminated the main tunnel of the mine. If any of the men they had been facing were still alive, Hausmann would see them silhouetted against the light.

Working fast, Reaper twisted the back of his Sure-Fire light, locking the switch in the On position. With the light held between his teeth and his M4A1 hanging down from its Chalker attachment, Reaper began placing his explosives.

There was not going to be any style or skill in this demolition job, Reaper was just going to blow the charges along with all of the explosives stored in front of him. Opening up the canvas top of the M183 demolition charge, he pulled out his Gerber DET 600 multipliers. With a snap of his wrist, he extended the pliers' head and unfolded the tool. Swinging out the detonator awl, Reaper stuck the pointed steel rod into the soft plastic explosive in the demolition charge.

Having poked two holes in the explosive, Reaper did the same thing to Hausmann's charge. Folding the tool back up, Reaper slipped it into his pocket and took a deep breath of the dusty air. In spite of the almost choking dust, Reaper calmed for a moment. He couldn't allow himself to make a mistake now. Pulling out a Kevlar pouch from his pack, Reaper opened it and took out a pair of electrical blasting caps.

The leads of the caps were already cross connected. Reaper slipped them into the holes in the C4 and then did the same thing with the other charge. Leading the wires back, he attached them to the terminals of his detonation timer. The charges were set under several of the explosive cases. Opening the top case of a stack, Reaper took out the nonelectric firing device that he had assembled with Hausmann's fuse.

Two twenty-foot coils of fuse had been attached to a pair of M7 blasting caps and M60 igniters already crimped to a fuse. That gave Reaper a ten-minute delay on the caps. Once more using his Gerber DET, Reaper punched cap wells through the orange wrappers of the Semtex blocks. Inserting the caps, he pulled the fuse igniters. In the beam of his flashlight, Reaper could see the lazy trails of smoke rise up from the burning fuse. Stuffing everything into the case, Reaper set it on the ground and stacked other boxes around it. Then he turned to the electric timers.

The red buttons on the cover of the black plastic box let him adjust the delay for the detonator. Pushing the buttons until 0–09 read on the dial, he hit the start switch. As the numbers on the nine-minute delay started to count down, he pulled the final safety pin from the cover of the arming switch. Flipping up the switch, Reaper armed the delay.

The rest of the men with Masque had disappeared. Either they had run when the flamethrower had opened up, or they were some smoldering piles up around the entrance to the mine. Either way, there was no incoming fire for Hausmann to worry about.

"Come on," Reaper said as he came up to Hausmann, "we've got to get out of here before the roof comes down."

The wooden support beams for the mine were all still burning after having been licked by Hausmann's flamethrower. The mouth of the mine was still open, the light told both men that. But it wouldn't be in less than nine minutes. They were standing in the muzzle of a giant cannon.

Chapter Twenty-seven

As Reaper and Hausmann headed to the entrance to the mine, they could hear the explosive thumps of 40mm grenades going off as they rained down on the hacienda. As they stepped into the sun, they saw a white GM Suburban stopped just outside of the mine. The doors of the vehicle were open and it was obvious that it was empty.

"Famine, War," Reaper said into the microphone of his Liberator headset. "Famine, War, this is Death. Over."

"Death, this is Famine," came over the headsets. "What is your location?"

"We are at point Charlie," Reaper said. "War is not to fire at the vehicle leaving this point. I repeat, tell War to hold his fire on the next vehicle leaving point Charlie. We are heading to the Hotel."

"Roger that, Death," Mackenzie said. "War is to hold fire. We are lifting fire now."

"Okay, let's take this big boy and get the hell out of here," Reaper said.

Without saying a word, Hausmann climbed into the passenger side of the Suburban after shoving the rear door closed. He tossed his pack to the center of the front seat as Reaper did the same. While Reaper got into the driver's seat, Hausmann looked around the vehicle. He had felt how heavy the door was and noticed how solidly it thumped shut. Looking toward the back of the SUV, Hausmann could see the shattered window and the edges of the material that surrounded it.

"Hey," Hausmann said, "this damned thing has armor."

"That will make for a safe ride," Reaper said as he shut the door. Starting the engine, Reaper was relieved to hear the roar of the motor. Then he noticed that the beeping of the alarm was still going off. He had turned the ignition key that had been left in the Suburban, so that should have shut off the beeping. What in the hell was going on?

"Holy shit!" Hausmann exclaimed. He had pulled his AN/UDR-13 radiac set from his pocket, The beeping alarm wasn't coming from the car, it was the radiation detector.

Numbers were flashing across the screen of the little device, but what they said wasn't of immediate concern to Hausmann. He turned around and looked across the backseat. There was nothing there. Craning his head, he could see into the cargo compartment behind the rear seat. Strapped in place were four white metal cans. The lid on one of the cans was bent and torn when the fragments of one of Warrick's Mark 211 rounds had ripped into it. They had found the radioactive isotopes.

"Jesus, Reaper," Hausmann said, "we have got to get out of here."

"That's exactly what I intend to do," Reaper said as he put the Suburban into reverse. "If the noise of that thing bothers you, turn it off."

Turning the heavy vehicle around, Reaper started out toward the hacienda. In the distance, they could see smoke rising from the fires started by Column's 40mm grenades. Not seeing anything he could do to change the situation, Hausmann sat back and watched the numbers change on the screen of the radiation detector.

———

When the head of their driver exploded, Santiago was covered by the spray of blood, bone, and gray matter that used to be the head of his sergeant. He grabbed the steering wheel and fought to bring the SUV under control before they crashed. In spite of a momentary flash of nausea at what covered his face, Santiago kept his composure and wiped the gooey mess from his eyes. Standing still in what he knew was at that point a great big target was the last thing he wanted to do just then, so Santiago grabbed Rodriguez's body and pulled it away from behind the wheel. The body flopped over with a wet sound as Santiago climbed over it.

"The isotopes!" Dr. Ammad said from the middle of the backseat. "They have the isotopes!"

"They won't do you any good if you're dead," Santiago snarled as he sat behind the wheel of the SUV.

The gate to the hacienda was only a few hundred meters in front of them when Santiago got the SUV moving straight once again. At any moment he expected to get another heavy round through the side window, but at least he had the vehicle between himself and whoever had been shooting. The incoming fire had stopped, at least as far as the SUV was concerned. If he had looked up at the wall surrounding the hacienda, Santiago would have seen how Warrick had switched his fire from the vehicle to the men firing up at the ravine.

As a man showed his head and raised a weapon, the big Barrett thundered out a shot. The head of the man would usually explode like a pumpkin hit with a sledgehammer a moment before the shot was even heard. It didn't take long before heads stopped appearing above the wall. Only weapons were being stuck up and fired toward the hillside. That's when the men inside the hacienda discovered that a Barrett loaded with Mark 211 rounds could shoot through adobe walls.

As Santiago smashed open the gate with the front of the SUV, what was left of Masque's men were abandoning the hacienda. Anywhere else was a better place to be rather than where grenades were falling from the sky and men died as bullets came through walls.

This was the end of things, Santiago realized, as he stopped the SUV and got out. The panic in the hacienda was complete. Even his mercenaries were abandoning the situation. The few who had been left in the hacienda were gone before Santiago returned. The damage from the explosions looked to him to be the work of 40mm grenades. It seemed like the U.S. government had finally decided to visit Mexico.

"We have got to go and save the isotopes," Dr. Ammad said. "They're irreplaceable."

Santiago just looked at the old scientist as if he were something found on the bottom of a shoe. He might be a fanatic, but Santiago certainly wasn't one, unless it concerned his personal safety. When Daumudi grabbed Santiago's arm and tried to spin him around, the ex-SEAL's hand came up, palm flat and fingers open. He drove the base of his palm up under Daumudi's chin, knocking the terrorist leader back in a wild stagger.

"So you think you can fight?" Hydar said.

It was the first English that Santiago had heard the man say. As he turned toward the huge bodyguard and crossed his arms, the man growled something unintelligible in Arabic and charged. The man's powerful hands were up and his fingers clutched for Santiago's throat.

The Glock 18C machine pistol that was in Santiago's right hand as he uncrossed his arms barked a short loud burst. The eight nine-millimeter rounds sounded like a single, stuttering shot. All of the 124-grain jacketed hollowpoint projectiles tore into Hydar's chest. The big man stood still for a moment with a surprised look on his face. Then his eyes rolled up in his head as he fell forward and crashed into the ground.

Dr. Ammad just stared at the dead form of his bodyguard. Daumudi couldn't see or speak very well at the moment. The blow Santiago had delivered had smashed his teeth together and brought tears to his eyes.

Reaching for the selector lever with his left hand, Santiago rotated the control on the slide to the single shot position. As he turned to an astonished Dr. Ammad and a hurting Daumudi, four quick rounds barked out of the Glock.

A single projectile smashed into each of the legs of the two men in front of him. Only the brittle tibia bone in Dr. Ammad's left leg was shattered from the impact of the projectile moving at over 1,200 feet per second. The shock of the large wound kept the pain away, but that mercy would last only for a moment.

Both of Daumudi's legs were knocked out from under him by the impact of the slugs. None of the major blood vessels in either man were hit by the shots, at least not as far as Santiago could see. Both men were on the ground clutching at their legs. They would not be a problem—or going anywhere without help.

Dr. Ammad succumbed to the pain of his wounds by falling unconscious. Daumudi looked up at Santiago with his face white with pain and shock.

"Why?" he said through clenched teeth. "Why?"

"You would think you were an Olympic figure skater," Santiago said. The reference was lost on Daumudi.

"Consider yourself and Dr. Ammad to be my election-year gift to President Bush. Perhaps your capture will help him get reelected. Besides, when the people who will be arriving shortly get here, they can deal with you and your wounds. That should aid in giving me more time to get away."

The logic and treachery of Santiago's statements

were something that Daumudi could well understand. He let his head fall back to the ground with a groan as the pain of his wounds washed through him. His plans for destruction were over. Nothing was left in front of him but a long interrogation and an even longer incarceration. The only thing that he could hope for would be to be taken to an American prison rather than a Mexican one. The final irony, he would have to lie there and hope the Americans would come and find him.

In their armored SUV, Reaper and Hausmann drew closer to the hacienda. Up in the ravine, Column held his fire on the Mark 19. He was accurate enough, but the big grenades could now take out friendlies as well as the enemy. With the lull in the firing, there was a crashing sound that came from the hacienda. Out of sight of the men on the hill, Santiago had taken the last armored Suburban and smashed through the back wall of the garage. Behind him, the fuel supply he had set fire to was starting to grow and throw black smoke into the air.

The smoke helped cover Santiago's escape and prevented Warrick from getting a clean shot at the fleeing vehicle before it disappeared into the hills south of the hacienda. With Reaper entering the field of fire, the sniper wouldn't risk a snap shot.

Coming through the gate, Reaper and Hausmann heard the announcement from War that a single vehicle had escaped the compound.

"Damn," Reaper said as he pounded on the wheel. "That's Santiago. I know it is."

"Well, who the hell are they?" Hausmann said pointing to the men on the ground. "That one guy looks like the man we saw at the truck the other night."

Going up to the two prostrate men, Reaper could see that the younger one was indeed the man they had targeted for capture. The other man was rolling around slightly as the wounds on his legs bled. Pulling a battle dressing from his trauma kit, Reaper tossed it to Hausmann.

"Bandage them up," Reaper said. "I'm going after Santiago."

"Reaper, you can't," Hausmann said. "I know that guy means a lot to you, but you can't chase him down in that SUV. It's hotter than hell from radiation. And we'll need it to get these two back across the border."

Before Reaper could argue his point, Mackenzie's voice came over the headset.

"Death, this is Famine. We've got company coming. It looks like the Mexican army is coming to check things out."

"How far?" Reaper said.

"Warrick says maybe ten minutes out," Mackenzie said. "Could be less."

Just then, the clock on the timer in the cave reached zero. For an instant, a tiny light on the black box shone in the dark. Then there was the rumbling thunder of several hundred pounds of military-grade high explosives going off.

At the hacienda, Reaper and Hausmann felt the

ground shake and then heard the rumbling roar of the explosion. Up in the ravine, Column stopped dismounting the Mark 19 and turned in time to see a gout of dust, smoke, and debris vomit out from the mouth of the Crystal mine as it ceased to exist.

Inside the mine, rocks smashed through the floor of the elevator cage and fell down into the depths. The roof of the main tunnel caved in for several hundred feet. It would be a major excavation job with heavy equipment to ever open that mine again. Far below the ground, the rumble of the shock wave moved through the huge cavern. Even the bodies in the death pit were shaken slightly by the blast.

At the hacienda, the living were working hard to make sure that they stayed that way. Helping Hausmann with the wounded, Reaper bundled Ammad into the backseat of the SUV while Hausmann put Daumudi in the front seat. The wounds of both men had been bandaged, and their legs and wrists tied with black plastic flex-cuffs, another item that had come with the Diamondback operators kit. The tough plastic cuffs would have to be cut off the prisoners to release them—something neither Hausmann nor Reaper expected to do for a while.

Both prisoners had been searched. When Dr. Ammad had come around, he found himself in the back of the Suburban he had wanted so badly to go after. And he could see the torn shielding of one of the isotope boxes. Gagging the now screaming doctor with a cut length of seatbelt, Hausmann looked the man square in the eyes.

"You wanted to dump that crap in the United States?" Hausmann said. "Now you can live with it as long as we do."

The rest of the hacienda was already burning violently. If the leader of the drug cartel was in there, he was welcome to the flames. Reaper was disappointed that they hadn't been able to search the hacienda for intelligence. But the heavy cloth bag he had taken from the younger terrorist felt interesting. The rough first aid that Hausmann had performed on the two men would have to be enough for the time being. It would not be a nice ride coming up for them.

Climbing into the front seat of the SUV, Reaper fired up the engine. Turning around in the big courtyard, Reaper knocked over part of a fountain before getting the Suburban heading back out of the gate. Once out of the hacienda, Reaper headed north toward his men, and the safety of the border with the U.S. only a mile or so away. Up in the ravine, all of the gear was being packed onto the Prowlers. The men didn't have the firepower to take on a portion of the Mexican army. Running away was the smart thing to do now that they had accomplished their objectives. There would be no more specific evidence that they had even been there outside of some spent cartridge cases. The State Department would be able to deny this operation easily— if the Prowlers and the SUV could get away.

"Famine, this is Death," Reaper said into the boom mike of his Liberator headset. Immediately, he heard back.

"Death, this is Famine, over."

"Famine, we have two wounded tangos, I repeat, two wounded tangos on board," Reaper said. "We are on our way to your location. I need you and your kit ASAP."

"Roger that, Death," Mackenzie said, "I'll be waiting. Famine out."

"Warrick," Mackenzie called out. "Take over my vehicle, I'm joining with Reaper."

Still lying on the ground, Warrick responded with a left-handed thumbs-up. His right hand was still holding on to his Barrett. He had heard the exchange between Reaper and Mackenzie over his own headset. For now, he was keeping an eye on the approaching Mexicans through the Unertl scope on the big rifle.

"Famine and Death, this is War," Warrick said. "I count six incoming hostile carriers. No armor, but at least three of them are armed. I count two heavy machine guns and one antitank weapon—looks like a big recoilless. They will be on target in fifteen mikes (minutes) or less."

Shit, Reaper thought to himself. There was no way his small force could take on even part of the Mexican military. And the political fallout from that kind of fight couldn't be ignored. Their only choice was to run, and run fast.

"Roger that, War," Reaper said. "Prepare to pull out."

Sparing a moment to glance at Daumudi, Reaper could see that the terrorist was in a bad way. His dusky Middle-Eastern complexion was an ashen gray from shock. There was only a moment that Reaper could spend looking at the man before he had to go back to concentrating on his driving. The big, heavy Suburban smashed its way through the brush heading up the hillside. If he slowed or stopped, Reaper knew that he might not be able to get the overweight armored vehicle moving again in the loose gravel and sand.

For every twist, turn, and jarring bump of the SUV, Dr. Ammad screamed into his gag. The muffled screams were growing thinner and weaker inside the noisy, dusty interior of the SUV. Thanks to Warrick's marksmanship, the rear window of the Suburban had been smashed out by the same .50-caliber rounds that had torn open one of the isotope containers. The air inside the SUV was thick with the dust that was stirred up by Reaper's driving, and sucked in through the ragged back window.

The dust was bad, but at least you could see it. That couldn't be said for the invisible poison in the air, the radiation from the open isotope container. All that Reaper and Hausmann could do was hope that the dose they were receiving would not be permanently damaging. The radiac meters in their pockets sat silently, counting up the radiation they had been exposed to so far.

Grinding through the gravel of the hillside, Reaper finally brought the Suburban to a halt in a cloud of dust at the side of the ravine where the rest of his men were. Pushing open the door, Reaper stood up and shouted to Mackenzie:

"Get in here and see if you can keep these two alive! The rest of you, saddle up. We are pulling out ASAP."

Having already shut and latched the case to the Barrett, Warrick stood up with the big weapon cradled in his arms. He snatched up the case with his left hand and trotted back to the Prowlers. His M40A3 was strapped across his back, bouncing at every step.

At the two Prowlers, Manors and Column were finished strapping down the rest of the gear. The engines of the two Prowlers were idling over as the two men helped Warrick secure his gear. The big Barrett had well proven its worth against the two Suburbans. It might be needed again soon enough if they had to fight their way out past the incoming Mexicans.

At the Suburban, Reaper and Hausmann were trying to help Mackenzie treat the two wounded terrorists. The ex-Air Force parajumper (PJ) had worked as a paramedic after leaving the service. His medical training both in and out of the military was more than useful now as he had his trauma pack open on the seat next to him as he tried to stop the bleeding from Dr. Ammad's broken leg.

A shattered splinter of bone stuck out of the wound torn open by the hollowpoint bullet. At least no major blood vessels had been severed, a small miracle given the four bullet wounds in the two men's legs. It didn't help Mackenzie's concentration in his task to hear the radiac set in his pocket start beeping as soon as he stepped inside the Suburban.

"The back has a bunch of cans in it," Reaper said. "One of them tore open and it's full of long silver rods. I think they're the isotopes. You don't have to stay in here with me—but I'm not leaving that crap behind."

"Get ready to pull out," Mackenzie said. "I've got wounded to treat. You just worry about getting us out of here."

The short, wiry ex-PJ reached into his pocket, clicked off the alarm on his radiac set, and then went back to strapping a pressure bandage on each of Daumudi's legs. Dr. Ammad was in much worse shape and would have to be immobilized for the trip out—or at least held as still as possible. Climbing into the backseat, Mackenzie started working on Dr. Ammad as Hausmann helped.

"Go," Hausmann said, his hands covered with blood, "we can handle this."

"Load up," Reaper shouted out the door. "Abandon what isn't secured. We leave now, follow me."

Sitting back down in the Suburban, Reaper went over his options. They were few, surrender to the Mexicans and face whatever they might offer, probably death, prison at the least. Or make a run for the border. It wasn't even a choice.

Stepping on the gas and feeling the big vehicle start to move, Reaper headed for the crest of the ridge. Well within sight on the other side of the ridge was the black fence line of the border. It was less than a mile away.

The escape plan had no finesse to it at all, no tricks. Reaper would drive straight for the border and smash the big Suburban through the fence. If drug runners could do it with old pickups, the massive armored Suburban would tear through as if the fencing were tissue paper. Then the Prowlers could follow through the hole he would make.

A simple plan, but they had to reach the border for it to work.

———

General Martinez was responding to an emergency radio call from Masque with his rapid deployment scout platoon. The men he had with him were all trusted people he knew he could depend on. If the arrogant Americans had crossed the border, they would find the going not so easy.

As they came within sight of the hacienda, Martinez could see that the place was in flames. So much for the funds that were going into his retirement. But the lone white vehicle heading over the ridge between the hacienda and the border, that was something he could go after and quench his sudden thirst for revenge.

The six open jeeps that made up General Martinez's convoy held more than two dozen men and their small arms. In addition, two of the jeeps carried post-mounted M2 HB .50-caliber machine guns. The last jeep had a 106mm M40A1 recoilless rifle on it. The recoilless was able to stop a heavy tank with one of its high-explosive shells. It could blow the truck in front of them to bits.

Ordering his driver to speed ahead, Martinez leaned back in his seat and hung on. Already, he was thinking about how he could take control of the local drug trade if Masque was gone. The thought gave him a warm feeling as the jeep he was in crested the ridge and the border stretched out in front of them.

Charging down the hillside, the six military vehicles

headed toward the border at full speed. Just a short distance in front of them, the white SUV could be seen charging across the desert. Now there were two other, much smaller, vehicles moving with the big white one. These were just dune buggies of some kind.

It wasn't the U.S. military or even law enforcement who had invaded his country. It was probably nothing more than a bunch of drug smugglers trying to increase their action by taking out the competition. This would never do and Martinez ordered his driver to increase speed.

As the big vehicle approached the border, it didn't slow down at all. The two smaller buggies fell behind the bigger one as it drove up to, and smashed through, the fence at the border. It had tried to escape into the United States. That just wouldn't work.

As General Martinez chuckled, the laughter died in his throat. Dozens of vehicles were becoming visible on the other side of the border. The white and green paint job on the trucks was very familiar to Martinez. It was the U.S. Border Patrol. And by the looks of things, it was the entire Arizona branch of the Border Patrol.

This was another thing entirely. Chasing down some drug dealers into the United States could be passed off as a mistake in crossing the border. Taking on a hundred agents of the Border Patrol would mean the end of his career at least, his quiet elimination as an embarrassment to the government at the most.

No, it was time to cut his losses. Telling his driver to stop, General Martinez raised his hand to call a halt to the entire patrol. As he watched, the white SUV came to a stop, the doors opened, and men stood up. From the back of an ambulance nearby, medical personnel in white shirts ran up to the SUV. Several men wearing odd-looking bright yellow plastic suits got out of a red van and walked up to the SUV holding silver instruments in their hands. They had clear helmets over their heads and faces.

Perhaps, Martinez thought, it wasn't a bad thing that he hadn't caught up to the fleeing vehicles.

EPILOGUE

Several days after their sudden return from Mexico, Hausmann was sitting at home reflecting on everything while Jarhead lay on the couch next to him. The big bulldog was enjoying having his back scratched and positively wiggled with pleasure. Laughing at the sight, Hausmann redoubled his efforts to scratch at the dog and was rewarded with a series of happy grunts and wheezes for his efforts.

Suddenly, Jarhead twisted around and jumped off the couch. He trotted up to the hallway leading back to the poolroom just as Reaper walked through it. Behind Reaper were two very big rottweilers bouncing along with their tongues hanging out.

"You know," Hausmann said, "you really put a dent in the vicious killer hellhound image I'm trying to cultivate in those dogs."

"Sorry about that," Reaper said as he sat down in one of the easy chairs.

"No you're not," Hausmann said with a laugh. "So, what's the story now?"

"Things are settling down now," Reaper said. "Warrick and Mackenzie are winging their way back to Michigan right now. The sheriff's office finally gave my people their weapons back, though they were really reluctant to. A call from D.C. apparently eliminated all of the problems, or at least told them we had the right licenses for everything. The sheriff didn't believe there was a license you could have for a grenade launcher and ammunition. He was told he was wrong.

"And Diamondback Tactical has their Prowlers back as well as a good report on how they stand up to hard riding. Manors is back on full duty, and with a promotion no less as well as back pay. Funny how someone much higher up in the food chain can convince a local commander to shut the hell up."

"Hey, that's great," Hausmann said. "What about our prisoners?"

"What prisoners?" Reaper said. "I'm not kidding here. It would be a real good idea if you forgot there was anyone else in that Suburban but the two of us. And as far as those boxes in the back go, they never existed at all."

"Okay," Hausmann said. "I can see that there isn't any use arguing with people I can never know. Since the doctors gave us a clean bill of health as far as our exposures went, I don't care about what even could have been in the back of that car. But just how the hell did everything happen down there at the border?"

"That's something I did get the word on," Reaper

said. "You know those satellites that we didn't get the pictures from?"

"Didn't get?" Hausmann said puzzled. "Oh, yeah, the ones we never got and never were wiped from my computer."

"Yeah, those," Reaper said. "It seems that someone in Washington was watching what was going on south of here. Just like in the movies, he could see people on the ground and vehicles moving in real time. When some boxes that don't exist showed up on the screen, they lit up the sensors like a baby star.

"The powers-that-be started communicating with a lot of different agencies. The Border Patrol was told in no uncertain terms that it would be heading for the border with everyone—that's every cook, mechanic, and secretary who wore a badge and could carry a gun—ASAP. When the word got out that one of their own might be in trouble, even the retired and off-duty personnel showed up. Including that Nuclear Emergency Search Team."

"Those were the NEST guys in the plastic suits?" Hausmann said.

"Yes," Reaper said. "They were already on alert because of the earlier information we passed on. When the balloon went up on the satellite, they were up and moving toward the border.

"Then there's the strange story of Valentine Dupree."

"What?" Hausmann said, "the snake bitch? What happened to her? They try to bust her for dope?"

"Hers is the weirdest story of this whole thing," Reaper said. "Apparently, she's been running dope for years. They found all the evidence they needed in her ranch house to close down drug dealers all over the country. When the Border Patrol cars came down the road to the Heart Ranch, she must have figured her time was up. At any rate, she panicked.

"Dupree climbed into her Lincoln Navigator and drove off into the desert. Where she was going to run to in that thing, no one knows. One thing's for sure, no matter what the ads say, that luxury SUV is not made for going across rough country. She may have run into a dust devil without noticing it coming up on her. The front of the Navigator is scoured like someone took a sand blaster to it.

"The blowing sand must have blocked her windshield completely. All she would have had to do was stand still for a moment. Just stop the car and let the dust devil blow on by. Instead, she kept going and drove herself right into a cut. Sank her front wheel to the axle.

"So again, all she would have had to do was wait and someone would have come looking for her. But no. To make matters worse for herself, she gets out of the car and tries to run across the desert."

"What happened?" Hausmann said. "Did she get away?"

"Nope," Reaper said, "and she never will. She's reporting to a higher court now. Of all of the stupid things she did, the final one killed her. Walking in the desert, she managed to step right into a den of Mojave rattlesnakes. They must have bitten her a dozen times. When they finally found the body, she had been dead from the venom for hours. And she wasn't more than twenty feet from her Lincoln."

"Well," Hausmann said. "They say that drugs kill."

"Not as well as stupid does," Reaper said.

"So everything's fine now?" Hausmann said. "We don't have to worry about any more ambushes, the law, anything?"

"I don't think so," Reaper said. "They never did get a report as to what happened to Masque. But the Cardenal Muerte cartel is falling apart. It seems that a computer disk showed up at the U.S. embassy in Mexico City. It outlined the whole cartel. If I didn't know better, I think that someone is trying to pay Uncle Sam off and keep him from chasing someone down.

"But the only thing you have to worry about is the IRS."

"The Internal Revenue Service?" Hausmann said. "Why would I have to worry about them."

"Remember that bag I took off that nonexistent person?" Reaper said. "Well, since the individual doesn't exist, neither does the bag. Your share of the diamonds that were in that bag should come to a good-sized chunk of change."

"Diamonds?" Hausmann said. "And we get to keep the money?"

"How do you think we manage to pay for all of the stuff we use?" Reaper said. "They're still discussing if we'll be able to draw on the reward that was offered on those two 'nonpersons' we brought for a visit."

"So what do we do now?" Hausmann said.

"How should I know?" Reaper said as he leaned back and rubbed Grunt's big head. "I'm on vacation."